FORGE of HEAVEN

Books by
C. J. Cherryh

FORGE of HEAVEN

C. J. Cherryh

AN IMPRINT OF HARPERCOLLINSPUBLISHERS

HarperCollins books may be purchased for educational, business, or sales promotional use. For information please write: Special Markets Department, HarperCollins Publishers Inc., 10 East 53rd Street, New York, NY 10022.

FIRST EDITION

Eos is a federally registerd trademark of HarperCollins Publishers Inc.

Designed by Katy Riegal

Printed on acid-free paper

Library of Congress Cataloging-in-Publication Data

Cherryh, C. J.
  Forge of heaven / C. J. Cherryh.—1st ed.
    p. cm.
  ISBN 0-380-97903-9 (HC)
    1. Human-alien encounters—Fiction. 2. Life on other planets—Fiction.
  3. Nanotechnology—Fiction. 4. Space warfare—Fiction. 5. Space ships—Fiction.
  I. Title.
  PS3553.H358F675 2004
  813'.54—dc22   2003049512

04 05 06 07 08 ᴊᴛᴄ/RRD 10 9 8 7 6 5 4 3 2 1

Contents

Reference

1

History

CONSIDER TWO BUBBLES in space, one the shape of *ondat* territory, the other the shape of what is human. Earth sits, not at the center of its bubble, but off center, at the farthest side.

This is the shape of things. The bubbles forever overlap, thanks to a human action. They forever overlap, since humans let the Gene Wars reach the *ondat* homeworld . . . since ruin overtook the heart of *ondat* culture, and the *ondat* went to war with humankind.

Concord Station sits in that zone of overlap. At Concord, humans and *ondat* keep anxious truce and watch, a situation older than all extant governments, all extant culture, all extant languages but one, in both spheres of influence. Time moves incredibly slowly here. But since *ondat* are patient, humans are compelled to be.

The Gene Wars ended here, ages ago, in a cold peace. The ondat maintain one observer at Concord Station—perhaps one. Humans, sharing the same station, have no way to be sure.

Cross deep space, now, to the deep places of human territory.

In the Inner Worlds, farthest bubble within the human bubble, Earth floats in a sea of biological change, still obsessed with keeping dry. Inner Worlds Authority, residing on Earth, restricts even the simple biotech that Outsider Space regards as a useful, even a trivial instrument. The Inner Worlds jealously protect what it calls the pure human genome, and frown on genetic modifications even of a medical, lifesaving nature. Every use of bioengineering technology in this region must pass slow and painstaking review.

Go back to the beginning of this situation, however.

In the larger bubble, and long, long ago, within that region of human territory that Earth calls the Outside, an anti-Earth splinter called the Movement broke from local authority, and broke in a way that forever alienated them from Earth. The Movement bioengineered humans, livestock, and agriculture—specifically to fit colonists for three difficult planets it hoped to claim.

Movement science had joined nanotech with biotech. It changed humans in ways that could be passed on. The Movement claimed worlds, and it meant to govern Outsider territory.

Earth quickly slammed down a total quarantine against everything Outside.

That meant that the far greater number of Outsiders who wanted Earth's help in this ongoing crisis were abruptly, and without consultation, cut off from direct trade. The next decades were a struggle for moderate Outsider governments to keep their own settlements alive, to organize some sort of government without Earth—and simultaneously to fight the Movement, which was mobile and difficult to track down. Earth began to use Outsider assistance in its own hunt for Movement bases, and reasserted its unifying authority over Outsider governments, but still refused any direct personal contact with places it considered contaminated, and that by then included the entire Outside.

It was not love of mother Earth that kept the beleaguered Outsiders fighting against the Movement. It was pure self-preservation, the knowledge that if biochange produced a disaster, it would happen in their laps. They formed a union of their own, centered at a station named Apex, and laid down laws that would keep trade going, independent of Earth and the Inner Worlds.

Driven farther out by a series of Outsider military successes, the outlaw Movement spread nanotech to another world, to secure a base there.

But another species existed here, previously suspected, but never encountered. *Ondat* landed on the world during this period, contacted these aggressively adaptive Movement nanisms, and unknowingly let loose disaster on their own species, a calamitous runaway that spread from them to their homeworld.

Ondat went to war, seeing no species or behavioral difference in Movement, Outsiders, or Earth.

Earth and Outsider forces understood at least that Movement actions, specifically the Movement intrusion into *ondat* territory, had touched off this war—and they moved quickly to dissociate themselves from the Movement. They joined the *ondat* attack on the Movement in space, they hunted Movement bases down to the last, and gradually the *ondat* seemed to accept that not all humans were hostile.

But in the economics of the war, badly hammered by the *ondat* attacks and Movement alike, the Outside had lost its newfound autonomy. In the process of protecting the Outside from infiltration by the Movement, Earth had maintained tight control of key Outsider sites, despite the new authority at Apex, and despite Outsider trade agreements. Earth ultimately asserted its old rights to install governors at every surviving Outsider colony, in the name of defense and negotiation with the *ondat*.

The Movement gained a number of recruits as irate Outsiders reacted to what they considered a betrayal, but it was a last flourish. The Movement fought a couple of sharp actions against the *ondat* and the Earth Federation, but they lost heavily, and this led to the suicide of three of its leaders.

The *ondat,* mollified by the fact human forces had helped defeat the Movement, drew back into their original borders, and conducted a shoot-on-sight but nonpursuit relationship with Earth Federation patrols.

That shaky border situation defined human and *ondat* relations for over three hundred years.

Federation law maintained a tight grip on Outsider colonies. Earth governors were there to stay. Ironically, however, the absolute isolation that pure Earthers maintained from Outsider worlds and stations (from which they took fuel and electronic information, but little else) allowed Outsiders under those Earth-run administrations the freedom to do pretty much as they wished in nanotech and genetics, synthesizing materials, creating life, creating whole servant ecosystems in limited environments—and simultaneously striving to fine-tune and limit these same systems. The Outsiders' stated intention was to rein in biological change on the several contaminated worlds, where, certainly, some Outsider descendants lived. They intended to prove that such worlds could be cleaned up.

Remediation thus became a word of hot political debate between Earth and Outsiders.

So did *self-rule.*

Meanwhile the Second Movement appeared as a political organization on several Outsider stations. Clearly it was a name chosen for shock value: it shared neither personnel nor history with the old Movement, so far as anyone ever proved. But it argued against Earth rule, and it argued against the quarantine laws. The intellectuals of the Second Movement, none of them over twenty-two at the time of the organization's founding, not only proposed to remediate the afflicted territories by throwing off all restraint on research, they talked about making a civilized agreement with the *ondat* as a route to regain Outsider self-rule. But two Second Movement founders, after a particularly unfortunate biocontamination runaway affecting Arc, the single Movement-run station, entirely repudiated the organization and turned in five of their radical subordinates. So the Second Movement had splintered, part going underground, into a clandestine radical group, part following the former Second Movement founders, constituting the relatively benign Freethinkers.

Freethinkers, with their music, their occasional prankish demonstrations against Earth government, and their flouting of station zoning laws, particularly—eventually provided a springboard and a backdrop for that other splinter, the radical chic, the Style, with its music, its fetish for nanotech creativity and personal embellishment. Both splinters thrived in illicit trade of various physical goods—smuggling, in other words, an activity that incidentally provided cover for the more dangerous radical underground, which began to call itself the Third Movement.

Like its predecessor, the Third Movement was well hidden in its outer shells of legitimate demands for freedom and self-rule. But it, too, died, in an attempted violent takeover of the remediation labs on Arc. Earth and Outsider forces fortunately prevented calamity there, and the last of the Third Movement leaders committed suicide with their followers.

The border tension between Earth and the *ondat,* meanwhile, continued, with occasional shots fired. *Ondat* did not communicate with humans, did not trade with, did not approach, did not tolerate humans. No one even knew what they looked like.

Then the *ondat* made a radical shift in behavior.

THE UNSPOKEN TREATY: EVENTS JUST PRIOR TO HAMMERFALL

Ondat never had communicated with Earth's ships, except to indicate, by firing at them, just where they thought their border was. Now the *ondat* began a program of nonviolent approach to Earth's warships inside human space, perhaps testing their peaceful resolve, or, some began to think, wishing them to follow their route.

Taking the risk, Earth did follow an *ondat* ship—to a hitherto unguessed First Movement base . . . on a world on the *ondat* side of the border. By all evidence, it had been there for centuries, and the *ondat* hadn't destroyed it; but they signaled that they were about to do so, with the implication, Earth judged, that they thought this newly discovered base represented Earth's enemies as well, and they were invited to join in the attack.

Or perhaps, someone said in a hastily called council, the *ondat* wanted to know what Earth would do about this find, so that they could judge Earth's behavior toward these human outlaws, and thus judge whether Earth had secretly supported this base in *ondat* space for all these years.

The situation on the one hand could lead to renewed war, which Earth was by no means confident of winning. Or on the other, it might bring peace and a fundamental change in the relationship between humans and *ondat*, to the relief of all humankind. All Earth had to do to gain *ondat* approval, apparently, was wipe out an inhabited planet—because human beings were scattered across the heart of the contaminated major continent, innocents born in the centuries since the Gene Wars, a population, moreover, that showed no outward signs of divergence from the human genome and that had no way to leave the planet.

The *ondat* waited. Earth hesitated. And desperately consulted.

Earth's ethicists were aghast at the situation, on purely moral grounds— while certain Outsider experts who had long studied *ondat* behavior raised another objection: that meekly committing an act of murder the *ondat* directed could set a bad precedent for the *ondat*-human future. A second set of experts from the Earth Federation also raised the point that this was a First Movement base, and that it might contain biological bombs that even today's Outsider science couldn't stop: the place was possibly more dangerous to them than to the *ondat*, if that population broke containment.

This was the surface debate. But certain other Outsiders, siding with the ethicists and those in favor of rescue, saw their chance at getting their hands on First Movement technology not only intact, but advanced centuries beyond their last information—because there seemed to be a high-tech establishment on the planet that still functioned. The planet represented a potential informational windfall, possibly even the key to the long-sought provable remediation.

Bitter accusations of Movement sympathies flew back and forth in the subtext of communications between the outermost Earth authority at Orb and the Outsider Council at Apex. But the strange coalition held, aided by a peculiar fact: Earth's military was powerful, but its bioscience had stagnated over centuries, under the quarantine laws. Earth functioned on faith that if the *ondat* ever mounted a bioneered threat in retaliation, Outsiders would be the ones to meet that threat, while Earth's powerful military pounded hell out of the *ondat*. And Earth joined the ones who favored study, which *Earth* saw as the moderate course.

The *ondat* waited through this debate, observed by one lone human ship—and eventually shoved a few small rocks out of orbit, their machines beginning to attach themselves to more ominous pieces of free-floating rock in the solar system.

Time was running out. Outsiders overcame their differences: the study proposal won out, and they went into urgent conference with Earth. If they could set up and work at a base down there, Outsiders said, they could find out whether there were still other Movement bases undiscovered, and maybe—as humans talking to other humans, in the face of the *ondat*, who were truly alien—humans could gain permanent control of this place and learn from it. Outsiders were willing to sacrifice two of their own experts to go down there to do it, with no possibility of return. The world was within the overlap of the human-*ondat* border. An Outsider mission could take responsibility for it, if they could just negotiate a deal with the *ondat* and promise to watch it. They could learn the nature of the threat that had existed in the first place—much of First Movement information was lost to war and time—and they could measure the threat that still existed. They could learn to communicate with the *ondat*.

Earth and the Outsiders attempted to present the proposal to the *ondat*, who sat, encased in their ship, still faceless, operating their robotics.

The *ondat* balked, while a few more rocks dropped. The *ondat*, through symbol transmission, apparently wanted assurances that the Movement ship on the planet wouldn't take off again, that there wasn't a conceivable means for Movement technology to escape the gravity well.

Negotiations dragged on. Outsiders took a new intellectual tack with Earth's representatives: most of all, they indicated, they needed to gain knowledge of the place and monitor its biology, along with any adaptive replication machines. They could help target the strikes.

Nanoceles, complex biounits of the Movement's creation, were a sort of life. They responded to evolutionary pressure, and would fit themselves for any changed environment. If the planet was devastated, they would go off program and become, in effect, true new life, at a bottleneck of evolution—

not inherently more dangerous, Outsider scientists argued, than life that evolved naturally. Certain capabilities would be trimmed off in a process of natural selection, and they would no longer be fitted to do what the Movement had designed them to do. In short, remediation might be possible for this and other worlds, including the *ondat* homeworld.

To do anything scientifically useful, however, scientists on the Outsider team needed at least a century to work on the planet, to get their hands on that tech and understand the original design before it mutated wildly under the scouring the *ondat* proposed.

And if they got that century, Outsiders swore they would share that knowledge with Earth and the *ondat*.

Earth joined Outsiders in last-ditch negotiations with the *ondat*, who had already chosen their missiles to crack the planet.

The Outsiders got forty years to work.

THE EVENTS OF HAMMERFALL

An Outsider team went down, a dive to prison without escape and, ironically, the assumption of a godlike power over a whole planet's future. The two scientists promised to report as long as they could, implying they expected to die in the scouring of the planet.

But the mission they intended was to get First Movement tech into their hands, build deep, and survive the destruction with part of the native population, and with their own laboratories intact. Their landing craft was capable of withstanding anything but a direct hit from one of the planetkillers or direct involvement in the consequent volcanics; and the Outsiders left not even that matter to chance, since Outsiders were helping target the strikes. The Outsider team onworld hastily burrowed a deep refuge, created surface modifications, took their samples, and set to work.

Foremost concern, Outsiders suspected Movement was still active on the planet: their first priority was to get any such highly trained persons into their own hands along with their lab records.

They were dismayed to discover that, indeed, not a successor, but an original member of the First Movement was still alive and still ruling after so many centuries. The Ila, as the locals called her, had intended to refurbish the Movement, build an ecology and an economy, rule a devoted population, and live quite well here. A new war? Possibly. A new culture? Slowly. Spaceflight? She certainly had the plans. Her science gave her the longevity. She just needed the industry.

But her plans hadn't gone utterly smoothly: the planet was short on metals and certain other key elements, making the synthesis of essential materials more difficult. More, the inhabitants, as generations spread out and adapted to the new planet, not only adapted to the harsh conditions, but developed self-interest and rebelled against her. The inhospitable planet itself hammered her other creations, destroyed them if they were slow to mutate and mutated them into problems if they were rapid to respond.

The Outsiders were right. Even with Movement active and in charge, it was becoming a new world.

The Outsider team saw the Ila and her records as key to their problem: and both resided in her ship, the half-buried center of the establishment the locals called the Holy City. Clearly that ship and that city were the one place on the planet from which they absolutely couldn't divert the *ondat* strike. They had to get that information out of the target zone.

The forty years was almost gone. Last-moment negotiations to stall the planetkillers fell apart. The Outsider team attempted to use the planet's own rebels to draw the Ila out or crack that citadel. That failed. As a last resort, they began to call in certain human residents of the world, in whom they had implanted communication nanisms, to save them and gather their knowledge.

But again the Ila thwarted them. She heard rumors of odd goings-on, and brought the affected people to her capital, endangering a major element of the Outsiders' plan.

But her bringing those particular people in brought the Outsider team an unexpected chance. Marak Trin Tain, a young man with leadership abilities as well as political importance, reached the Ila in person. Through him, using the implanted tech, the Outsider team delivered a warning to her, to evacuate her base and seek shelter in the east.

It was a warning Marak Trin Tain didn't wholly understand, but the Ila certainly did. She evacuated the city and saved her records as a bargaining leverage, exactly what the Outsider mission wanted.

The *ondat* attack had already begun. The Outsider team continued to try to stall the planetkillers, claiming one of their team was out in the desert and in trouble. Whether or not their appeal actually delayed events, or that the larger planetkillers, coming from farther out in the solar system, lagged behind others that served as ranging shots, Marak and his party, including the Ila, reached the Refuge before the first true planetkiller fell on the other side of the world.

So the Outsiders got their hands on the Ila, on hundreds of years of records, and on a great number of refugees.

The hammer came down. And the world became a volcanic hell.

The Outsiders continued to transmit new discoveries to ships in orbit—and the *ondat* seemed to accept their presence on the world so long as that stream of knowledge flowed. Earth didn't leave the vicinity, nor did the Outsider ship break contact with their team from orbit. Nor did the *ondat* leave. There were things to learn. There was a lingering threat here to keep an eye on.

The *ondat* understanding of humans was insufficient to let them reason out quite what humans were up to, after everything that had happened. But humans were perfectly willing to indicate that they would not lift the team off the planet, nor visit them, and that they would establish a permanent base in orbit to guarantee that permanent state of affairs.

The *ondat* evidently believed this—as long as *ondat* stayed to guarantee it, too. A station grew. Earth naturally moved in an official to govern it. The Outsider Council established a matching governmental structure aboard. The *ondat,* still unseen, set aside a section of the station and moved in a capsule which became incorporated in the structure, and ultimately integrated with it.

The name of the new station was, hopefully chosen, Concord. A trade route was set up, from Arc, to supply it.

Below, the planetkillers had done their work. The impacts had sent shock waves through to the other side of the planet: volcanic plumes melted hot spots in areas of weakened crust. Vast lava flows choked the sunlight planetwide in thick clouds of noxious vapors. The planetkillers had vaporized undersea carbonates in the sea off the west coast of the inhabited continent, killing the food chain planetwide.

The hardiest life survived in the depths of the seas and the crevices of the earth, along with extremophiles of various sorts, some of which were likely foreign, imported by the Ila, some native, both unpredictable in their potential, given the conditions that prevailed.

The world had a lengthy course to run before the atmospheric balance reasserted itself . . . not, however, as lengthy a course as might have been without the nanisms that now played their part in an accelerated evolution.

Observers up on Concord remained hopeful, but highly skeptical.

CONCORD AND THE NEW AGE

Concord itself grew over the centuries, an establishment mostly Outsider, still with the colonial government Earth installed and maintained—and, unique to Concord, at least one, and perhaps a handful of *ondat* observers. This arrangement made it an overwhelmingly important station, a very influential Earth governorship, and an equally potent Outsider chairmanship, in many ways independent from the Outsider Council at Apex. No one was sure about the *ondat*.

On the planet, life reasserted itself and interlaced in biological cooperation. The doors of the Refuge opened and human scouts traveled out into a vastly changed world, to hand-spread more seeds prepared by Outsider science—and to shed their own nanisms into the world, hoping for the best. Seeding operations began to spread hardy plant life the Outsiders claimed contained remediating nanoceles, creations intended to spread throughout the biosphere, attracting and eliminating certain of the runaways, themselves changing and reproducing into beneficent microorganisms.

Nothing dangerous in the original sense had yet turned up—but, certain doubters could point out, there was necessarily one place where the Ila's nanoceles still flourished: in the Ila herself, and in a handful of other survivors, whose lives had passed ordinary human limits, notably Marak Trin Tain, who was the earliest and hardiest explorer of this new world. *He* became a contact point for the observers aloft; *he* became a known quantity, a continuing, reliable guide, about whose doings the *ondat* were extraordinarily curious, whose activities they wanted to know, at all points—one single human being, a benchmark, perhaps, about whom their records were continuous, who perhaps embodied their understanding of the species with whom they shared, and did not share, a station.

The original team likewise availed themselves of that long life. They had become living laboratories of Outsider attempts to contain the Ila's science. The nanotrackers, potent against the runaways, failed to attack the First Movement modifications in the Outsider team and in the Ila—a circumstance that some pessimists aloft called proof of the danger inherent in First Movement tech, and others, more optimistic, called proof of the fine control the Outsider team already exerted, on their way to remediation.

The Outsider team simply said it was not to their advantage to kill themselves—since with those internal nanisms, they were, in effect, immortal—a rumor that caused nervous shivers far beyond Concord.

Nobody wanted a return to the bad old days of the Gene Wars: no one wanted the *ondat* to resume their attacks or retaliate in kind. The *ondat* seemed happy as long as they had regular reports from Marak Trin Tain, and apparently cared little for communications from the station itself.

But rumors of immortality scared Earth. Earth, overpopulated as it was, could see social collapse if the immortality modification ever reached the black market ... and only the information needed travel. The Outsiders' entire hope to remediate the political situation with the *ondat* hinged on their team's efforts to rehabilitate Marak's World—and on the contact they maintained with the *ondat,* and on the *ondat's* fixation on Marak's successful, healthy life. The Outsiders wanted no provocative new tech to exit the world, but they were glad enough to know their team was as immortal as Marak—the team, by now, having a tremendous accumulated knowledge ... and being, like Marak, one constant that transcended the careers of individual administrators in orbit.

So everyone stayed. Everyone carried on above, on Concord, as if this ages-long occupation of a ruined world and a handful of immortals were the modus vivendi they had discovered. To Concord Station, the curious situation was forever, a condition of life like light and warmth, essential, but the maintenance of which happened outside the understanding of nine-tenths of the lives inside Concord's spinning wheel. The population had diversified far, far beyond the scientific mission.

Commerce went on. Human lives did, briefer than what they observed. In the mind-bogglingly long time since the Gene Wars, new civilizations sprang up. Governments and institutions rose and fell. Languages and cultures changed. The Ruined Worlds deep inside Outsider territory grew stranger and stranger, one with continents nearly covered in algaes and slimes, one with a population that could no longer be called in any sense human.

Marak's World, however, showed signs of health. The population had been ordinary humans in most particulars: they still were. The surface of the world was metal-poor. Newly arrived metals, largely aimed to miss the area of human habitation, were mostly inaccessible to them. That had not changed. But the reawakened geologic forces that were rearranging the planet would change that picture, bringing up metals from the core—slowly, over time only the immortals could survive.

Meanwhile the Refuge maintained a few aircraft of fused fiber; it used trucks of metal, fused fiber, and cast ceramics. It had brought down fusion for its own needs. It harnessed water, wind, biomass, and solar power, the latter fragile in the vast, long-lasting sandstorms. Fuel cells provided power for outlying installations, but the fuel cells themselves used scarce materials. Life showed signs of health in this new age. Technology struggled, not according to ancient patterns, but making ample use of exotic, synthesizing nanochemistry. For civilization, it was still an uphill climb.

The Concord Station that now monitored the planet was the third station to orbit there, the other two outmoded and abandoned, the *ondat* having transferred their section as a unit to each in turn. A fourth station was under construction, a subject of the usual debate and wrangling, but nothing important was likely to change when the population migrated over to it. Concord still spoke the language it had always spoken. It still believed what it had believed. The *ondat* still sought their daily information on Marak. Only outward appearances and trends underwent revision, never the laws that governed its interaction with others.

Life was comfortable for all concerned at Concord.

Biological change on Marak's World was a slow process . . . and a constant guarantee of employment.

•

ii

Positional Map

Not to scale

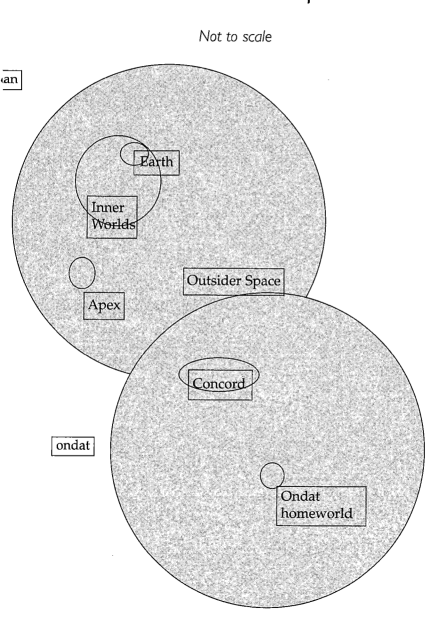

˙˙˙
iii

Power

EARTH AND ITS ENVIRONS

EARTH, WITH ITS FEDERATION of the Sol System planets and moons, Luna, Mars, et al. Its current center of government: Adacion, in New Brazil, its legislature comprised of representatives of ten regional earthly councils, plus five space-based councils.

Earth maintains strict immigration control over its space. Its large military establishment, partly robotic, enforces the Quarantine Laws.

Earth appoints governors for all stations, except Apex. Earth made the Treaty that ended the Gene Wars, and Earth continues to enforce Treaty Law.

It does not permit immigration and does not trade in material goods.

THE INNER WORLDS

From roughly twelve lights of Earth outward to a distance of twenty lights: three successfully colonized worlds and fourteen stations in the area are administered by Earth governors. They are much more Earthlike than Outsider in philosophy and law, and impose purity laws nearly as stringent as Earth's.

OUTSIDERS

Comprising the bulk of the human species, Outsiders remain nominally under Earth government, as regards Treaty Law, but govern themselves and trade freely.

APEX

Apex Station, the military and governmental center of Outsider culture, orbits an Earthlike planet, Apex Prime, which has been successfully, though sparsely, colonized.

The Apex High Council elects the Chairman General, the chief executive over Outsider Space. The High Council, called the Apex Council everywhere but on Apex, appoints the Supreme Judiciary as well as the twenty-odd chairmen who serve as Outsider executive authority on stations throughout Outsider Space. These chairmen share civil power with Earth-appointed governors on various stations, and have authority over Outsider citizens, whether in trade or civil law.

THE RUINED WORLDS

Four sites, including Aldestra and Luzan, inhabited worlds, once subject to ill-advised terraforming, and carefully monitored from orbit. Direct contact is not permitted. Aldestra possesses a seasonally nomadic culture. Luzan's population clings to life.

OTHER OUTSIDER STATIONS

Orb, Arc, Serine, Momus, and the other Outsider stations all have a bilevel government. Earth-born governors serve as the station executive, overseeing maintenance, heavy manufacturing, and trade, and ruling over a separate society of Earthborn and Earth-affiliated citizens, who are generally financiers, traders, industrialists, technicians, occasional religionists, and providers of specialized services—all well-educated, generally well-monied individuals. Earthers are relatively few in number on the stations they govern—a layer of technical administration serving to keep the station mechanicals working and guaranteeing stability. Like gravity on a planet, it costs relatively little, has assured a firm footing for a long time, and no one is particularly interested in challenging it.

More numerous, Outsiders reside usually on a separate deck, with their own trading associations, hospitals, social services, and mercantile endeavors, their political factions, and their labs—that essentially defining item of Outsider culture. Outsider trade and use of biotech nanisms make Earthers very reluctant to mingle with the darker elements of Outsider communities. This guarantees that real law enforcement rests with the Outsider Council and the local chairman.

CONCORD STATION

Marak's World might be counted as a fifth Ruined World, except for the extensive remediation efforts that are an ongoing basis of Earth-Outsider-ondat cooperation, on which the all-important Treaty rests, and no one ever suggests failure. Its solar system, of which it is now the sole life-bearing planet, lies within that region of unintended overlap between *ondat* and human space.

Concord Station is an important trade partner of Apex, Arc, and Orb. It speaks a language ages-vanished, and all incoming media have to be translated for the majority of its citizenry.

Concord's governor is, as elsewhere, Earth-appointed. Its Outsider chairman is Apex-appointed. No one understands how the *ondat* observer is chosen . . . but one exists here, making Concord unique among stations: *ondat* ships visit here, another anomaly. The total *ondat* population at Concord is fewer than five—humans think. No one asks or knows what their power structure may be, how long they stay, or what they report to their distant authority. No one has ever gotten a clear view of an *ondat,* though shadowy images are in classified files.

The Planetary Office installation, whose director is appointed by the Apex Council and who reports to that body, is unique to Concord. The PO, as it is called, constitutes an Outsider authority independent of ordinary station administration, one specifically charged with overseeing remediation efforts on Marak's World.

That three nations and two species can coexist here argues that an *ondat*-human peace, like planetary life, is evolving slowly. There seems to be progress.

But remediation, and therefore the peace itself, is still in doubt.

Forge of Heaven

1

GROZNY WAS WHERE LEBEAU Street mingled with the Style, where the low haunts of Blunt Street flowed into the Trend and rubbed shoulders with the rich and carefree.

Heart of the Trend on Concord Station, Grozny Street, where the Style walked side by side with gray-suited, slumming Earthers from exclusive upper levels, the ruling class making their own statement in shades of pearl and charcoal. Flashing newsboards warred, streaming stock and futures tickers under cosmetic adverts and the dockside news. A ship from Earth was coming in. *That* was major news, rare and interesting, but it didn't immediately affect the Trend, and it didn't affect Procyon, né Jeremy Stafford, walking home from dinner, an easy stroll through the neon and the crowds.

There was Jonah's Place, and The Ox, there was Right Ascension, Farah's, and La Lune Noir, there was The Body Shop and the Blue Lounge—and the Health Connection, which cleaned up the Body Shop's done-on-a-whims. There was Tia Juana's, the Ethiopia, and the high-toned Astral Plane . . . not to mention the exclusive little shops that sold everything from designer genes to boots—and there was The Upper Crust, that very nice little pastry shop that Procyon did his best to stay out of.

The whole station came to Grozny to relax—well, except those solid citizens content with the quiet little establishments in their own zones, or with the output of their own kitchens. Most daytimers to Grozny took the lift system into the Trend. Very few citizens had the cachet or the funds to live here.

But Jeremy—who preferred to be Procyon—had the funds, a fact clear enough in the cut of the clothes, the precious metals of the bracelets, the small, tasteful modifications that an observer might automatically suspect were at issue here, since the body was good-looking.

He was twenty-five and single. He was a former Freethinker turned Fashionable because he liked it, not because he lived by the social tyranny of the Stylists. And he was fit and in condition the hard way, not because he had any great fear of mods, but because of a certain personal discipline. He spent every third night working out at Patrick's Gym, every next night taking laps at the Speed Rink, and only every seventh night carousing with friends down at Tia Carmen's or wherever else their little band of affluent young professionals decided to gather.

He had turned toward home tonight from that seventh-night gathering, warm with drink and the recollection of good company. Home was a little behind the main frontage of Grozny, so to speak, a T-shaped pocket, a pleasantly lit little dead-end street called Grozny Close, which protected its hundred or so apartments from the traffic and rush and the slightly higher crime rate of Grozny Street proper. Number 201 Grozny Close, sandwiched between a highly successful lawyer and a retired surgeon, had a blue door, a shining chrome arch, and a tall orchid tree that Grozny Close maintenance changed out whenever its blooms failed. The whole Close was a riot of such well-kept gardens, and the air consequently smelled less of the restaurants out on the street and far more of the lawyer's gardenias.

The button beside the door knew his thumbprint and let him in, and after the security system looked him over and decided he was absolutely the owner, the floor lifted him up to the main level, the middle one.

It wasn't a huge apartment. It had fine amenities—the wall-to-wall entertainment unit in the main room was his life's greatest extravagance, the one he personally most enjoyed. But, being he'd had a few drinks, it was upstairs that drew him more than the evening news, which he knew was going to be full of speculation on that inbound ship and no real information at all.

Boring stuff. And he was too tired to order a sim, which cost, and which would run longer than he would stay awake. He took the few steps up, undressed, and slipped into the floating, drifting serenity of his own bed.

Eyes shut. Perfect. Not a care in the world.

Except—

Damn.

Eyes wide open. His parents' anniversary. He'd forgotten to get the requisite present.

"Sam," he moaned. Sam was what he called the computer. "Sam, day reminder for 0830h, onquote: anniversary, endquote. Night, Sam."

"Good night," Sam said sweetly, not questioning the enigma of the note. "Sleep tight."

His mother had used to say that. Whimsy or guilty secret, it put him in a mind to rest, so he assigned it to Sam. Sleep tight.

Duty was done. Work tomorrow. Life was very good.

MORNING BECAME A suspicion in the east. The beshti set to munching the nearby brush, a noisy activity, distraction to a man trying to sleep in his tent until after the sun rose. But so was a wife with notions of lovemaking. Hati was determined, and Marak Trin Tain never refused that request.

That took its time. Hati got her due, and more, and the night watcher politely left them alone, always there, but inattentive. Marak lay afterward with his wife in his arms, eyes shut, listening to the beshti at their breakfast, listening to the boys begin to stir about in the dawn.

Boys: the young men of this generation, two of them with well-grown beards. Young blood was anxious for adventure, willing to cook and pack and heft the big tent about. Marak could show them what they couldn't learn in the Refuge. He could show them the old skills, the knowledge that had kept their ancestors alive. He could tell them about the desert as it had been and as it was, and they drank in such stories.

Young people nowadays were ambitious to recover the world, living in notions the old stories gave them. A few, yes, wanted to be technicians and stay in the halls of the Refuge forever. But a good many more wanted to go adventuring and slip the well-thought law of the Refuge for the absolute freedom of the horizons.

They would not, however, escape the watchers in the heavens. Their reach extended and extended, aided by new relays, and the watchers often foretold events that had used to surprise the world. Part of what the young men loaded onto the beshti with the tents this morning was, in fact, another relay tower, which, unfolded to the sky, anchored to the rock and powered by the sun, made contact with such adventurers as themselves much more dependable. And that made the Refuge much less worried about them.

Marak himself had watched the hammer fall, when the *ondat* had brought retribution on the world. Hati had seen it. The two of them together had seen the rain of fire in the heavens, had seen ice fall in the desert, had seen the heavens wrapped in the smoke of volcanic fires beyond the sea, and the air turned to suffocating poison.

Through all of it, they lived.

They lived, while the earth and even the sea died and stank of corruption, deprived of light and clean air, leaving life only in the depths of vents and the cracks the hammerfall had made.

They had lived to see the first rockets go out, bearing spores on the raging winds and landing the first relays.

They had seen the rains fall and the air begin to clear. They had seen the desert change and flow with water, seen volcanoes belch out molten rock, seen the world crack and new rifts begin to move.

They had seeded the land and shed life into the waterways that ran down to the sea.

And, eventually, chafing at the restrictions of the Refuge, they had saddled up the beshti and gone out to see their handiwork. To this day, when something was in the offing, he and Hati found themselves a handful of willing young people to go with them—not that they needed the help, but company on the long treks was welcome . . . and safer. And it passed on the knowledge into the generations that lived and died around them. The two of them were immortal, for all practical purposes, immortal as the Ila, who shut herself among her records and dealt in knowledge for what she wanted; immortal as Memnanan, who served her with remarkable patience and remained mostly loyal . . . immortal as Ian and Luz, who were older than the fortress in the sky, but not as old as the Ila. Ian and Luz ruled the Refuge, and their word was law, though they spoke very seldom in matters that regarded the tribes.

They, themselves, Marak and Hati, ruled all the tribes. There were long periods of dull routine in the camps around the Refuge; and there were times when they shook the dust of the ordinary off them and rode out into the world.

But whatever they did, they had the watchers in the heavens with them, in their heads, hearing what they said, making records. Ian and Luz could speak to them, through that means.

And they had that other observer, the Ila's au'it, the recorder of their travels, herself both old and young. She slept, or not, in the shadows of the tent near them.

But from the caravan master to his boys, the younger company was awake and rolling up their mats. The youngest boy began to make tea, while the master packed for the day's journey.

There was enough light now to claim it was daybreak. A great event was imminent in the south. The Southern Wall had grown fragile, and lately trembled with quakes. Consequently they hastened to extend the relays toward that region, widening their view of the world in that direction.

A beshta complained to the coming sun, protesting its day's work.

"If we get up," Marak murmured into his wife's ear, "the boys can strike the tent."

"If we refuse to get up," Hati said, "we can strike it after morning tea."

"The Wall may break, and us not there to see it."

Hati sighed. And sighed again, and sat up, her dark braids, gold-banded, falling loose about her face and swaying against his cheek as she leaned to kiss him. "Up," Hati said. *Hup*. That word they used to the beshti. And he gathered himself up. A clean, cold wind was blowing. It would turn hot by noon.

THE SHIP INBOUND was the *Southern Cross*, Constellation class, Earth origin. That meant weapons, which meant enforcement, which sometimes meant a political presence that outranked a system governor. Routine ship-calls from that distant source arrived only once a year. And their current year was far from up.

Setha Reaux, who *was* system governor, consulted his records, anxiously searching for something regarding that ship, its recent business, and its possible reason for showing up all the way to Concord, to this most sensitive post outside Earth itself . . . where, if a ship arrived, it was not just passing through.

The Outsider Council was clearly tracking that arrival. Reaux had a call from Antonio Brazis, Chairman of that body and director of Planetary Observations.

The resident *ondat* official, Kekellen, had likewise noticed it, and sent one of his or her enigmatic queries, which had gone to technical committee for analysis, and a careful answer.

Setha Reaux, consequently, had spent last night in the office. He had a call from his wife backed up among the queries from various departments right now. He had postponed dealing with it, as one more straw on his back, likely the breaking point. He'd made over ten drafts of a message to that inbound ship, but, unable to find the right words, had sent nothing to it as yet. Now he feared his failure to salute that ship at first sight might in itself be seen as arrogance or cowardice, and he increasingly believed he had to do something.

A massive globe-garden sat cradled in the corner of the office. Most such globes were small, islands of pure Earth genes, a few algaes, a little wisp of life. Add a moving creature, and complexity increased. Add light and warmth, and life carried on, microcosms of Earth's evolution, from salt seas to life on land. His globe, imported at great cost from Earth itself, involved anoles, quick, flitting creatures that fed and mated, birthed and died and fed the plants that fed the creatures that fed them.

Concord Station itself was such a bubble, not as successfully self-contained. *They* had governments that came from the outside and, if not carefully managed, fed on Concord itself.

He drafted another message. He stripped it to the bare, necessary bones: *Setha Reaux, Governor of Concord System, to the captain of arriving ship* Southern Cross:

Welcome. We look forward to receiving you, and hope that this visit will be enjoyable.

There. Less was more. No speculation, no apology for delay, just general good wishes, his willingness to cooperate, his total blithe innocence of threat . . . or the fact he should have said something eight hours ago.

And he *was* innocent of wrongdoing, damn it, except a few questionable items some real stickler for accounting might fault, if an audit started looking for excuses. There were the sports arena solicitations, but they were entirely legal—he was sure they were legal, and he and the board had made peace last year.

Nothing *that* piddling small could have brought an Earth ship out here.

Promotions came out of such unscheduled visits, but his governorship was already the highest rank a man could attain. Some aspirant in some lower post, but with high connections, might, on the other hand, get a promotion upstairs, to his doorstep—Reaux's perpetual nightmare: that the urgent need to move somebody's nephew out of a sensitive spot, reasonable enough at the other end of the telescope, could eventually get said nephew promoted upstairs to trouble his life—or even to replace him, since his political connections had been in the prior, more reasonable administration.

Never say absolutely it couldn't happen. Governments did incredibly stupid things at long distance, and this one had certainly done its share, but his displacement was unlikely. The fact that Concord was the most sensitive spot in the immediate universe— the one in direct contact with the *ondat*, who could still, in a misunderstanding, devastate human civilization—meant that Concord's governor most often rode through governmental changes untouched, no matter what craziness—even minor wars—convulsed and overthrew the Inner Worlds.

As for the arena controversy, and all of local politics—silly small issues obsessed Concord's local news services precisely because Concord had no close connection with events outside its own perimeter. That insularity was why a stupid social tempest in the sports club blew all out of proportion and bounced through every governmental department. It was why the president of Concord Bank and Trust, Lyle Nazrani, had fired the head of the CB&T's corporate finance department, and then was all over the media in a campaign of high-profile interviews laced with innuendo.

Stupidity. Lyle Nazrani might even try to lodge charges, but

Earth wouldn't give a damn about the luxury seating in the arena or the ownership of the suppliers. It would never question the finance: more to the point, Lyle Nazrani, colony-born, didn't have the personal connections on Earth to make that issue a threat. The ship had certainly stirred the local rumor mill, made a major to-do in the media, and unsettled the markets. That was the sort of collateral damage this ship could produce just by its appearance, trouble for him to deal with long after it left with its own business settled. But of all possibilities, Lyle Nazrani's political ambition surely *wasn't* why they were here.

One surety was that if this off-schedule visit had disturbed the *ondat*, that was a problem with far-reaching repercussions, a problem that concerned more than Earth's authorities. Foreseeing uneasiness in the Outsider offices, he sent Chairman Brazis one very short message; in effect, call me, *stat.*

He had answered Kekellen, sent a message to the inbound ship, and invited consultation with Brazis. Now he had to feed something out to the news services, whose initial clamor for interviews had now devolved to half-wit speculations on the incoming ship. So-named well-placed sources had leapt up to recall every forgotten piece of business in his administration and the prior administration that might be at issue—including the construction of the new station and the sports arena, damn them one and all. One news broker in particular he had marked for his personal wrath when all this blew over. And the news had to be diverted. Given something else to cover. Some other headline. *We have sent a welcome to the inbound ship, and anticipate a constructive meeting:* constructive was a good, a positive word. Let the commentators gnaw on that one. He sat at the center of an informational web and managed it as skillfully as he could.

He'd stayed at his desk, he'd ordered supper and now breakfast in. The news services were lurking out there to catch him on any transit he made between home and office. He had three different terminals active, heard reports from various agencies, went over the last six years' tax records, and wondered extraneously if he could call in a personal favor from an editor to keep a certain senior reporter's series on finance from airing. He didn't want any current quotes floating through the news services.

Chime of an incoming contact from his secretary's office . . . the uninvited input passed through Ernst, and most minor nuisances stopped at Ernst's desk. The major ones, unfortunately, didn't.

Reaux unhappily pushed the button. "Yes?"

"Your wife's on, sir."

He'd called and told Judy he'd be doing an overnighter. He *had* called.

Hadn't he?

"Put her through." Deep breath. He heard the click. "Judy?"

"Setha?" There was upset in that voice. *"Setha, she's* blond*!"*

Their daughter's hair. He dimly recalled an argument. Kathy's desire for a new haircut. An appointment at Whispers, begged for by his wife.

All of which was a thousand k from current reality.

"Judy, have you looked at the news since yesterday? There's a ship from Earth coming in."

"It's platinum blond!"

Kathy had gone blond. He couldn't imagine Whispers doing something like that without consultation.

"Judy, just calm down. It's just hair. It's not a mod. It grows out."

"I want your support in this! I don't want you making any more excuses for her!"

"Not a single excuse. Didn't the shop call you first, for God's sake?"

"She didn't go to Renee! She ducked her appointment and went to one of those walk-in places!"

Their daughter Kathy, blond. Olive skin, dark eyes, and the best shops—and blond. It was an appalling thought.

But not a thought on a scale that could engage his attention today.

"Judy, just calm down. Take her to Renee and get it fixed. Buy her a new outfit." So his fifteen-year-old daughter bleached her hair. It was one more shot fired in a generational war. His wife, a queen of society whose conservative taste ran to pearls and gray suiting, hadn't radically changed her hairstyle in twenty years. Now Judy ran up against a daughter who had her mother's iron will and a dose of free spirit from God knew where. Kathy's ideas came bubbling up in color combinations that—her mother's words— belonged down on Blunt Street. Kathy thought that was a good thing. Judy didn't. The argument was loud. Judy's demand for obedience in matters of reputation and appearance was inflexible.

Personally, he felt sorry for his daughter.

On an ordinary day.

"I can't just take her to Renee! Renee has appointments! And I can't take her into Whispers like this, in public!"

"Renee can come to the apartment, can't she? Just explain the problem, pay the woman off—buy her theater tickets. It can be fixed, Judy. Just use your imagination. And don't call me with the details. I have a serious problem here. We all could have a serious, career-ending problem if dealings with this ship blow up, and I can't think with the two of you going at it. Just take care of this yourself. All right?" Calm, quiet voice, against Judy's panic. It was a secure line. Security saw to that, constantly. "Take a deep breath. You have my complete support. Call Renee. It won't take that long. It'll all be fixed."

"I don't know why she does these things!"

"It can be fixed. It's not an illicit. She's not pregnant. Go do it, Judy. I love you."

Click. Judy hung up, not happy. Judy was going to go have herself a cry and call Renee, and cry some more after that.

Trendy, too-tight clothes. Too much makeup. Kathy was fifteen-going-on-twenty, and Judy was trying to keep her socially respectable in a crowd Kathy had the brains and the family connections to rule with an iron hand, if she ever set her mind and her energies to it. Notably, Kathy could toss Ippoleta Nazrani and her little fuzzy-sweatered clique into social oblivion in another year, *if* Kathy didn't squander the social capital she had before her taste caught up to her budget.

He relied on his wife to bring on that day. He detested Lyle Nazrani. He truly detested Lyle Nazrani, and particularly Lyle's wife Katrione, without whose vitriol the whole arena scandal would never have existed. And he extended it to their social queen daughter, the bane of Kathy's young life.

"Ernst?"

"Yes, sir. I do copy. I'll try to handle anything she needs. Breakfast is here, sir."

Well, something went right.

*   *   *

0915H. EARLY TO WORK. With a pile of diet wafers and a snack bar balanced on a saucer in one hand, a pot of caff in the other, and a notebook under his arm, Procyon navigated the door of his basement home office, elbowed the switch, and let the robot turn the lights on.

He let the door shut on auto, set down his load on the cabinet, and settled into the depths of his work chair without spilling anything, step one. The automatics had turned the room-ringing monitors on. The second of two transcript sticks dropped into a tray.

Step two, arrange his notebook and set spillable items into various holders. Step three, pour a cup, settle back, and take a sip, first good caffeine hit of the morning.

Step three, pop the sticks into the reader.

He flicked a finger to scroll the transcript past his view of the room, transparent mode, floating in air, so they seemed—so he could still see the relay monitors. He had implants—could see one thing in one eye, one thing in the other, and still see through both to account for what was going on in the screens, but he didn't like that much input at once while he was still on his first cup of caff. He coordinated the transcript vision to both eyes . . . visual, because he wholly detested listening to audio acceleration. The jabber, even computer-sifted for significant bits in emphasis, gave him a headache. He preferred the civilized act of reading.

And reading, this morning, turned up an interesting discussion Marak and Hati had had with the caravan workers last night. He wasn't sure whether the information in the discussion was new to the record, and thought probably it wasn't—astronomical probability it wasn't, in fact, in the long history of this post—but it very much interested him, to the point he conceived a notion of writing an official memo expanding on those remarks about preimpact wind patterns, relative to something else Marak had once said on *his* watch.

It might get more attention than his last effort, which had turned out not to be news to anyone else in the PO.

Second sip. Personal ritual as fixed as the station in its orbit.

He counted himself beyond lucky to get his assignment, let

alone to have day shift. After midnight down on the world, when staid, scholarly Auguste was online, didn't produce much activity—well, not the truly significant kind—except in the mornings. If there was any of the three shifts he had rather have, it was Drusus's, whose watch was during the station and planetary evenings, when Marak often grew philosophical, or discussed plans with his companions and his wife. But his shift was certainly next-best, full of the midday's activity.

And important, God, yes. His job, with his two associates' effort, was the most important thing that went on in all of Concord, and not only in his own estimation. It might not be the most exciting, in the day-to-day conduct of things as certain people would see it, since they were watching—in the slow, day-to-day scale of mortal humans—the re-evolution of a planet, on a geologic scale. More to the point, they recorded and analyzed the day-to-day doings of the one living individual who mattered most in the Treaty, the one ongoing life that for some reason kept the *ondat* themselves intrigued and watching. Marak had lived through the Hammerfall. He was still alive. Mountains rose and eroded away. Tectonic plates moved. And Marak went on living, and the *ondat* went on sitting here at Concord, watching, and refraining from war.

Procyon Stafford was the latest of a long, long, *long* line of observers.

And the transcript that came to him said that things were routine, that Marak and Hati had reminisced during Drusus's watch, slept through an uneventful night on Auguste's, risen and ridden out with their companions in the tail end of Auguste's, all this in intermittent contact with Ian, back at the Refuge . . . that absent-minded flow of information passed between two men who had been sharing random remarks for all of time, and who long since had learned to finish each other's sentences.

The transcript said Marak and his party had gotten under way a little late in the day, for them. Marak, when he was out in the land, believed that a day began at whatever time the terminator swung near enough to be a hint on the horizon—that kind of *late.* Which meant Marak had been up and moving for, oh, about five or six planetary hours by now, without saying much at all. None of it was unusual, especially not in Marak's scale.

Auguste's transcript ended with the note: *Small discussion relative to landmarks (ref 288) and plant growth, which Marak declares to be common graze and false pearl plant, no samples taken.*

Note: the release of insect life (see my note: ref 122) has not shown up here, but it must exist nearby, since windblown seed from the graze plant has reached this point (ref 1587) . . .

God. Typical Auguste, whose style crowded more words onto a thought than he personally liked, but Auguste did have a clear vision of the ecology, was dead-on accurate on his references, and usually had intelligent suggestions and comments to inject.

Windblown, Auguste reminded them, in answer to his own naive suggestion of his last watch. *Wind*blown, which he just hadn't thought of. Things on the station didn't ordinarily pick up and travel—at least on the macroscopic level. But a field of graze plant was not going to reproduce if insects didn't find it, and it couldn't be here if insects hadn't had something to do with it—or—of course—the wind. The wind and the insects. A textbook case of life constantly paving the way for itself. Procyon felt his face flush, reading Auguste's untargeted comment on his suggestion yesterday, that he thought the unsupported graze plant must be an earlier seeding, when it turned out—trust Auguste to have his references, and a mind like an encyclopedia—that no one had visited this area in ages.

Thus proving Auguste's theory. And proving the newest member of the observation team wasn't clever enough to make observations—yet.

Survival on Marak's World was such a complex, interwoven thing, so many things to think of, so foreign to his way of thinking. A plant died without bugs, and the bugs needed the plants to get food out of the elements. The one needed the other to reproduce, and the other needed the one to live at all. The wind carried the seeds *and* the bugs, and if bugs and seeds got in the wrong order, the bugs were certainly worse off, not being able to live at all. Penalty of being higher up the food chain.

He absorbed the data. Beyond the data, he tried to imagine what it was *like* to stand on the planet surface, like Marak, feeling an earthly wind on his face, experiencing a rush of air that wasn't a fan-driven draft from an open vent, but rather the product of heating and cooling and the rotation of a planet. He tried to adjust his lifelong thinking—admittedly only twenty years' worth—in terms of things that moved on the wind as well as by gravity and a thousand other interrelated causes that a station-dweller might not think of. He wondered what it was to watch the stars go out because the world was turning toward the sun, and he imagined what it felt like to see that first suspicion of dawn come over the edge of a convex horizon.

He loved the thought. He swore he'd volunteer to go down without thinking twice, if they ever had to replace Ian or Luz, as, who knew? *could* happen—if Ian or Luz fell off a cliff. He was sure he could adapt to living forever. He'd like to live forever, no matter the documented downside of that gift and the questions about sanity that consoled those of them that lived and died in normal span, up here on the station. He was sure he could adapt to immortality quite nicely. He'd ride the open land for years, just getting acquainted with the world. Of course Marak would teach him. He'd find the new seedings they'd let loose on a ravaged planet. He'd see lightning from underneath, and listen to thunder with his own ears, and watch the spread of species by means space-based humans just didn't ordinarily think about, and he'd spend the first hundred years just riding around watching things, before he even got down to taking notes.

Daydreams, those were. No station-dweller was immortal, and no one went down to the planet. No one ever went down, that was the very point, the reason Concord was here in the first place, staving off war and *ondat* craziness. The world below, Marak's World, was a permanent sealed laboratory, and three governments' armed forces saw that it stayed sealed, no matter what happened elsewhere, no matter what governments did, no matter what cataclysms came and went. Concord swung around Marak's World, and, like Marak's World, Concord, too, changed very, very little from what remotest ancestors had known.

Planets? There were worlds in Outsider Space you could land on and live on if you wanted to stay on them forever, but Procyon had no interest in those: they were just as isolate as Marak's World, but the stations above them were, from all he knew, strange, secretive, and focused on a trade in oddments. The people down on those carefully guarded worlds might have been human once, but the one culture struggled with agriculture that wouldn't cooperate, mines that collapsed, and native life that wasn't amenable to their presence, while another was nomadic and barely surviving the violent winters, not to mention the ones where humans hadn't survived at all. No, no interest in being assigned to any of those stations, not in this Concord-born researcher.

This world—Marak's World, that had been the focus of interspecies controversy, this technology-ravaged world—was the most human of all the colonized planets. It was self-ruling, managing its own environment through all the changes, and its changes were progressive, building up, not just churning away at the edge of catastrophe. Granted, one human lifetime wouldn't see it: but Marak's World was improving constantly from the days of the Hammerfall—was hauling itself up out of the years of destruction and making itself more than viable, while *ondat* and humans watched. It was a pace of change that, so certain authorities believed, had encouraged *ondat* to become friendlier. The *ondat*-human relationship did change, however slowly, and the *ondat* communicated, these days, on the third station to bear the name Concord.

A long, long watch. Teams did archaeology over at Mission One station, and brought strange things to the museum, oddments that few people could even figure out, and some of them were stranger still, leavings of the *ondat*, that today's *ondat* scarcely recognized. Stations had been orbiting Marak's World, yes, that long, since the Hammerfall, and the world below them had many, many centuries yet to go before anyone remotely contemplated unraveling the quarantine or changing the treaties that depended on it.

But change did happen. And for a watcher who'd only just begun on his job, there was hope that before he left it, he might see a few more klicks of grassland grow, and a settlement or two spring up.

Meanwhile he had constant pictures from the camera sites around the world: the ceiling-high half ring of monitors that surrounded him gave him a constantly shifting view, a few from inside the refuge, another out on the volcanic islands, where smoke generally obscured the view. One observation station sat high above the seacoast, where waves broke against jagged rock, and yet another up on the high plateau, where sand still flowed off the edges. He could shift any one of these cameras to the transparent view in his contact lenses, making one of them his momentary, if dizzying reality. He did it, when storms swept in. He loved the lightning, particularly, and the rain.

0955h. He was about to become recording angel, that particular presence in the heavens that watched over Marak, recorded his information—and advised him in case the wisest man on earth ever needed advice from orbit.

Procyon ate the wafers—the bar was lunch—then poured his second cup of caff and re-read the more interesting details of Drusus's transcript from last evening to midnight, waiting for the handoff.

Marak had promised Ian last week that the party would be well up the heights today, wending their way on a safe approach to the Southern Wall. When it came to schedules out in the wild, Marak tended to be right, and today, in fact, he was well along on the very thinnest part of that spit of basalt and sandstone that rose like a spine between the southern basin and the deep cut of the Needle Gorge to the north.

Day sixty-four. Marak said he meant to set up an intermediate base unit on this spine of rock, positioning a new camera so that the Refuge could monitor this curious dividing line between river-cut Plateau uplift and the sinking terrain of the southern pans.

And after that, proceeding along that curving spine, he'd take another twenty days to reach the Wall and set up the most important observation station, with camera and global-positioning equipment. Hitherto the Project had only observed the situation at the Southern Wall from orbit, or in the seismic records, the latter of which said that the downdrop fault that edged the Wall was increasingly active—that fault being the reason Marak was going the long way around and avoiding the lowland pans. Speculation was that the combined forces of a moving plate would rip the Southern Wall apart, and if that happened, the pans of the Southern Desert would be a floodplain in a matter of days . . .

Not to mention what might result as the colliding plates sorted out precedence. One might override the other. Mountains, volcanics, might result. Geologists were extraordinarily excited, in their longsighted way: on a scale of geologic change, there was a certain urgency in the signs in the earth . . . which pointed up the fact that right now they had no camera in the area. They'd landed one, that had lasted a week, thanks to an imperfect positioning: it had fallen to the notorious violence of the winter storms. Ian had his next rocket in preparation now, and had fretted and fussed and wished Marak would stay around the Refuge and let it all be done by robotics, instead of trekking out to a region of current hazard. But Marak disregarded Ian's objections and went to watch personally the dynamics of a restless land, the unstable nature of a wide basin below sea level, a burning desert suddenly opened to icy antarctic water. Never mind science, Procyon suspected: Marak wanted to *see* it.

So did he. He spent his off-hours reading the bulletins that flowed from geology, from metereology, from biology, disciplines that had suddenly acquired immediacy for him. All that icy new sea would be shallow, quickly warmed by the sun, cooled by winds off the Southern Sea, meteorologically significant—and, when it happened, in his lifetime or three watchers along, it would be a laboratory of biologic change right in their own laps, when the icy water, with its life, met the superheated pans and lay there for a few centuries, breeding new things in the shallows.

But continental plates moved at their own pace . . . gave signs of imminency, and then might refuse to move for a decade or so.

Which—a sigh, a return to mortal perspective—was something for the immortals, not two-years-on-the-job watchers still trying to justify their existence.

A glance at the clock. Coming up on 1000h.

With a thoughtless effort, Procyon tapped in, a simple shunt of blood pressure behind both eyes and ears.

Triple flash of light. That was his personal signature, coming in. Double flash exited. That was Auguste, outbound. It was a courtesy they paid Marak, just to let him know without disturbing him.

Hati's watchers weren't active but every third day, at the moment. It was vacation for them, during the days she was constantly close to Marak. It was only when that pair separated that Hati's watchers enjoyed full employment.

The teams all took their turns, however. His three-man team had a five-day rest coming up, oh, in about two weeks, when Hati's team would be on full-time for at least eighteen days straight.

That was the other benefit of this job—frequent and lengthy furlough, to let nerves rest and overloaded senses readjust to the world he lived in. In his two years on the job, he'd been on three months of furlough.

For now, officially on the job, he settled back in his chair, let the caff cool just a little, and shut his eyes. He couldn't *see* the world through his taps, but he could hear it through Marak's ears, and the cameras let him imagine the sights. He picked up a gentle creak: saddle leather. Two voices conversed, one, Marak's, he could definitely understand, one distant and generally hard to discern. That was Hati. All day long he lived with that accent—that very old accent, that never changed because it had living speakers. It didn't change, and, consequently, Concord's language didn't change. It was always what it had been, no matter what the rest of the Outside did. He had to be careful, however, about picking up the onworld lilt in his own speech, a giveaway, in a program very careful not to give away the identities or occupations of its most critical personnel.

Marak and Hati fell silent for a long space, and he picked up just the sound of the beshti. In front of his chair, the view of onworld monitors endlessly cycled in hypnotic, fractal regularity. In most of the monitors the sun was shining. Near the seacoast, rain spotted the lens, and up in the saw-toothed Quarain it was snowing, while the islands to the west were, as usual, obscured in volcanic smoke and steam. One gray spot in the cycle of monitors indicated a relay had come to grief this morning, gone out of service: Procyon noted its number in the sequence and bent forward and flicked buttons. The actual location of the site was up on the high desert plateau: he marked it for autorepair or eventual replacement, both technical functions outside his domain.

The site had been hammered by hail, maybe. Or cyclone. It was at least one of the sites in fairly convenient reach of the Refuge, not in Marak's direction on this trek, however. It was a relay that—he checked the record—Memnon's fourth daughter had set up on her last trek in that direction.

That was old, then, five hundred years or more. A wonder it had been still functioning, as was. He put the whole problem into his report for Brazis. Auguste had missed it—unlikely, since Auguste rarely dropped a stitch—or the malfunction had just happened.

The monitors kept *him* sane in this job, confined in a viewless room. They lent him a sense of utter freedom, of wandering the planet below at any slight moment of boredom. While Marak was in range of cameras, as he was within the Refuge itself, he could maintain a schizophrenic identification with Marak and his surroundings, and with Hati; when Marak had been there, he had seen, sometimes, Ian and Luz and more than once, the Ila, who, diminutive and beautiful, was the scariest individual he had ever imagined.

For Marak, he held the mental image of a man in his thirties, more often than not wrapped in the robes of his long-lived tribe, which Marak preferred. Marak's people learned new skills, knew computers and bioscience, hydroponics and engineering, mining and manufacture, the old ways and the new. Most of Marak's people wore clothing that was far more conservative than one saw on the station, but certainly not desert robes. These generations stepped aside and stared in awe when one of the Old Ones, young as themselves, walked through the halls of the Refuge, a breath of the past in their body-swathing, tribal-patterned robes, with the aifad, the veil that kept moisture in, dust out, and thoughts private. Talk stopped. Imagination—came up against a wall.

They were all special, the surviving Old Ones, suffering no age, no death except by mishap so severe and sudden their internal nanisms failed to make repairs. They passed their longevity to their children not by genetics but by infection; and could bestow it on strangers as well, but they rarely did that, as hard experience had, so the literature said, made it clear that generations more focused on a mortal timescale did not easily adjust.

The world, since the Hammerfall, had reacquired a biological clock. Latter-day lives ran by nearer and nearer expectations of outcome, and began to think that several days of waiting was long.

The original Old Ones not only had learned Outsider science, they had a personal memory of the Hammerfall: that was one thing. The Ila, oldest of all, had the memory of the Gene Wars and the Landing, and had originated the nanisms that had reshaped the ecology, a life span that staggered the mind even to contemplate. That handful of immortals had a community that transcended old feuds, had a shared perspective that somehow anchored them in time, a shared reality from which they were all born and from which they seemed to derive their curious sense of scale. He had read Marak's personal views on the subject, in which Marak swore he'd beget no more children, and give no one else his gift: it was too hard, Marak said, for the later born, without that cataclysmic event of the Hammerfall in their past.

Why? Why was it hard? What had the immortals all seen, that made that moment the changing point? Procyon yearned most of all to ask such questions, sure that there were more than the obvious drawbacks to immortality that a callow twenty-five-year-old could think of. He was sure there was a word somewhere in it that could give him a far different perspective than he had, a perspective that might be useful in what he did—so useful, so immensely useful, he might become an expert, an oracle in the service of the Project, if he had it.

Brazis would have his hide if he spoke to Marak unbidden, that was what—well, except for weather warnings and the like. If Marak ever wanted to exchange views with him, philosophically speaking, Marak easily could do that, and so far didn't, and thus far showed no interest in doing so, which would likely be the rule forever.

Marak apparently liked him, however. Marak had chosen him out of a hundred possibles, not the most experienced watcher on staff—in fact, the least. Not the brightest, maybe, certainly not graced by the best record in the Project, being only third-shift watcher of one of the youngest of Memnon's line, aged six, and having gotten into the Planetary Office by the skin of his teeth in the first place, despite his lack of connections inside the Project. He didn't know *why* Marak liked him. He certainly wasn't the watcher the Chairman had wanted Marak to pick, he was sure of that—but the regs said all possible choices had to be in the pool when one of the seniors chose, and the ancient agreements said it was absolutely Marak's choice to make, end of statement.

So after sifting through all availables, Marak had picked him, for reasons Marak never had to explain, and the rules, most tantalizing, never let the subject of that selection ask.

The little he did know—Marak's seniormost watcher, the day watcher, had died of old age, time finally overtaking even the most highly modified in the Planetary Office. Marak, Drusus had told him, didn't want somebody senior, coming in with perspective and history with him, and especially didn't want someone with a long record of intimacy with any other of his contemporaries. Marak, he overheard in the Project hallways, zealously avoided politics and kept his own counsel. And the same whisper among the watchers, some jealous, said Marak might test him for years before he said a thing to him of a personal nature.

Or Marak might never talk directly to him at all. He knew it must frustrate the Planetary Office that Marak wasn't talking to his daytime watcher in the frank, offhanded way he'd talked to the last one. A source of information had gone. And all he could be, all the PO could be, was patient, and hopeful, and meticulously correct.

He didn't know where his career would take him, though he doubted he would be shunted aside, as he'd been moved from his last assignment, unless he did something extravagantly objectionable to Marak. So he had a certain security, being as high as he could get, while getting a major vacation now and again, enjoying his work as the dream job, and being paid exorbitantly.

The drawback—there *was* one true drawback to it all—was that he couldn't tell anybody on the outside what he did for a living. Watchers—Project taps—worked inside a security envelope that, if you breached it, would just swallow you down and never let you out again, in any physical sense, let alone the informational one. So assuredly he had no desire to break the rules and end up living his entire life as a shadow in the farthest recesses of the Project offices.

And what was that job? He monitored Marak's whereabouts, activities, and observations, he took notes, he made his hour-by-hour transcript, he passed that on to Drusus, who passed it on to Auguste, who passed it back to him, as watchers had done, time out of mind. He was a highly classified instant communications system and still an observer-in-training, but he never forgot it was a dangerous planet down there, and his attention to what he did could conceivably make a difference between life and death for a man on whom the integrity of the Project depended, a contrary and independent man who'd lived longer than any human mind could grasp.

His job, in effect, was keeping tabs on God, or such a god as the planet had, besides the Ila, besides Luz and Ian.

And learning. Fast. Marak, when he was in the Refuge, had encounters with people with various agendas hour to hour, and it was his job to consult with other watchers and suspect who was up to what. When Marak dealt with his own family, in their enclave— or with the Ila—where politics was definitely at issue—transcripts were a fast and furious production. A tap knew a mistake could racket to the halls of government.

But this, this venture into the outback, was six months of pure wonder, observations, close work with the science departments, instead of other taps. Marak traveled out into the world with his wife, enjoying the days, observing a land whose scale of change was more like his own life span and Hati's.

Out there Marak could say, as he had yesterday, of a certain landmark—it's almost all worn away now, the way some people would say, Hmmn, that frontage was painted green yesterday, wasn't it? Or, The camelia's in bloom. How nice.

His job, his enviable job, was watching God watching the world change.

Third cup of caff. Take a walk around, stretch the legs. Take a break. Meddle with the displays. Tinker with a 3-D puzzle he had laid out on the counter days ago. Take a note or two. Since the tap was audio, mostly, and one-way, at his selection, he could do that, while keeping up the transparent transcript he was building. There were other aspects he could use, including voice from his direction, simply by talking aloud and letting the resonant bone of his skull carry the sound to the tap, but such contacts were rare. He wasn't supposed to talk aloud during his hours of observation, in order not to annoy Marak. He used a keyboard, used a tablet, drew and typed in a rapid code. Across the station, in various apartments, in various offices, the day's records grew and sifted from one office to another, everything from repair requests to weather reports and geology.

His notes by midmorning were mostly botanical, the latest involving a patch of low scrub of a kind, greenbush, that Marak remembered personally seeding north of the Needle River, oh, six or so hundred years ago. Reference available to Procyon's casual scan said it tended to be a precursor species. It put down roots, and lighter seed that blew up against it lodged, grew, and fought the precursor species for water, if water was scarce.

Scarce it was not, on the Plateau, and would be less so if the Southern Wall cracked. As the climate changed, precursors and new plants would live and fight each other for sunlight, until their strongest descendants won. But that was in the future. Marak said he was seeding several other plants as they passed, a ground cover, stubweed, and a taller type of shrub, blue dryland windwalker, that, Marak said, might rim a someday sea.

Procyon keyed up images of those plants, too, getting his own picture of what Marak intended and the sort of growth Marak foresaw covering the thin sandy skin of this rise. He *didn't* want to make another statement Auguste could gently imply was foolish.

And he was insatiably curious.

Crazy, his younger sister had said about him. Way too serious. Enjoy life. Who cares about classes? Cut out. Party.

He did enjoy life, precisely because *he* knew what those plants looked like, because he was planning a way to get into an intelligent dialogue with Auguste in this next report to prove he wasn't a fool, and because he knew, because Marak hadn't needed to give his conclusions aloud, but had—that he'd been purposely given a tidbit of information. A living god thought his curiosity was worth rewarding, the way he had rewarded his predecessor's. Finally.

And *that* inspired him beyond all expectation. Curiosity was his life. Curiosity made him enjoy getting up in the morning. Curiosity made him dive right in even before the alarm went off—

Hell!

Anniversary. The parental anniversary.

He'd come in here, isolate from the house system, before Sam gave him the scheduled reminder, and he hadn't remembered to tend to it before work.

He made a note on his hand, as something he'd carry out of the room.

He could take care of it. He had an idea. Courier delivery. Peace in the family was the important thing.

Marak and Hati rode, meanwhile, talking quietly, and Procyon listened, only listened.

Eavesdropping on God. Tagging along like a five-year-old, learning everything in the whole world as if it were new, and sometimes almost forgetting to type his notes in the excitement of the instant.

They'd come in sight of the rim of the Needle River Gorge, the edge of the western lowlands. They had reached the narrowest part of the rocky spine, from which they could see the deep of the gorge on one hand and the expanse of the pans in the other, both at the same time.

God, that had to be a view.

"GREEN," MARAK SAID TO HIS wife and his companions, looking back down the curve of the long ridge of rock—desert pans dizzyingly far below on one side, and now the eroding deep of the great gorge on the other side of this resistant, ancient lava flow. He added, for his young watcher, "As far as the eye can see."

Marak rode comfortably, foot tucked in the curve of the beshta's neck, rocking gently to a rhythm as steady and eternal as his heartbeat, the line of their caravan still ascending that narrow spit that was part of the Plateau, which became, ultimately, the Southern Wall.

"Green-rimmed like the Paradise," Hati said, meaning the river of the Refuge, where fields and farms and orchards had skirted the first dependable water of the midlands desert, to welcome the refugees in the days of the Hammerfall.

Plants always came first in their plan. Plants that cleaned and replenished the air, not only plants on the land, but algae blown out onto the vast oceans, mats of algae in shallows, life of more complex sort running down with water from the free-flowing streams of the midlands. Marak understood these things. Hati understood. That was the work they did, slowly remaking the world in a way the *ondat* might one day approve, and grant their descendants peace from a war they never began.

They'd seen the rockets go out, trailing fire into the dusty clouds until they were a white and vanishing glare. Such rockets burst far away and showered algae bloom high into the furious winds. Over and over and over, year after year, Ian had sent them out.

They had seen the snow come down, and the hail fall, sometimes breaking rocks, the hail of those days was so large. They had seen monstrous whirlwinds dance across the lowlands, vortices within vortices, whirlwinds that, carrying sand on the high plateaus, would strip an unprotected body to bone as they passed.

From the earliest days of the Hammerfall, rains had begun in the high desert, and the winds dried the rain, and sent it high up into clouds that rained down again, until, year by year, since the great destruction, the wind kicked up less dust. These days, gray-bottomed cloud swept off the heights in regular systems, clouds carried on the winds at the edge of heaven.

These days, dependable streams of water fell in a thundering spray off the escarpment, in a chasm that widened year by year, and, conjoined, they flowed down to the Needle, carving a deep gorge on its way to the sea, working its last bends closer and closer to penetrating this ridge.

They had seen the rains fall until the air itself changed, until, these days, they wore the a'aifad more often against the evening chill than the blowing dust that had been the rule in oldest times.

They had ridden the eastern lowlands hundreds of years ago, finding lichens on once-barren rocks, and scum on the pools. They had carried samples to Ian and Luz. The Ila, on first hearing of their discovery, had avowed herself uninterested. "Tell me something more than scum on the ponds," she had said, affecting scorn. But she had surely heard, this power who had loosed her own makers on the world in one single pond of free water. And all through these ages, Ian and Luz had watched her very carefully, as if she nursed some secret store of trouble she could loose if ever the world grew amenable. Certainly she might to this day possess knowledge she had never given to them. That she did have such knowledge, Marak was certain.

But Ian and Luz had knowledge, too. They had changed the

world with their skill. On their account, the Ila's great enemy, the *ondat*, had called off their war with the world, and only watched from the heavens, waiting, waiting, for what outcome those who dealt with them claimed not to know.

The land went on changing. The *ondat* seemed satisfied, for now, at least.

The beshta under him had struck a steady pace. Hati's strode side by side. The boys rode easily behind, with the pack beasts all rocking along at that sustainable rate that could cover considerable ground in a day, climbing up the long, gentle rise of the spine. Machines could go many places where riders might suffer great privation; but Ian lost a good many of his precious drones and robots to uneven ground, to weather and dust, too—metal and materials that had to be searched up out of drifting dunes at great labor . . . by riders, who had to go after the failures.

And as for the little rovers, their solar panels blew apart in the winds, liquid fuel had to be brought to sustain them, grit from the unseeded places got into their works, and they failed. After all was said and done, in Marak's opinion, despite Ian and his clever synthesizers, riders were still the best.

Riders fared best here in rough land, for instance, where there was very little space between one fall and the next.

A good day in the heavens, a good day on earth. And the Refuge was far behind them and mostly out of mind for days on end.

"The green has spread down to the river terraces," Hati said to him, when a deep erosion in the rim of the Needle Gorge afforded them a view of those terraces, hazy with depth below, and indeed a careful eye could make out a gray-green, spiky sort of growth they called knifeweed because of the look of it, a stubborn, wind-blown plant that had outfought the shifting sand in patches throughout the lowlands, growing tougher year by year.

So it grew on the very rim of the Needle Gorge, and now below it.

"Knifeweed," Marak named it aloud, for Procyon, "patches all through this place and well down into the gorge."

There was a great deal else of new growth, some of it unexpected. Where he rode now, well up on the spine, they had never gone, only seen it through eyes in the sky.

For those who lived forever, something new was oftenest measured in rivers and rocks. And to his eye this dark basalt underlying the red and gold land across the gorge, newly dotted with green and gray, this was already a place of change, a sight already worth their coming. Here, ancient volcanic flows were exposed and uplifted, the red cap worn away—only on this side of the gorge. It was a fault line, and a great one.

But not for long, this beauty of contrasts. The long-lived began to have a certain sense of timing, apart from Ian's machines and the opinions of the heavens, and Marak's said greater change was imminent, perhaps this year. Perhaps this very quarter of the year, all the life that clung to a foothold here would meet a new challenge. The earthquakes had assumed a rhythm he had seen before, and if he bet, as some of his foolish descendants loved to do, he would say it would be soon.

Count among those signs Ian, perhaps seeing better than his machines, too, who quibbled about his going out on this ride, foreknowing he would lose the argument.

"Go," the Ila had whispered, when she heard about the debate. She had even hinted at going with them—the Ila, who would bring all her accompaniment of tents and attendants and recorders, her cooks and her wardrobe and her comforts, not to mention her often-voiced opinions. He had not wanted her along. So he and Hati had spoken to a handful of the young men, and they had packed up the requisite equipment, thrown saddles on the beshti, and gone speedily over the horizon without further discussion with anyone.

The Ila, he had heard, had chosen to be amused at his escape, and possibly had rethought the strenuousness of the journey, or possibly had not wanted to leave Ian and Luz unchallenged in the Refuge, likely to make decisions in which she would have no direct part for months. The Ila had generously wished them, through their watchers, a good journey, and was content that they had at least taken her au'it, a woman as ancient as themselves, and in the Ila's service, a recorder whose book now had become many books, full of the most extraordinary things.

They rode carefully and well back from the rim of the deepening gorge, and this passage, like all others, the au'it recorded, writing as she rode, having given up the precarious ink for a self-contained source, but never relinquishing the weighty book she balanced on her knee, like those many, many books before it.

The Western Red, a sizable river, poured through the gap into the Needle just east of them, where the rim of a second great river chasm split the southern face of the Plateau and joined the gorge. That seam in the earth stretched hazily off into the distance. From here on, only the wind and the rain had touched this ground since the Hammerfall.

And this, Marak reminded the younger riders, created a certain danger. For centuries a rock layer might stand, undermined and precarious, balanced against wind and rain and gravity, but not against the added weight of a beshta's pads. So they kept the beshti back from the rim, not letting them meander to the fragile rim, no matter their longing to snatch a mouthful or two of the greenbush that grew there.

They rode where the high, improbable rim of the Needle Ridge broadened, until they had a good, level space around them. Greenbush as well as knifeweed had spread here, in sand and soil that endured in patches across a layer of sandstone. It was sparse and tough foliage, gray, mazy clumps rising up off a tough and knotty base growth. Beshti could use either for graze.

"Here for the base unit," Marak said to Hati and to the others, having brought the party to a halt. All about him he surveyed that unobstructed field of view, from the low-lying river gorge and the red land on the other side, to the bare, eroded sandstone spires falling away to the south, down to the wide pans, apart from this strip of ancient basalt.

This broad place on the ridge was where they would put the critical relay, which might even make contact with number 105, lost out of range to the south, so they could perhaps gain its attention to effect an autorepair. So Marak hoped. At the very least, it was time to set a relay, since contact with the Refuge was perceptibly fainter. And there was, at this height, in that broad sweep of his eye westward, a rim to the sky.

That was not good.

"This is a good broad vantage before the Wall," he said. "Set up the base. And bring out the deep-stakes."

The young men looked, all of them, apprehensively westward,

as they ought, when he said that about deep-stakes. They gazed at just a faint dirtiness above the horizon.

They should have seen it. Now they had.

DEEP-STAKES. TIME. Damn, *time,* and it was just getting to what would be a rapid deployment, just when Procyon had a screen cleared and ready for that new monitor Marak was setting up. He'd known it. He'd known it would work out that way. And what was this about deep-stakes, the irons they used to anchor shelter in a blow? Weather showed nothing but a small line of disturbance off the sea.

The tap came in from Drusus, the clock showed 1802, and Procyon moved, realizing pain. His left leg had gone to sleep.

"They're well out on that rocky spine, now, between the Needle River and the pans," he said aloud to Drusus, hiding his disappointment, since he knew Marak could overhear them talking. "They're at the site. Marak's asked the base be set up. Then he asked for deep-stakes."

Flash of light. Quadruple flash from Drusus. *"Coming on a serious blow, I'm afraid. And they're still setting up?"*

Drusus was taking up his watch in a similar office in another apartment, far across the station. Drusus would actually see the new landscape and the camp the instant the new relay and the camera installation turned on, if they got it done before dark. If weather didn't intervene.

"Looks like."

He, on the other hand, had to wait until morning to find out what happened, and he would very likely miss the deployment. It would take a bigger blow than seemed likely from the weather reports to prevent the base unit driving its legs down. It took only an hour.

But he had taxed his brain and his eyes enough over the last eight hours. A flutter in his left eyelid and a leg gone to sleep confirmed it. He was officially booted out of the tap. He hadn't quite shut down yet, as he multitasked his transcript and Auguste's belatedly over to Drusus—they should have gone half an hour ago.

He had a rapidly burgeoning headache, he'd been paying such

tight and constant attention. The average tapped-in line worker in, say, a bank, sat with his ears plugged and his eyes shut, focused on a single audio interface and admitting no alternate possibilities to confuse his brain.

He, on the other hand, did multitask. He didn't ordinarily take *all* the information simultaneously available to him, but close to it, and when he had to, his brain ran a large number of tracks quite handily: get the transcript out, get the board shut down, were the final two. All those daily repeated tasks, the same daily-routine keystrokes, the hindbrain could handle on autopilot.

Drusus had been, it turned out, by a glance at the clock ticking away in his contact display, two minutes late tapping in. Neither of them was sinless, him for hanging on and Drusus for showing up late. But Drusus had delayed to get an updated weather report. Not entirely a favorable one, as it had developed a bit beyond the last he'd pulled down: he could see that when he demanded it. The front they'd thought would miss—wouldn't.

He slid out of the chair, gathering up the used cup and plate, thinking about the cold front, and spotted the note he'd scrawled on his hand. Which otherwise he'd have completely forgotten, given the depth of his concentration.

Anniversary.

Damn. He'd been ready to think about restaurants. About de-buzzing and recovering the sensation in his right foot.

"Procyon is reluctant to leave us," Marak said, at the edge of his conscious attention, and Procyon felt himself flush, embarrassed to be caught between here and there.

"Good night," he said to Drusus, "Good night, Marak. Forgive me, omi." With that, he did entirely tap out, doing the little blood shunt behind the ears that shut the contact absolutely down.

Contacts lost their internal lights, too. He took out the case from his pocket, cupped one eye and the other, dropping them into solution. Didn't take those out on the town, no. And the foot was *still* asleep.

He'd been more wound up than he'd thought, so excited about the prospect of that new camera set up for a close-up of the area and taking his notes on the new growth he'd lost track of the weather he was supposed to be monitoring: he was embarrassed about that, in cold afterthought, *ashamed* that he hadn't tracked that weather change, which was a major part of his job.

He'd gotten lost in his imagination, was what. He had his own curiosity about the land—the Needle River Gorge and the narrowing spine of mudstone and sandstone layered with flood basalt that arced around to the Southern Wall—that actually became the Southern Wall, when it reached the coast. He'd missed giving Marak an earlier warning. Marak had had to tell him. That wasn't good.

But Marak *had* seen it. And they were well set, and prepared for what wouldn't be a blow of any scale such as in the old days. It was worth embarrassment, was all.

And when he should have been pulling down the weather report, he'd been deep in geology, reading the charts—he hadn't known what the atmosphere was about to send down, but he had been tracking very, very accurately the stability of the ground on which Marak proposed to camp, and he had sent that over to Drusus, in its entirety.

One scientist said the ridge might be an old crater rim predating the Hammerfall. A more prevailing opinion said it was uplift right along with the Plateau across the gorge, but another said that failed to account for the flood basalts. He'd gotten all but visual impressions through Marak's intermittent conversation and pored over his own maps of the lava-capped spine of rock that might or might not be Plateau Sandstone, carved to near penetration by the Needle River on one side and deeply faulted on the other. It had become a spired escarpment on the side of the alkali pans to the south, but the core of the spine was an outpouring of what had to be very ancient basalt, on Marak's side of the Needle. The curving spine where Marak had camped stood a good quarter kilometer above the gorge and nearly that far above the pans, on the other side of the escarpment, strata all tilted toward the south—

All of that spoke of geologic violence, immense geologic force that, in conjunction with those flood basalts, had predated the *ondat* attack, in a previous period of vulcanism, on a planet whose plates had been locked, immobile. That was very, *very* old rock, that spine. It was an access to incredibly old rock. He imagined Geology was in a froth at the moment. He anticipated requests for samples, and almost took it on himself to request Marak collect them.

He had notions of a very presumptuous memo, was making notes on every geologic hint Marak gave him about the age and orientation of the strata there, whether the rock that had been eroded off the spine was actually the same as the Plateau Sandstone across the gorge, as most geologists thought, or whether it was more like the floor of the pans, where there was also some suspicion of deep volcanic rock. In either case, the basalt layer was much thinner than they had thought. That meant an exposure of—granted extreme uplift—much older rock below?

And dared he, two years on this job, and with only a recent course in geology of the region, contact Geology with his speculations? If it was not Plateau Sandstone, if the oddly formed spine was actually an exposure of a piece of an older coast that had rammed in here during a previous tectonic activity, they might get something of a magnetic record of prior orientation of the spine. More, in those exposed lower strata of the spine, there might even lurk a fossil record, life predating not only the *ondat* but the Ila's own interference in the ecosystem. That was the Holy Grail of planetary explorations. Fossil records were incredibly scarce, in the one inhabited area of the planet where they could get to them to collect them.

He hoped he was going to get a request from Geology tomorrow, when they'd read Marak's observations, and more, when the new relay put a camera active on the site, and Geology got a much closer look at the area . . . he had an idea they would make urgent requests for all kinds of samples.

But, God, when the Wall did break, they might well see the flood penetrate through cracks and fissures right into the Needle Gorge, flooding it all, along with the pans, carrying away the spine, so if there was any older record in the rocks, they would lose it once that happened.

So Marak needed to get those rock samples.

And *his* monitors *and* the room lights were about to turn off. He had to leave. If he didn't clear the room before the systems wanted to lock down, the tap supervisor would tell him about an overstay in no uncertain terms.

Morning was soon enough to make a memo to Geology. It had to be. He wanted, tomorrow, to get a library search on southern fossils. He wondered if he dared pursue it all the way to Geology.

Maybe to Chairman Brazis' office. *Hello, sir. I'm Marak's junior-most watcher, with two years of basic geology. I think I've just found prior life.*

Ambition had some sensible limits.

"Board, key out. Door open." The system had a voice lock, and it answered. The screens simultaneously went dark, all around the room. When he came back in the morning, and only in the morning, the door would let him in, at earliest, 0930h. The fact was, he didn't actually rent this apartment: Planetary Observations owned it. Specifically, the Project did, and had made its own alterations, and he wasn't allowed down here or onto the downworld tap except at his strictly regulated hours of duty. The Project didn't want its taps negotiating their own hours or collaborating with each other on their reports.

So his day's work was done, forcibly so. He let the door lock behind him and took the day's cup and saucer upstairs to the main floor to put into the kitchen washer, all on autopilot. He was still thinking about that landscape Marak had described, still imagining that river gorge and the strata of the spine as he went upstairs and shed the work sweats.

He took a quick pass through the shower, dry-cycled, and bare-assed it to the closet for a thoughtful change of focus and a major change of clothing—a nice combination of blues and brown, shirt, pants, boots, and jacket. Hair—it was dark brown the last while—in easy short curls, nothing fancy. Eyeliner was permanent. The rest he was vain enough to maintain as nature provided, unimproved, with its few little flaws. He didn't do seek-and-destroy on fat cells: the gym burned them off. He was actually a kilo light when he consulted the scan, and dessert was consequently an option tonight.

An acceptable, if not a high Trend look. The brown shirt was a pleasure to the skin—and by now he began actually to feel his own skin again, and be sure where his feet were, after the daylong immersion in the tap. The mental solitude of a luxury apartment was delicious, a luxury the Project afforded after a flurry of multitracking and prolonged deep concentration. But solitude and silence would get truly stale before the evening aged much.

Hell, get the mind off it. He wasn't *supposed to* think about the job after hours. Wasn't supposed to get together with the other taps and discuss things. His personal speculations—well, the spine had held for ages. It wasn't going to go tomorrow. He could get office time next downtime, to do his extended reports when Hati's taps were on and he was off. He could send out a modest note to Geology then, granted only Geology did wake up and ask for samples.

"Sam, I'm going out."

Sam's response was a single chime, not a single word from the computer after noon and before 2200h. His choice, that silence. He wasn't in the mood for a cheeky damn bot if his day was going badly, and he didn't like inane pleasantries if it was a really good day and his mind was still, as it was now, exploring the planet he'd just left, dancing down the ridges and wondering if that line of mudstone Marak had mentioned was in the sequence he hoped it was, and most of all hoping that there was time to do the work . . . if they missed getting samples when Marak was going out to the Southern Wall, they might still get some when he came back, which might be along the same route, a few months from now. Those rocks weren't going anywhere.

"Down, Sam." *He* could speak to the bot. It just couldn't answer. Sam chimed. He walked onto the lift area and rode it down to the front door.

Outside, in the Close, the lawyer's gardenias wafted heavy perfume to his senses. He nodded to the otherside neighbor tending her roses, a nice lady with not a clue what he did for a living or why a healthy young man left his apartment only in the tag end of the day. She was retired, but spent much of her time writing for a culinary society.

The occasional polite nod was the only regular interaction he had with her or his other close neighbors, whose dossiers he had read, and he had rather not know them better. The PO liked it that way. And he did his own part for anonymity, having nothing in common with the lawyer or the retired lady or, God knew, the rest of the honest citizens in the complex. He didn't look hostile or odd.

He didn't bring home suspicious visitors. He didn't attract police, play loud music, wear his hair in spikes, or set off fire alarms. He was, in fact, relatively faceless in this pricey neighborhood of people who had, occasionally, children with problems; who occasionally threw big parties, who occasionally had noisy divorces and shouting matches on the doorstep, bothering everyone—as he bothered no one. He was Procyon, just Procyon, as the Fashionables chose to be, just Procyon, whose job nobody actually knew, or ventured to ask, and who, they might think, probably did his work by computer, since he wasn't a Stylist, but lived like one. He only went out in the evenings. But few people besides the lady with the roses were home during the day to think about that. It was a neighborhood adequately respectable and not too worried about the character of anyone with the credit to be living here, which was, he was sure, why the PO decided this was the ideal place to install one of its protected talents.

Just off Grozny was his own ideal place to live, too, and he'd picked it off a very short list of PO-owned properties—close enough to the action, but not in it, so he could walk out of the Close and right onto this fashionable end of Grozny Street. The location was a dream for a young man who came out of a day's isolation hungry for life.

He let the general traffic and the muted noise of voices ease the accumulated tension behind his eyes. He could call any of his friends, if the common tap in his head didn't have its output channel permanently blocked. Anywhere he walked, he could get still get music on the common tap, he could get art, he could get talk; but he declined them all, cherishing the silence and privacy inside his skull. If he was like anyone else on the street, he could be tapped in, all the time, and some who only skimmed life certainly lived that way, moving constantly to their own music, talking to their personal taps, checking with a spouse about a grocery order or making an assignation with a lover, never alone in their heads, never—he suspected—*thinking* any long, deep thoughts in their lives. Himself, he *used* a tap all day long for a living, and now that he was off-line, the very last thing he wanted was abstract shapes dancing in his eyes or the latest band blasting its relentless rhythms into his chair-weary bones. He wasn't thinking deep thoughts either at the moment. He just wanted to walk along in internal silence and let his brain float neutral for a while . . .

Well, give or take the burden of the dreaded anniversary gift, ink still surviving on his hand. The question was whether to make the gift personal, something he could really enjoy giving, or just give up, get something with a high price tag and be done with it.

But a personal kind of place that would also courier the item to his parents' door—that considerably shortened the list.

He was tired of fighting his parents' taste. There were greater problems in the universe, and the parentals he was convinced wouldn't remember next month what gift he'd gotten them this year or last, as long as it didn't scare them or offend them. And he wanted peace in the family. He opted for the sure thing.

Down Grozny to 12th, and up 12th to Lebeau—Glitter Street, the Trend called it, containing most of the conservative shops, frontages that competed in crystal, glass, gold, jewelry, and utterly useless knickknacks for people with far too much money. It catered to Earthers, particularly, who liked shopping on the chancy edge of the Trend—or to those who imitated Earther taste, which, he admitted sadly to himself, pretty well described his mother. He'd long since given up trying to impress his father with what he picked, and as far as impressing his mother, it wasn't so much the gift that mattered, it was the package, it was the label. It was his parents' thirtieth anniversary, and if his father was a cipher to him, he at least figured how to please his mother—and *that* would please his father.

It was all on him, as well. His sister certainly wasn't going to acknowledge the parental occasion. But he kept relations with the family well polished not only because it was the right thing to do but because it was the sensible thing to do. They were dull, but they were solid as core rock, and depend on it, if things ever went wrong in his life, he'd have family, imperfect and unpleasant, but family, loyal as you could ask. They had their virtues. And maybe, if he ever totally misjudged the universe and messed up his personal life, he'd have someone he could query about his own biases, or at least analyze theirs from a mature perspective—he was old enough now to see them as people, just people, like other people. He'd had his stint at rebellion. Now he tried compliance, top to bottom. He decided he'd give up trying to get them nice things, arty things, real art, from live people who'd admit they'd made whatever-it-was. It's a pot, had been his father's most telling judgment, when he'd tried to explain last year's gift. His mother had put flowers in it.

So this anniversary, after the fiasco of the last one, he learned. He went straight into Caprice, picked out a completely useless hand-cut crystal egg in Caprice's signature style, such a piece of uninspired commercialism that his sister would have thrown up. He paid the extravagant price on his own credit and ordered it delivered to Ms. Margarita Nilssen and Mr. Jerry Stafford Sr., of 309 Coventry Close, D1088, before 0815h on the 15th of May.

That was tomorrow morning, before he even got out of bed.

The clerk offered the optional gold-embossed 5.95c gift card. He signed it *With love, Jeremy & Arden,* which was fifty percent a lie and a bit of wicked humor. His sister would be outraged.

So, there, he'd done it. He smiled nicely at the salesman, who hadn't had to work at all hard for his commission, and walked back out onto the street, free, unburdened now, and taking his own sweet time.

Best he could do. It wasn't a pot. A former Freethinker rebel had paid good money for a hand-cut Caprice egg, and the station still turned on its axis and spun about the planet it guarded. Was that a sign of advancing maturity?

All-important point, he'd bought that expensive, logo-bearing card, and signed it with his own hand, the personal touch. It would arrive in its envelope of crisp cream vellum, as fancy as if it were going to the governor's wife, and stand beside the egg on a conspicuous shelf for at least a month. As long as his mother was in a good mood, everybody was happy—and if the parentals were both happy enough, maybe he could claim he'd drawn overtime at work and skin out of the gruesome family dinner of overcooked meat, overdone vegetables, and his mother's special fruit salad.

God, he really hoped he could finagle his way out of that dinner. He detested his cousins. He wasn't fond of the uncles and aunts. Most of all, he didn't want to stand smiling through the usual battery of questions before hors d'oeuvres . . . Have you seen Arden, dear? Well, yes, Aunt Faye, he had, but he'd have to say no, he hadn't, or the next deadly question was Where?

And . . . How's the job? His father would ask at some point in the evening, as his father asked every time they met, and he'd smile and say the job was fine, then change the topic.

His parents were good and devoted sorts—not that he was sure they still loved each other, but they'd stuck together for thirty years, being good religious people and the descendants and relatives of generations of good religious people. Children were the one achievement that they were instructed by God to create with their lives. His father, after whom he was named, Jeremy Lee Stafford, was a station mechanic, which was right next to a tech, as his mother would always say.

Good pay, his dad would say, looking askance at a son who lived at a very, very fancy address, who didn't tell his father what he made per year, or explain exactly what he did, beyond that he worked in computers for the government. Key-pushing wasn't his father's idea of a high-paying job.

Then his mother would convert the question back into how Arden was getting along, and whether she'd found a job, completely oblivious to how Arden was really getting along, and unaccepting of the fact that Arden was never, ever going to get a job.

Your sister could have had a *nice* job, their mother would say (he had the conversation memorized), meaning a job in the plastics shaping factory where their mother was a line supervisor. Their mother had virtually assured his sister an entry level position in household furnishings, with a clear track to good promotions in design if she took the company study program. Arden had run away to the streets the day of the scheduled interview, a fact to which their mother never quite alluded, but his father did, if he ever got into the discussion. *She should get a job,* his mother would say sadly. Followed by, with that honeyed sweetness usually reserved to herald a new baby: *We're so proud of you.*

All because, yes, he clearly had a job of some kind, and he sent them presents, hand-thrown pots and all, and occasionally showed up at the family gatherings wearing a nice suit and talking computer games with his cousins' rotten kids, who believed, like the aunts and uncles, that he was some kind of computer expert—after all, he'd gotten a technical scholarship to university and actually graduated, while his missing sister had set her heart on fashion design, which the aunts and uncles all agreed was frivolous.

Live in the real world, the parents would tell them both, and they both got the lecture at every mention of fashion design. So he'd graduated with a technical certificate in communications systems, and his younger sister hadn't gotten any certificate at all, after her three years in fashion design.

Compared to his sister's, his relations with the parentals had been sterling. Then, last unavoidable paternal birthday, he'd made the great faux pas. No, he'd let slip when pressed, he didn't go into the office every day. He did wear a suit when he did. But he usually worked at home.

That entirely upset his parents' image of him. Last he heard from the cousins, his anguished mother had told the aunts he was doing *part-time* work for the government. His father acted odd when the topic came up, which his mother finally confided to him was worry about the money he had and the address he had.

I have enough, he'd assured her. I'm doing all right. It's a scarce specialty. And his mother had said, two months ago, We're sure you do, and then confessed his father worried he was involved in organized crime.

God. From one crisis to the next. He wished he could actually breach security and tell them in strictest confidence what he did, that he was day watcher over the whole reason for Concord Station existing.

Then his father would look him straight in the eye and ask, with undefeatable logic, *So if you're so damn important, why don't you do it in an office?*

And his mother would decide "strictest confidence" naturally included her sister.

He increasingly didn't want to go to the anniversary dinner. Other thirty-years-married people of his parents' generation might think of going out to a romantic dinner for their anniversary and even make love afterward. No chance of that. His parents invited all the relatives and their kids to an enormous supper, to sit in the cramped living room for hours discussing sports and even more remote relatives, most of them deceased.

Worse, at some time in the evening, particularly if he once spoke his mind to his young cousins, the talk would get around to religion, that other great divide; and if he ever expressed an honest opinion violating their notions on that, his mother might ask again, in a hushed voice, if, working for the government, he was *modified*.

And if he ever answered that question with the truth, he'd have her praying for him daily.

If she saw Arden these days, they'd all be on tranquilizers.

He took 11th Street back down, a walk past two-story apartments. Cleaner-bots scuttled, small half domes moving busily wherever walkers were scarce, gathering up here and there a discarded wrapper, a little accumulation of dust. A handful of giggling, overfunded pre-pubes from upstairs, whose responsible parties probably hadn't given a damn in years, taunted the bots, slyly tossing small bits of trash to attract them and trying in vain to tip them over. The teens were police bait, oblivious to the watch-cameras.

He left them to their folly, strolled back onto Grozny Street at the busiest intersection on restaurant row.

La Lune Noir. He was in a mood for the pastries. Best desserts in the Trend.

Now he was in a good mood.

2

AN ANOLE LOUNGED IN PLAIN SIGHT, belly down on a rock. Setha
Reaux, having missed lunch, had a cup of caff, a muffin, and tried
to steady his mind as he contemplated his bubble world. The lizard
contemplated him from the other side of the glass.

The incoming ship had answered his queries, finally. *Special Ambassador Andreas Gide to Setha Reaux, Governor of Concord. We will remain here five days for consultations. We look forward to a brief and
productive conference.*

Consultations. Business. Special Ambassador. An official, this Mr.
Gide, with an unstated mission.

His first relieved thought was that there was no indication, at
least, of an audit, and no summary request for records. After an all-
night scramble, and all morning going through files, he had all the
tax records accessible and immaculately clean if there should be a
question. All the Council meeting logs. All the communications
with the various business interests, on-station and off-. He had gotten it all organized in thirty-six hours, in the face of that oncoming,
silent ship. He'd gotten the arena records in careful context, along
with the time line of phone calls and conference agendas, which
proved his case on the construction of the new station, in case there
was a question on that front, locally or otherwise.

But nothing about this arrival looked like an operations audit
after all, as that message indicated. He couldn't say he was exactly
disappointed to hear there was a Mr. Gide with some sort of con-

sultations in mind—mortally relieved, was more the point—but after a night and a day in the office, he was frayed, underinformed, and most of all frustrated.

A flood of inquiries had hit his desk early when this ship had turned up, local agencies wanting to know what everybody on the station wanted to know: what was going on and why an Earth ship was here off schedule. The price-fixing board had immediately swung into action, of course, and the securities and exchange people had put in a night of overtime trying to scotch speculation on ordinary goods and luxury items. Everybody was discommoded. The fashion shops likewise were probably organizing flood sales on their newest items. When the regular Earth freighter touched the station in its annual visit, information on the mother world's fashions came with it, and things changed rapidly in the *haut ton* shops.

This unexpected midyear arrival created an economic flutter in the damnedest places.

Technology futures naturally went softer by the hour: Earth technology was also a wild card, and one never knew what would show up in that market when Earth injected its Inner Worlds creations, patterns, and patents into the station's data files, extracting automatic payment as they went.

Every ship traded. Even warships traded. Earth couldn't physically touch the physical goods of an Outsider station, but patents and patterns for synth programs went back and forth on a two-way trade, some of it in Earth-owned goods on another Outsider station, some of it in stock futures, some of it in actual substance off-loaded from an Earth ship, just nothing taken aboard. Earth always bargained hard for what they sold, and had a monopoly on the finest synthesizer patterns, those that enabled molecular synthesis on say, caff and fine wines, patterns that subtly changed from year to year, each variation available at very high cost.

In that trade, Earth had a bottomless gold mine, and the buzz was already out that there was, inbound, a new liqueur and a very fine Merlot pattern, not to mention an exciting and rare offering, the pattern of an aged wine from an estate collection: the ship's command levels and the mysterious Mr. Gide might not have communicated a damned thing, but the trade office had certainly gotten communication from the ship's trade officer, so ordinary business and moneymaking wasn't beneath this ship, was it?

And what was currently going on in the substrate of the trade office was the ordinary flurry of intense, small-time negotiations, the trade board and individual license houses engaged by voicelink with the ship's trade officer, who would work to obtain what he wanted and to pay as little as possible for it in goods and credit.

Reaux had sent a personal agent on a fast, discreet round of face-to-face meetings with key corporations, stating, quote, we regard this as ordinary trade and intend strongly to defend local interests—and implying, of course, the reciprocal, but unspoken: *if* you defend us if asked any nasty questions about our administration—just a little happy talk to confirm that, yes, the governor was certainly on the local corporations' side, and they would all stand united, nobody being negotiated out of what advantage they held in their creative property, and nothing radically changing in the economic climate. Only granted they themselves hadn't done something to bring on some sort of inquiry from Earth, the government would defend patents and negotiate for all companies equally, none sold out at disadvantage for the benefit of another no matter how Earth tried. He could be tough. Had been, on one notable occasion.

As for the stock market, the various moderating systems had engaged as they ought, and functioned as designed. Bulk commodity selling was impossible once those regulations went into effect: that was always the worst hit that could follow rumors of a new technology or a major sale, but the automatic safeguards had slammed that brake on the minute the ship turned up, and consequently there was no need to stop regular trading as that ship glided toward them. There was even a modest wave of profit riding the event, small speculative buying of certain companies' shares.

So the ship looked to carry on ordinary business, midyear as it was.

So what was this oddly timed contact from Earth? A Mr. Gide? And consultations?

When had Earth ever *consulted* its governors?

That unusual word was worth looking for. Reaux put the computer to searching all the Earth ship calls since Concord's founding, precisely for *Consultations*. That took a few moments, during which he drank off the cooling cup of caff.

Chime from the desk unit. *"Sir."* Ernst. *"Your wife is asking if you'll be home for supper tonight."*

"Put her on," he said, and hearing the contact made: "Judy?"

" . . . supper. Are you going to be home tonight?"

"For God's sake, Judy." It *was* past his ordinary quitting time. He didn't think he could make it through another overnighter in the office. "Well, I think it's remotely possible, but I can't think about that right now."

"It would be a very good idea if you could come home this evening and say how nice Kathy's hair is."

That bad, then. "I'm trying. I'll try, Judy."

"Dinner at 1900h. I'm cooking."

Judy was *cooking*. And dinner was fairly late. She hadn't made it to her job today, he made that a good guess. He remembered the prior controversy. Judy had snared their daughter Kathy, she'd have called the hairdresser in, heavily bribed to silence, and Kathy's hair was still tearfully controversial. He could read between the lines. Kathy was recalcitrant and Judy wanted backup.

A message crawl hit his screen. *Brazis* was on his way up the hall at this very moment: Antonio Brazis, head of the PO, local Chairman of the Outsider Council, his opposite number in station authority.

Dortland, his own head of station security, and Redmond, from the Trade Board, were next on his agenda, and they were going to have to wait, clearly, if Brazis was coming in. Ernst had been tracking all these matters, and shot this vital information to his computer screen in bold letters on a black background before he could make a commitment to his wife—and have to break it.

"Dinner at 1900h is possible. Possible. I might be late. I have no way of knowing what this ship business is, or when they'll decide they want to talk. And I've got meetings."

"Setha."

"I say I have appointments, Judy. People are on their way to my office. Heads of departments. We have problems. That Earth ship. Our daughter's hair, I'm afraid, is very much a side issue today."

Silence on the other end. Judy knew when she'd pushed him absolutely too far. She wasn't happy, but at least she didn't sulk out loud.

"Likely 1900h," he said, trying to mollify that deadly silence. "If not, be sure that something unexpected happened." He had a dire thought, just before he thought she might hang up on him. "Judy? Judy, whatever you do, *don't* talk to the media."

"Why would I talk to the media?"

"Because of that ship! I'm not talking to the media, I have no particular answers for them, and it's remotely possible the media will hang around the apartment trying to get information or just the temperature of the household to have something to report. We have a serious matter here, Judy. Turn on the news, for God's sake. Don't answer the phone. Don't answer the door. And don't let Kathy leave. As happens, it's a very good night to eat in, and I've got to come home. I'm exhausted."

Small pause. Not a happy pause. *"1900h,"* Judy said, and broke contact.

It wasn't just a day. It was an unmitigated two days of hell. The ship came on, unhastened, uncommunicative, across several AUs of untenanted space.

The anole got up on his legs on his branch, expanded his throat, and displayed to a rival.

Damned well that's what it was, that inbound ship: like the lizard, a display of power.

One Andreas Gide, ambassador with special powers. An off-schedule show of force, making them sweat. The simple ability to launch a ship this far, on a special mission. Lizard on a branch.

The context search had produced a result on his screen. Ships arriving for *consultations*, in the long history of relations, inevitably came because of tension between the *Apex Council* and Earth.

Scrolling through the dates, it had meant much the same even before the days of the Earth Federation, while it was still a question of Inner Worlds versus Outsider colonials.

Politics changed. But the stress lines on the charts, dictated by who lived where and where the trade routes went, didn't change all that much. Location dictated politics, and *consultations* at Concord were always ominous, always, thus far, involving some tension between Earth and the High Council at Apex, several times because of some perceived misdeed regarding *ondat* relations.

Well, not at Concord. He'd heard of no problems with his on-station Outsider Council counterpart, the *ondat* representative was perfectly quiet, and he didn't believe whatever brought Earth inquiry to them was a valid suspicion. Some sort of accusation could always turn up, instigated by politicians with an axe to grind, something could be going on elsewhere, but Concord was incredibly remote from most of human interest.

And, God, he didn't need problems with Brazis, who was a competent, quiet administrator, to color his lifelong term of office.

He didn't need any Ambassador Gide—political ideologues with ambitions were always to fear. Earth was known, occasionally, to stir things up on the fringes to make some political point at home.

Spies were also to fear, individuals who might have damning reports to give such a ship, but they were always present, people either sent here by various interests ranging from commercial to political—his chief of security, Dortland, had given him a small watch list—or persons born here and ambitious for advancement they couldn't get under his administration: his personal list of the latter ilk started with one Lyle Nazrani, who had his financial fingers in the new station construction, who was high up in the banking industry, and who'd raised hell about the arena contractors and a dozen other issues in the new station construction, anything to get on the news. *There* was a man who'd lose no time getting a private interview with Mr. Ambassador Gide, and Reaux was equally determined not to let that happen.

Say what Earth would, however, and no matter what politicking might advance some party on Earth or some ambitious idiot on station—the *ondat* presence had a major say in matters on Concord, too. The *ondat* always had a major say at Concord, and might just very easily decide, for at least a decade, that they viewed Concord as still within their sphere of territory, in which case . . .

In which case the shadowy presence that existed within their sealed section might pull that section off, as they had done, once and twice in the worst times of Concord's history, when the whole fragile peace had nearly shattered. Let Earth remember *that*, if Earth wanted to interfere with Concord's smooth running. The *ondat* might suddenly move in a warship and exert a greater power over Concord administration and over what ships came and went, all Earth's ambitions be damned, and never mind the local human economy. That had happened more than twice—economic disaster, from which Concord had taken decades to recover.

And no one wanted to think of a situation that might cause that quiet presence, that sometimes amusing, sometimes sinister presence, to wake up and become actively involved. They lived with the *ondat*. Concorders saw the sleek, frighteningly massive ships that slid up to the station at irregular intervals and did their business, saying nothing, having no intercourse with any human. They knew that, beyond the walls of that independent section, something lived that veiled itself in shadow, in ammonia-reeking murk, and carried on inquiries that made no human sense . . . *no one* played politics with the *ondat*. That was the very point of Concord's neutral existence, was it not?

And, pressed to the wall, faced with a threat, as he'd reminded himself last night in the throes of the tax records—he did have good relations with the *ondat*, with (the only name they knew) Kekellen. Earth would be well-advised, would it not, to leave that situation undisturbed?

Kekellen had sent him a message yesterday through the symbol translator: *Ship Earth?* Meaning, roughly, What in hell's this untimely ship doing here, and should we care?

His own linguists had replied: *Ship Earth unclear word. Reaux talk this ship. Talk Kekellen soon.*

Soon.

Well, that was a stall, no question, and sufficient to the day the trouble thereof. Those pesky abstracts like *soon, if,* and *why* had taken the linguists and the *ondat* ages to work out. He ordinarily hated it when his experts used abstracts to Kekellen. Stick to solids, he'd say. Keep it concrete, especially if it's an emergency. Don't seem to promise things.

We have a situation with the *ondat*, he could legitimately say, however, carefully citing that message. Keep it quiet, please, Mr. Ambassador Gide.

That was the ultimate power of a Concord governor, after all, wasn't it, the ultimate argument for keeping Earth's fingers off

Concord politics—the ominous foreign presence that sat, cocooned in its own segment of Concord Station, occasionally insinuating its robotic errand-runners past what had once been a tightly sealed barrier. The *ondat* had, in the last century, breached whatever moderate quarantine had once existed, had begun to do so during the last two governorships, beginning with random inquiries to ordinary offices and citizens . . .

And lately taking delivery of orange juice, table salt, live lettuce, and eight canisters of chlorine, which it just confiscated from various shops and storehouses. Figure *that* one. Last week it had taken a sculpture from a good neighborhood. It scared hell out of the merchants. No one claimed to understand it.

He should report the sculpture theft to the Earth ship. Let them worry about it.

No QUESTION the *see me* from the governor's office had to do with the ship incoming. The invitation suited Antonio Brazis, even at this late hour. He was just as anxious to see Setha Reaux and know what Reaux knew before this untimely ship got to dock and sent its electronic tentacles running into their affairs.

He hoped to hell that Reaux's personal fund-raising peccadillos hadn't caught up with him. As governors went, Reaux was a good one—not immune to influence peddlers, especially close to the construction interests that formed a real power base in a station currently building its own replacement; but he had to maintain his own power base, and he was a sensible and honest man where it counted, regarding the overall welfare of the station. Infighting always swayed governors: wealthy expatriate Earthers arrived on Concord to assume what wasn't, after all, a popularly elected office; and life-appointed governors grew corrupt primarily because they were outsiders in the lower-case sense, foreigners incapable of function if locally stymied and opposed. A man wanted to have allies, and Earth might appoint its governors from Earth itself, counting them more loyal, but local Earther descendants chose Station councilmen in hotly contested local elections, and oh, believe there was favor-trading, if a governor really wanted to get anything done, let alone done on time.

Outsider chairmen, for which Brazis was truly grateful, had no such considerations: the High Council at Apex life-appointed both the head of the Planetary Office and the Concord Chairman, both offices, in his case, vested in one person, and yes, local Outsider citizens held elections for civil posts and local Council, just like Earther citizens, though with far less fire and drama. The Earth governor thus remained forever at the mercy of his legislature, which directed day-to-day operation of station systems, managed trade with Earth and the Inner Worlds, and maintained control over the police, customs, and legal systems. In effect, a governor could ask, but had the devil's own time enforcing policy, if he had not played the local game of favor-trading.

Not so, Brazis's own office. *He* traded no favors. Concord's local Outsider Council, lacking any power to regulate station operation, was more a debating society, handling zoning regulations and public services in its districts. Concord's Outsider Chairman presided over the Outsider Council and appointed the head of the civil police in Outsider districts.

That, on most stations, was that—Outsider government wielded very little power over the station's external dealings.

But on Concord, there was that other office: the Planetary Office. *The Project.*

And the project director, holding absolute authority over the Project, necessarily held police powers and regulatory authority, not only equal to the Earth-appointed governor's authority, but authority that could actually override the Earth governor's decisions, where it affected the PO's operations or Project security.

Brazis being both local Chairman and Project Director was not to Earth's liking: that had been clear when he took the second office. Earth officially didn't like that combination of powers—in fact, Apex itself was divided on the matter, which had carried by one vote—but it stood, and it was useful when it came to putting his foot down. He had been at Concord for thirty years. Earth was still unhappy about it.

So now Earth sent an off-schedule mission and Reaux wanted to talk to him. Consequently, he had to wonder in which capacity, and whether he would have to put his foot down, or just listen to some financial confession of the governor's, an appeal for understanding—

in which case he would listen, and back the governor, for what it was worth, if it accorded with his interests, and the governor would almost undoubtedly explain to him how extremely it did.

What was more worrisome was the remote possibility that this incoming, very expensive ship had intentions that were going to annoy the PO. He hoped not. It had been a tranquil thirty years.

The governor's sweeping body scans, in the long office hall approaching the governor's suite, were fast, discreet, and asked no permission, setting off a flurry of small beeps and protests from his electronics, internal and otherwise. Brazis took no umbrage. His security was armed, he wasn't, and, by no means on his first visit here, he knew where to leave his escort, at the entry to the governor's suite of offices. He walked on through the last doors alone, into Ernst's little wood-paneled kingdom.

"Mr. Chairman." Ernst instantly reported his presence to the governor, got up and opened the governor's office door the low-tech way, with the button. "Sir."

No waiting. No social dance. Governor Reaux rose and met him with a little bow, if not a contaminating handshake . . . he *was* still native Earther, even two decades into his office.

"Antonio. I so appreciate your coming. Tea?"

He'd been on the go since the ship business had hit the horizon. Which was yesterday. "Tea sounds good," he said. He didn't have his scan with him—didn't, as a rule, trust private dispensers, especially when he couldn't watch the preparation, but an Earther staff wouldn't slip you anything but a chemical problem. Reaux wouldn't have an illicit nanism near his precious person.

"Did you run the media gauntlet?"

"They were out there, no way not. I'm afraid my visit will be on the news. I said it was a courtesy call. They were noisy and unconvinced."

"Mmm." Reaux poured the tea himself, from a dispenser tastefully concealed next to the extravagantly expensive lizard globe.

Fascinating creatures, Brazis considered them. They'd come all the way from Earth, intact, in a long-ago administration, and the globe had run for, reputedly, a hundred and fifty-odd years with minimal intervention. The lizards stared at him. Little predators, a whole food chain. A man who superintended the program that re-seeded and redeemed the planet had a great admiration for the balance requisite in that globe.

Reaux served him tea in Earth-import ceramic, antique and fragile. And sat down behind his desk for his own first sip.

"You've made inquiries about the ship inbound," Reaux said.

If there was one thing Brazis continually appreciated about Reaux, it was his straightforward, no-time-wasted approach. "Yes. But I'm sure your information is better. My problem or yours?"

"Frankly, I don't know. They claim someone with ambassadorial status aboard. A consultation. You aren't expecting anything like this, are you?"

"No reason, I assure you."

"A five-day visit, routine in length if not in timing. If there is anything on your levels you know that's going on—I certainly hope you'd tell me."

"Not a thing." He hoped his eyes were clear all the way to the back of his brain. The Chairman of the Outsider Council naturally knew a dozen things, including the names of unruly groups and certain individuals who might decide the visit of a mission from Earth was exactly the time to act up, either to get local concessions for their peculiar points of view or to create a racket clear to the Chairman General at Apex. "Naturally certain elements will be excited. They might think of something on the spur of the moment, but I doubt they're prepared to carry anything off in an organized way. My security is out and about. Do you think you can possibly keep Mr. Nazrani off the news for five days?"

The Earth governor didn't get to twit the Outsider Chairman about *his* peculiar security problems without taking a shot in return. Reaux accepted the jab with a wry, unamused laugh.

"I know enough to make him nervous."

"But no one of your enemies is nervous enough to act rashly, dare we hope?" Brazis said. It wasn't Nazrani and the sports arena they were discussing now. It was their own intermingled affairs. The whole sociopolitical structure of Concord was in fact a geodesic, dependent on its little lines of tension. Pinned together by its own sins and the knowledge of those sins, that web held strong and steady, against most minor disturbances. The current cooperation had never been challenged from the outside.

Witness that Concord, ancient as it was, remained a continual point of uncertainty in a very old and essentially stable arrangement. There was Earth and the Inner Worlds, there was the Outsider territory, and those got along.

But given Concord's unique existence in a bubble inside *ondat* space . . . distant governments, if they were sensible, wished only a report of unending tranquillity from Concord. "We'll certainly support you, if that's what you're asking. We consider your administration progressive and sensible over the last two decades. We very much value our working relationship."

"I'm flattered." Reaux could hardly be entirely flattered to hear he was greatly valued by the other side of this ageless détente. Small smile. "But don't tell them that."

"By no means. I'll swear you're a son of a bitch and I detest negotiating with you. I'll exit past the media swarm frowning and angry. Do you have any clue what this portends?"

"Nothing," Reaux said—which Brazis doubted. "Do you?"

"Nothing." His own dance on the brink of the truth.

"It may be some political hiccup on Earth itself. Such things are difficult to foresee. We can only make sure Concord is secure, from whatever internal sources disturbance might come. I ask again: you've heard nothing."

Maybe it was time for a little half-truth. "The Council at Apex has absolutely nothing to gain from disruptions at Concord. This is the important point, it's always been true, it continues to be true, and you can assure Earth of this. The local Outsider Council, disregarding all the little trade questions we discuss with your Council, has an overriding interest in continuing stability here. We like our governor very well."

A small tight smile, a little nod. "As we like our local Chairman."

"If what's arrived is Earth's own problem trying to stir up something for home political value, it assuredly doesn't need to involve us. This ambassador—"

"Gide is his name. Andreas Gide."

"Mr. Gide should do his business, ask a few questions, take a physical tour, I suppose, to say he looked or advised. And then go home. They do this, don't they, every time they need to shore up their own political capital? 'We have a mission to Concord, we've investigated subversive activity.' I've seen one before this, in my predecessor's time."

"What did they do?"

"They ask a few questions, take a physical tour. And go home. It scares hell out of Earth's internal factions, is my theory. Just meddling around out here near the *ondat* diverts attention from whatever they're up to at home, and it's far enough away nobody can possibly prove a thing. The game's always the same."

Deep breath. "My records indicate some sort of Outsider trouble."

"Did they actually say that?"

"The word they used for the reason for their trip was *consultations*. I looked it up. They always say that precise word when they're investigating Outsider trouble."

Certainly information worth logging. "I can assure you their excuses are one thing; their intentions are likely for domestic capital. This is the last place either your people or mine want controversy."

"Antonio. I want Blunt Street quiet. Very quiet. Bottom line, I want no trouble they can point to."

"Earth demonstrating its god-given authority does provoke a . certain natural sentiment on Blunt."

"I want it astonishingly quiet. I know you can do it. I can't stress enough how important it is that you do it."

Clearly this was why Reaux had called him here: keep it quiet and we stay friends. Reaux was worried, whether on specific information or because it was the man's nature to worry extravagantly.

"I advise you," Brazis said, "with the friendliest of intentions— keep your secret police off Blunt."

"Then you need to have your own police thick down there. Quietly. Discreetly. Without our visitors noticing it. Without stirring up Kekellen's questions, God help us. You know me, Antonio. You know I mean it in the friendliest way, about trouble down there. My predecessor let Blunt get way out of hand, as was. They'll remember that. It's in your interest as well as ours not to let the old Blunt Street situation make any visible resurgence. We've made a great deal of progress in our two administrations. I don't want it all unraveled because *now* Earth gets some notion to find fault with your government over something that's no longer an issue here."

It *was* the trade question, smuggling, at the back of Reaux's worries, Brazis would bet four months' salary on it. But Brazis didn't find smuggling an issue to be discussed, not here, not now, not in this context. Truth to tell, he had his own very uncomfortable feeling about Blunt at the moment, for reasons completely aside from that inbound ship, and any rash attempt to bring down the iron fist of Earth there could do particular damage to quiet investigations already in progress.

Fortunately the governor had a sense of how things on Blunt worked, too, and had given him as clear a signal as he could send without coming out and saying so, that he intended to divert attention away from Blunt.

"I don't want it unraveled, either," Brazis said. "The business with the old network has been delicate for years. What agency sent this Mr. Gide?"

"I don't know. I'll find out. I just ask your cooperation for a few days."

"You certainly have that. Just leave the police work and the surveillance to us. You won't see my agents. But I assure you they'll be out there, in contact in ways you don't have, and they are efficient." He already knew one man he wanted to talk to personally, one of Apex Council's little gifts, operating there currently completely independent of his office. But the existence of an Apex operative delving into whatever he was into, down in the Trend, needn't concern Reaux's office. "I'll fix it."

"Has Kekellen queried you?"

"Yes."

"How did you answer?"

"I said *Earth ship. Not Outsider.*"

"Tossing the ball into my court." Reaux said with a little compression of the lips. "Thank you, Mr. Chairman."

"Absolutely. It *is* your ship inbound."

"A good idea to confer and compare, your experts and mine, if we get any stir out of the *ondat*. At least until this ship leaves."

"But not to coordinate answers. He'd know. I'm quite sure he'd know." Their resident *ondat* sent random inquiries, when he, she, or it was disturbed, and might ask a plumber on three deck what he thought of this inbound ship, if Kekellen took the notion. Contacts with other tiers of society might completely violate Outsider and Inner Worlds notions of security, but if Kekellen specifically queried a plumber on three-deck, he wanted an answer. University experts might get involved helping that plumber answer the letter, and there was a hotline to help such individuals, but that man had to answer in his own name, or Kekellen went on sending, jamming the system, to the detriment of all station business.

That was another kind of *ondat* trouble, one he was sure their governor didn't need demonstrated in front of the incoming ship.

"That's a point," Reaux said. "That is a point. But I hope you'll consult with us. At least cross-check what's being said. Or asked."

"And shall we cross-check what's being said back and forth with this inbound ship?" Brazis asked.

"I'm sure you'll know."

"Oh, make it easy on us."

Reaux heaved a visible, a desperate sigh. "Our offices have a good relationship. In all honesty, Antonio, I don't know why this is happening. But if trouble does turn up, yes, I will communicate with you. I hope it's reciprocal. If you hear anything."

He leaned his arms on the chair. Considered the question. "All right. Let's have a valiant try at honesty. I have a situation I'm keeping a particular eye on, down on Blunt. You'll only mess things up if you send anybody down there to check up on it. If I identify a troublemaker, he'll be off the street for a few days on a warrant for spitting on the street. Our police are extremely efficient. Keep your people out, and I'll tell you what I find out. Do me another favor. *You* feed Kekellen enough basic information to keep him from querying our personnel and asking us questions we can't answer."

"Oh, now—"

"Nothing detrimental and nothing to do with that ship. We're busy just now. We have a developing situation down on the planet."

"Of interest?"

"Not political. Geological. We're about to have a new sea, give or take a few decades. Or maybe sooner. Maybe much sooner. I'm getting alarms from the geologists. I've sent a briefing to your staff. I'll send it to your office if you're curious."

"I'll query them. I'm sure it'll be in a briefing." Reaux made those small movements, fussing with items on the desk, that began to say that new seas a decade removed were farther from his personal interest than that inbound ship or some fool of an activist down on Blunt. Given his doubtless full schedule, geology was likely very far from his interest. And the interview was over. "As for your person on Blunt, no difficulty, if you say so. I will appreciate your honesty."

"We'll exchange information as it becomes available."

"Excellent."

"A pleasure." Brazis stood up and the governor stood up, mutual courtesy. They didn't shake hands. "Visit *my* office when this is over."

The governor of Concord never visited him in his own territory. The protocols—and certainly that residual Earthborn fear—kept Reaux from accepting Outsider hospitality. It was an ages-old official situation.

Reaux just smiled, as generations of governors had smiled benignly, and gave vague promises for a visit someday.

The bubble they lived in had its set of balances, its food chain, and until a high-level Earth ship showed up, the governor's office was largely preoccupied with the internal business of its own society. The Earth governor never gave up a shred of his dignity, thin as it sometimes was, and never admitted that his power didn't effectively extend to the fifth level of the station he ran. The Outsider Chairman never gave up a shred of his power, which was vested, in his case, not only in a population vastly outnumbering the Earther veneer on his station, but in an office that could impose martial law on this station and forbid that inbound ship a docking, no matter their objections—if he wanted to use it.

He didn't. He bowed to the governor, walked out, exchanging pleasant words with Ernst, and picked up his highly modded security escort on the way out.

He swept down the hall, back through the ambush of competing news agencies. His frown was sincere, and annoyed, his answers terse.

"Consultation," he said. "A frank exchange. No further comment." It was politic, for the news, that an Outsider Chairman not be seen smiling and happy after a visit to a governor.

His own lift-car was waiting at the nearest station, with another of his security team aboard, holding that car private, making sure it wasn't diverted or switched, it went without saying. He escaped the swarm of reporters and cameras, got in and sat down as the door shut, his two bodyguards standing. He heaved a sigh, as the car set into motion.

And still didn't smile.

He didn't have to tell the governor that Blunt Street was a potential problem. But the wide universe, of which he was well aware, in his capacity as local Chairman, had stresses and strains of far more import than the opinions of some young local idiot who'd read a political tract.

That didn't mean some eloquent young idiot inspired by a random occurrence like this ship-call couldn't light a dangerous fire, and he knew it and Reaux knew it.

More to the point, and the current thorn in his side, the Chairman General at Apex had sent one of his observers to Concord to carry on a very deep investigation of affairs on Blunt Street, two years ago . . . covertly inserting his agent, as the CG tended to move. Not covert enough to prevent him finding it out: whether that lapse was intentional or not, Brazis had no idea, but he viewed the CG's ongoing investigation as a potential problem and an inquiry from Earth as no help at all, if the two crossed.

Magdallen was the agent's name—or at least the name he was going by on this mission.

Time to talk to the Council's deeply lodged ferret. No question of it.

He tapped in and contacted Dianne. "The Council's man," he said. "Down on Blunt. I want to talk to him immediately, in my office."

"Yes, sir," Dianne said.

He'd never talked to Magdallen. It had seemed politic to keep his distance and pretend he was unaware of Magdallen's activities, considering that the investigation might run under official doors as well as down on Blunt, and that they might even hope—the CG's personal, long-held hope—to find that he wasn't handling that dual office with complete efficiency. Just let the man rummage quietly about for the CG and leave without a word, he'd thought, previously. He'd had no intention of talking directly to Magdallen, less of appearing to put pressure on him to suppress whatever findings he might make.

The ship's arrival changed things. If Earth was investigating at such great trouble and expense, it was time to ask questions of the Council agent and give certain clear directions. Missed communication had done harm enough in human affairs.

ARDATH WASN'T ON Procyon's personal tap—she couldn't be, since the nanoceles in his body were government issue and classified, so classified they'd demolished the output communications tap he'd gotten in his Freethinker days, in those few months of breaking away from family influence and doing stupid teenaged things. Nowadays he couldn't explain his lack of ordinary personal communication to the universe at large—well, at least he couldn't give the real story on it. Certain friends suspected him of going tapless out of respect for his parents' religion; even his sister had accused him of lying about having a tap and just not wanting to hear from her, the family black sheep.

Oh, he'd gotten one, he'd admitted to her finally, but it had broken down when he went to work for the government. There was a government reason he didn't get another one. He didn't want to talk about it. It was upsetting to him.

If *that* didn't tell her the government had wiped the output portion, he'd thought when he said it, she was deaf to hints.

Then she'd started worrying about him. Then she'd understood just a little of the constraint he was under, and forgave him. She could contact *him* if she needed.

And as things had gotten to be, even without the output tap most people had, he could still usually find her, because Ardath was by no means a quiet presence on the street.

He hadn't made it to the desserts at La Lune Noir yet. He'd decided, after taking her name in vain on the gift card, that it was a good idea to let his sister know about it, on the exceedingly remote chance Ardath, née Arden, had uncharacteristically intended a filial moment, a gift of her own for the occasion. They all lived their little fantasy of family, peaceful so long as Arden believed what she believed, that he was a cog in the bureaucracy, so long as the parents believed what they believed, that they'd brought up good, ordinary children and that Arden would come around to their view of the universe the way her brother had. The way it didn't do at all to have the parents see beneath the scenery, it didn't at all do to have Ardath's lively curiosity or her sense of indignation engaged on his case.

So he went through the usual dance of *not* looking for her, just happening into and out of her usual places—at this hour it was cocktails and dinner, indisputably, and he let slip he was meeting her, dropping the word in three different high-priced restaurants.

"*Pro*-cyon?"

Isis. He stopped, among the evening traffic of minor Fashionables. He cut a fine enough, though quiet, figure. But this was one of the Style, whose glittering gold bodysuit used a drifting glow to trick the eye into believing it saw skin. Green-eyed Isis hailed him on the common street, merely brushing his arm as she melted aside into the neon of the Astral Plane. Her music was her own. Her body moved to it, hips swaying, a liquid vision in retreat.

"Procyon." Sweetly. It was Spider at his elbow, then, one of Ardath's intimates. Originally male, Spider. Now even his lovers weren't sure. "Are you looking for Ardath?"

"Maybe."

Spider, whose naturally black skin glistened with sparks of color, likewise brushed by him and touched his sleeve. "A message?"

"Oh, a visit with my sister. *Family* business."

Spider, beautiful dark eminence, nodding with plumes, gave a flourish toward the Plane. Wait for her inside, that meant, and Procyon walked casually into the not-quite-door of the place—a set of reflective columns, light dimming progressively to eye-teasing shades of magenta and blue and deep shadow. The floor disappeared into black and reappeared in blue around a turn. Rhythmic vibrations flooded from the flooring up to the bones—enticing a customer to switch his commercial tap on and get the music from the local relay. The vibrations quivered against the skin, little discharges from the pillars. And from overhead, puffs of air teased and caressed.

He didn't tap in. He didn't hear the subliminal commercials or the music. He went to the bar, ordered wine, slipped his hand into the reader that debited his account twice the price of anywhere else on Grozny, and scanned the establishment.

The clientele ranged from Fashionables to bankers, elaborate elegants with fiery tracings on bare skin, and the occasional Earther in a gray pin-striped suit, zipped close and collared in sober black. There were living plumes, lately: that was the new chic, replacing hair. There were skin-shadings, finger-caps, and exotic hair-mods. A bony young man with magenta hair drew cold stares with a pair of green glowing-soled boots that left lime green tracks where he walked—not a happy sight, that boy's style, tragedy waiting to happen, if certain Stylists met him, but it was also his choice to be here, and one wondered if he knew the notice he gained was so highly unfavorable.

The wine arrived. He'd ordered a middling Outer Worlds Sauvignon, twenty a glass. It was, indeed, middling quality on his own scale, but in the Plane the average customer paid such prices unquestioningly, not for the wine, but for the spectacle of the elegants and the Fashionables, the walking adverts of various upscale emporia—not to mention the grotesques, whose choice was body-sculpting and augmentation of a risky but trend-setting sort. Spider verged on that class. Many successful Stylists did—the difference between Stylist and grotesque being the individual's sense of where that tasteful line was—and the general response of the Trend to the whole. Spider set trends for his admirers. So did Isis. Eyes fixed on them when they crossed the room, and people who wondered what shop sold what they wore needed only scan the fashion news of the week, and wonder if they dared. Shops thrived on Spider's patronage, and happily claimed to be the origin of certain unique items.

A stir attended a new arrival into the Plane. Heads turned. His turned more slowly.

Ardath was amazing. The plain black suit might have graced a corporate Earth auditor, except it glossed like satin and had an open throat. To answer their mother's question, yes, she was *modified:* patterns came and went on her skin, a delicate surface glow of flickering pale violet and gold. Her hair had the texture of straight silk thread, skeins of shining black silk done up in twists of lavender and blue and gold. Her eyes, with augmentation that didn't, at the moment, show, saw him plainly in dimmest light, no question. She rippled her surface glow, a little shiver of pale color, as she glanced at him and recognized his presence.

But then the cat-suited owner of the establishment intercepted her. She let the owner take her hand,, and walked about with him, being shown a table set and waiting for her, with a low centerpiece of crystal and exotic blooms. She touched the chair, smiled in acceptance, caressed the owner's arm, and made, perhaps, a request.

Wine arrived for her, not, he could be sure, the middling one. A handsome young waiter brought it, and Ardath sat and sipped it, listening to the owner's passionate monologue as he sat opposite at the table.

When will she get a job? their mother asked plaintively. At sixteen, Arden Stafford had been on the Street. At seventeen Arden had disappeared into it, and Ardath had emerged from that chrysalis, a young Fashionable immediately turning heads.

Get a job? Ardath had whatever she wanted and paid for nothing. She had the best wines, the best suppers, for merely walking into the Plane and being herself—Ardath, a Grand Stylist, one of the chief arbiters on the street, of what Fashionables should be and do. If Ardath even spoke to a Fashionable, that person's public esteem rose, and if Ardath turned a cold shoulder to a certain look, that person's stock plummeted in the Trend.

So with establishments. Wherever she dined, the place thrived and raked in the money. If she lived in an apartment complex, it profited, and that complex had a long waiting list for rentals at inflated prices. If she wanted a modification, she had it, gratis, and the doctor could as well move into a fancier residence and take on assistants. Theaters, style shops, restaurants, accessory shops, jewelers, all begged her attendance and offered her gifts. She let most such offerings fall untouched and unrebuffed. Grand Stylists made no mistakes, and what they noticed, let alone what they adopted for themselves, they chose ever so carefully.

She knew he was here, no question, and Procyon waited. After a few moments with the owner, she rose from the table, made her obligatory tour of inspection, briefly noting this and that person, chatting amiably with Spider, pausing to tip up the face of a young female hopeful and look critically, then smile. Ardath was never cruel. It was always positive notice, encouragement to what pleased her. Young Fashionables regarded her with worship and flocked to her vicinity in droves, wearing their best, all in a hope sometimes gratified for no plea at all, only the spontaneous honesty of her judgment.

His own dark tones, shirt and coat, matched her somber dress. He was glad of that accident as she slipped up and joined him at the bar. He'd known if he was going shopping uptown he wanted no flamboyance in any shop frequented by Earthers, but if he subsequently visited his sister, modest plumage definitely served. He by no means wanted a visual conflict with Ardath, by no means wanted to attract her kind of notice to his inexpert choice of style.

She leaned an elbow on the bar. Her skin settled on the lowest, slowest flicker. Blues melted back in curling, gold-edged shapes around her features, making of Ardath's natural clear complexion an Arden-mask, his sister's real face, revealed for him for the moment.

"Procyon." The voice had grown sweeter and lower over the last year. Even that was modified, and sounded like power in restraint, no longer his sister's voice, or even her original accents. "You look very well tonight." Seeing that she was beyond the Style, if she wanted to take her brother's hand, even to smile and compliment his modest, off-the-rack, though pricey suit, no one could fault her. Her fingers lingered on his, on the three handmade rings that were his personal vanity. "And what brings elder brother asking questions?"

"Oh, the annual parental occasion." He was just a little pained by the continuing performance, by the continual diminution of Arden in Ardath. "I just thought you'd like to know it's taken care of. A friendly advisory."

"Do I care? Let me see . . ."

"A truly déclassé crystal egg will find its way to the parental door tomorrow, with a Caprice label."

She drew back the hand in dismay. "Oh, shame, Procyon!"

Now it was his sister's voice. And he smiled, having scored.

"I confess. I did it. I doubt they'll see the humor in it. I signed both our names."

Very few people took any liberties with Ardath these days. He did. He saw the indignant fire in her eyes and the frown on her lips, and was immensely gratified to see the little girl for a moment, his outraged little sister in the Stylist's mask.

"*Jeremy and Arden.* In eighteen-point engravure. We were very proper. Mother, by the way, patiently asks whether you have a job yet."

Lifted brows. An uncontrolled gold flush washing over her cheeks spoiled the carefully modulated tendrils of color. Then outright laughter roused a sparkle of blue and gold, dancing like fire along her skin. No need for big brother to take her on a guided tour. She knew she'd been tagged, by someone who knew her well.

She said, with hauteur: "I hope you reassured her of your own orthodox circumstances."

"Oh, I did. Certainly."

"What *do* you do these days?" Tag, and tag. "You're not flopped down with those Freethinkers again, are you? Not embezzling from banks."

And she got no more information than usual.

"Still just pushing keys for the government."

"And wearing fabulous silk shirts." A touch drifted across his collar. "That *is* nice silk, big brother. Imported?"

"Expensive, expert keys for the government." A sweet, false smile. For revenge, she ran him through the everlasting familial maze: what do you do, where do you work, why the secrecy. "Expensive keys for very many hours. Slave labor. But I won't intrude my decadent Freethinker self here. Dessert at La Lune. I've dropped a bit of weight. I have it coming."

"La Lune Noir. Nice place. Drop my name there."

Meaning the establishment would give him his dessert and dinner just for the notice of Ardath's brother. "No. No, little sister." The false, sweet smile became true. "I pay my own way. And I don't want a personal following. I only thought you should know I've taken your name in vain—your birth name—just keeping those parental doors open."

"I won't visit them. I won't ever. You're entirely wasting your time."

"Life's long. Things change. And please don't trouble to damn

Caprice. They exist to please our mother. It's ever so good someone does."

"Oh, don't talk about her. It's a boring topic."

"She's a good person. So's our father, for that matter. Don't get too improved to remember that they gave us a good start."

"I don't remember that. I don't choose to remember it. Our mother used up that credit."

"Will you forget me? Will I get just too boring to cross your mind?"

"Never." Light danced in her eyes. Likely a number of chemomachines did, and music attended her, unheard by anyone outside her skull, music along with her personal messages. He saw from time to time how her eyes flickered with external input. She'd become the center of her own electronic universe, a very active internal universe of lights and signals and transmissions. "But *Caprice*! I could just *die*."

"Oh, don't. I'm sure you have something else to do this evening. I'm off to La Lune."

"On your own card, silly brother."

"It's just money. I have plenty."

"Mysterious, always mysterious. Are you actually going to the parentals tomorrow?"

"I'm hard to catch. I'm sure there's a gruesome dinner in the works, tomorrow off shift. I intend to disappear for at least six hours. Overtime at the office."

Slow, wicked smile. "Do they think of me often?"

"The parentals? They always ask how you are. I lie and say I see you often. I tell the truth and say you're doing fine."

"I'll bet she prays over me."

"Not such an unloving thing to do, midge."

"You're so brave, to go there."

"Oh, not that brave. I sometimes miss vegetables boiled to mush." Sometimes he longed for a parental voice. He was human. He experienced nostalgia. He wasn't that sure about Ardath. She had had yet to grow into her emotional adulthood when she fled a career in the plastics plant, and something in her had never ticked over to love for her origins, only roused a rebellion more bitter and more lasting than his. If she didn't cure that anger, she'd carry a lasting scar that nothing could cure—a part of her, he feared, that never would grow up. Lately, too, he detected a troubling chill, a remoteness he didn't like in her, and he suspected a first twist around that deep scar: he might be the only one who could talk to her that knew what her growing up should be. So he didn't give up the battle.

But no one took up an inordinate amount of Ardath's time. Her fans were hovering. It was time to get out of the way.

"I feel the urgent need for dessert. I'll leave now. Have a wonderful time, sis."

"So déclassé." She kissed him on the cheek. The whole restaurant must notice. The old warmth was there, and his sister was there, not yet warped by the anger or the changes, and that pleased him. "Why don't you just get a tap like every other reasonable person in the universe? Your department won't know. They can't rule your whole life."

"Government rules, government restrictions. A third time, government restrictions, and, trust me, they would know, darling sister. I know I'm not convenient. But my job's how I afford to go into these trendy places to see my dear sister. And you always manage to know when I'm looking for you. So somber today. You so *clearly* dressed to match me."

No one else would dare that impertinence. Her lips parted a second time in shock, her eyes flashed. And being his sister, she laughed aloud and hit him on the arm. "Silly Procyon. Go entertain yourself." Her skinlights curled closer and closer to her features, well controlled, now—over lips, tip of nose. Eyes lingered last, changing subtly from dull native green to pale, gas-fire azure. "Be good."

"I'm always *good*," he said solemnly. "Virtuous is another matter."

He left half his glass. He walked out among the reflective columns, out toward the street, the cynosure of every eye in the Plane. He was an encounter he was sure Ardath would have to live down tonight, oh, at least for two minutes; but she had the personal force to do it with complete aplomb: it was why he dared needle her.

Not exactly what Brazis liked, his skirting through the kind of attention that surrounded his sister, but on the PO staff's advice, he wore that public notice like a mantle, just another camouflage. *No* one high in government service sought public attention—so perhaps it made him less suspect. He walked out into the normal neon light of Grozny and down the street, momentarily enveloped in a string of dancers that melted past him, then stepping around a band of preteens clustered around a bench, kids likely not going home tonight and maybe not going home for the next number of nights—until the police rounded them up, asked them where they did belong, and billed the parents.

Most teens out at this hour were simple sessions-dodgers or young half-day factory workers on off shift, plus the more or less honest daylighters, who studied their hours or worked their hours and then played as hard as their finance let them, no one at home caring. They weren't generally a problem, but you didn't lay a credit card down on a counter and turn your head when that sort was about.

A few Freethinkers congregated at the corner—you could tell the type by the grimy, threadbare casuals, their own statement of style, their contempt of money. He didn't know the faces: those had all seemed to change in the years since his sojourn there . . . but then, he'd been transitory in that group. He'd attended only two meetings, long enough for disillusionment to set in; he'd quit them in three months, seeing nothing that interested him there.

And he'd made a full confession of his former associations in his government résumé, so he wasn't open to blackmail. Brazis reportedly didn't take his admission for a problem. Intellectual flirtation, he'd called it, in his interview. The rest who'd shared those grimy rooms at Michaelangelo's claimed they wanted to change the universe, but they spent their meetings nitpicking their own election rules and taking up collections for legal fees for extremist idiots. Mostly they sat around swilling cheap beer, complaining that everything the government touched was corrupt, and proposing no societal fix that could survive their own personal habits.

Well, so now he was working for the corrupt government himself, well, working inside it, on a critical job, and he had a very different view of how much actually did get done by officialdom, hour by hour, day by day, to keep the station running, never mind the corruption that threaded its way through human affairs in every endeavor—including Freethinker elections.

Maybe Freethinkers were leaven in the societal loaf, and shoved public opinion into progressing a healthy few degrees a century, in a society otherwise far out of time with the rest of the speeding cosmos, but otherwise they had no power, and Chairman Brazis just did as he did, and moved society in his own, far more powerful way. A former Freethinker strongly suspected Brazis had his own shadowy spots; but Brazis made the Project work, and did his job, and was, meanwhile, fair to his staff. A former Freethinker held a niggling suspicion that purity of life and purpose was the most suspicious thing in a public official. A former Freethinker began to think that the real world had far more layers than he'd once thought.

Well, but he was growing layers, himself. Secrets. Things he didn't admit. Ardath grew more and more apart from him. He worried about her, but as yet thought of nothing he could do but live within her reach, and wait, and keep to his own venues except on rare occasions of purpose. Like the parental anniversary.

La Lune Noir wasn't on his sister's list. Too near Blunt for high fashion, but sitting on Grozny, purveying its fancy food at a modest price that didn't upset his old Freethinker sense of economy. It had that kind of clientele, not quite in the Style, rubbing elbows with the fringe of the Trend.

And it had that beautiful showcase of desserts, right in the window.

He walked in and, being as he was a regular, his regular waitress nabbed him and showed him right to his table, his preferred place near the vid screen. "The usual?"

"Everything."

He loved not having to think much on his off shift. He liked La Lune for leaving their patrons music-free and vibration-free, to bring in their private choices on their taps, or not.

It meant the place was hushed, except the noise of adjacent conversations, the clink of glasses, and the occasional crash of a dish.

"Damn!" from the kitchen. He laughed.

That was La Lune.

A trio came in during his supper, danced on the transparent floor, to music the lot of them shared, and he recognized in that set three of his old Freethinker friends, who'd likewise left the den and prospered obscenely, by Freethinker standards. Marcus

Liebermann was a medtech and Danny Casper was a paralegal. And Angie Wu, who'd recently married Danny, had become that archenemy of Freethinkers and terror of every marginal shop on the street—a customs cop.

They waved at him, he waved at them—he exchanged a few words with Danny and Angie and Mark when the music changed and they left the dance floor—how are you doing? Seeing anybody? New job? And from him to Angie and Danny: Congratulations on the wedding.

Seen any others of the old gang? however, was anathema as a question. He'd kept his distance from these three, and didn't socialize. They didn't have that much in common anymore, didn't occupy the same stratum of society.

Polishing more than a handful of social contacts cost more energy than he had these days, and he was glad that his three old acquaintances didn't propose to join him in a dinner well under way. He enjoyed the last of his entrée, drank a second glass of wine, shut his eyes in the general noise of quiet conversations around him, and let the tension flow out through his fingers and toes. He was trying not to think more deeply about Ardath.

He remained concerned about the changes in her, however, which seemed too many, too fast. He worried about the day she'd age, and how she'd take it, and where she'd go, when his own career was a very healthy, government-funded, extended lifetime—so long as he didn't personally piss off Brazis or commit one of the hundred and one fatal rule infractions.

Not hard rules. No theft. No drugs. No illicits. No criminal associations. No dinner with three old friends over there—not because they weren't probably completely respectable, these days, but because if he did, they'd have government investigators raking over *their* pasts, maybe to their detriment.

All his friends had to pass muster. And intimate relationships outside the department just couldn't happen.

That was the killer. You could work out arrangements for a personal life in government service: a prospective mate could be sucked into the offices, given some adequate job, and earn an equivalent security clearance, but you'd better be damned sure, thoughtful, and permanent about your choice. Divorce that mate, and you might both be reassigned somewhere less nice within those office walls. The PO didn't like attachments or tag ends that hung out into the ordinary world . . . especially tag ends that hung out down in the Trend.

And if a tap should get fired from his job, worse thought, he got to spend the rest of his life wondering how the world down there was getting along, what that sandy plateau was becoming, how the people he'd come to know almost as family were doing in their day-to-day lives—and no one in the Project would ever give him those answers. Lose his security classification over some infatuation? Even a passionate attraction? It was like a musician agreeing to be cut off from music if he fell in love inconveniently—or ever changed his affections. It was a painter agreeing to go blind if he fell in love. It was the one cruel downside of his extravagant lifestyle, and it had happened more than once in the long, long history of the department. A significant number who'd fallen afoul of the infamous Rule 12, the personal relationships rule, and gotten into some insolvable personal entanglement, had subsequently gotten in trouble with the Project's secret police, or spiraled down with drugs, with drink, with a series of unsuccessful relationships inside the Project, spreading disaster around them as they went. Or they just ended up discreetly killing themselves.

Nasty line of thought. He wasn't going to let himself make that fatal mistake. Wasn't going to associate with anybody outside the walls. Wasn't going to get fired. No way. No relationships outside the Project. If you were going to be a tap, you had to come in young and full of hormones, that was one thing, and that fact gave the Project trouble. He'd applied just for a job, his hope when he made the try: just a job and a good salary, in computers. But his application kept getting shunted through to other departments. When his application had gotten up as high as it could get, and when he'd found out he was under consideration for the Project, he'd been stunned; when he'd learned he might become one of the taps, he'd been scared as hell.

But attracted by the pay scale. Give it that. Attracted by the security. So attracted he'd been like every other tap that had come in from beyond the security wall: he'd been seeing the glamor and ignoring the other facts of his proposed life.

But when he was actually about to get the tap, Brazis himself had had a sobering talk with him about Rule 12. He'd been bone-ignorant, but still ambitious. Having seen his parents trying to make ends meet on two salaries, and seeing what he could make if he went that track, he was blinded by the prospect. He'd sworn on a stack of mission statements that he'd remain faithful and true to the department, avoiding all outside entanglements forever and ever, amen.

They'd run a further battery of drug, health, and psych tests and opted him in, seeing something in him, he supposed, that he never could figure, and completely ignoring the Freethinker business, which he'd thought would be a deal-breaker. He'd been eclectic in his studies, unable to settle, except for the certificate in computers. He'd hoped for employment in the technical wing and ended up opted in behind the security wall as that most rarefied of Project entities, a tap.

Then, Marak having made his pick, contrary to all Project hopes, Brazis had had a quiet fit and called him in for another interview, asked him excruciatingly pointed and personal questions for an hour and stared at him for another few minutes as though he were something under a microscope. He'd tried hard, since then, not to have another interview with Brazis until he'd put a few successful years behind him in the job he'd risen to. Maybe a successful paper or two. Maybe a geological memo going somewhere. He wanted something extravagantly positive in his record, to justify Brazis's signing off on his assignment.

He knew he was bright. He knew he was incredibly lucky. He knew that an eclectic academic background was one of the assets that had gotten notice from the Project, but utterly outrageous chance had landed him in the assignment he had. He personally liked Marak . . . if you could like somebody on his scale . . . he more than liked him: he found in that strange, calm personality a stability that he'd never had, a matching curiosity that opened his mind to question after question, an insatiable hunger for knowledge he'd never known could be accessible. But now that he'd found his place in life, he absolutely dreaded anything that could threaten that good fortune. Meetings with old friends and his extended family always left him anxious, remembering what he'd been, where he'd been headed, where he was now, and how fragile the whole structure was.

Crystal eggs, parental expectations, and the cold, impenetrable wall behind which the PO worked. He didn't *want* the PO raking through his immediate relations . . . or making trouble for Ardath.

Damn, he wished he hadn't had to tap out on Marak today when he had. He hoped there'd be a perfectly functioning new camera waiting for him tomorrow. He could imagine those vistas, the red river gorge, the long steep fall to the pans on the other side, and the trembling knife-edge of the arcing ridge between. He could imagine the slow movement of tectonic plates that had created the place, the flow of lava in geologic ages before plates became locked in place, before the hammerfall had set them free again . . .

"I always see you alone," his waitress said, picking up the remnant of his dinner. "Are they friends of yours?" With a nod at the other table.

"Old acquaintances."

The young woman lingered hopefully, stayed to talk, and Procyon, at first irritated, not wanting any closer communication to spoil his nonrelationship with his favorite waitress, still fell into her game. There was no departmental rule against sociability, and he liked her well enough—played at her little flirtation, but only just, and, mindful of Ardath and her kindness to the hopefuls, he didn't give her any real encouragement to escalate the game. She was maybe twenty. Bright. She got good tips. She'd find whoever she was looking for. Someday.

She offered him dessert, gratis. As if he were Ardath. He didn't know what to do about that. He hoped he hadn't encouraged her too much—that she didn't have further plans.

He made his selection, a burnt cream. "I don't think my patronage is going to bring in floods of Fashionables."

"No," she said with a wink. "But you know people that will."

Damn. Damn and double-damn. It wasn't his personal attractiveness. It was Ardath the girl was courting.

Tag, Ardath would say, long-distance, you're it.

*   *   *

No SEALED GLOBE. A light panel and rows of orchids. Forgiving plants—they survived drought long enough to live when business was routine, and they survived being overwatered and overtended when a crisis came. That meant they survived in Brazis's office. Nothing else could.

A crisis had arrived, and he watered his plants, one and all, distracted into the hope of a bud stem emerging. The new cattaleya had proven amazingly cooperative, even luxuriant. The oncidium had produced a new plant, and rested, and now that trouble showed up, and a temporary glut of water, he was sure a number of the rest of the collection would soon think about blooming.

He fed his darlings. He carefully removed an old leaf. He discarded the detritus and wiped down the lighted shelves himself. Housekeeping, fearing for their lives, refused to touch them. He refused to have cleaner-bots anywhere in the office.

Agent Magdallen had been busy when he called on him to come in. *Busy,* Magdallen had had the temerity to inform him.

Agent Magdallen might have been extremely busy, Brazis began to think, ever since that inbound ship made the news.

But his plainclothesmen had nabbed the man and outright laid down an ultimatum: come in, or spend the next ten days in confinement.

"Agent Magdallen is here," Dianne informed him sweetly—his dragon at the gate, Dianne, who would also have assured that Magdallen entered the secure offices inconspicuously, on some other office's summons, and without untidy items in his possession, or she'd break his fingers.

What happened inside this set of offices, Governor Reaux's security couldn't penetrate, often and earnestly as it tried.

The door opened. A weary-looking older Fashionable in a black coat came in—stood for a moment observing the orchid-tending.

"You needed me?" One shoulder straightened. The other did. Magdallen stood a little taller. Brazis watched the reflection in an aptly placed mirror strip, and saw hawk-nosed Magdallen grow subtly younger and slimmer by the moment. The long hair slowly lost its white streaks in favor of healthy black.

Needed him. Hell. Magdallen had never been on his needed list, among gifts the CG had sent him, but he was stuck with him. Talent came in from the Chairman General and a local chairman dealt with the offering until it decided to go away and spy elsewhere.

"This ship," Brazis said, sparing a sidelong glance. A very sharp glance. "Do you know why this ship is coming in?"

"No."

Short and sweet. "Not our local business?"

"I'm sure I don't know. I can't examine its origins. Or its passenger lists."

Magdallen was here on a ghost hunt, and was surely powerful, but not as powerful as Magdallen thought, that was the point Brazis meant to make.

"Tell me. Does 'sir' ever pass your lips?"

"Sir."

The tone did it. It finally did it. Brazis put down the watering pitcher on the edge of the credenza and brushed off his hands, facing the subject squarely.

"Agent Magdallen."

"Sir."

One suspected sarcasm. Magdallen might be used to local authorities running scared of him and his backers. Brazis didn't personally run scared of man or devil. As head of the PO, technically entitled to a seat on the High Council, he didn't flinch at an inquisitive auditor, not in any particular. Nor did he worry too much who was currently sitting behind the Chairman General's desk at Apex. CGs came and went, and might fall from office. So might a local chairman; but from his position as Project Director, only Ian and Luz acting together could remove him, so long as he lived.

"Don't parse missing negatives with me, Agent Magdallen. You may have come in here with the High Council's blessing and a kiss on the cheek from the Chairman General himself, but I assure you the Council won't appreciate a foul-up here, and if that ship and you or your business here have any remote causal relationship that's going to touch me in either of my offices, I want to know it before I set my local security into motion. Let's not treat Earth authority to the spectacle of two Outsider investigations tangled in each other's operations, shall we not?"

"I remind you you have no binding authority over me."

"No binding authority. But a preventative authority—that I do have, and you're within a hair's breadth of discovering it. You may be the Chairman General's personal valet for all I care, but you're a damned nuisance to the Project Director in this moment of crisis, and if you're determined not to cooperate with our needs, you're about to annoy me in ways that won't possibly benefit your career in the future—trust me. I want to know definitively what you're nosing about in on Blunt, I want to know why you have at least two apartments and two alternate identities down there. I want to know the gist of that investigation and what it's turned up, and especially I want to judge for myself whether Earth might have launched an investigatory mission bearing some remote relationship to what you're doing. My clearance is higher than yours. In my capacity as Project Director, I want to know. It's moved beyond your orders from Apex and into a crisis on my desk. Is that a clear enough request for you?"

The business about the alternate identities was a little secret Magdallen hadn't expected to have laid in front of him, Brazis bet on that. There had been just a little change of expression.

"Someone else *should* know," Magdallen said slowly, as if he'd reached a decision. "The Chairman General said you were capable in a need-to-know situation."

"I'm incredibly flattered. Compliments to the CG's foresight in telling you so. I assure you this is that situation. Talk. What the hell are you doing messing with the Freethinkers?"

"I don't know what this ship is. I hear the word *ambassador*. I think that's cover. I think this intrusion is more inquisitory than representative. I'm not sure what agency might have sent this person and given him this cover."

"And the Freethinkers?"

"Rumors run the little channels, among the petty smugglers. There's been a whisper of illicits that Earth's detected at Orb. It's possible that's brought an inquiry in."

"Smuggling." It was too ordinary. Brazis didn't buy it. He hadn't liked Magdallen before, and he liked him less for hedging after promising him the truth. But in truth, there was one kind of smuggling that would involve Earth in two seconds. "Are you talking about biostuffs?"

A hesitation. "Yes."

That actually *could* explain it. It wasn't, however, the only conceivable answer, even for Magdallen's presence, and he wished he hadn't steered Magdallen so conveniently into suggesting it was the obvious—and maybe misleading—problem. "All right. So I'll play along with this theory. But it's a theory, not ascending to fact. What else do you know?"

"Nothing, at this point. I must point out, sir, your bringing me in like this jeopardizes my several identities and makes it less likely I'll find out anything."

"I'm sure you'll recover handily. Know nothing, do you, after all this time ferreting about in our understructure?"

"Nothing solid, I regret to say. I'm pursuing the theory I named."

Brazis saw he wasn't going to get cooperation, and would probably get a cover story if he pressed. He hesitated to divert Magdallen's energies by giving him one more falsehood to manufacture and maintain. And if he gave the man space, and let him know he was allowing him that, he might get more from the man in future. "All right. Chase your private theories. Do your job—whatever it is. But hear this. I want information from you in return for my patience. And if you make any policy-threatening move without telling me, I'll send my own message to the CG, and it won't be understanding of your difficulties. I'll warn you now, I'm doing a quiet crackdown on the street. You're hearing this advisory a quarter hour before I send the pick-them-up message—an hour, if you'd answered my original summons. If the pickup is likely to disrupt your operations, you'd better identify those operations to me before I give that order, and I'll make a few careful exceptions."

"Go light on MacDougal's, between 10th and 11th. I have operations there."

"Noted. I know it well. Here's a reciprocal bit of advice. The governor's a friendly. We don't want to lose him. If you think to the contrary, say so now, and we'll talk about it fully and frankly."

"I don't contradict that opinion."

"Good. Now let me give you some information. *Earth* may well want to lose this governor, but I assure you *we* don't. His fall from grace would generate all sorts of difficulties. Not insurmountable ones, but damned inconvenient, and apt to have repercussions. He's upset local power games, made some factions very angry, had a major falling-out when he entered the financial games that were the eternal rule here, and powerfully annoyed the clique that runs the banks. In the process, he's done a great deal to put the brakes on the graft that's gone on here for generations. Consequently he has enemies, none from Earth that we know about, and I doubt Earth cares that much what he does; but there are locals with strong motives, shall we say, to make him look bad while that ship is pursuing whatever business it came to pursue. *Not* an advantageous result for your career, Agent Magdallen, if you should knock over that stack of breakables. So stay out of the way of my operations, if you don't have anything to do with this ship. See to it that whatever you value down on Blunt stays invisible and inactive for the duration. That's the long and the short of it. Your opposite number among the local Earthers is just as likely to go after suspects on his own list, given a little free rein by the governor. Be discreet."

"Dortland"—that was to say, Reaux's chief of security—"seems to have no idea I'm here."

That was worth a long, cold stare. "In my local experience, Agent Magdallen, saying someone has no idea is a very dangerous presumption. An equally dangerous presumption's that you know all my agents. Or the governor's. Or even Dortland's, who may be a separate operation from us or the governor. I've long suspected that. Do you think I'm a fool, Agent Magdallen?"

"No, sir." More subdued, a far more cautious answer.

"I'm not a fool, Agent Magdallen."

"I assure you of the same, sir."

"Good. *Good.* So what's my ultimate answer, from you, as to why petty smuggling would bring an answer clear from Earth?"

"Smuggling of biostuffs, and maybe not petty. That's not theory, Mr. Chairman. It is going on. I know that. Earth is upset, but not panic-stricken. Nothing got through their barriers. Nothing was ever directed at them. I can at least assure you this has nothing to do with your governor. And I'm somewhat doubtful the ship's visit offers him any personal threat."

"If you learn any differently about their business here, I want word. I don't insist you come here, but I want word, and I want it within the hour you learn it."

"I trust—in your own expertise, sir—you know that's not always operationally possible."

"Call it a moral goal, Agent Magdallen. Attempt to achieve it. I'm sure you have unguessed capabilities."

A little nod, a kind of bow. "I'll keep in touch, sir."

"Good." Brazis picked up the watering can off the slate-surfaced cabinet. "Thirty minutes, Agent Magdallen, and certain people will start disappearing off the streets for the duration of this visit, or longer. I trust your scattered people and interests will respond to the warning I'm giving you. Do we agree?"

A little nod from Magdallen. "I can manage that. I'll trust if I do say release someone—someone will somehow escape."

Brazis looked at the man. This wasn't a fool, or a man who'd push him—now. As well have an agreement with him, whatever he thought his powers were. "I think we can manage that. Contact me at need. Perhaps we can manage a much closer working relationship hereafter, Agent Magdallen. Since I can safely assume your target isn't me, you can somewhat reliably assume mine isn't you."

A little bow, not a word of answer, no love lost.

But there existed now, for mutual reasons, a cooperative agreement.

3

A DECENT TIP TO THE WAITRESS, including the price of the gratis dessert, and so help him, if Ardath ever projected her pricey presence onto La Lune and ruined this place in some misguided sense of charity toward her brother's favorite restaurant, Procyon swore he'd go into mourning.

Not that the staff would be sorry for a rise in tips. Maybe crashing dishes and no music in restaurants would be the new fashion statement. Maybe there'd be a new chic, for the slightly distressed environment.

But Procyon doubted it. Any new ownership would fire the staff for breaking the crockery, and they'd install that damned Rhythmique apparatus, grim thought, to pound rhythm into the floor. Then they'd triple the prices of the food, advertise up and down the street, and it just wouldn't be La Lune anymore.

Damn, damn, and damn. He should call Ardath and absolutely threaten her life if . . .

"Staff alert.

"We have an Earth ship inbound for docking. You may have noticed."

That was loud. Impossible to ignore, blasting through the tap. He'd stopped dead on the walk, as if he'd been hit with a stun, and recovered, trying not to be conspicuous.

Brazis himself. The voice always sounded different coming over a tap, the way people didn't naturally know what their own voices sounded like outside their heads; but it was Brazis, from the inside,

Brazis, talking to the whole staff, no matter where they were, and Procyon looked stupidly toward the ceiling of the corridor and its bright lights. He hadn't known there were secure tap relays all the way to the bag end of Grozny.

But of course there would be, now that he thought of it. Brazis had his agents working in all sorts of places where trouble might hang out. They had to have some way to report in, off the common tap. There might even be secure relays on other levels of the station, for all he knew, wherever Brazis might have interests.

"Be discreet. Stay out of questionable places."

Did La Lune fit that description? Intrigue wasn't his forte.

"Best if you could all stay in your residences the next few days. Take this very seriously."

The old man seemed actually worried. An Earth ship was coming into dock, and they were supposed to go home, pull the lid on, and stay there.

All right. That was a clear and sobering order. He started walking. Home it was. No show. Eating in and living in for a few days, he could do that. He could stop by the store and pick up a few items, and he'd be fine. He certainly didn't want any trouble with admin or the old man, and reality had just jolted into his path, with an advisement that had to include police and everybody associated with the Project, a regular take-cover, as if there were something going on that threatened all of them.

But insatiable curiosity was his profession. He wondered what unprecedented thing was going on, involving this ship from Earth, that produced this kind of order.

He dipped into the common tap for the moment, wondering if there was any sort of news bulletin he hadn't picked up. But all he heard was talk about a garden show, and a new music shop opening on second tier. He shut it down and cast an eye to the running newsboards as he walked Grozny toward home.

The Earth ship was coming into dock in the slow way ships did. Whatever it was, it would be here by morning.

The rich dessert wasn't resting quite as easily on his stomach. His world was running so very well. Change wasn't good. Any change at all in things as they were wasn't good. He didn't want any Earth ship bringing emergencies and take-covers without any rumor what was going on.

Cheese. He was out of cheese and pasta makings, his standard recipe for domestic survival, in a fancy kitchen synthesizer woefully basic in patterns, since he'd never really used it for more than caff and breakfast.

Maybe he'd stop by the store and get one of those frozen cakes the store sold, from its own kitchen. That would fortify his spirits in his hours locked away. And it wasn't as if he wouldn't hear things: he'd gotten news the rest of the station hadn't. The Project would keep him informed. He'd hear something more, surely, when he went back on duty tomorrow morning.

But he was in confinement, otherwise. If there was a parental potluck, he was assuredly going to miss it. That was a plus.

He shouldn't answer any calls. And his mother would, of course, call, and then worry that she couldn't get to him.

He should send her a note—his religious mother not, of course, having a tap—he should send something casual, like a card, to forestall her questions. He could send a courier note from the grocery.

Short and sweet: *Dear Mum and Dad, extra work at the office. I'm on mandatory overtime, a computer blowup.*

So they wouldn't possibly connect it with the inbound ship.

Wish I could be there. Congrats. Love, Jeremy.

Damned good thing he'd sent the crystal egg.

HOME. THANK GOD, Reaux thought, home past the cameras and the media hounds with a well-rehearsed statement—*we have an ambassadorial visitor, and expect a brief visit and consultation*—then safely, solitarily, home. The smell of Judy's grilled fish permeated the rooms as he hung his day coat in the closet. He hoped for scalloped potatoes. He hadn't had potatoes in forever.

And a glass of white wine. Maybe two glasses. It had been a day. It had been, he remembered, *two* days. And he was home. Safe.

The ship was on approach now, for docking at about 440h. It had become tomorrow's problem. Tonight his wife had decided to cook, and thanks to that decision and a small crisis with a beautician, he had the privacy and comfort of his own well-secured walls around him, instead of a restaurant where the media might insert a lens in the table bouquet. It damned sure beat takeout and a nap in the office for a second night. Whatever Judy's personal reasons, whatever fuss she was having with their teenaged daughter, it was a very good night for her to have resurrected her culinary skills.

He found her in the kitchen, in an apron, pushing buttons on the grill and looking domestic and frustrated, her meticulous coiffure a little frayed. He came up behind her, having gotten half a surly glance, put his arms around her—still no yielding—and kissed her cheek.

"You can pour the wine," Judy said.

He saw the wineglasses—two—on the white tile counter. He pressed keys on the fridge: it delivered the chilled wine, and he slipped the bottle under the opener. Hiss and pop, as the wine began to breathe.

Wonderful sound.

"Pour it," Judy said. "Pour me one."

Not good. Not celebratory, that was sure. He poured two full glasses and handed her one.

"Our daughter," she began.

"Dye didn't solve it?"

Mistake. Judy took a deep, angry breath. And took a large gulp of the expensive wine before she set the glass down on the counter. Thump, face averted, both hands flat on the counter. "Setha. Setha, *your* daughter—her friends—her friends, Denny Ord and Mark Andrews . . ."

"I know them."

"Clearly you don't know them well enough! They've been arrested. Swept up in a Freethinkers' dive down on Blunt!"

A moment of panic. "Kathy wasn't involved."

"Kathy was with me."

"Good." Deep breath. "Good sense of her."

"Do you understand me? Our daughter has friends in *jail*."

"They're both from good families. I'm sure they were doing what all young people do at one time or another, slipping down to the Trend. She wasn't involved in it, and their parents will get them out of their mess. It'll all pass."

"I want some support, Setha! I want some backing here!"

"I'm sure I'll back whatever you think needs backing, but I'm operating on short information, at the moment, Judy. She wasn't with them, and I'm sure the boys haven't done anything but be in the wrong place. It will all work out."

"You don't understand!"

"I know I don't understand, Judy. I'm asking for information."

"Her *friends*, this Denny and Mark . . . I'm forbidding her to associate with these people. Forbidding her even to speak to them, ever again! I want your backing in this. I want her school sessions changed! I want her to transfer to St. Agnes!"

"That's a little extreme, isn't it? If you haven't seen the news, Judy, a lot of people are getting swept up on Blunt at the moment. Nine-tenths of the people hauled in may be innocent, maybe even just passing on the street, and nobody's even going to notice if two teenagers got into the sweep. There's a security watch on. They're pulling in everyone who's anomalous down there, no proof these boys are actually guilty of anything at all but bad timing. I certainly don't think there's any need to pull Kathy out of a school where she's happy."

"She's running with the wrong people, Setha! She bleaches her hair, her friends get arrested—three guesses, Setha, where she was supposed to be today, when she *didn't* get arrested! With them! I'll bet, with them!"

"Judy, proportion. Proportion."

"She's cut sessions before now to go down there! Did you know that? She's cut three sessions this month, and the school didn't report it, because *they* didn't think it was significant, and I just happened to see her attendance record when I excused her out today to get her hair done! That's what's going on, Setha! I can't quit my job! I *refuse* to quit my job because I can't trust my own daughter to be at sessions without checking up on her every minute! If I can't trust her to go to sessions or to be home when she's supposed to be home, what can I do?"

He took a deep swallow of wine himself. "We can certainly have a talk with the school administrators about their reporting policies."

"I stayed home from work today. I had Renee come here, and I made it abundantly clear I didn't want this bleach job talked about in the shop."

"Did it work? The dye?"

"It's at least better. And then when Renee left— Have you seen Kathy's closet?"

"I—no."

"Things that don't fit decently, low cut blouses—she's asked me for clothes money three times in the last month, and what she buys is a disgrace, an absolute disgrace, Setha! Sweaters down to here." A measurement low on Judy's own elegantly bloused bosom. Which generated a grease stain on the mauve silk to which Judy at the moment seemed oblivious. "Pants that show everything! Shoes you can't walk in! Tees with crude language and shorts that wouldn't make decent underwear! I took her shopping after Renee finished."

"That sounds like a good thing."

"I took her to lunch. We had a perfectly nice lunch. Then I took her down on Lebeau, to Marie Trent's."

Judy's favorite shopping venue, where the establishment brought outfits out one at a time, modeled on live mannequins, and served tea while the systems constructed your purchase to fit your own physique and your own coloring.

"What did we spend on this venture?"

"Plenty! Her hair styled, a manicure, and Jeanne Lorenz jewelry. And then she didn't want the clothes once they made them. Marie Trent herself tried to explain to her that she does have too much bust and she could stand a little sculpting, and meanwhile she should deemphasize that feature with a perfectly beautiful look for her. Kathy said to Ms. Trent's face that *she* could do with bigger breasts and her shirts all looked like sacks. At that point, Ms. Trent said I could take her out of the shop, and I tried to, but Kathy threw a fit, a screaming *fit*, Setha! I was so embarrassed. I've never been so embarrassed in my life. And Kathy wouldn't leave the shop. Kathy kept saying, quote, no bitch could throw her out, and nobody could talk to her that way, and that she was your daughter . . ."

"God."

"Oh, yes, *your* name got into this. Now, are you worried? Kathy said she knew grotesques on Blunt with more taste, this, when another customer had come into the shop! Ms. Trent threatened to call the police." Judy was shaking. She picked up the glass and almost slopped the wine over the rim getting another sip. "I can never go back there, Setha. I can never go back there. I don't think I ever want to leave the apartment again in my life!"

"Judy." He did feel sorry for her. Glass and all, he put his arms around her. "You have to go back there. Tomorrow. I'd advise an apology to Ms. Trent and a very large purchase. Break the budget."

"I don't know why Kathy's acting like this, Setha, I don't understand it!"

"I'll talk to her." At the moment he had Judy in his arms and a wineglass precariously crushed against her bosom. He disengaged carefully. "Are you all right?"

"I need you to be home and deal with this!"

He was suddenly aware of a burnt smell. "I think the fish is done."

"Damn!" Judy burst into tears and grabbed the oven door.

"I'll talk to Kathy." It was an escape. Judy was about at the screaming stage herself, and it didn't do to push her to communicate. As Judy should learn about Kathy someday, except they were too much alike. Two queens couldn't possibly sit on the same throne.

Cutting school sessions and sneaking out into the real netherside of Blunt, however, was a serious matter. A screaming fit in Marie Trent's was serious on another level, an exposure to gossip that did his wife and daughter no good, and him no political good at all under present circumstances, with the media on the hunt and frustrated. He'd better call Marie Trent's himself, apologize profusely, and buy something extremely expensive for Judy, trusting Marie Trent had Judy's sizes in the computer.

He could do all these things *after* he'd dealt with Mr. Andreas Gide, tomorrow morning, assuming the ambassador's ship arrived on schedule.

God, Judy and Kathy could time things amazingly. One night he spent at the office, and they were immediately at each other's throats.

He took the lift up to Kathy's hallway, walked to Kathy's door. Hesitated. Knocked.

"Kathy. It's your father."

"Go away!"

"Kathy, I've got a ship from Earth on my doorstep and your mother's burning supper downstairs. We need to talk."

"No!"

"I heard about Marie Trent. I sympathize with your position and I'm not sure her clothes are your style, but can we possibly avoid stationwide media coverage?"

A heavy thump. Something hit the wall. Little thumps then as bare footsteps marched to the door.

It opened. Kathy stood there flatfooted, a beautiful teenaged girl in a gray, too-old-for-her skirt, a chic white silk blouse half-unbuttoned and hanging its tail out to the left, and her hair an unKathy-like and shocking red-brown, with her olive complexion. Behind her, the closet was a disaster area, clothes, mostly black and gray and white, flung over the bed and onto the floor, along with a confetti of fabric bits on the floor. His daughter's chest was heaving. She had a scissors in her hand.

"She threw out all my clothes and put her damned castoffs in my closet!"

He heaved a sigh. "We'll find your old clothes. Put down the scissors."

"She says she put them in the disposer! Those were my *favorites*! She hates me! Everybody hates me!"

"Damn. Look, Kathy." He put a hand on her shoulder. Kathy flung it off, a hazard with the scissors. He took the implement out of her hand, reached in his pocket and extracted his wallet, and now that he had her slight attention, drew from that mesmerizing object a credit card, holding it up between them. "Kathy, I'll give you five hundred on my card. Just go buy something on your own tomorrow, without your mother. I'll excuse you out of sessions."

Five hundred had secured his daughter's solid interest. She wiped her eyes and took the card.

"I just don't know why she can't leave me alone."

"I'm on your side, right down to the point you cut your sessions, which is in the school records. On that score, I have an objection. Cutting up your clothes . . . I can almost sympathize with that. They don't suit you."

"I hate them!"

"The clothes? That's evident."

"The school. The damned school! I hate them, too!"

"Don't use that language, please. What's the trouble?"

"They're a bore, and they're always finding fault, no matter what I do."

"Ippoleta Nazrani?"

"Is a skinny-ass whore."

"Language. Language, Kathy."

"*Mignette.*"

"Pardon?"

"I want to change my name. I want to change schools."

"Why?"

"I'm bored. I'm bored, bored, bored, *bored* with those fools."

"Boredom rather well damns your own imagination, doesn't it?"

"I don't care. I don't like always having to watch what I do, watch what I say, all because *Ippoleta* is so good and so sweet. She's a lump. She's just a lump. She'd wear these things! I won't!"

"Kathy."

"Mignette. I want to be Mignette. It's what my friends call me."

"Mignette." It was always something new with the female of the species. She wanted to change her school and change her name. As if that would solve it all. "I hope I'm still your father."

"Mother's not my mother." A furious kick at the detritus of fabric snips on the floor. "Not anymore! And I haven't got anything to wear and she says I'm not to talk to Denny and Mark, who are the *only* intelligent people in my whole class. And she embarrassed hell out of me with this *stupid* haircut and this *stupid* dye job and I have to go out in public and have that *stupid* woman tell me I'm fat because I have a chest and she doesn't!"

"You know, Kathy—Mignette—I completely sympathize about the remarks. But you can't pitch a fit in your mother's favorite shop. She took you there because she cares about you and she wanted to give you what she thinks is pretty."

"She took me there because she thinks I'm fat, too, and she doesn't like my clothes and she hates my friends and she's thrown out all my stuff, and she just drives me *crazy*, papa, she just drives me crazy!"

Now it was tears. Hormone wars, he'd about bet, fiftyish wife and teenaged daughter, who physically took after his side of the family. He gathered his outraged daughter in his arms and hugged her hard. "There, there, Mignette or Kathy, you'll have five cee to go fix this tomorrow. You're a good kid. You manage pretty well, all taken together—you don't do drugs, you don't do illicits, you usually don't do things that I have to explain on the news and I appreciate that, I respect it, I really do. You can just come by the office tomorrow when you get through and show me what you've bought. And I'll talk to your mother."

"She's not my mother, I tell you!"

"I'm afraid you're stuck with biological fact, darling girl, you're hers as well as mine, which is why you're always fighting with each other. I want you to wash your face, tuck your shirttail in, and come downstairs."

"No!"

"You can't starve. I'm sure it's a lovely fish, even a little singed. Just be my sweet daughter and learn to be a diplomat."

"I don't want to be a diplomat."

"What *do* you want to be someday?"

"I want to be rich, and buy anything I want and not have to be polite to anybody."

"I'm Governor of Concord, and I absolutely have to be polite to everybody. Money and power won't do that for you, Kathy-sweet. Mignette. Nothing ever excuses rudeness. Not yours and not your mother's, and I hate it when you do this to each other. Temper always makes a mess of your surroundings, and if you're smart, you mop it up as soon as you know about it. Now go wash your face. Put on your robe, if you don't want to wear what you have on—I trust your bathrobe survived the scissors—and come down to dinner and be nice to your mother."

"I can't!"

"Katherine Callendish-Reaux, you will. You can and you will. Listen to me." He set her back sternly, hands on her shoulders. "I have a headache. I have a backache. I had a cold supper last night, damned little sleep in my office chair, and interviews all day with every power broker on Concord, from Station Security to the Outsider Chairman. I've had an absolutely hellacious two days, I've got an ambassador from Earth arriving tomorrow, and he could conceivably decide I'm not to be governor anymore, and you're not to have a nice apartment or any nice clothes, or any father for that matter, do you understand that? That's how serious it is. So if you'll do me the moderate favor of giving me five days of tranquillity in this household, no matter what you have to say or do with your mother, I'll be so deep in your debt I'll buy you a shop full of whatever your heart desires and let you dye your hair blue if you like. Just hold the lid on for five days. Please, baby."

"*Mignette!*"

"Mignette." In calm, perfect earnest. Hormones were raging, no question. Not a word he said got through. Or would, until the adrenaline ebbed. "Come on. Tuck it in and come down to dinner. Your mother will be vastly relieved."

"I don't want her relieved about anything."

"Come on." He knew his timing. He set a hand on his daughter's back, steered her out the door. "Shirttail."

She made a one-handed, halfhearted shove at it, and slouched ahead of him down the stairs barefoot.

Judy had the table set. Table, yet. It was a once-a-year occasion, table-setting, never mind the fancy inherited import china. Judy looked sidelong at her daughter and forbore a comment.

Good, he thought. He pulled back a chair for his daughter at the side of the table, pulled back Judy's, at the end, and they sat down to a still-passable grilled fish.

They were a family tonight.

Maybe it was auspicious for tomorrow that, within the household, his diplomacy had prevailed.

GROCERIES. The essentials. A frozen cake, imported chocolate. Heavy synth packets that he had to have for pasta and cheese . . . well, and some fancy bread, which looked good. He could have called it in and had it all delivered, but deliveries had a way of showing up when he was locked away downstairs in an office Brazis didn't want advertised to local merchants; and if he didn't get the delivery when it came, he'd have a message requesting a time for redelivery, which wouldn't work out any better. There were a lot of conveniences on Grozny that just weren't convenient, if you lived only a block from the store and didn't rule your own communications on the common tap.

A little déclassé to be lugging one's own groceries, his sister would say. But she wasn't here to be embarrassed.

And in-person shopping always turned out to be more complicated than phoning in. He wasn't good at resisting nicely displayed treats. Last-moment packet of custard cups. Patent really grown berries from Momus at 29.95 the box. He was feeling sorry for himself.

His bills were paid up, his messages were all answered, every day. It was going to be just him, the kitchen synthesizer, and the e-channels for the next several days of enforced solitude, no questions asked. Grim.

He ran his items down the track, stuck his card and his hand under the reader to pay out, then hefted the heavy green bags, careful not to crush the delicate berries, and headed out.

Straight into public view—public suddenly meaning a handful of faces he'd ever so rather not see.

Algol was an old Stylist, verging on a grotesque. The left side of his face was black, the right side red. The designs that ran between were very nicely done. That effect was what saved him and made it art . . . but there were whispers of an illicit gone way wrong twenty years back that had had to be covered up very expensively, and that had left certain sexual side effects.

Not so Algol couldn't muster a coterie of hangers-on—tough sorts, the sort you'd shy away from during the odd hours on Blunt, which was where they usually hung out.

He didn't want this encounter. But he clearly had it.

"Little dog." That was Procyon's namesake star in vulgar terms, lesser Dog Star after the Hunter, as Earth saw the ancient sky. Algol was very educated, a walking encyclopedia of bits and tags. But the split defined his personality, too, bi in every department. "Hunting what, little dog?"

"Box of milk."

One of the hangers-on stepped into his path. A second and third blocked him in, little punks trying to prove their usefulness to the center of their universe.

"Procyon. Procyon who works for the big dog. What does *Brazis* say about this ship?"

"Somehow I don't get that information." If the punks started a fight, he supposed he just had to take it and hope the store called the cops to save him. Brazis didn't like government employees, especially taps, throwing punches or getting arrested, and he'd now been way too many hours awake and had his nerves too jangled to put up with this. "There's a ship. That's all I know, demon prince, and I got it off the reader-boards. What have you heard?"

"Not a thing. Not a thing, little dog." Cheap theatrics, Algol moved a hand and the flunkies opened out.

He didn't bolt. His life was secrecy. He was appalled to hear Brazis linked to him—but maybe Algol meant it only in the general sense, in that he worked for the government, hence the Chairman. He tried for information. "Come on. You've heard something. Think it's the governor's problem? That arena business?"

"Not a sure word on the street," Algol said. "Brazis's snoops raided Michaelangelo's this evening, just walked in and threw everybody out. Does that possibly say something to those in the know? Those who work in government offices?"

Michaelangelo's was the chief Freethinker digs. *His* old digs. And Algol's. God, did Algol think his job was with the slinks? That he was an informer?

"Somebody in Michaelangelo's wasn't what they wanted, after all, that's what it says to me, and they went elsewhere. I wouldn't know. Go home, why don't you?"

"Word is Reaux's dogs and Brazis's slinks are out together in plain clothes, and they've ordered the untidy questioners of authority out of sight, out of mind. *Callisto's* disappeared."

"Oh, well. They're just picking up fools, then. I wouldn't worry. I wouldn't stand on the docks with a placard saying *Freethinker* tonight. I wouldn't and you wouldn't, and I'm sure they'll let Callisto out someday."

"Michaelangelo's is closed to nonresidents for a week."

That was unprecedented. "Interesting."

"There's a sign in the window. Somebody's already flung paint on it."

"Then it's probably a good place to stay away from. Paint clings."

"No sympathy at all from you for your old friends, little dog?"

"None for fools. I don't intend to go down to the docks to protest Earth rule. If some do, they can look to spend a few nights behind locked doors, and I'm not going to protest that, either, when it happens. I like my own bed."

"Your own *lonely* bed, little dog."

"My nice safe bed, demon prince." The sacks were heavy. He shifted them in his arms, a defense, a weapon, if it came to it. "My loss, I'm sure, but I'm happy enough. I wish I knew what was going on down on Blunt, too, but I don't."

"What's going to go on, little dog, is a protest. The Chairman thinks he can shut down Michaelangelo's, and shut down businesses he doesn't like. The people are going to rise."

"The people are going to get their cards ticked, if they get caught. Here's a piece of my advice, for free. Stay out of trouble."

"Never."

"Well, at least I wish you luck. I hope the cops miss you—unlikely as that seems."

"Coward. Slink."

"Not a slink. Prudent, demon prince. Innocent, and planning to stay that way."

"Little dog's scared."

"Little dog's just going home. Good night, good luck, and don't get caught."

"So kind." Algol waved an arm, letting him pass. "Run home. Run home. No need for the police ever to arrest little dog. He arrests himself. Is *that* these huge sacks of groceries?"

"Hunger pangs," he said, and escaped, with predatory eyes on his back.

Well, if you wanted the official line, read the newsboards. If you wanted to know the craziest rumor on the street, ask Callisto; but if you wanted the best and most accurate, you went to Michaelangelo's and just sat and kept your ears open.

Which now the slinks had shut. A week's shutdown, arrests, and the problem ship hadn't even docked yet.

He arrests himself. Not quite, though it stung. And he didn't like it that Algol came to *him* asking about Brazis. He'd put it out that he was what he'd applied to be, a computer tech, not admin; and damned sure not a slink for the government. The street apparently questioned his cover. And what the street questioned—God knew, it could be serious trouble for him and his residency here if the light stayed on him too long.

He wanted to get home and become less conspicuous. Out of sight, out of mind, and he planned to stay far out of that one's mind.

Maybe, too, he should report in to the PO and say he'd been approached by a questionable source, but he didn't want to target Algol to get arrested—Algol and others might make that connection with him, if that should happen. Algol might well be one of the prime police targets already, and he didn't want word running the street that he'd ratted Algol—God, no. He liked living.

He headed into Grozny Close, where his own neighborhood security cameras checked him out, where the likes of Algol and his muscle didn't dare come, if they were half-smart.

He began to realize he was holding his breath. It came short as he let it go. His grip on the packages was iron, threatening to crush the fragiles.

He reached his own door. Entered. Sam lit the hall and silently lifted him to the heart of his own safe, secure apartment.

He dumped the sacks on the kitchen counter, threw the few frozens into the chute and let Sam read all the labels and organize things in the freezer and the Synthomate. The off-program boxes needed more attention: he had to be coordinated enough to scan the labels through the hand reader and coordinate them with their data, a fussy job, but there shouldn't be frozens in that lot. He decided he was too tired and too frazzled to tackle the other sack tonight, except to send the fragile berries—they had survived—into the vegetable storage unit. He left the rest of the sack sitting on the counter and flung himself down on the couch, to sit and stare blankly at the entertainment unit—not to turn it on, just to stare at the wall-sized screen, letting the past hour play in his memory.

He didn't want music, he didn't want images. He just wanted to let all input channels rest a moment before he even thought about hauling himself up to bed.

Damn, why did Algol come to him to ask about Brazis's intentions? That chance word had thoroughly upset his stomach.

The message light abruptly started blinking, that unforgiving red eye on the center top of the entertainment unit. Something told him he really didn't want to know what it was. Algol said there was a problem on the streets. It could be Ardath slipping him a warning about Algol. It could be some old friend with a com- pletely unrelated query. He earnestly hoped it wasn't Ardath with a problem.

Or—God, the parentals, extending their invitation to the deadly potluck.

On the other hand, he had posted the excuse to them by courier, right when he started shopping, and if they'd gotten it, the mes- sage courier having gotten there, they might be inquiring further. He was safe from such invitations, and had his excuse. He'd been called to work. He needn't tremble at the mail-light, if that was what it was, and he bet that it was.

"Sam, give me the message."

The entertainment unit came live, all that wall-spanning space to display, hanging in midair shadow: *Look/eye official/important hu- mans on station. 20900Kekellen. Hello.*

Cold chill.

Kekellen, for God's sake. Kekellen.

The cold chill went through him, a breath out of the dark. *Everybody* was stirred up. He was stunned. Shocked, so that his heart renewed its thudding pace.

Well, it was somehow understandable that Kekellen passed in- quiries. He'd never gotten one of these before, but other people in the department had, and in his case, he'd been prepared to have it happen: the *ondat cared* about Marak, if one could assign a word like that to the *ondat*. They'd made inquiries of his predecessor. He'd been warned, seriously warned, that it could happen.

In this case it probably regarded the ship incoming. Maybe everybody in the Project had gotten the same message.

Still disturbing. He had no idea at all what it meant. It wasn't for a PO tap, even one of Marak's taps, to figure out on his own, that was sure. He had to trust the experts. The goal was to avoid a sec- ond, follow-up query from Kekellen. That, he understood from rumor, was where it could truly get spooky.

God, he hadn't needed one more worry. He captured the mes- sage, relayed it to the head of his division, then, an attempt to settle his nerves, sank back on the self-adjusting couch, turned on the entertainment unit and rapid-scanned the news, finding what he had expected—absolutely nothing informative. The governor had made a statement. He searched it up.

It said exactly nothing.

Damn. The frozen cake was in the bottom of the bag. He hadn't put it in the fridge.

He got up, rescued it. It hadn't thawed yet. When the mart froze something, it was frozen metal-hard, no question.

"Sam. Fridge. Cake. Frozen." He loaded it in and the fridge took it in, a little whirring, finding it a spot.

And, twice damn, the service light on the fridge freezer went orange, forewarning him the cake was the last straw. Within a day or two he was going to have to empty the thing, open the service door, and clean the system, a domestic nuisance he'd last performed—

Well, it had been last year, he recalled, when he hadn't put a sauce bottle lid on straight. Something oversized he'd shoved in recently must have broken, jammed, or gotten knocked over, somewhere in the fridge works. Damn and damn. He didn't dare call a cleaning service.

And he was tired of waiting for the shoe to drop. "Sam. Message to parents, conditional: if they call asking about a message I sent. Onquote: *This is your loving son. I trust you got my note. I'm called into the office tomorrow early. I wish you both a happy anniversary, all the best. Wish I were there. Have a very nice time. Regards to all the aunts and uncles.* Endquote."

Chime. Sam had swallowed the message. If his parents called, following his note sent by courier, they'd get that as an answer, and give up calling him at home.

"Sam, turn off the set."

Chime. Off it went.

He gathered the basic strength to climb the set of eight shallow steps, and slogged upstairs to bed.

"IT WAS FOUL," Mignette said, lying on her bed, tears puddling in her eyes. "Foul."

"Special you weren't there, at least, Minnikins," Noble's voice said, on the phone Mignette had tucked in her ear.

"I wish I had been. I wish I'd been arrested along with Tink and Random and my dad had to get me out."

"That's why I called. Tink's dad got a doctor to come and say he was on meds and he needed to get out and they still wouldn't let him. You have to get your dad to get him out."

It wasn't good. Mignette didn't want to talk to her dad and explain how stupid Tink had gotten himself canned and needed official help, because a store was going to file charges. Her dad would frown at *her* and maybe side with mum if he ever heard Tink had boosted a bracelet off a store—the fool was wearing it when they raided outside M's, and there he was, in the can, and a parental *and* a genuine med excuse couldn't get him out.

At the moment, she hated Tink, who was Denny, and stupid, stupid, stupid. He pulled this right when her own credit was shaky.

"I can't get him out. My dad's mad at me. I've used up all my good-points for a month."

"You've got to. Your dad can stop it if it doesn't get any further. Random was with him. And we were all at the table and we're probably all on the vidder. Mignette, where's your soul?"

"Was Random with him when he did it? In the store?"

"I don't know."

"He was. I know he was." Mignette rolled onto her stomach. Tears ran down her nose, and she wiped them. She slept in the nude. The air from the vents chilled her skin and she felt as if she might throw up.

"How do you know?"

"Because he's a fool. And if he's going to be a fool, Random's got to go along, I'll bet he did. And they're probably both in *that* store's vidder doing it. They haven't got a brain. And I can't do anything, Noble, I swear I can't."

"Out with mumsy today?"

"Shut up!"

"Out getting fancy stuff? Don't care about your friends?"

"I can't help it!" She heard a noise somewhere in the house and dropped her voice to a whisper, thinking it might be her father, down in the kitchen. She wasn't supposed to be getting phone calls in the middle of the night. "You can talk, and don't you take advantage of it. I can't, right now. I think I heard somebody out of bed."

"*Your mother?*"

"Dad, I think." She was very still, talking in her half whisper. She had a lock on her door. She was sure she'd locked it.

"*Sure they haven't got a bug on you?*"

"No."

"*You truly sure?*"

"I'm pretty awfully sure." She strained her ears to hear down to the kitchen, wishing she was amped, but she couldn't get any useful mod like that, not while she was living at home. She couldn't do anything with mods at all, not even a common tap, and they'd dyed her hair this awful red-brown, like sludge, and she wanted to cry. The fish had been awful. It had been a living thing, and they killed it and her mother tucked it on a plate with a flower arrangement, burned side down and expected her to eat it, because Earthers ate live things, and it was *class*. "I think he's gone back to bed."

"*You've just got to do something.*"

"I can't, is what I'm telling you. Mum and I are having a fight, and Dad won't listen. He just gave me his card."

"*You got credit?*"

"I got a little. Five cee."

"*You're beautiful.*"

"Don't tell me that." It reminded her about the hair, which, if Noble had seen her on the street, was just too humiliating to think about, and, more than that, it was permanent dye, Renee had said so. The chemical when they were doing it had made her sick at her stomach and the nasty perfume in the dye was in every breath she breathed now, complicating the nasty taste of the fish on her tongue. "You only care because I've got money."

"*Meet me down at 11th in an hour.*"

"The hell I can." She didn't want to explain how she looked. She couldn't stand mirrors. Not until it grew out.

"*Scared?*"

"No."

If she went down to Blunt, she could buy a mod for her hair, a mod that would let her say what color it was for the rest of her life. Or she could buy one of the fat-nibblers, that would let her eat any-thing at all, as much as she wanted.

Or a real multichannel tap. Which got you fevers and headaches for a month or more while it took, but after that, her mother *would* disown her and she'd have to go to the street to live.

While Ippoleta ruled the scene on the block and would probably sniff and call her déclassé, all the while saying *her* genes were pure.

"Maybe I'll buy a hit on Ippoleta and get *her* infected with a mod."

"*That would be a laugh.*"

"Ippoleta's so good, Ippoleta's so smart, Ippoleta's so haute class the instructors all fawn on her. I could just puke."

The instructors were all part of the social clique, was what. And her father didn't remotely understand what she was up against, in that school full of his enemies.

"*Know what I might buy?*" Noble drew her into the fantasy. "*A tap.*"

"You think your parentals wouldn't know if you did it?"

"*They don't know what I do. I bet I could even get a tap and just not let it show.*"

"You'd puke your guts out. I heard a guy once did it at sixteen and he was in hospital for six months. You'd be sicker than hell. On the other hand—surface stuff doesn't do that, most times. I might do my eye color. I might be like that Stylist and have my eyes go all colors. I'll bet my parentals never would know if I kept them brown at home."

"*I wonder how you see in the dark if they glow like that.*"

"It's on the iris, not the retina, silly." She knew some things from science sessions. If it could possibly involve mods, she was inter-ested.

"*I still wonder if you don't see the light from them. I'd think you would.*"

Having a glow in her eyes didn't sound so attractive, under those terms. She turned the tables. "So what would you get besides a tap?"

"*Me? I'd get a mod so I'd never get drunk.*"

She giggled. "Then how would you have fun?"

A small dull silence. "*Well. I suppose. But I could drink all the beer I like.*"

"Then you'd need a fat-mod. And all that beer still wouldn't get you drunk. So where's the fun in that?"

"*Hell. Come on down here, rich bitch.*"

The parentals would kill her if she did. She could get based, completely based for a month. "Can't."

"*11th and Blunt. Right now. Scared?*"

"Not scared. Just don't want to."

"*Scared of her shadow. Nice little Kathy-boo. All talk and no action. I'll call you back when I'm there. You'll change your mind.*"

"Go to hell." She pulled the phone out of her ear and, deprived of body heat, it would beep out on Noble, who was a slime.

She hated her life. She really hated it.

4

THE WIND HAD KICKED UP at dark, as Drusus had forewarned, and a perverse and wicked wind it was. It would have made the extension of the antenna uncommonly difficult, if they had tried to outrace it. It was likely to cause damage if they tried extending before the dust fell, and that and the need to get the deep-stakes driven and the guy wires on the relay station anchored had made them postpone that task.

The boys were entirely frustrated, having looked forward to calling their sweethearts and relatives back at the Refuge, but the desert and the weather made for patience with certain things. There was always time, in Marak's way of thinking, and an immortal who could love the sound of the demon wind thumping and booming at the canvas and revel in the sand hissing off the tent at night was far happier and healthier in his life. An immortal who could meet occasional frustration and not see in it the pattern of all his past frustrations was the one who would survive the longest. Some who had the gift lacked patience, battering themselves against all adversity, increasingly finding malevolence and divine obstruction in small accidents.

Those who adopted that opinion grew more bitter and strange by the year. They eventually wandered off from their fellows and lost themselves in a solitude where only the dunes changed. They mattered less and less once that happened, and all but the oldest forgot them.

Or they did as Memnanan's great-grandson had done, before he died: he'd destroyed an entire laboratory and taken three lives before he'd gone down, angry at his life and his long train of reverses. It was sad and pointless, the waste of a life that could have meant something and that had held so much promise. But Memnanan refused to change himself while the world changed around him, and saddest of all, everyone was relieved when Memnanan was gone, even, one feared to say, Memnanan himself.

So a wise immortal embraced the howling wind and the dust out here in the wide land as he embraced his wife. And he took the delay as a variation in a world that otherwise was too stable, and cherished the reverses that inevitably came as absolute proof there were still surprises to be had in the world—since without surprises, immortality grew unbearable. Memnanan had shut himself away from the desert, sealed himself in his work, and met small reverses with increasing anger in his metal corridors. Lack of humor, Marak believed, had been his undoing, right along with confinement under a roof.

But there were, mortal and immortal, those blessed with the true spark of curiosity. The boys they had chosen for this trek gathered close on this night of wailing wind and begged for stories, to carry the old tales forward to their children.

Hati told the best stories. She had a gift for it. She painted the great storms of ages ago. She told a half ring of listening faces by lanternlight how, in those days, the dark, sand-laden wind wore metal away and stripped flesh from bone in an hour. She told how the tribes had had no battery lights, only flame that flickered perilously low as the great gusts sucked the very air out of the tent. There were so many ordinary things this generation had never seen or felt. She told them about villages that now only turned up as half-buried ruins, and how life was then, villagers making gardens in soil-filled stone basins, to waste no drop of water.

Every word of memory was precious, and Hati never recited: she told the tales with her heart for another generation of eager faces, so many generations by now that the individuals within them grew difficult to remember. Marak himself struggled with names, and mistook people alive now for people generations dead, attributing to the new and innocent, too, the baggage of lives past.

Perhaps he cared less for individuals than Hati. Perhaps he saw them as an endless succession of similar lives, so that one generation of listening, earnest youth filled the place of another within the tent, and nothing was lost forever.

He loved young people in general. He was particularly patient with the young ones who volunteered for such long treks with them, young people whose questions repeated the silly questions of generations before them and whose jokes echoed the amusements of generations stretching away into trackless time. Truly new jokes grew like the mountains, slowly, out of cataclysm, and lived for centuries, changing as they aged. When the wind blew and they were shut in like this, they soon wore out the jokes they had, but a wise man laughed all the same, and meant it, simply because they were alive.

Drusus had said the storm would spend itself by morning. And like most southern storms in these years, the wind lessened enough for them to wrap up close and go out under the morning sky to see what the wind had done to their plans, and how deep it had piled the sand around the base of the relay unit.

The new day was still filmy with the lightest dust when they went out of the tent to see how much they would have to dig. Sand had blown through the anchor legs of the observation station, but the station sat undamaged, deep-anchored. Sand had completely buried the greenbush of yesterday, except that along the rim, where the windblown grains had fallen into the gorge. The beshti had gotten up when they stirred out of the tent. The beshti would sit like lumps through the worst of the wind; but now, confirming the storm was fading, they gathered themselves up on their long legs, stretching themselves, shaking the sand out of their coats, weaving their long-cramped necks about and complaining. A beshta complained if the wind blew, or if the sun shone, or if it disliked a smell in the air, and if one beshta complained, the rest complained about its racket. It was an ordinary morning.

There came, however, a strange lull in that ritual complaint, heads lifted, shadows in the red-brown haze of shaken coats, all the beshti staring in one direction.

There were no other beasts in the land but their kind. There was no moving creature walking the wide world for the beshti to take sudden alarm like that.

And seeing that ancient, instinctive alert in a herd made ghosts by the filmy dust, Marak's nape suddenly prickled in ancient alarm.

"Quake," he called out, and began to move toward the herd. Hati moved. The boys stared about them as if they could discover the oncoming threat somewhere in the lingering dust.

The beshti were tethered to a long-line. If they hit that rope it would foul and there would be wild chaos, not to mention broken bones. Marak gathered his own beshta's halter rope and unclipped it from the line. Hati did the same. The boys were a little behind them.

A shiver ran deep in the earth. It reached his feet. The beshta shied as the rolling shake began.

He grabbed the beshta's halter rope up close to the chin, pulled his beshta's head down and around against its shoulder as it squalled. Other beshti tangled with the long-line and went down in a flailing heap, and the tether-line snapped right off the deep-irons. "Get them!" Hati yelled, not a hurt yell, a furiously angry one. "Cut the line! You can never hold them all!"

Marak half saw, in his own struggle, in dust like mist, another battle going on, beshti scrambling up, two and three together snapping free of a line unable to withstand their strength.

Hati had held on to her beast's halter, too, and the fouling tether line had popped her beshta hard with a flying knot, then wrapped about its hindquarters, driving the beast mad. The boys struggled to coordinate their efforts, which beshta to free, which to attempt to hold. One boy reached Marak, as he struggled to bring his beshta's head around and down to the gust-clouded sand.

Downing a beshta was one thing. Keeping it down was another trick. Marak sprawled over its bony jaw, pressing its jaw and neck to the sand as it kicked the boy who'd helped him from the wrong side.

The boy had courage—he crawled back again and added his weight to the flailing forequarters.

"Use the aifad!" Marak yelled, too busy keeping the boy from getting killed to use his own. The beshta heaved, trying to roll, and kicked his hind feet at the air with all his might, while the fool boy fumbled about, thinking that he should use his scarf to blind the beast, without the practical experience to get it there across another man's body. The earth heaved, the beshta struggled, and Marak pinned its bony head with all his strength, covering its eyes with his arm, suffering a hard nose-butt into his gut.

The boy must finally have used his head and gotten the hind feet tied with the strip of scarf. The beshta, deprived of vision, hind legs bound, smothered first under his coat and now another boy's late-arrived aifad, finally quit struggling, lay panting, muscles hard, waiting a chance to explode if he had any notion which way was up.

"Hati?" Marak asked, half-blind and teary-eyed from the dust, and not daring, at the moment, to risk his grip by turning his head.

"I have mine," Hati said. "The others all ran." She was not in any way pleased. "Fashti, help Marak."

Fashti arrived to add his weight to the struggle. All the other boys but Argid seemed to have gone to Hati's aid, and they had, in sum, two of their beshti caught, held down by a weight of bodies as a second rumbling became a general shaking.

It went on and on. Then quit.

"The others broke the ropes and ran," Fashti said, out of breath. "Meziq has his leg broken, I think."

"They didn't take the tent. They didn't take the food or water." Marak found himself short-winded. Long since he'd fought for his life, or taken a beshta's knee in the ribs. It was a curious, even exhilarating feeling. "We have two beshti. We'll catch the others. Are you all right, Hati?"

"Very well," Hati said. "Which shall we let up?"

"Mine." He didn't have to explain anything to Hati. Everything was a mystery to the boys. They'd doubtless heard what to do, but never had to depend for their lives on the old wisdom. A man afoot was a dead man, and getting only one beshta down and secured meant they could catch the rest . . . if things went well.

Now it was a matter of getting their two beshti up and saddled, which meant letting go very carefully and only one at a time.

"Let go," he instructed Argid. "Loose the hind feet when Fashti brings my tack. Move easily. Don't hurry."

There was a quick to-do, sorting tack, and Fashti brought the saddle. Marak eased his pressure across the beshta's eyes, and it wanted up all at once as the boy loosed the hind feet. Long legs started to flail, looking for purchase.

It rolled upward. He gathered himself up with a death grip on the halter and kept the beshta's head exactly where it had to be to assist the beshta up without its breaking its own bones or a by-stander's. It had to get its front feet tucked and its hind feet under it, first.

Up it came then, reliant on his pull, dependent on him all the way, and continually under control. While he held it steady, Fashti bravely eased the saddle pad on, as another boy waited with the saddle.

"Watch that girth." It was swinging free, and the beshta's patience with objects hitting him in the groin was slim at the moment. The beshta was ready to explode, and another shaking in the earth could send him sky-high. Fashti made a fast reach under, risking his head, and got the girth strap threaded through the steel ring. Then Fashti hauled up hard, once, twice, three times. The beshta, however, took it with a deep sigh, wove from side to side, beginning his general lament at the winds and the dust and the thunder of the canvas tent, and most of all at his own deep misfortune, being caught and saddled when all but one of his mates had run, lured off by a young rival male.

"Lai, lai," Marak said, as a parent would to an infant, while hanging on to the rein with all his strength. "Argid, get hold of his head on the other side."

The saddle was on, straight and secure. Fashti handed Marak his long quirt. He let go the cheek strap, slipped the quirt's loop onto his wrist, and tapped the beshta's foreleg, keeping the long rein in hand. The beshta offered a partial, distracted obedience, answering to its training and extending its left leg in a bow. It was more interested in getting up, pulling and turning, but the slight bob it gave was enough. Marak seized the mounting loop, hurled himself up like the tribesmen of old and landed firmly in the saddle, rein in hand.

"Let him go," he said immediately, and reined the beshta in a circle, pulling its head around against its own deep-chested body.

The beshta only managed a little lurch forward and around, a motion that, in the veiling dust, took them in the general direction of the canyon rim.

"Fool," he named it, and used heel and rein to hold it back. "Help Hati," he said to the boys, and the whole process began again, getting their second beshta up onto her feet and saddled.

Hati got up to the saddle as a little jolt hit: a tall rider and a long-legged beshta necessarily swayed in the aftershock. The two beshti staggered, squalled and fought the reins, heads aloft.

"How is Meziq?" Marak asked the boys from his high perch. His dust-hazed view of the camp moved from windblown canvas to the relay installation as the beshta under him restlessly turned half-about and squalled. He saw Meziq lying beside the tent, the other boys hovering over him.

"The femur is broken, but not through the skin." The boy who stood up, bare-faced, to report it had a sand-scrape on his cheek, and a renewed gust of wind battered at him, rocking him on his feet. "We shall take care of him, omi."

The stack of baggage and saddles was safe. Their supplies and water were safe in the tent. They had two beshti. In the old days, even if the worst happened, a man only needed to stay in camp with the only water in a wide, arid land. The runaway beshti would tend in again in a matter of days to get a drink and a browse, leaving it to a man's cleverness and strength to catch one and afterward track down the others.

But the land had changed. Water and new green growth abounded down in the river chasm on one side and down among the pans on the other, the latter sheltered from this miserable northwest wind. Marak had no question what thoughts would come into their furry skulls once the panic of the quake wore off.

And one thing more he could predict. The young male, Fashti's, would assert himself over the females of the group the moment he was out of range of Marak's senior bull. Tolerated until the mass escape, he would find new and rebel thoughts entering his thick young head. He needed no water their former masters had to supply, and being with the females, he would keep the females with him, moving farther and farther from the threat of combat.

So as master of this small band, Marak had his own choice. They could pile food, water, and small canvas on their two beshti, having set up the one relay and disposed of its heavy components. They could abandon the other relay yet unset and the bulk of the supplies as a cache for a later mission to the Southern Wall, such supplies as might survive the intervening storms. They could try again next year.

But that quake had been strong, a forewarning, it might be, that they had no next year, and going back now was not Marak's first choice. Meziq could live and heal while on trek in either direction, back to the Refuge or on to their final site, where he could sit and heal. And which direction they went now, in his intentions, depended solely on their catching or not catching the fugitive beshti.

"They will go down to the pans, likeliest," Hati called to him over the thunder of canvas. "They will go down at the first opportunity, away from this wind."

"No question," Marak said, and looked down at the boys caring for Meziq. "Set it, splint it. Wrap it with matting. Keep him still until I get back."

"Yes, omi."

If he now only cut his hand, if he set the bone straight and bled the makers in his blood into Meziq, he might greatly hasten Meziq's recovery.

Or kill him with fever. That sometimes resulted. In either case he would change Meziq's life. That always resulted, and it was worth Meziq thinking long and soberly about the consequences.

"Keep the tent," Marak said further, "and finish the work here. If one or two beshti should come back, and you can get them, do, but take no chances and do not try to follow us down. Stay here in comfort as best you can and save your resources." He and Hati could talk directly to the watchers in the heavens. The boys could not, but they had the relay installation at hand, and could communicate with the Refuge by means of their hand units with no trouble at all, once the relay was up and working. They needed only get the power cell charged. "Finish the setup, call Ian and get his instructions. Find out what may have happened to the Southern Wall and use your wits. Expect more quakes, and trust Ian to advise me. Be moderate with food and water, and check the deep-stakes of the tent at every shaking. We shall need rope, supplies, and canvas. And a pistol."

"Omi," they said earnestly, and ran to do his bidding.

With the uncertainty of the earth, he elected to stay in the saddle, he and Hati, having the boys pass them up a couple of good coils of rope, enough to constitute lead ropes for the two key fugitives, the young male and the senior female of the escapees. Food, water, a small medical bundle, else, and a simple roll of good canvas, in case worse weather came through before they got back to the tent—that was the rest of the supplies they needed. They could survive without any of it, but the nights were cold with the wind sweeping in off the southern ocean, and he foresaw several nights on this trek, very possibly.

Absolute prudence, the rule in the old days, would have left one rider with the camp itself—but try to persuade Hati to stay behind, in anything less than direst circumstances? She would suggest he could stay, she who was of the tribes, blood and bone.

And would he have that? No. So there was no need going that circle.

Meziq was his worry. He rode near the boy, where he lay in pain. "Three days, Meziq. Endure three days and from a clear head, when I come back, ask me favors, if you think you must."

On that offer, he turned his beshta away. The canvas thundered in the wind, and Hati, moving ahead of him, was already a red-hazed ghost in the dust.

They rode away, tracking the fugitives easily and quickly so long as the tracks lasted in the blowing gusts, intent on overtaking the beshti on the straight and narrow of the spine.

But the tracks soon led to a slot on the south side of the ridge and vanished.

It was a long, sandy slope they had noted on the way to their camp. The tracks went down it, down toward the pans, vanishing among sandstone spires, along windswept terraces.

And the wind, in the trick of that slope, came up in their faces, a different wind, that carried the warmer air off the pans.

"Auguste?" he said.

His watcher, Auguste, had listened in silence through all this, not saying a word—usual, in Auguste. But now Auguste failed to answer him.

Perhaps the storm and tricks of the high atmosphere had made the relay uncertain. They were very near the outer range of the other relays. Once the wind sank and the boys ran up the antenna on the relay station and got the battery going, his watchers, he was sure, would all at once have a great deal to say, much of it exhortation to return to camp and wait for rescue.

But for now they were on their own. Ian and Luz could oblige them by warning of further hazards and advising them the extent of the damage . . . once they were back in contact. No doubt Ian already knew about the earthquake.

"The young bull thinks he is master," Hati said. "But he is not easy about it. He knows the old bull is back here."

Small chance that the young bull, having his prizes headed down land, out of scent and sight, would come back on his own for a fight. He followed the females, damn them, thinking he led them, and they had done what beshti would do, going toward graze and most of all, water, down to the pans, where beshti were always most comfortable. Once they smelled that warm wind, all thought of the camp would fly right out of their heads.

"We have no choice," he said.

So they rode away down the slot, headed onto the spired terraces above the pans.

Silence in his head was a curious thing.

It felt like old times.

09 1 0H ON A NEW DAY, and the Earth ship was now three hours at dock, all its attachments made. The *Southern Cross*, its name was, declared to be a research vessel. And carrying light armament.

Armament. That was uncommon. That might say something about the ship's capabilities, but it still said nothing about its purpose here, in this most sensitive zone . . . inside what was, after all, *ondat* territory. If its arrival at Concord, even with light weapons, was in any wise a gesture aimed at the *ondat,* it was sheer folly, not even to be contemplated. If it was, as history indicated, a little gesture aimed at the Outsider authority, it was still provocative of the *ondat*. Neither was acceptable.

Setha Reaux meant to make that point early and strenuously— once he found out what the ship was up to.

Ambassador Andreas Gide held the explanation of what was going on, the only source of explanation that would reach Concord's deck, and Setha Reaux, dressed in his immaculate best, had headed down for the main-level personnel reception area to meet him, as far as meetings could go, once the necessary connection was made. But just as he got under way, security called with an emergency advisement, informing him, to his great dismay, that Ambassador Gide had left the dock on his own, refusing all advice, and headed up in the cargo-area lift system. The exit that particular lift bank afforded would be a seventh-level public station next to the Customs administrative offices.

What in hell was Gide doing?

Reaux immediately changed his car's destination. He was not that far from the offices in question. He reversed course and went up.

And, a little breathless from the requisite walkover from a 53rd Street station rather than try to route over the Customs Plaza, Reaux arrived, planted himself in front of the bank of lift doors at Customs Plaza, watched the levels tick off on the digital indicator of an inbound lift, and drew a deep breath as Gide's car arrived. Intercept successful.

The lift doors opened. A chest-high ovoid vehicle trundled out. A fog of melting condensation still hung about the vehicle's cold plastic surface, a shifting mix of violets and blues that flowed like oil on water, showing no window.

Then, astonishingly, the machine extruded a violet bubble, which quickly swelled up into a head-and-shoulders simulacrum of a middle-aged man. It had a surly, heavy-jowled face and shoulder-length hair, all shining violet and fuming with cold.

The mobile containment was no surprise. Elaborate and heavy as it was, it *was* the suit which Gide would wear continually, but the usual mode of interaction of such containments was a simple holo cube on the front. *This* unprecedented innovation, this vanity, this shape it presented to the outside world, reminded Reaux of nothing so much as the fabled Sphinx of Earth—the head and fore-arms of a man on the body of a beetle, a smooth, shining carapace, both sheathed in that continually shifting oil-slick plasm.

Whatever that substance was—and in his tenure on the edge of *ondat* space he thought he'd seen all there was to see—it gave off cold vapor, and didn't encourage an exploratory touch.

The head, in its light fog of condensation, looked around, and one had to wonder whether Gide, inside, actually saw his sur-roundings via those eyes, or whether Gide was looking at him on screens through entirely different receptors. Whatever the medium, Reaux was willing to bet that the sensors in that carapace compared very well to an Outsider's internal augmentations, that they saw into the extremes of the spectrum, that Gide could hear a pin drop—literally—if he wanted to. And he also bet that the ap-paratus recorded. Oh, depend on it, that shell recorded and even-tually transmitted information back to the ship.

But the lift hadn't delivered the ambassador to his office, and the ambassador had utterly ignored the official advisements to wait on dockside, as if to assert he went where he pleased and saw what he wanted. Maybe the ambassador *wanted* an official embarrassment, *wanted* to look around, and to be able to start their relations with an official fuss about protocols.

Well, he and the lift automatics had outmaneuvered that try.

"Ambassador Gide." A little bow, a little out of breath and try-ing to look serene. "I'm Governor Reaux. Welcome to Concord."

The sphinx-face stared at him. Liquid blue ice scanned him up and down. Blue lips drew further down at the corners. "A long, *un-attended* ride." The ambassador *was* trying to provoke an incident. And the thick Earth-ethnic accent jolted a compatriot's memory, sowed self-doubt. "Well, well," Gide said impatiently, "are we going to have to put up with tedious ceremonials here and now, at this late hour? Get on with them, if we must."

"If you wish not, Mr. Ambassador, it's certainly easy to dispense with them." And give due notice to departmental heads, shivering in the dockside cold. "You're welcome in my office, two levels up from here." It would be pushing it to say the ambassador had mis-taken his destination, or to hint that the peculiarities of the lift sys-tem, which needed a citizen code card on the dockside lifts, had foxed the ambassador's solo attempts to breach security and dumped him right on the plaza where any common non-citizen had to go.

The sphinx-face looked around the area, looked far to the left, and again to the right. "This is Customs Administration. Where is my residence from here?"

"This is the main foyer for those who have to file visa affidavits, Mr. Ambassador, who need a temporary card." He refrained from saying, fool. "Customs is certainly superfluous in your case. We can go from here either to my office, or straight to your residence." Impossible to offer food, drink, or even a soft bed to their visitor. What one of these rigs actually wanted was general connectivity and a secure place with wide doorways, which could be any apartment or office thus equipped, where there were adequate connector-slots. But Reaux had rather have this visitor well-protected. Constantly. And soon. And *hell* if he was going to issue Gide a code-card to let him come and go from docks to residencies at will. "If you'll share a lift with me, I'll escort you myself wherever you would wish to go."

"My requirements?"

"Exactly as requested, a secure apartment with broad accesses, on the lesser-gravity deck, in the heart of our community. It has all the connections, a secure line to your ship." The shell was, in its way, a bubble of pure Earth environment extended from the ship—a bubble that the ship extruded onto their dock and up into their station, since never, never, never could Mother Earth contaminate anyone, but the mere breath of station air would contaminate the purity of their visitor. Gide would leave that extravagant shell behind in a few days, discarding it like some outmoded chrysalis on the dock, as the ship took him in and sealed him behind its pure, uncontaminated hull, never having contacted the station's air or water.

Then all the intriguing secrets of this simulacrum might be available to them to be extracted, if there were any secrets in it that they didn't already have, and by the look of it, there might be plenty. Earth might not particularly care about the expense or the knowledge shed along with that carapace, not relative to the value of the awe it generated among mere station-dwelling provincials, and assuredly it wouldn't want it back, no matter it was perfectly possible to decontaminate the thing. Earth and Inner Space didn't covet a stray molecule of Concord's air, let alone suffer its other microscopic contaminations, ever, in any form, or in symbol, to enter their ships or their lungs. The fuel they bought on station all burned in an antimatter furnace, utterly annihilated. They traded, but they traded in programs and data. God forbid they ever, ever touched a damned thing.

Supercilious sods. Had he been one of them—ever?

"My apartment," Gide said curtly. "Now."

"Certainly." With an iron smile.

Earth didn't speak Concord's language—no one else, in fact, did that—as Earth didn't breathe their air. And Reaux was very sure now not only that he knew what language Gide spoke as a native, besides that of the Commonwealth, but what accent. *They* shared a birthplace. Not that it won him acceptance from Gide. From the first time he'd taken a post outside Earth, the very first time he'd drawn the air of the Inner Worlds inside his lungs, he accepted being doomed to live no closer to Paris than the Inner Worlds. From the first time he'd set foot on Serine, truly in Outsider territory, for a higher post, even the Inner Worlds became barred to him. That sacrifice was the only route to career advancement for a man of modest means—and in his case, the path to power, the ultimate that any station governor could reach, the most sensitive governorship, the highest, the most isolate. He was accustomed to making decisions on his own, dealing one-on-one with the Outsider authority at Apex.

He had power . . . until this higher breed of Earther, like Mr. Gide, with his doubtless upper-class accent, showed up, a power whose incidental report could even conceivably damn a governor for removal. A long-sitting governor, and Reaux was that, inevitably lost touch, and Concord more than most. He had no complete guarantee what party on Earth Gide represented, what beliefs Gide supported, what faults Gide came here to complain of. A governor's sin might consist only in belonging to the wrong faction, the wrong dogma, as administrations rose and fell on Earth.

It was a hellish system, a system ages entrenched, vulnerable to slow corruption that no one on the outside had the power to fight

and no one on the inside ever understood enough to challenge—
that was the absolute hell of it, and he had halfway forgotten that
visceral fact of politics until he came face-to-face—so to speak—
with this ostentatious display of Earth's power. Good appearances
were everything. Substance was rarely at issue. Any whisper of a
governor sympathizing too much with the people he governed
was grounds for suspicion. A governor getting along well with the
Outside was suspect for that fault.

In Reaux's own carefully concealed opinion, it was a system that
hadn't come to disaster only because Outsiders, who profited from
Earth's occasional confusion, lived very comfortably with Earth's
governors in occasional fear, and had no reason to push for anything different.

He'd been too busy to be panicked until now, now that he was
confronted by a presence clearly designed to intimidate, and now
that he found no hint of courtesy extended toward him or his station. He was very glad not to have begun their meetings by telling
Mr. Gide his arrival in the Plaza was his own stupid fault.

The sphinx glided along beside him in surly silence, down the
short distance to the next bank of lifts. For the moments it took to
get Mr. Gide to safety, the whole lift system in this quadrant of the
station had to be frozen, a condition they would have avoided had
Mr. Gide routed himself where they wanted him. A few Customs
supervisory staff stood back, watching, securing the area, not intruding. A few news recorders bobbed in the air, a carefully managed presence, no human agents intruding here with a babble of
questions. Some powers even the news feared.

The sphinx entered the car, turned, facing the door. Reaux barely
managed to get himself and his two bodyguards inside with it,
where it had grandly placed itself.

"Code 12," Reaux said to the system, and the car smoothly engaged and gathered speed. It wasn't an address code that that simple
number represented. It was a set of preset operations, instructions to
the lift system, security moving to cordon off areas of transit as
they passed and concentrating efforts in areas where they were
going, getting them back where they should have gone.

"Remarkable technology, that of yours, Mr. Gide." He wondered
could there possibly be sensory input from the car's surface that

might appreciate the fine surroundings he had arranged for the man—as distinct from the utilitarian offices that might adequately have served the machine itself. "It's certainly a striking application."

"Useful," Gide said coldly. So that conversation died, assassinated.

"If there's anything you wish to see while you're here—" Reaux was determined not to babble, but made one more effort, in case the man was simply overtired. "—of course you've only to ask."

"I'll let you know."

In his native tongue, he asked: "How are things in Paris?"

"As usual." In that language. And nothing more. Dead silence. No cordiality. No human pleasantry from what might be a compatriot. And it was that aristocratic, academy-educated accent he had suspected.

He truly didn't like this man, Reaux decided. He hadn't been sure, but he was rapidly solidifying his opinion that Gide's presence was not friendly to him. He remotely feared he might be the object of an Earth-originated political sandbagging—in which case, Gide would certainly find fault with minute details, and even try to meet with Lyle Nazrani or God knew what other thorn in his side, second and third generation as they were, and ordinarily not acceptable sources.

But he wasn't without his defenses. He decided to challenge the threat head-on, foolish or not. He asked, again in his native language: "What actually brings you here, Mr. Ambassador?"

"Classified."

"If I can possibly be of assistance in your mission, I'll be happy to put my security personnel at your disposal."

"I'm sure you will." Conversation thudded to a stop.

The car, thank God, likewise reached its level and sector, and stopped. As it opened its doors, more security waited for them, in a large corridor, a towering ten-deck vista distinguished by interior landscaping, balconies graced with flowers and vines that spilled luxuriously over the edges. It was an Earther district. It was one of two such residential zones—*not* the one where he had his own apartment. He'd wanted distance between himself and Gide, no hint of personal invitations. Given Kathy's current state of rebellion, and given the hair, which by Kathy's attitude, could be green tomorrow, he was very glad to have his teenaged daughter half a kilometer removed from the Earth envoy, no commotions on the doorstep, no teenaged swains below Kathy's balcony putting on a show for the neighbors.

And he was equally determined now that he wouldn't bring Gide near Judy, near his belongings, to criticize what he saw, doubtless ever so inferior a circumstance than Mr. Gide was accustomed to. *Damned* if he'd invite this monstrosity into his home.

"Pleasant," Gide said, however, viewing the architectural, floral marvel of Concord Street. "Pleasant enough."

"You'll note recognizable species," Reaux said, addressing Earthly prejudices, head-on, doggedly pushing the local virtues, and the truths Earth rejected. "All the species genetically pure. Three hundred years of tests, not only here for aesthetic value, but as an ongoing biological experiment, on the one station of course potentially most exposed to unfortunate elements. The plants remain quite clean. The human population and test animals, likewise."

"Very impressive display."

"Thank you." Finally. A reasonable reaction out of the man. Maybe Gide had a human heart. Maybe he'd felt stupid, about ending up at Customs. Maybe it was the middle of his sleep cycle. "This way, Mr. Ambassador, if you will."

They entered a gardened close, past hundred-year-old trees and blooming shrubs, a tropic paradise. Reaux had particularly hoped this display would soothe and please their visitor.

"And in less clean areas of this station?" Gide asked. "No problems there?"

"No runaways on the entire station, nor in its two predecessors, ever." Technically answered, but correct. "We're quite fanatic about our checks and inspections, Mr. Ambassador. We've had a few incidents in years past, but nothing has ever gotten past our defenses. And here we are . . ." They'd reached the door of the sole apartment that owned this tropical nook. "A trilevel apartment, sole dwelling in this close. I hope you'll find it comfortable. Broad doorways throughout. Security you can set to your own codes. It's a Berger system—I trust you're familiar . . ."

"Adequately. Not the best system, but I'm sure adequate against what your local threats can muster."

Reaux set his jaw and smiled resolutely as security personnel remotely opened the door. Gide could set the lock to his own voice—not that the system was in any way likely to mistake his physical appearance. He fervently hoped the mistaken foray to the Customs Plaza would discourage further adventures.

Gide glided in. Again that curious turn of the sphinx's head, this way and that.

An upward look, then, to the towering internal balcony of the apartment, with its artificial skylight, the illusion of Earth's blue sky and cloud, with plants cascading off the upstairs balcony rail. Little difference between the garden outside and this one inside, in abundance of flowers.

"Unique among stations I've visited," Gide said. "Excellent."

"I'm very gratified." He actually was—and despised his own gut reaction. He hoped Gide might quit the games and get down to business now. He glanced at the security agents, shifted his eyes toward the door. They sensibly took their cue and retreated outside.

The door shut.

"Security will be within your call, sir. Should you wish anything, at any hour, they will bring it."

"I've come onto this station to see what's here. If I only wished to be locked in a room, I could have spared the expense and the trouble of this rolling containment. I shall come and go as I please."

"Of course. Absolutely as you please." Stubborn. So bringing station transport to a halt once in a day wasn't enough. Dortland's men would follow discreetly, however, if Gide left the apartment.

The sphinx turned 360 degrees, glided forward to examine a precious vase.

Extruded a fuming blue-violet hand and picked it up.

Astonishing. The simulacrum wasn't just an appearance. It had hands, eyes that, yes, by that look aloft, must actually see. The hands could touch. Could they feel? Had they strength to crush that vase as well as cradle it?

"Local pottery?"

Distinctive zigzag pattern, a fine blue glaze. "Imported. Based on transmission from Aldestra surface." It only appeared to be native clay, one of the Ruined Worlds, art objects being all the rage these days, traded between Orb, Apex, and Concord. Ferociously expensive, part of an estate, like this whole apartment. One hoped Gide wouldn't drop it. Or take it for an insult that the thing was here.

A native-world item in Gide's apartment, however harmlessly a replication. Security setup had had an utter lapse of common sense.

"Interesting." Gide set it carefully down on the table. His grip had left frosted prints on its surface, condensation of moisture in the air.

That grip . . . could do that. Could burn skin.

"From Aldestra surface," Gide said mildly, "but a copy?"

"The analytic portion of the technology was soft-landed. No actual material moved from the gravity well. Only the holographic information. It's completely synthesized, including the clay. And scanned for any biologic inclusion."

"And locals on Aldestra surface know how to run the apparatus."

Aldestra wasn't reputed for civilization. "They don't need to. They put in what we image we want. They get something in return."

"You trade in such things."

Reaux gathered his courage and took a deliberate chance, plenty to lose, but nothing ventured, nothing gained, he decided. "Aldestra Station has extensive trade in native art. Perfectly clean and proved clean over a long period of time."

"Curious notion. *Curious* notion. A whole human universe stranded on those planets. Their intellectual invention, largely independent of the cultural stream from Earth, must be very diverse from the norm. Yet the thing has the look of native terrestrial artifacts."

Scary, dancing down the brink of anathema. "A pot is a pot, I suppose. Made on a wheel, it's round."

"Is it?"

"Made on a wheel? So I'm informed. There's a good deal to recommend their efforts. Their *artistic* diversity."

"And their genetic diversity?" Pointed question.

"Absolutely never gets off the planet. As nothing gets off Marak's World, below us."

"Certainly this art object is a climb up the ladder for Aldestra.

But genetically, do we think, is this new culture, this new genetic model—a climb up the ladder for the human race?"

"Some say—" This was getting dangerous . . . and Reaux took another small chance, aware of numerous political and religious positions native to Earth, and probing for exactly what intellectual affiliations this Gide might have, "some say that remediation might well involve thorough re-speciation, so we *can't* affect one another."

"And is the resultant humanity human?" No answer, only an old, old catechism.

"I leave that to the scientists and the ethicists."

"Such populations would be suited for their own worlds. But would they be human?"

"Again, that's for the experts."

"And the other life on their worlds adapts to this new humankind, and not to us, and therefore becomes harmless to us, if not to them." Drily, like a recitation. "I'm familiar with the argument, Governor, I assure you, but I also assure you Earth will have a strong word or two about any implementation of contact with a subset of our own species. Did genetic diversity from us protect the *ondat* from disaster?"

"Clearly not." Signal. Strong warning signal. So Gide did *not* subscribe to that model of remediation, which had enjoyed a certain popularity in his youth, and from time to time over centuries. A traditionalist. A conservative. One could imagine Gide taking damning notes inside that carapace. "But it was nanomachines that did the harm there. An artificially accelerated system that adapted to what the nanisms found."

"As they can do harm anywhere."

"I merely cited a theory, not my belief. I thoroughly agree that continued isolation—"

"Do you subscribe to the theory that outside presence and protection actually retards natural remediation? That by watching over and assisting such populations we save lives that evolution might well cast aside? That we thereby prevent beneficial change and adaptation? Is that your belief, that we should all but *abandon* remediation and let nature simply take its course in all affected biosystems?"

He regretted, now, ever engaging Gide in this train of logic. "As a governor appointed to maintain isolation, sir, I by no means hold that belief."

"Do you think we *should* permit human evolution to operate unrestrained among Outsiders?"

Another set of traps. "Stations function to moderate and observe Outsider change, precisely *without* creating ourselves any sort of problem. Certainly the Outsiders I've talked to locally share the opinion it's a beneficial restraint, having us as the oversight. I by no means take the notion as far as you suggest . . . or if we do retard the evolutionary process for all of humanity, I certainly consider it beneficial."

"And if we interfere with natural process by our acts of prevention?"

"We make haste slowly." Old adage. Safe, he hoped. "Progress happens."

"While we plan—even hope—to let Concord native life crawl back out of a contaminated sea."

"Contamination which locals don't catch. Neither virulence nor runaways. Ample opportunity, but the Refuge on Marak's World has no outbreaks to speak of."

"Minor outbreaks."

"Easily treated."

"And on the station? Never?"

"You're surely aware of our record. Nothing uncommon to the rest of the worlds. What the *ondat* experience here is beyond my reach . . . I assume that's always been true. They haven't complained." A pointed reminder to this aggressive visitor that the Treaty on Concord was a constant concern—and should be his. He took another chance. "I hope your mission here doesn't involve any perceived threat."

And had it turned bluntly aside, with another attack. "Tell me. How *do* you get along with Antonio Brazis?"

Double thump of his heart, which he was sure Gide could hear. Only the truth. Only the truth, when dealing with this rolling laboratory. "Tolerably well."

"Are you worried about the Outsiders?"

Truthers were certainly at work, analyzing every breath and

heartbeat, able to pick them up from half a room away. One leading question, and the man could read him. His lenses could likely
see the movement of his irises. His amplified ears could hear the
fluctuations in his voice. He'd been foolish to keep talking. The
man had his pattern and might have picked up numerous touch
points. "We govern the station where the Treaty works most
clearly." That was the ages-old mantra. "And we watch the watchers. We have reasonable arrangements with Outsider authority,
and the whole system still works."

"You watch the watchers. Curious you should mention that particular matter."

Dangerous questions. Incredibly dangerous. Peace or war questions, anything that involved disruption of the taps. Reaux wished
he were anywhere else. "I'm not sure I follow."

"The PO," Gide said. They'd drifted into their mutual language.
Now Gide switched to the ancient language of Concord. Visitors to
Concord didn't routinely speak it. But Gide clearly did. Gide was
here, prepared, and fluent, never having visited here before—not
unprecedented, but it argued for a terrifyingly specific preparation
for this mission, this place, this population. "Isn't that what you
call it? The PO?"

"The Planetary Office," Reaux said. "Yes."

"The head of the Planetary Office is also the local Outsider
Chairman."

"Yes, currently."

"Besides being a member of the Apex Council."

"If he's PO Director, that goes with the job."

"Your opinion of him?"

Opinion. He'd never formed an opinion of Brazis, nothing that
he could put thoroughly into words. "Cooperative. Cooperative
in station affairs—cooperative, actually, in administrative matters." Was *Brazis* under some suspicion? He rated Brazis as too
smart for that, too smart to create an incident. There was no motive for him to do that. But God knew what Apex Council might
have done.

"A busy man, stretched very thin by all these powers, one
would think."

"He delegates, delegates quite a lot, in fact. His proxy routinely sits on local Council and another, I suppose, though don't know, at Apex. Chairman Brazis seems deeply involved with the PO. Handles it quite hands-on, as happens, as much as I know about his work. At least I never find him surprised by a situation."

"A competent man, in your judgment. An active manager. I take it you view him somewhat as an ally."

And this was preparatory to what? Going where?

"A scientific administrator," Reaux said, "but not specifically a scientist. A political administrator, but not political." He found no sense in this thread of questions. "Is there some grounds for worry about him?"

"In continual close contact with a world that has, perpetually, a member of the First Movement in residence. You might observe that, too."

"Yes." Meaning the Ila herself, immortal and changeless. He absolutely didn't know now where Gide was going with this, but he didn't like the direction. Not at all.

Again the hand extruded, and touched the pot, leaving condensation fingerprints. "Do you get pots from Marak's World, too?"

"Pots and fabrics. Replicated, of course."

"Primitive. Yet one is given to understand a certain portion of the populace is quite technologically skilled. Even sophisticated."

"That's so." Ominous turn. If Earth was taking an interest in the PO's domain, it was an outstandingly bad idea, bound to have repercussions clear to Apex. "The tribal arts provide a certain sense of identity. So I understand. A sense of community."

"A certain persistent conservatism?"

"I don't see that has any application to conservatism in our sense, Mr. Ambassador. The downworld inhabitants are fitted to their own world. They have their history. Their culture is not ours."

"Yet stationwide, you share their language."

"Yes."

"Doesn't that provoke a feeling of community?"

"Among us, among stationers, yes, it's a signal difference, us from other stations, but not one we share with them."

"In fact, you share the Ila's language, the language of the First Movement. And the culture you support down there is the culture of the First Movement—is it not?"

Formless implications at every turn. And now this nonsense. "Necessarily, I suppose, since it's the one we have to deal with."

"Necessarily so, because the language doesn't change. There are living speakers of a dead language—down there."

"Hardly a dead language, sir. As you observe, it also has a million speakers up here."

"The language of the First Movement. A very, very dead language everywhere in civilized space. And freighting some very old concepts within its vocabulary."

This was approaching ridiculous. "I'm not a linguist, sir. I speak it because I have to communicate with a station that speaks it. As the *ondat* themselves, I might add, have an investment of knowledge in it, and also speak it. Without it, we couldn't communicate with them, either."

"Do you possibly think its thoughts?"

"No, Mr. Ambassador. My *culture* is Earth. I assure you I think the thoughts of a person born in Paris."

"While you support a living museum and collect pots from the Ruined Worlds. Immune to time. Literally immortal. Resistant to change." The sphinx moved off, touring the room.

"Sir," Reaux said to the sphinx's back, "I gave Earth up, Mr. Ambassador, not because I don't love Earth, but rather because I do."

"A pretty speech."

"I was born in Paris."

"You married a colonial, however."

"My wife, sir, is first-generation. Her grandfather, Martin Mandes-Callendish, is the second son of Astrid Jorgensdottir, head of . . ."

The sphinx turned slowly and faced him across the room. "I know the Mandes family. Very respectable."

At last, a personal connection. Approval. Thank God. Dig long enough in the foreign service, and there tended to be some personal connection recent enough to touch. "She'll be delighted to have any news of them, I'm quite sure."

"Her grandfather is quite well placed, isn't he? One assumes the family exchanges messages."

"With every ship." Reaux didn't like this tactic—pretend ignorance, and then reveal a far deeper knowledge once he answered Gide's question.

"Information flows throughout the system." The sphinx glided back toward him and stopped. Extended fingers toward the vase. "Information down to the atomic level."

Now he had an inkling what this revolved around. "I assure you, anything that we replicate here is pottery or fabric, containing absolutely nothing else."

"Replication that was not permitted, in the beginning."

"We deal in fractals of reality. It's completely reorganized in the process. It can't transmit unintended information, and it relies on a technology which I'm told is extremely reliable in that regard, that there's no more chance of accidentally replicating a nanism than there is of a five-year-old coming up with the formula for chocolate. Are you suggesting there *is* a hazard?"

"The information, Governor. The information of a pot still on Aldestra is in this pot."

"Still not carrying nanotech. I assure you, those records reside down on the planet, and no nanocele and no nanomachine ever goes through replication."

"Not as a contaminant in a pot. But the information that produces the pot—is just information. Are you so sure what you're saying is true—is true?"

"Information doesn't get off the planet. It does not come to our labs, sir, in any way, shape, or form."

"Old Earth families still maintain their ties." The sphinx moved toward him and rested. It had only a face, at the moment, no arms. "One might say that, too, about old Outsider connections. One wonders if they ever go away, either."

"There's been no breath of it. Has there?" Reaux caught a breath and pursued the question to the end. "Are you suggesting—are you possibly suggesting someone might transmit something of that nature from the planet? The only people that communicate are the Project taps."

"Exactly."

"I can assure you they're very thoroughly screened."

"I'd rather have that assurance from the head of the PO."

"I have no authority to ask him to meet with you. I can't guarantee it."

"You can ask, however."

"I can ask." He was stunned, over all, with the implications in Gide's assertion: information. Data, escaping the planet, not through replication, but simply through one of the taps physically writing things down. But those were not simple notations. Was that what Gide was suggesting? Was *that* crackpot notion what had brought a starship out here off schedule?

"The *ondat*," Gide said. "*Kekellen.* Is that how he says it?"

"He or she, we don't exactly know." God, another threshold he had to defend, while his stomach was still riled from the last inane maneuver. "He, by convention. Let me say, Mr. Ambassador, I strongly discourage any direct address to his office. Even through our experts."

"Come now. I'm told this entity sends out inquiries to local flower shops and food vendors. That he has robots making occasional forays out into the station."

"And takes orange juice and liquid chlorine, the combination of which I don't want to imagine. We don't understand him, and this office has worked with him for generations. This entity surveys the entire station at random, for his own reasons. If he wants something, he takes it, and we absorb the cost. That's Treaty business, and I have to stay by my understanding of my duty, sir. If he does contact you, I urge you in the strongest terms, consult with my staff, and we'll gladly assist you."

"You refuse my request to speak to him?"

"The *law,* Mr. Ambassador. I have no choice but refuse."

"I'm duly impressed. The correct answer."

Damn him. These were demeaning games. Exceedingly demeaning. And wearing very thin, considering the performance at the plaza. "If you're satisfied with your accommodation, Mr. Ambassador, I'm sure you'd like to rest. I have to get back to my office."

"Premature, Governor. I assure you I have no designs on the *ondat*. But I do come with a purpose, and I do require your cooperation in achieving it."

"In every regard, sir." Pots. Fabrics. Nanotech replication. And taps connected to First Movement tech, writing complex formulae by hand. "You have only to make the request."

"The Outsider who deals with Marak. This is a new man."

"Reasonably new."

"I'd heard the old one had died. Natural causes, I assume?"

"Very advanced age."

"Knowledge and prior agreements undoubtedly went with that individual."

"The taps, Mr. Ambassador, are completely under the PO. And they don't, to my knowledge, have any ability to conceal any business from their own authority. They're intensely monitored."

"This new man. I want to see him."

"Mr. Ambassador, I can't possibly promise that."

"You say you have a tolerably good relationship with Chairman Brazis. Get his cooperation. I want this man here."

A damned diplomatic disaster.

And did he confess to Brazis what the scope of this inquiry might be? "I'll have to contact the Chairman. And I can't at all guarantee he'll consent."

"This tap is a very young man, I understand. An untested young man. Jeremy Stafford is his name, isn't it?"

"I'd have to look up the name. I'll assume you do know."

"The selection of taps is governed entirely from planetside, isn't it?"

Was he implying something wrong or dangerous in that selection?

That a First Movement survivor, on the planet, might have affected that selection?

Impossible.

"I'm certain the Chairman doesn't install questionable people in a position to be selected. Downworld may not run background checks, but I'm very sure the Chairman runs thorough ones."

"You have great faith in him."

"That he wouldn't install someone who wasn't under his orders . . . I have every confidence."

The sphinx nodded. "Exactly."

"What are you saying, Mr. Ambassador?"

"In absence of an interview with the principals themselves, Governor—which I wouldn't expect you could arrange—I've come here specifically to see this young man. Get me that. Tomorrow morning at 0900h. I rely completely on your resourcefulness."

God. Intrigues and accusations. He trusted Brazis's essential honesty more than he trusted this stranger, this heartbeat-reading monster. Two years to get information to Earth and back. Two years. It was plausible, nearly, that the ambassador was telling the truth—that it was news of this replacement that had launched his mission. The time line could work. Just barely—if the ambassador had left Earth like a shot.

But it could work much better if the ambassador had been visiting worlds somewhat closer, and diverted here on the continuation of a mission. "I'll talk to the Chairman," Reaux said. "That's all I can do. I can't possibly guarantee you his response will be positive."

A tone of mild surprise. "But I take you completely at your word, regarding this close cooperation. I expect it." A hand lifted, an ancient emperor waving off a courtier. "Good day, sir."

The man-half of the sphinx ebbed down, became featureless carapace. The whole surface turned from blue and violet to shining gold, smooth-shelled beetle.

Reaux hesitated, wondering if a good-bye would even be heard, and asking himself if he was possibly that great a hypocrite. In the end he said nothing, and, tight-jawed, let himself out the door.

His security escort was waiting, by the palm trees in the garden.

Talk to the taps. Talk to one of Marak's taps, for God's sake. Suspicions of First Movement tech leaking through their contacts with the planet. Subtle accusations, threatening the foundations of civilization itself.

God! What did a man straight from Earth know about Marak and Brazis's staff? What judgment could Gide possibly make on what he had never tracked?

Except he came fluent in a language difficult to learn except on Concord, clearly prepared for this inquiry.

Knowledge, however, of what went on day to day in the life of a man, Marak, who'd personally seen the last gasp of the Gene Wars—or the woman the human worlds simply called the Ila, who might once have been Ilia Lindstrom, a combatant in those wars—what could Gide really know, when lifelong students of their biographies were frequently puzzled by their actions?

And the *ondat,* mention of whom Gide had passed so casually, untroubled by threat? Fool. Earth came along periodically brandishing some new idea, confident it knew best, sure of the brilliance of some new theory of how the universe ought to run.

Now Earth wanted to get directly, hands-on, involved with a Project tap, because replicated pots and fiber were visually identical to the originals and Marak's newest watcher was exceedingly young?

The investigator seemed well-enough prepared he ought to know better—if he weren't neck deep in some damn theory, some assumption or some set of orders that wouldn't let him budge from his purpose. That was worrisome in the extreme.

Earth and its quarantine had frozen their own genetic type like a fly in amber, defining by exacting law what was human and what was not. Earth, they'd declared, didn't evolve anymore, would never evolve again. Nor would the Inner Worlds. Any deliberate genetic change was anathema. Any natural mutation was examined with great suspicion. Natural change in the human genome was allowed, but . . . scrutinized.

On record, he'd agreed with the premise that there should be an agreed, broadly defined standard of what was human in the Outside. Humanity was capable of being each other's predator if they grew too different, or, if re-encountering a profoundly variant group, apt to produce tragic problems in their offspring. He was Earth's appointed governor out here, and he was bound to enforce certain boundaries.

But was a policy of no-change going to profit a species that wouldn't flex, as if pinning down the genome, they'd forever reached the be-all and end-all of what was human? The theory was that humans were aptly fit for a cosmos that changed locally but not universally, and therefore evolution was no longer a good thing. But he'd slowly changed his opinions in a lifelong journey from the center. He'd begun to think that Earth, while disparaging Concord's ancient language, was itself as stuck in that ages-past era as the immortals on Marak's World—the latter of whom at least had a clear memory of catastrophe, and who lived in a changed and changing world. Earth insulated itself from Outsiders who'd gone on evolving, Outsiders whose genome, escaping the bottleneck of the emigration from the motherworld, showed, yes, a modest diversity from Earth's standard, but the protections were extravagant, more to drive home the point than to protect Earth from any real threat. Granted, Outsiders had taken hellacious chances with deliberate tinkering with the genome, and, yes, deliberately modified planetary settlements had come to grief in very tragic circumstances, not least of them the Hammerfall, but Outsiders didn't legislate the surviving planetary residents out of the human species.

Earth was legitimately worried about some imported problem hitting its ecosystem, the mother of all human environment, but over such a span of time and distance there were human groups whose divergences arguably had less to do with nanoceles and engineering than just isolation—isolation while eras of Earth's internal confusion meant no ships had called there, eras when the whole system of trade and genetic exchange had broken down and left pockets of Outsiders completely stranded. In those dark ages, some stations had died altogether and some had developed unique looks, unique accents, odd political institutions, all of this. Were all these less than human, when you could drop most of them back into Earth's gene pool and they'd become mere lumps in the batter, not anomalous except in their concentration of certain traits?

Reaux didn't ordinarily entertain such rebel thoughts, not all at once. Gide had provoked them to the surface, and outright engaged his temper. Adapted to live out here? Well, yes, he was. He'd become adapted, mentally, if not physically. He had a daughter here, who had developed notions more in agreement with the Outsiders than with her own family, and that was what happened to pure Earth households this remote from Earth. The children *did*, some of them, go into the Outsider gene pool.

But did he love his daughter less, because she wanted to live on this station, because this station was her entire future?

Ask Judy how the purity laws worked—Judy, whose great-grandfather's branch of the family had purged certain of their own relatives, banishing Judy's own mother from the Inner Worlds to the Outside, because her genetic tests had failed the standard and a contact was suspect, third-hand. Judy, born at Arc, had married into the political elite—but never quite salved that social wound.

Was her exile fair, or beneficial to the species? Had those questionable genes contaminated Kathy?

And for specimens—the Earthborn out here were by no means the prettiest, the swiftest, the best-looking or the brightest. Outsiders in general tended to be in far better physical condition than first generation Earth exiles, or than Mr. Andreas Gide himself, Reaux was willing to bet, inside that shell. It took a strong ego to live out here among the beautiful and the bright . . .

One only needed take a clear-eyed, unprejudiced look at Concord. One could see on this station how it all ought to work, in Reaux's not humble opinion: not only Earth-exiles and Outsiders in daily face-to-face contact, but the *ondat* peacefully resident among them *above* a world where the absolute worst had happened.

And nothing else catastrophic had happened to humans down there. That was the very point on Concord, wasn't it? That was the very point, after ages of watching and waiting for another runaway to break loose—nothing happened. Hospitals could remediate eighty percent of the most serious mistakes individuals made down on Blunt, absolutely clean bad bugs out of a human body. The other twenty percent, well, those that survived, were under close watch, and didn't spread their problem, and weren't self-modifying or transmissible—nothing they'd found, ever, had been on that level, nothing like First Movement nanoceles at all.

Certainly *some* level heads in the Inner Worlds saw all those facts in operation and recognized a state of affairs that contradicted near-religious dogma back on Earth: the Restorationists had been a flourishing party that actually talked about relaxing the Purity Laws in the Inner Worlds. The problem was, the majority on Earth were scared—had been taught to be scared and were kept scared by precautions like Mr. Gide's. And in the last ten years the Restorationist Party had unhappily suffered murders and scandal on its staff, and was now being outlawed by Earth's legislatures, in region after region, with whispers that such behavior was what one got for bedding down with such thinkers.

A slight cynic—and Reaux had long counted himself in that camp—suspected covert sabotage and planted evidence. A politically savvy cynic could wonder if a more restrictive regime was gaining a foothold on Earth, taking advantage of the Restorationist scandal. A paranoid cynic might even ask if this visitor that had come here to Concord so conspicuously making demands might represent those interests. Gide might be looking to stir up a cause célèbre in the very place Earth feared most.

And that could not be good news for the governor.

Damn it all, remediation itself *was* genetic change. Remediation was the whole basis for the human-*ondat* treaty he was supposed to be administering out here, out of one side of his mouth, and now he had to avoid saying anything or doing anything that indicated that was the case.

Sometimes, with a certain periodicity, the universe just went crazy. Maybe there was such a thing as too long a history for a species—or too much recorded knowledge of where they'd been for any human mind ever to absorb it all. Fashions recycled. Political movements did. Ideas did.

But fear of the *ondat* would surely protect Concord from the greatest insanity. It had a way of reminding fools, in the breach of basic rules. And a clever governor could survive out here, independent of the madness at the heart of the system, because ultimately, nobody dared interfere here.

One thing Reaux did take as an article of faith, what he called his own rule: that if two parties followed rigid party lines long enough, the political parties would actually switch positions on some essential issue and each of them end up defending the position the other side had used to defend. Political migration, he called it. The opposition consequently picked other issues, until the other party moved onto that ground, too—because as public consciousness advanced, political parties usually took on the very behaviors and alliances they had once most loudly decried—perhaps because those were the issues they had most passionately focused on and most thoroughly understood.

It was why he resolved he had to talk to Brazis honestly about this situation, and if Brazis was halfway reasonable, it might force him to make common cause with Brazis regarding this Mr. Gide, before Mr. Gide did something incredibly stupid in the service of some political party on distant Earth.

Dangerous. Dangerous in the extreme to approach Brazis. The ambassador's ship had presented credentials electronically. Beyond a doubt the ship was from Earth, not the Inner Worlds, and beyond a doubt it was authorized at highest levels. Gide's credentials were therefore solid.

And a governor, however right, couldn't just out and say, twice, as he'd tried to do, Excuse me, do you really realize the repercussions of what you're doing? Do you realize your stupid foreign prejudices are leading you to insane conclusions about perfectly ordinary situations?

He couldn't say, even once: No, sorry, you're patently out of line and I'm not going to let you do what you've come hundreds of light-years to do at the behest of your remote, stupid, and abysmally ignorant party leadership.

Politicians. Scientists. And guns, assuming that ship was prepared to enforce its opinions. Gide had raised certain legitimate questions about planetary security, given a certain loosening of laws about replication techniques that meant, yes, if they weren't careful with that technology, some fool someday could attempt to replicate First Movement tech—but they were careful. The Refuge didn't let technical information off the planet, and certainly the requisite underground laboratory to create a threat didn't fit in a shopping bag. So where on Concord did they think an illicit operation resided?

In the taps, of course: Earth wanted to be suspicious, so it had to find a focus for its suspicion. Of *course* some tap was taking notes so voluminous they'd mean a sizable bundle of storage and getting them past the room monitors. Of *course* someone had bodged a replication apparatus designed to fractally reproduce, say, a pot the size of one's head, into one capable of producing an item so small and exacting that the creator couldn't even find it without a labful of equipment unrelated to the replicators.

On the other hand, maybe someone on that ship was educated in the actual technology, and after a cursory glance and a romp through station records, would have to find that there was no basis in actuality for those suspicions. Maybe Mr. Gide would ultimately be forced to listen to his own experts—if anyone on the mission dared advance any truth to the contrary of Mr. Gide's party's foregone conclusions of what it was going to find.

But once he called Brazis in for conference, as Gide himself requested, then ultimately Gide and his party *would* be forced to listen to the Outsider Chairman. Brazis had the right, the Treaty-mandated right to tell Mr. Gide, sorry, no, you aren't talking to one of my people.

And if the ambassador persisted or tried to bully the Chairman, Brazis was the man who would tell Mr. Gide to present his credentials in hell. Brazis had a notorious temper, and he had an armed and independent government to back him. It might be a new experience in the universe for Mr. Gide, to be told that Earth's rule didn't extend to the PO.

What the *ondat* would decide was going on, meanwhile, with this ship arriving and Mr. Gide throwing his weight around was another worry, and one that couldn't wait for events to make the matter a crisis. He had to figure how to tell Kekellen in advance of any question that they were on his side regarding any disturbance the ambassador or that ship produced . . . without inciting the likes of Lyle Nazrani and his friends to charge that there was any chancy politics going on in that message-flow. No intent to sabotage Mr. Gide. Oh, never.

God, what a situation.

Being an honest Earther, he didn't have a personal tap. He did have a coded-relay phone in his pocket, and he flipped it open as he reached the safe interior of the lift. Storage blinked, jammed with fifty-six messages, as the scroll informed him. Small wonder: every department on the station wanted information. Ernst, however, was doing his job and, when he pressed the button for a breakdown of those messages, only four had actually gotten through the sieve and into the for-your-eyes basket.

He checked them as the lift made its sideways trip to its destination. Judy and Kathy—sorry, *Mignette*—were having another round. The Trade Board had inquired, complaining of an outrageously low opening bid on a new plastics synth. Dortland sent a report up from Blunt, and, yes, the *Southern Cross* had indeed invaded a sensitive area with a probe and just blitzed an expensive and delicate system with the finesse of a solar hiccup. Technical people were on it, repairing the damage.

He phoned Brazis.

"This is Governor Reaux. I need to speak with the Chairman, immediately."

Inside that apartment, he was well aware, Gide could already be sending other probes into their communications, trying to by-pass their security by eeling his way through wide-open domestic systems.

Well, Gide could guess again: they weren't wide open. Gide would hope to establish a private link with his ship that would let the ship in its turn try to get into their systems. It had all happened before. There had been protests from companies, from the PO, and from the *ondat*, on those occasions, angry protests that racketed all the way to Earth and Apex. And he had no plans to file a protest again, not using *Southern Cross* as a courier, at least. No, he was meditating a scathing letter to be carried by the next regular contact ship, on which his letter might not be lost.

"*Governor?*" Brazis himself answered.

"My office. Please. Immediately. I need to talk to you." He hung up, not wanting to commit anything else to the phone system at this particular moment, hoping Brazis would realize the reason for such a cryptic invitation, drop everything, and come.

Perhaps the quick exchange did leave detail behind to be sifted by Earth's investigators.

A record of his call, oh yes. That would exist inside their secure network, which might be a target of a probe.

But hadn't Gide just requested him to talk to Brazis? To use his diplomacy to gain an interview with a certain young tap?

He was guiltless, whatever that ship's probe turned up.

The lift slowed to a sedate stop. Dortland met him at the exit—his chief of security, thin, gray fellow who wouldn't look remarkable either in a riot or a board meeting, except the eyes, which were likewise gray, and never held a vestige of liveliness.

Not his favorite person, Dortland, of people he dealt with—no sense of humor, not even at the grimness of his own position. Dortland was just what he was, and Dortland's whole world was dependably what Dortland imagined it to be, the universe that Dortland created around himself: bleak and full of treachery and problems. Reaux always felt like taking a very long walk after he'd had to deal with Dortland, but at the moment Dortland took the walk with him, their two bodyguards lagging far to the rear.

Dortland reported in a low voice about the activity of the ship, which was nuisanceful but not destructive—yes, the ship had gotten into the network and fried that one system. It wasn't critical and didn't damage their security. Yes, the *ondat* had sent another query when that happened, but the office that dealt with such things was dealing with it, and Kekellen didn't sound particularly disturbed, only curious.

The notion upset Reaux's stomach.

"And what did Gide want, sir?" Dortland asked.

"Hell if it's that clear," Reaux said. "He wants Marak's juniormost tap on a platter, is what he wants. He's upset about replicated pots and he's afraid of bugs coming in with them."

"That's not technically possible."

"That's what I understand. More to the point, he's worried about taps taking notes from the onworld First Movement. As I understand, such notes wouldn't be easy to hand-take or to hand-carry."

"It could be done, in computer storage."

"You think it *has* been done?"

"Not likely, without our notice."

"So, outside of the usual paranoia about rogue nanisms, what's he after?"

"Clearly, this junior tap," Dortland said. Who had no sense of humor. It was worth a second glance, to be sure, but Reaux decided in the negative. No sense of humor, and an imagination utterly devoted to predicting other people's mischief.

"I've called Brazis in. I'm trusting him to say no to the interview with this young man, and that's that."

Dortland frowned and concentrated on the walk ahead of them, toward his office and inside.

A middle-aged woman in a gray courier's uniform sat, prim and proper, in Ernst's office, and stood up as he entered.

Outsider tap-courier. She was clearly waiting for him, dispatched from some location likely on this level. He didn't like that.

But it was Brazis's personal presence—in a sense. And secure communication—it certainly was that.

"Governor Reaux, sir," she said. "I'm asked to mediate your request of the Chairman."

"Hell," he said, peevish. He'd wanted Brazis in person—he hated dealing this way. But if he insisted, he'd raise warnings in Brazis's very wary security. "Can you manage here?"

"Yes, sir."

He didn't at all like it that a PO courier's relays operated inside his office foyer, inside all his electronic shielding. He didn't think Dortland liked that either.

"Where's your base unit?" he asked. "Point of fact, you're not supposed to be operating up here."

"It's amped a bit." It might be Brazis speaking through her. "Ordinarily we don't. But it's convenient, today."

Bloody hell. He didn't at all like the notion of Outsider relays in his ceilings or anywhere near them.

"Dortland. You can be in on this."

They moved inside. Shut the door between them and Ernst.

"Antonio?" Reaux asked.

"Yes?" from the mouth of this passive gray-clad woman, the antithesis of Brazis himself.

"The ambassador wants to interview one of your taps. One of Marak's taps. One Jeremy Stafford. Which I'm sure you're not going to permit."

"Why? Did he say?"

"He's got some intel who this tap is. That he's young, and in this post. This is apparently some matter of concern. Is there any reason this young man would be a concern?"

"Curious. Very curious."

"Is there a reason we should think anything's wrong with this young man?"

"I'm disposed to find out. When does he want him?"

Brazis's curiosity. Brazis's damnable curiosity, which had had him meddle more than once in an investigation. No, no, that wasn't at all the answer he wanted.

"Why would you possibly agree?" he ended up asking Brazis, and Brazis, through his living transceiver, answered:

"This ambassador has come so far on his mission. And I'm sure he'll give something of his intentions away, just in the questions. When does he want this person?"

"As soon as possible, I gather. I don't like this. If you're going to agree to this, and I very much advise against it—"

"I understand that. But I'm extremely curious."

"Curious!"

"Yes."

"I want to see this young man first. In my office. Antonio, I have to stress—there can't be any provocation."

"Soul of discretion. This is a young man who deals with very volatile personalities on the planet. He understands diplomacy and certainly appreciates the value of understatement. I doubt there'd be physical danger to him in meeting this person. Would there?"

"I'd earnestly hope not. No, I don't think so."

"Then I'll send him to you and let you make the exact arrangements. I must say I'm interested in the outcome."

"Antonio,—" he began to say, thought of telling him frankly what the ambassador implied about his operation being full of leaks. But while he was drawing breath to do just that, the courier shut her eyes and opened them again. Her expression changed.

"Excuse me, sir," she said. And turned to leave the office.

"Damn it." He *hated* tap-couriers. They jangled human nerves. You couldn't delay one. You couldn't get anything additional. They cut out on you. Rudely.

And on a second thought, he wasn't that sure that he should forewarn Brazis of what Gide intended.

But after the woman had left his office, on a third thought, he wished he had done it. What if this kid—this tap—found out his governor had strongly indicated Brazis shouldn't send him, and spilled that fact back to Gide?

Governors didn't often resign the Concord office. They died in it, more than once under very mysterious circumstances.

"Curious," Dortland said, echoing Brazis.

"Curious. I'm sure he's *curious*." In both meanings. He never had liked Dortland. He decided today that he *truly* didn't like Dortland. The man had ice water for blood. Ran risks involving others and didn't give a damn.

But the man was efficient. And intelligent. Give him that.

"Am I going to have to say no to this interview on my own?" It was still an option. "Dangerous, but an option."

"You've gone this far. You might just see where this goes, sir," Dortland said, "and keep meticulous records—in case this investigation widens. I would in fact have advised against your interview of this young man beforehand. Since it will take place, I'd record that session, under seal, to prove exactly what was said."

"Who is he?" Sharp question, sudden focus of thought—on the Outsider Council at Apex, and simultaneously on the byzantine maze of Earth and Inner Worlds politics. "*What* is he allied with?"

"Do you refer to the Chairman, the ambassador, or Mr. Stafford?"

"Gide. Mr. Andreas Gide. What possibly authorized a ship to come out here?"

Dortland never varied expression. "Some important entity, some body of very great resource and ample finance."

"A political party."

"Or some other entity who has a ship of this sort constantly at its disposal."

"The Treaty Board." That suggestion was completely askew from surmises of Earth party politics. "Do you possibly think? The Board, or someone trying to prove something to the Board?"

"It might be," Dortland said.

"Do you have that information?"

"I don't have it, but I suspect it, rationally."

The Treaty Board sat aside from ordinary Earth authorities, which came and went, and combined and recombined. The Treaty Board was monolithic, quiet, and rarely moved or voted, or even surfaced, in its age-old existence. Most of its members were decrepit, dull, and scholarly, and most residents of the Inner Worlds and the Outside went about their business oblivious to the Treaty Board's function in the universe.

But when that board did stir, when it raised any question that the Treaty, its sole business, might be endangered by some policy or action, governments shook and wise politicians thought twice and changed their tune as fast as they could dance to the other side. Nothing could generate panic in the economic markets like the Board stirring to life. Alone, it *could* argue with Antonio Brazis's authority, if it wanted to invoke its powers. It *did* deal with the *ondat*, and with the agreements of performance that kept that ancient situation contained.

And what other Earth entity *would* logically be investigating any serious whisper of First Movement data getting off the planet . . . and doing it with an armed ship as backup?

"Get your stock out of volatiles," Reaux muttered, "if that's the case. This isn't a political setup. They're serious. They're damned serious. Do you suppose Brazis agreed to this because he *suspects*?"

"Let Mr. Gide meet with this young man," Dortland said. "That's my advice. You're this far into it. Don't falter."

It was worth a shiver. He still didn't like the prospect. But he'd asked Brazis. He'd gotten his answer.

Damn Brazis for saying yes. But now, twice damn it, the suspicion Gide held might be solid, and if it was, *he* wanted the answers.

A BREAKFAST BAR, a sandwich, a piece of cake and a pot of caff, precariously balanced, but Procyon had the entry to his in-apartment office down to an art. The very minute the security system would let him in the door, an elbow against the switch, a rotation of the body, entrance achieved.

After which, every morning just before 1000h, he set his breakfast and lunch down on the counter, poured himself that first cup of caff, and reclined in his working chair, feet up, to read the transcripts. This morning he had an agenda, research to do.

The room-encircling bank of monitors showed him everything from remote islands to the halls of the Refuge. He couldn't command their search for a new one, not until he came on duty. They merely showed him what Auguste saw, at the moment, in his office several streets apart from his residence.

Nasty weather had moved in on Marak, in Drusus's account. Marak's party had set up the base unit, but *hadn't* gotten the antenna up last evening. They'd taken to their tent and gone to sleep as the storm hit. That front they'd hoped would go slightly north, hadn't.

And after that there was a very short file from Auguste. With the storm, disappointing news, had come a long communications blackout, lasting most of Auguste's watch since midnight. Sand blasted into the air created static. Better if they'd been able to establish all their planetary relays by satellite. But there was upset with the *ondat* every time they added a satellite. It took an act of God to get a new transceiver aloft, and here they were, communications-short and downed by a sandstorm.

Well, damn, Procyon said to himself. No new camera image from the area yet. He glanced past the images that floated before his eyes, to the rest of the monitors, scenes from off across the continent, stations either remote-dropped or precision-set by Marak or one of his people.

One of the stations, two sectors east of Marak's position, had its lens completely obscured by blowing dust. The storm front had moved that far. Which probably meant it was clearing over Marak's camp.

Auguste, still working, had sent over his partial transcript. The section of Auguste's record that he could access was still brief, uninformative: storm and silence.

Well, damn and damn.

Then, from the tail of the general record, Ian's, at the Refuge, and half an hour later—he saw there'd been worse than weather. An earthquake had hit the region this morning, a major one, with an epicenter, the team thought, in the Southern Wall, the very area they wanted to set up this string of relays to monitor.

Not unexpected, in the gross sense. Not a surprise. But a very strong movement.

An earthquake felt like an emergency stop in the lift system. That was the way he'd heard it described in his studies of planetary geology: a lurch, only with a shaking component that lasted about a minute or less. Structures fell down, poles whipped about, the taller the pole, the more violent. A tent could even pop a rope loose, and in a stormy wind with the dust flying, *that* certainly wasn't a good situation. Canvas would bell and buck, possibly break loose and blow completely away.

Marak could certainly deal with that eventuality. He'd dealt with far worse. But the relay had clearly gone to secondary importance in their morning . . . witness Auguste was, in what trickled in minute by minute, still having trouble making contact with Marak, and his account of the quake slowly came trickling in, so voluminous and laced with research inserts it obscured the essential facts. From Drusus's report, they had quit setup last night because daylight was going and a storm was coming on. And that had turned out, Auguste said, to be fortunate: an earthquake that strong, had the antenna been up without the bracing, might have added to their troubles, especially if they were in mid-process of the extension.

But things were surely all right down there. There was no one more experienced with rotten weather and the high desert than Marak and Hati.

The quake seemed right on that fault that followed the Southern Wall. And right where they *didn't* yet have a camera. Marak would be very upset with that.

Procyon read, ate his breakfast, waiting for 1000h.

The clock showed two minutes to go. He waited for the final transcript from Auguste before he tapped in.

The last of the transcript came in. He skimmed it—Auguste had gotten a fleeting contact. Marak and Hati were riding off from the camp, pursuing beshti that had run away in panic, all but two of their beshti having taken off. One of the men had a broken leg and cracked ribs.

From falling off? From a kick? Or from an accident with a collapsing tent? The situation was ongoing. The report was unclear.

Not good news at all. The last of Auguste's report was cryptic, unrefined, from a tap trying harder to listen than to write his transcription, trying to make sense of intermittent contact, unable to maintain a coherent communication. Auguste had spent the last of his watch in contact with the subdirector, who'd shunted Auguste into contact with Ian at the Refuge, regarding Marak's situation. Hati's intermittent watcher had been called to duty as backup, but had gained no contact, either. Auguste blamed their distance from a working relay.

He was coming on duty into an outright emergency—well, not a huge one: the communications dropout was surely the storm as well as distance, and Marak seemed to be doing what he had to do, which was to catch the runaways. But certainly it was an exciting event, a chance for him to actually work a situation. In anticipation, he watched the clock tick down the last seconds.

1000h. He made the slight effort to tap in.

And didn't make contact at all, not even with the tap.

That was a curious sensation. Just silence. Was the tap-manager wanting Auguste to stay in charge a little longer, still trying to reestablish solid contact?

"Procyon Stafford."

The Old Man's voice echoed in his head. Brazis himself. Speaking directly to him. Why did his heart suddenly pound? Had something happened to Marak?

"We have a problem, Procyon. There's a situation on station and unfortunately you've been selected. I want you to report to Governor Reaux's office."

"To the governor, sir?" Total change of direction. Didn't the director know the staff had an emergency working? Didn't he know Auguste had lost contact, after an earthquake?

"The governor's a reliable ally to the PO. Don't offend him. Do you know any reason why an authority from that ship out there would want to talk to you personally?"

"To me, sir? Ship?" He talked aloud in order to talk to Brazis, and knew that *me, sir?* wasn't an adequate, even an intelligent answer. But *ship.* The docked ship. "No, sir. I haven't any idea why. I have no idea. I don't know anybody from Earth."

"The ambassador's name is Mr. Gide. Mr. Andreas Gide, from Earth. He likely views you as new on the job and vulnerable—maybe someone he can bully for information he shouldn't acquire. He's likely interested in Marak. Needless to say, we're not pleased at this attention, but we're curious. And very wary. Don't take this meeting lightly."

"No, sir. I couldn't possibly. Take it lightly, that is. I can't talk to him, can I? I'm not supposed to."

"You can. You will. And you'll do it intelligently and observantly, just as you do your job. Go to Governor Reaux's office and get further instructions. He's managing your visit. I'm sure he has the address."

He was utterly appalled. "What am I supposed to say to this person, sir?"

"Answer his questions—consider him as equivalent to the governor, certainly no higher than that, but be very polite. You have skills of observation. He knows who you are and what you are. You know the Project rules. And you have a proven discretion. Use these assets."

"Yes, sir. But . . . you know there's been a major earthquake down there this morning. Marak's out of touch. Am I—?"

"Auguste has the situation in hand. The contact is intermittent, but he has it. Marak's situation is entirely manageable. Marak is very confident and Auguste is volunteering to extend his shift to meet Drusus halfway at noon. Don't worry about it. Don't think about it. I want your mind on the job at hand, which I assure you is far more critical to the Project."

"Yes, sir." He was concerned, humanly concerned, for a man down on the planet who in many ways had grown closer than family, and, no, he didn't want to be shunted off on any other job, especially one where he could get into politics, where he could make a career-damaging mistake he couldn't remedy. "Can I come back later and trade shifts with Drusus, sir? I'm sure I won't be that tired. I want to know how this comes out."

"You're to talk to the governor, and then the ambassador. Find out what Gide wants and why he has an interest in you. And you'll debrief to me after that. I'm telling you to concentrate on this job, not the other. I trust you can use that professionalism."

Stern reprimand. Refocus. Fast. For his career's sake. "Yes, sir, but can you tell me what I'm supposed to be listening for with this person?"

"This Earther from way high up in his government has come out here specifically asking questions he knows he shouldn't ask—which is interference with Outsider government and interference with the Project and the PO, of which Apex takes a very dim view. Take mental notes on his questions, his attitudes, his implications. Forget nothing. Commit yourself to nothing. Give nothing away, the same as to anyone on the street. Is that a clear enough explanation for you?"

It wasn't. He felt a rising panic. He didn't want to sound uncooperative. "Yes, sir."

"You have an immediate appointment at Governor Reaux's office, in person. Dress modestly and appropriately. Don't contact any friends or relatives while you're under that ship's observation, as I assure you that you will be for the next five days. Don't answer questions relating to Project affairs, not with the governor and especially with the ambassador. You already know what you can and can't talk about. For all we know there are a dozen bugs and all manner of truthers inside the governor's office or inside the ambassador's shell, so keep calm. Don't be overawed by the gov-

ernor—don't trust him, either. Don't talk about your work or your per-
sonal life with him and don't talk about department business, no matter
how nice and social it sounds. And damned sure don't get friendly with
the ambassador or get led down corridors where no-answer means they hit
something sensitive. If truthers are an issue with the governor's office, bet
they'll be in full force when you're with the ambassador. In short—follow
the rules you always follow, find out what he wants and what he thinks
and admit only to what he brings up that's within that level of knowledge.
Don't even think of tapping back to the PO while you're in either office,
remember every minute detail you're asked, and don't tell the governor or
the ambassador a thing of substance. You're a tap. You know how to do
what I'm asking of you. You have that kind of memory."

"Yes, sir." A shiver ran through him, as if the room had gone
way too cold. He decided he had the picture as clear as he was
going to have it. He couldn't imagine what the governor or the ambassador would want to talk to him about *except* his work and the
department's business, which he was ordered not to talk about.
And he had no inclination to say anything about his personal life,
or the personal associations the department had forgiven him,
even to his own department head.

Could it be *that*? Could his assignment to Marak have come into
question, because of those old associations, his Freethinker days?

That was a truly terrifying thought. But it was Earth, not Apex
asking the questions. Earth couldn't make any decision regarding
the Project. Earth, once he thought clearly about it, wasn't that big
a threat to him no matter how much they wanted information.

"Go," Brazis said. *"Say as little as possible, and remember everything."*

"Yes, sir." He tapped out. He got up from his chair and numbly
gathered up the items he'd brought in, to take back to the kitchen.
Breakfast wasn't sitting at all well on his stomach.

Dress appropriately. That was a major problem, too. He worked
in sweatpants, socks, and a tee. His Trendy go-to-dinner clothes
certainly weren't going to impress any Earther at 1000h in the
morning.

He did have his reporting-to-the-office suit. The suit his parents
wished he would wear every day.

He rode the lift upstairs to deposit the day's unused snacks back
into storage.

Reaux was going to give him further details when they met: that was simple enough to grasp. The governor, who didn't—wouldn't—couldn't—use a tap, wasn't going to use the phone to transfer information to him, either, and a personal courier from the governor, coming here to Grozny Close to deliver him a message, would start gossip racing from one end of the Trend to the other. So it was better, his going there.

And as for the level of what he was allowed to say—*no* had to be his favorite word for the occasion. *No* and *no, sir.* Security wouldn't allow a member of Brazis's staff to discuss any sort of Project business, or even what he did inside the Project, outside the department's secure environs. Brazis was right. That instruction wasn't hard to fix in his head: it was the rule he lived by. His own father couldn't get the truth about his job out of him. He wasn't about to give things away to Earthers, just because they asked.

And for that matter, and a cold second thought—these being Earthers, and neither the governor nor the ambassador having any internal tap, they wouldn't completely understand the tech involved, its limitations or its abilities, and they wouldn't like disrespect.

That was what he was dealing with—ultraconservatives. Think of the parentals—and their priest. Black suits and no earring, no flash on the fingers. Like dinner with the parents and all the relatives at once. Like a family funeral.

With the possibility of some really scary, state-of-the-art truthers, constantly reading everything he said and probing for what he might be hiding behind every blink of his eyes.

Don't even think of tapping back to the PO while you're there . . .

A hack? The PO's system being a completely different piece of equipment than the public tap system—that made interference with it a whole different operation than the common variety of tap-hackers, whose routine business contacts—and their customers—ranged from Earth security to the criminal underworld. The public tap system was worm-eaten with hackers—which was why the Project tap absolutely had to be a whole different system on every level.

And because the Project tap was nanocele-based, for all the ages of its existence, it remained unhackable—so the PO insisted. So far, the Project was impenetrable.

But if anybody thought of hacking it—if anybody was going to try that—that effort, if concentrated on him, might do physical damage. He'd felt overload—he'd felt the tap-output spike when he was recovering from the implant, when it was brand new. He was going where he couldn't even *think* about using equipment that was supposed to be absolutely secure, equipment that was as natural for him to use now as his sense of sight or hearing. It had bioelectronic components, notably the relays that interfaced with the nanocele. That meant electronics *could* interfere with it. Could attack it.

Scary games he'd been dragged into. Marak's World held the only politics he ever wanted to study. That world ran smoothly in the hands of those that had managed it forever, and he was at orbital distance. But now if his one teenaged flirtation with Freethinker idiots had somehow attracted the attention of authorities outside the Project, damned right he was upset. He had a right to be upset—and tooth and nail, he'd fight any implication . . .

Only if he had to. He had to remember he *had* Brazis's political protection. Brazis wasn't going to have Earthers of any stripe telling him who to assign where, or demanding he fire anybody. Brazis would hire two more questionables right off the street tomorrow if only to tell Earth to go to hell.

And, always a fact of the universe, always, both inside the Project and wherever the Treaty itself was at issue . . . *Marak* had the ultimate say about his taps. Nobody, absolutely nobody, challenged him to a duel of wills.

No. He was safe. Politics couldn't remove him, no matter how this went. Earth could throw a screaming blue fit and it wasn't going to scare Outsider authority, let alone Marak, who could shut down cooperation for a century or two and annoy the *ondat* in the process. Marak's displeasure could shake an economy. Ruin a career. A dozen careers. Bring down governments.

Which only argued that an otherwise very junior tap should just go in calmly and confidently, do what he was told to the letter, keep his eyes and ears wide open as requested by the only authority he answered to, and do his job without making his superiors any unnecessary trouble. It was scary, but it wasn't fatal. He just needed to look good, sound respectful, do it and get back.

Dark suit. No flash. He went upstairs, opened the closet,

searched for the dark blue shirt that went with the parental-approval suit. He searched the whole closet three times and finally located the missing shirt in the shadowy back end of the freshener, where he recalled he had put it after the last holiday dinner with the parents and the relatives.

He found the conservative collar, dug up both matching socks. Head to toe, he became a good boy, as churchly-straight as possible, void of any breath of the Trend—

Well, except the hair, but he wasn't going to cut that, not even for the Earth envoy. He clipped the locks back into head-hugging simplicity.

Rings. And earring. He stripped those off and put them in his house safe. No hint of show or display of extravagant salary. No controversy. No hint of arrogance. No problem. He looked sober as clergy.

5

THE TRACKS HAD tended down along the terraces, over drifts of sand, then grown dim on sandstone. Marak and Hati looked for signs at several opportunities for their fugitives to have taken another downward path, but they found none. The wind-blurred traces led instead across a vast flat sheet of sandstone, staying on their level. This gave them hope that if the dust should settle a little, they might catch sight of the group. They quickened their pace.

They advised the Refuge to advise the camp. The relay had gone up. Auguste said so, and communication had now become reliable. "The leader of this band," Marak said, "will be skittish. This may take a while."

His own old bull would not have bolted repeatedly and zigged and zagged along the terraces. The young one had. And the herd, indecisive as their new leader, veered slightly southward now, generally down the long spine, still on this level of the terraces. Sandstone spires rose ghostly and strange in the lingering dust, and generally obscured their direct view of what was ahead, even had lingering fine dust not hazed the air.

Marak had faith that even the spookiness of a new herd leader had to steady down with repeated tremors. But right now their young bull would bolt at every shaking in the earth, every breath of wind, taking the females farther and farther from the old bull he had robbed, and would do so until the females grew annoyed with his skittishness and grew slower and slower to follow. Beshti had their quirks, but they were predictable in their ways.

About the watchers in the heavens, however, Marak was just a little concerned. He expected Procyon, in the ordinary cycle. He discovered he had Drusus instead. Something strange had happened in the earth, and now something else strange had taken place in the heavens, at a time when he most wanted his information flow to be ordinary and dependable. First his contact had gone on and off, intermittent in the storm. That had steadied, and now other things seemed unreliable.

"Is Procyon well?" Marak asked Drusus, when first he came in clear. "Is he taken ill?" Hati expressed her concern, too, to her watcher, Carina, who joined her uninvited. That was the measure of worry on Ian's part. They suddenly had watchers left and right, Hati's called back to duty, but his not the one he expected.

"*Brazis has sent him on an errand today*," Drusus answered his inquiry. "*A request from an Earther lord. Earth seems concerned with his appointment because of his young age. Procyon will pay his courtesies to that person and return, either today or tomorrow. The Earther lord is considered benign. There is no reason for worry, and this is an inquiry, not a matter for concern. I hope, omi, you will accept my being here early, today.*"

"We understand," Marak said, to end the protestations. He was, at the moment, at a difficult traverse, on a strip of sandstone scarcely wide enough for safety. He had his answer, but he remained annoyed and just a little suspicious—halfway moved to demand Procyon's immediate attendance, never mind the affairs of lords in the heavens, who had no right to demand the attendance of persons who lived under his personal protection. He knew about Earther lords, he had experienced them, that they were prone to nose about and interfere where they could. And this request was damned ill timed.

Lords and directors came and went in that place in the heavens that by all description was like the Refuge, all corridors, plain walls, and lights, with here and there a garden, by what Marak had gathered. There the *ondat*, too, once hostile, thanks to the sins of the Ila, lived and watched over the world with some suspicion, still dangerous—but Earth, at some distance, being the birthplace of all humans and even the beshti and no few of the now-extinct vermin, thought its history gave it a special right to send out its governor to rule this metal world.

So the Ila said, along with much else he had read in the Books of the Record.

But Earth certainly picked a time of great nuisance to make its demands. He knew his own right not to be annoyed by what happened above—particularly where it regarded his watchers. He wanted Procyon with him today—the cheerful young watcher who even in his routine weather reports managed a heartening enthusiasm. Drusus was the director's man, full of rules and cautions. He had the niggling suspicion someone thought Drusus was the watcher he should have right now, since the quake—and that suspicion more than annoyed him. If he thought the boy's inexperience would be a hazard, *he* would make that call. He was determined not to blame Drusus for the situation, but he could blame Brazis, when he had time, because he was not at all sure there *was* an Earth lord.

Meanwhile, however, he could try to moderate his temper and find out the truth of what was going on.

"Procyon is paying court to some Earth lord," he told Hati, who could be overheard, but who could not overhear Drusus. "No long venture, so Drusus assures us. He's come in early to fill Procyon's place."

"So," Hati said, frowning. Hati was an'i Keran, Keran tribe, quick to the knife, even in these latter days when the land grew wider and water was no longer a matter of dispute. "Today of all days, and without consulting us. We can well remember such favors." Let the director and the Earther lord hear *that*. Hati had an opinion of her own, and, unlike him, felt no obligation to be reasonable.

They were neither of them happy, at the moment. They had another aftershock, and their fugitives took out down a slope—they came on the tracks, a wide wallow in a breakneck sand-slip. There were no beshti lying dead at the bottom, which argued they had made it.

But it was a chancy ride, and they had to do it. They worked their way down, and tracked the runaways southeastward, while Drusus kept prudent silence.

The wind was less down here, at least, and haze was less in the air, but they had been cautious coming down, and their fugitives almost certainly opened a wider lead, breaking low brush—a sparse, low-lying spiny growth that spread like fingers from a single plant, and branched and rebranched among the rocks and on the sand, putting down new roots—a warfare like that of nations, vegetative dueling for broader and broader territory. The weed actually poisoned the ground to discourage its competition, and made a thick mat that cracked and broke as their beshti crossed it, behind others that had cracked and broken it in passing. Beshti, who ate most things, found no attraction in this stuff, which the Refuge had never chosen to seed, but which survived and thrived since the hammerfall. And now it helped obscure the ground and made footing less certain in precarious places. It hid holes and crevices.

"Prickle-star," he said to Drusus. "It smells like graze and burns the tongue. One of the worst things will thrive, and the succulents gain no foothold here, in consequence."

He felt another aftershock coming. The beshti felt it. It was a hard shaking, and long.

"Stronger than the last," Hati said.

The young men up on the spine, minding the tent, were surely getting an education they had not expected on this tame journey.

And their fugitives, invisible among the spires, would not have stood still.

"Another quake," he said to his watcher.

"*Are you all right?*" Drusus asked him.

"Well enough," he told Drusus, amicably. "It was stronger, however."

Hati was used to him talking to his voices in moments of crisis. She talked to her own, today, and told her watcher to let her alone, that there was no difficulty. She was never patient with them. They reached a place of vantage, above the dust-hazed depth of the pans. And an area of darker dust showed in the haze below.

"Can you see them?" he asked Hati. Hati had risen up with her knees on the saddle in their pause, to have a look with a collapsible glass.

"Yes," Hati said. "Well away down the slope, toward the next terrace."

"Where are you, omi?" Drusus asked.

"Two terraces down toward the pans," Marak answered, and tapped his beshta with the quirt, as Hati dropped down to the saddle and put away the glass. They both started down.

"Have the beshti gone off again?" Drusus asked, annoying him with questions.

"What else would beshti do?" he answered shortly, then amended the answer. "They have gone down, risking their necks. The gorge rim was too steep for them. This is not."

"It's too dangerous to go down, omi," Drusus told him. *"The quake was not minor. Ian believes the Southern Wall is about to fail."*

It took a moment to reach his attention. Then did. "Ian thinks the Southern Wall may have cracked," he said to Hati, but he thought she might have heard it from her own watcher. Her jaw was set in a deep frown. And he abandoned his annoyance with his watcher. "Is it breaking where we thought, Drusus?"

"The epicenter was out under Halfmoon Bay."

"It was at Halfmoon," Marak said, for Hati—all he needed say to convey extreme chagrin, because the Halfmoon area of the Wall was their planned destination, the point where the spine they were on intersected the Southern Wall.

It was the site they had thought would be a safe place to set the next relay.

"Observers are less sure now how or where the Wall will crack," Drusus said to him. *"Don't go down into the pans, omi. The director thinks it best you come back up to camp and let Ian send a mission out from the Plateau, not with trucks. He says he can put Alihinan aware and have his riders bring beshti to your camp. . . ."*

And have someone bring more beshti up from the Refuge to Alihinan, clear up on the Plateau, on the other side of the Needle. "Which will take a while. If the Wall has cracked, the spine itself may grow unstable, and we have a man lying in camp with a broken leg." His beshta's descending strides jolted under him, a chancy descent of a loose, sandy slope. "We stand a better chance by catching our runaways." As haze wrapped them about, obscuring all but the solid shapes of the sandstone spires. "Has the Wall shown a breach?"

"Not yet."

"Then tell me when it does."

"Omi, when it comes, where it comes, they think now it may become a far faster, far wider breach. An entire section of the Wall may fail at once. The displacement in that first event may have been as much as ten meters."

Drusus's usual stolid, quiet voice was not stolid or happy at the moment. A cataclysm of icy water was portended to break through, not far to the south, but right where they might have been standing, if they had been a number of days further advanced on their trek. They would have been camped on the Halfmoon section of the Wall, setting up their relay when it changed relative elevation by ten meters.

Maybe there was reason the director had moved Drusus up in the daily sequence.

"Ian says he is this very moment preparing a rocket," Drusus said, *"to soft-land a relay at Halfmoon. You have no need to go on."*

Ian had *had* to relay that to him. They had disputed the matter of the rocket hotly before he left, he and Ian, Ian intent on using their sole prepared rocket to set down the relay, before establishing fuel dumps and small manned way stations to take various missions there by truck, a very quick process on one end and a very slow business of establishing a land route on the other, a three-year program with trucks making successively more distant fuel drops, and getting to the Wall eventually. Machines had to be supported by more and more machines. Sand buried fuel dumps. Fine dust found its way into intakes and engines. Landbound machines broke down. Flying ones crashed in inconvenient places and someone, usually with beshti, had to trek after their irreplaceable metals. Marak maintained he didn't need three years to prepare the way for a small, self-sustaining caravan. He could get a firsthand look at the Southern Wall while Ian was still getting under way, and without risk of an airplane or expending another rocket in a very chancy and rocky area.

He would have been right—if he hadn't lost the beshti. If he'd used Ian's metal-centered cable to secure the beshti, instead of softer, safer rope.

If, if, and if.

He hated it when Ian was right. He could limp home with the

two beshti they had and all his party could survive with limited canvas. He could give Meziq the makers, set the leg, and have it healed before they got down off the spine.

But they weren't that far from their fugitives, and they weren't beaten yet.

"Ian is urging us to take the conservative course and walk home, and perhaps, eventually, someone will meet us with beshti," he said to Hati, their two beshti side by side for the moment. "He says the Wall will crack at Halfmoon."

Hati shrugged. "So Carina says." Naming her own watcher. "Ian is launching his rocket. Likely we shall still set up our other relay ourselves, after Ian's silly rocket sits down on a rock, like the last one. Several caravans can carry back its metal, if it survives the flood."

"They want us to go back upland and give up this chase."

Hati looked across at him, with those beautiful fierce eyes.

"I don't think so," she said.

THE GOVERNOR'S OFFICE was entirely terra incognita. Procyon walked a corridor where he had never in his life looked to go, a hall lined with doors reputed to be antiques salvaged from ancient governors' offices on prior Concord stations. They were carved in flourishes, and might even be real wood, not plastic. The vases in the niches were definitely imports, maybe antiquities, too, the sort of objets d'art that even his mother wouldn't put flowers in. The reds and blues were deeply glazed, the gilt amazingly bright. He tried not to look impressed.

Glass doors protected the end of the corridor, clear and thick, and probably able to go opaque at the touch of a button. They said, in lettering that hung glowing with an iridescent water-pattern in the glass, SETHA T. REAUX, GOVERNOR OF CONCORD.

Those doors admitted him without his doing a thing but approach them. A second set of doors, also antique, let him into an inner office where a thirtyish official—tall, blond man, prim sort, with close-set eyes, and nothing, absolutely nothing but a bud vase on his desk—looked him over as if he'd come to steal the silver.

"Mr. Jeremy Stafford," the man said.

Not even Brazis called him his registry name. But he was, in fact, Jeremy Stafford Jr.

"Yes, sir. I'm supposed to see the governor. Chairman Brazis asked me to come."

"The governor is expecting you," the man said. "Go on in."

The inner door slid aside for him. With the feeling he was going behind more doors than he possibly liked, farther and farther from familiar territory, he walked in, onto fancy import carpet, facing a stout, gray-haired man he'd only seen on the vid.

It was a surprisingly small office, with amazing antique furnishings. A huge life-globe. He couldn't forbear looking at it once, and again, seeing a small movement inside. Antique printed books, in massive shelves.

Reaux rose from his desk, offering a welcome, a little nod, if not a handshake, and Procyon's instant thought, on looking into the man's face was, *He wants help, and he really hates doing this.* He gave his own little bow—you never reached for an Earther's hand: they went into hysterics—and produced as friendly a smile as he could manage, given his situation.

"Mr. Stafford," Reaux said. "Thank you for coming. Do sit down."

"Yes, sir." He sank into the opposing chair, hard, but padded. The dark brown leather under his hands might be real.

"Brazis says you're one of his best."

"One of his newest, sir. I hope I do my job."

"I understand you were a Freethinker."

God, was that the issue? "I attended a couple of meetings when I was a kid. I left. It was my idea to leave."

"In the remote past."

"Remote, yes, sir."

"Six years ago."

"I'm twenty-three, sir. Not to be argumentative, but six years is a fair number of years ago, out of twenty-three. I was sixteen, seventeen, then, and stupid."

"I hope this particular curiosity is now satisfied."

"I didn't agree with their ideas. I think they're wasting their lives."

"Attracted by the Freethinker style, then?"

"No, sir, by the ideas, on the surface, but when I got to hear the details and the reasoning, I didn't like what I heard. And I haven't had anything to do with them since."

"Sixteen. And interested in the ideas. You were remarkably precocious."

"I was curious. But I didn't agree with them."

"What did they say, in particular, that you didn't agree with?"

Shaky ground. He wished now he'd skirted this topic with more determination, but didn't see how. "They talked about justice. But they were more interested in debating their own rules. And they cheated in their own elections. How were they going to give justice to anybody, if they cheated to get into power?" It was out of his mouth before he realized he was talking to an elected official. He wished he hadn't said that last.

"A sensitive young man."

"I don't count it any credit to me for being there. They're not what I wanted. Not what I want now. That's completely done with."

"You have a tremendously important position these days. One naturally, yes, does understand the curiosity of youth. The flirtation with ideas. That's even commendable. Seeing through them, more so. But let me be very frank here. If you have any lingering acquaintance with anyone in that organization, I earnestly advise you tell . . . not me. I know I can't ask you for that level of honesty. But tell your Chairman. This is extremely serious. At very least—if you even remotely know someone in that organization, don't contact them on the street for the next four days. If I could make a request—don't entertain or be contacted by anyone with ties in the Trend *or* on Blunt for the entire duration of this ship's visit to Concord. Their monitoring may be extensive, and you wouldn't want to give them any false impression of you."

"I understand, sir. I have no friendly contacts among the Freethinkers. And I have no trouble agreeing."

"Has the Chairman told you there's a political development involving you?"

"That the ambassador wants to see me, yes, sir. The Chairman told me that."

"Chairman Brazis apparently believes you might successfully carry off a little inquiry. That, doing the job you do, you're smart enough to avoid saying anything provocative while you're there. He also says that you have considerable powers of recall."

"I'm not allowed to talk about my job with anyone, sir, I'm sorry."

"You are a tap."

"I can't talk about what I do, sir." By his tone, the governor, curiously enough, seemed to list the tap among his assets. Most Earthers felt differently.

"A particular kind of tap, allowing you to do the very important job you do—which at governmental levels we do know, Mr. Stafford, and have no interest in creating difficulty for you."

"I'll have to tell the Chairman you asked me, sir, with all respect."

"You acquired this tap after you left the Freethinker orbit and you trained to use it, so successfully so you are where you are. Is it active now? Could it be active now, if you wished?"

"I'll convey that question to the Chairman, sir. When I leave this office."

"I'd like to ask the Chairman a question."

A little harder jog of the heart, a warning. "No, sir. I won't say what I can and can't. But I'm not a tap-courier and I don't mediate messages."

The governor gave a slow smile. "Brazis said you were no fool."

A test of his discretion. If there were secure relays here, in the governor's own office, he wasn't aware of it, and he wasn't going to tap in here and now to test it. "I try not to be a fool, sir."

"Has the Chairman indicated to you that he doesn't trust my office security?"

"No, sir. Not to me, he hasn't."

A little frown of annoyance or thought, then a smile that seemed somehow more genuine than the one before. "I've had it gone over minutely. I don't find any relay. But you can tell Brazis I and my security are a little annoyed at the fact a tap-courier can operate here."

"Yes, sir." That one could was news to him.

"Are you cut off from contact with Marak at the moment? I'd certainly hope that's the case."

"Again, sir, you'd have to ask Brazis about that."

The smile hardened. "Again, Mr. Stafford, you have very good instincts. I'm impressed. So. Let's get down to business at hand. Mr. Andreas Gide has come all this distance specifically to see you, it seems, and Brazis is agreeable to that interview. We're both curious what this off-schedule visitor is up to, and what he thinks you represent. We both recognize the danger you may run in going in there, not utterly discounting any physical danger, but I doubt it. So does Brazis. Let me supply you other facts, which a young man of your political awareness can surely take to heart. This isn't a scheduled ship-call. It came as a complete surprise to us. This high-ranking person purposely travels an extreme distance, at extravagant expense, and his first request is to see the youngest, newest tap connected to Marak himself, a tap who happens to have a Free-thinker background, however far and faint in his past. I'd be far more comfortable if you had never visited a Freethinker den—if I could send him a young man with no past entanglements. But that's not the situation we have, is it?"

"No, sir, but it is far in the background."

"Do you comprehend that the repercussions from any mistake, any slip of critical information, could be extreme in this affair? That I have great misgivings in sending a twenty-year-old, no matter how intelligent, to handle this? Your mind is probably extraordinary. I'm very impressed. Your experience, however, is limited. And this man is very sharp."

"I can't imagine what this man wants from me, but I know one thing. I can't contact Marak for him. The Freethinker business is done with, it's no secret to the Chairman, and I can't be black-mailed or surprised in that. In the main, sir, I don't know anything particularly secret. There are a lot of people in the Chairman's office he could have asked for that have data on the Project. But I doubt they'd be volunteered for this. The only thing that bothers me is that I don't see why he'd settle on me, except maybe he thinks he's got something on me in the Freethinker business, or that I'm new on the job and he thinks he can intimidate me."

"*Can* he intimidate you?"

"No, sir." No hesitation. He was very sure where right and wrong lay, by the sacred Project rule book. And he wasn't required to do anything but show up and avoid answers.

"I hope you can report to me what questions he asks."

"Chain of command, sir. I report straight to the Chairman, and that's exclusively where I'll report unless he instructs me otherwise. You can ask him, and he might let me debrief here."

"Smart young man. Remember what the ambassador asks even if you don't understand the question. Remember exactly what he says, the very words, and manage not to answer him. He *is* fluent in your native language. You may not appreciate how extraordinary that is. But it indicates to me that he came here well prepared for this interview. Say as little as possible. Claim you have to consult: you do. Set up a second meeting if possible, which may give your Chairman and me a chance to confer in the interim."

He was supposed to miss one session with Marak. Not five. Not ones after that, in endless debriefings. It was an appalling prospect. He didn't want to be used for this. But he didn't say that. "If the Chairman agrees to that idea, sir."

Reaux pushed a button on his desk. "Mr. Chairman?"

"I'm following this." It was Brazis's voice over an ordinary phone. And Procyon knew, first, with a little jump of his heart, that he'd sat here, with all his confidence, failing to detect he'd been spied on, by such low-tech means and by an Earther. But he was sure, his heart subsiding to a more confident beat, that he'd said absolutely nothing he shouldn't. He lived under observation. He was, in that sense, used to it, never knowing, when anyone talked to anybody in the offices, whether they had a tap, and whether somebody not present was hearing most of it. Brazis had warned him explicitly about truthers. But he'd passed. He hoped he'd passed.

"Procyon."

"Yes, sir."

"Voices can be synthesized. You should constantly remember that."

Deep blush. He felt his face go hot.

"Yes, sir."

"I agree with the governor: arrange a second meeting if you can. I'll confirm all these instructions later, so you can be sure they're mine."

"Yes, sir."

Not only physical lines, in dealing with Earthers—a trick he hadn't straightway thought of—but physical tricks he'd not had to worry about, either, in discriminating truth from lies, like faces and voices that weren't real. Earth didn't use taps, but he'd always heard Earthers had tricks. Faking identity was a near impossibility where the secure taps were concerned. But among Earthers, behind the governor's doors, where there were no secure taps, proving one's identity, yes, had to be a major concern.

"An escort will pick you up tomorrow morning at 0900h," Reaux said to him.

"Tomorrow." He'd already missed today. "And, sir, the Chairman won't want attention drawn to my apartment—"

"—at your area lift."

"There are two. The one at 11th and Lebeau. It's far enough away."

"The 11th and Lebeau station, promptly at 0900h. You'll know my man by a code word. He'll call you Mr. Jones when he meets you. He'll take you to the ambassador. Dress modestly, as you are now. The ambassador's name, again, is Andreas Gide: you can call him Mr. Ambassador, or Ambassador Gide, or just plain sir is quite adequate. He'll assuredly try to unsettle you. He'll almost certainly confront you about your past associations. Be prepared, but don't be glib. Let me warn you in advance, his appearance is imposing. You'll face a plastic display, a chemoplasm on a containment shell, which may have unguessed sensors and recording devices inside, and truthers, but don't try going in on sedatives. That always shows. At all points, you'll have Brazis's protection, so rest assured, Gide can't harm or threaten you: he'd fear the consequences, in terms of international law and Treaty law. Brazis is relying on that point, extremely, and so am I, in principle, so I want you to understand what is at risk. Unfortunately in certain departments this ambassador outranks me, so it's not likely I can help you if this goes badly. At all points, listen far more than you speak, and encourage the ambassador to talk. Draw him out, if you can."

"I understand." He wasn't sure he did have the full picture of what he was up against. But he saw he had no choice. He wanted to get through this. He wanted it over, for more than just getting back to the business on the planet. He wanted himself back in his own life where he belonged, safe and out of reach of powerful strangers.

"Thank you, Mr. Stafford. I very much appreciate your cooperation."

"Sir." He rose and gave a little bow, understanding he had just received his cue and the interview was over. "Tomorrow. 0900h."

Trouble now, trouble of all sorts if he didn't handle this well, and meanwhile all hell had broken loose on the planet, and he only hoped Drusus had told Marak it wasn't his choice to be absent right now. But he couldn't even choose his own cover story: he'd have to learn it from Drusus, and he'd have to live with it. Business behind the security wall wasn't something he could explain to Marak later—since they weren't supposed to inform the planet about the station, or about its politics, and this certainly fell under business behind the security wall. If Drusus didn't handle it right, he could find everything on end and Marak mad at him when he did get back on duty.

But it was no place to think of that. He paid his courtesies solemnly, received the governor's polite acceptance, and made his exit past the secretary, not happy, no.

He walked out down the corridor and into the general administrative zone, where he thought there might be tap relays if there were any on this level. There he made the blood shunt in his skull, the coded single long effort that contacted Brazis's office.

Brazis himself had several aides who shared one of his tap codes, aides who took notes and handled what amounted to nuisance calls from workers who didn't quite have the level of emergency they thought they had—or sometimes handled real emergencies that Brazis couldn't get to fast enough.

"I want to talk, sir," he said to the empty air, conscious as never before that there might be physical eavesdroppers or lip-readers around him, picking up his side of any conversation. "This is Procyon." He walked quickly for the lift, and then thought that, too, was audio- and video-monitored, particularly if the governor was tracking someone. Computers once set on his trail could track him through every common tap relay in the station. Whether that had any physical connection with tap relays that weren't supposed to be operating up here, he had no way of knowing. "I'm going to the lift, now. I'm anxious to talk about this. Instructions?"

No answer. Either he wasn't getting through because there wasn't a Project relay in this area, or nobody in Brazis's office wanted to talk to him here. He caught the lift down to more general territory, changed to a common public lift where he knew for a certainty there would be secure relays and little likelihood of spybots.

But he didn't make a second try at Brazis's office until he was safely down in the thick foot traffic at Seventh and Main, on his own level, where Outsiders alone maintained everything that needed maintaining, and where any Earther attempt to bug the place would meet quick detection and entail nasty repercussions.

Then he didn't have to try to reach Brazis. Brazis found him.

"*Procyon.*"

"Sir."

"*Good job up there.*"

"Thank you, sir." His heart pounded.

"*What he requested you, do. This constitutes your confirmation. I did hear the conversation—mechanically speaking.*"

"Yes, sir." Considering there was still a danger of lip-readers or listeners, he just listened to the tap, which no one without a tap from the same source could get into.

"*This isn't a situation you asked for by word or behavior. It's political, and I'm relatively sure it's Earth pressing for some advantage, and using any anomaly they can find to justify whatever they're after. It's far from certain you're in any sense the real center of this inquiry. You're going to have to use all your wits on this one.*"

"Yes, sir." God. How had he gotten involved in this? Why him? And he desperately wanted a briefing on the downworld situation. "Quick question, though, sir. I'm not going to relax this evening. Would it remotely be possible for me and Drusus to switch shifts? Or at least let me have the current transcript. I don't want to raise questions with Marak that I can't—"

"*Use your wits, I say, or a missed session could be the least of your worries. Concentrate on the business at hand. I applaud your devotion to duty, but Ian knows exactly where Marak is. The new relay's working. We're in reliable touch with him and with his camp. Ian says the camp is geologically sound despite the shaking. Drusus has explained your absence to Marak. You're covered down there. Concentrate absolutely on what you have to do in this interview. If you make a mistake of any kind with this man, let me make it clear to you, you'll hear from the High Council, the Chairman General, and from me, personally. Do you understand that?*"

"Yes, sir." Soberly. Heart pounding harder. "I do. I'm frankly scared."

"*Understandable. Are you at all flattered this Mr. Gide came here asking for you?*"

"No, sir. I'd rather he hadn't. I've thought and thought. I can't imagine a reason."

"*Don't be overawed by his attention. The man is a diplomat. He may be exceedingly gracious. Don't go off your guard. I'm sure he can threaten. Don't be spooked.*"

"Yes, sir."

"*I wouldn't send you into this if I didn't have confidence in you. You want to know why I agreed to this.*"

"I do wonder that, sir."

"*Consider. He's here at extravagant difficulty, making an extravagantly provocative request, which he knows I could say no to, absolutely. Probably I should refuse him, and I think Reaux expected me to. But he failed to get an issue on that. And we know one thing: we're not talking about a fool arriving here on a personal whim. This will be a very clever man with an agenda we don't know. He comes with Earth-based credentials, not just Inner Worlds, intruding into Project business, which means he and whatever he represents have stuck his neck way, way out. Earth has very many institutions. We don't know which one this Gide actually represents, and we may never know. But if there's a clue to be had as to which faction is sticking its nose into our affairs, I want to know it. It could be someone looking for an issue to raise back at Earth, to reinforce their politics. It could be a legitimate anxious inquiry into your background, which we both admit has a shadow on it.*"

"Yes, sir." He was beginning to have fears that ran under doors he couldn't possibly open.

"*Expect state-of-the-art truthers, which I can guarantee were running all the time you were talking to Reaux. Are you in fact up to this, or do you need to have an attack of something contagious?*"

"I'll do my best, sir." *I don't know* didn't get you points in the Project. *I can't* might lose them.

"*Observe, don't interpret, just as you do on the job. You don't want to know too much about this. Deeper knowledge could very easily bar you from places you want to go in your life. Let me play politics. That's my job. Yours is to go on being innocent, and in that innocence, to protect the*

Project from an inquiry Earth isn't allowed to make. A further piece of information. You'll continue to be shut off Marak's tap for the duration, for security reasons, not because we don't trust your integrity, but because we don't want them probing it."

He was appalled. "Can they possibly *do* that?"

"The signal's within the electromagnetic spectrum, and they can certainly try it. If it happens, don't cooperate and get out of there fast. You know the rules. I don't want to frighten you further, but if they physically grab you, don't cooperate, and leave if you can, with whatever force you need. If worse comes to worst, trust absolutely that we'll get you out. I'll contact Marak if I have to. It's one reason I dare send you in there. I have no doubt we'll get you back safely. Just don't make me have to do that."

"Yes, sir."

Brazis tapped out. Gone.

My God, Procyon thought. He felt sick at his stomach. He didn't know why this business had arrived in his lap, except his teenaged stupidity in getting into a questionable group, in listening to ideas different from what he'd heard before—it was his only real sin in his whole life, politically speaking, in any sense that would ever reach to Earth's files. One mistake, and it came back to haunt him. He wished this business were all over with, and for the rest of his life after, he swore he wanted to live as far away from Earthers' notice as he could get.

We'll get you back safely, kept ringing in his ears. And, *Mr. Jones*, for God's sake.

What did Brazis think he was going into?

MAGDALLEN HAD SHOWN UP—on time for his appointment, give or take five minutes, but Brazis was in a touchy mood at the moment, touchy enough to keep an Apex agent waiting in his outer office. Several reports had flashed across his desk in the last while, most notably Marak's irritated reaction to Procyon's continued absence.

Worse, Marak, having followed the trail of the runaways to the brink of the ridge, was now well down on eroded terraces and sand slides, stubbornly proceeding where, Drusus informed him, underlying sandstone could crumble without warning. Marak had a few notorious flash points: deception in his contacts, mechanical devices in general, and Ian second-guessing his firm decisions at the head of the list. Left to his own devices, Marak might have given up the pursuit and come up again to take other measures; but then *Ian*, who had his own flash points, had gotten hot about Marak's decision to go down off the ridge, Drusus had seen fit to relay that to Marak, Marak had gotten hot in return, refused Ian's help, saying he had the beshti in sight, and now it was clear that hell would freeze over before Marak gave up and retreated.

It was already a delicate business, keeping what happened on Concord away from Marak's lively and very experienced interest, while pursuing an investigation about Earth's poking about in matters it should never touch—that was one thing. But Drusus, damn him, had straightaway committed them to a particular line of explanation that involved Earth—admittedly within the allowable degree of latitude, but letting Marak know that Earth was an issue in Procyon's case. And if Marak did find out what was going on up here, he'd find it out while he was already feuding with Ian, again thanks to Drusus's decisions.

The juxtaposition of issues was like fire near explosives. The very last thing any of them wanted now was Marak, already in a temper, conveying to the Ila, whose relations with Earth were ancient, unpleasant, and always full of acrimony, that Earth was now interfering with their taps, potentially including hers.

That would fry the interface. Absolute disaster. He wanted to strangle Drusus, who hadn't been aware how dicey things were.

Ian and Luz, meanwhile, already quarreling with Marak over methodology, were monitoring the aftermath of a second very strong quake to the south. Everything Marak had come south to observe was now in full career, a spectacle that had the geologists glued to their posts in anticipation. Over a matter of hours two high salt waterfalls had sprung out on the inward face of the Southern Wall, white threads presaging a far greater flood. Icy polar water was tearing itself a wider access to the hot southern pans of the inhabited continent. Marak had lost his bet with fate—source of half Marak's temper, Brazis had no doubt. Ian had proven right: they should have used the rocket in the first place, and now Ian rushed to get a backup relay soft-landed on the Wall itself, a tricky bit of targeting, while the landscape out there was changing by the hour.

The northern end of the basin itself might have dropped another half meter relative to the Southern Wall in the last strong aftershock, which had the geologists on station scrambling to revise their predictions both of the extent and speed of the event, and of the consequences to anybody in that region, notably Marak and his stranded party. A major inland sea was arriving in what had long been mountain-shadow desert, deepening over an unknown amount of time, depending on how much that sand soaked up, for starters. The mountains in the northern part of the basin were predicted to become islands. The frozen southern sea, a weathermaker for the southern hemisphere, was in the process of acquiring a shallow, sun-heated annex, which, the meteorologists said, was going to mean fog. Mist. Rotten visibility, that was already obscuring the site of the break in the Wall.

And as for Marak, the need to reassess his party's situation and cope with the aftershocks *might* distract him from asking more closely about Procyon for the next couple of days; but it wasn't going to improve Marak's mood or the ease of dealing with him.

Meanwhile *he* had the inquisitive ambassador *and* Francisco Magdallen to deal with. An Apex Council agent poking about in the usual habitats of trouble was a common enough nuisance throughout the territories, just the Council keeping tabs on Concord Station to confirm what the Chairman of Concord and the director of the Project patiently and correctly told the CG was the truth.

And to top things off they had the arrival of this Andreas Gide, who wanted Marak's tap for a face-to-face interview. So to speak. Did he now believe that Magdallen's presence was coincidence?

Trouble didn't just come in threes: it gathered passengers as it went, and crashed nastily into bystanders.

He deliberately calmed himself. Had a few sips of caff, which had cooled enough by now not to scald his mouth.

He tapped in, a simple contact with his aide, Dianne, outside. Dianne escorted Magdallen into the office.

The man had clearly responded in respectful haste. The gray coat mostly covered a shirt that belonged on Blunt, the shoulder-length curls were done up in a clip without benefit of a comb, and the eyes, brown at their first meeting, were outrageous green, a green purchasable in cheap shops. Brazis didn't take it for granted those particular lenses were cheap, or without augmentations, or that they were locally-bought lenses, at all. He proved it by a fast tap at a button on his desk.

Clean, however. No transmissions.

"Mr. Chairman."

"Agent Magdallen. Have a seat." Brazis waited, and poised himself comfortably backward behind his desk, arms on his middle. "So what's your news this cheery day? I would expect there's news for me, with all this going on."

"Gide is on the station in an unfamiliar containment vessel. I don't know its capabilities, but the bizarre impression it creates where he travels is surely part of his intentions. To intrigue us. To intimidate. To make maximum stir here on the outer edges of human civilization."

"And among the *ondat*, a demonstration of technological wonder."

"Forever the *ondat*, yes, sir. But one doubts they're awed."

"Gide has asked to see one of Marak's taps. The youngest. Procyon."

"Procyon." Magdallen frowned. By his look, he actually hadn't known about Gide's summons of the young man, which argued that his major sources tended to be in the environment where that shirt was ordinary.

And one could then hope that Reaux's office didn't, at least, leak information too quickly to the Outsider streets, no matter where else it might go, among Earthers.

"Did this Gide give a reason for this request?" Magdallen asked.

"A whim, he would have us think. A five-hundred-light-year whim brought him here to ask for an interview with a, for all practical purposes, junior tap."

"Perhaps Earth doesn't like such a young man in the office he holds," Magdallen said. The man had an annoying habit of not quite looking up when he spoke. "Or perhaps Earth doesn't like what they hear of *this* young man. Who does have unusual contacts present and past, of which I'm sure you're aware. He has crossed my area of inquiry."

"*What* area of inquiry?"

"Into the Freethinkers. What did Governor Reaux have to say?"

Was he querying the agent, or the agent querying him? Magdallen was quick to provide an excuse for knowing about Procyon's past.

"What contacts?" he asked Magdallen sharply. "What contacts does Procyon have that possibly concern your investigation?"

"His sister, whose contacts are numerous, some low, some high. I looked him up, sir, for the Freethinker connection into high places. He is an anomaly."

"He can't avoid being that." Brazis considered the question Magdallen had posed to him, considered the source and the set of motives, none of which he quite trusted in this man who didn't work for him. Tell him? Encourage confidences? Or slips? "As for Governor Reaux, who just had an interview with young Procyon, we talked. We shared nothing but the basic information. We're left to assume Gide is putting his nose into Outsider affairs—and through Procyon, possibly into planetary affairs, more critical still. If not into this Freethinker interest of yours."

"That is a question."

"Can you answer it?"

"No, sir, not yet."

"I don't take such an intrusion into our affairs matter-of-factly. But yes. What about this Freethinker connection?"

"I have numerous inquiries going on. None that bear fruit. May I observe, sir,—you had to consent to this interview."

Brazis rocked his chair slightly, irritated by the stone wall, increasingly not liking that diversion—or the implication of fault. "Yes. I did."

"Clearly you have a reason."

"Curiosity." Deliberate cold answer to the authority this agent represented. And to any report he might be drafting. "Tell me, Agent Magdallen, what is Earth doing here? Who is Andreas Gide, and does he represent anything legitimate or changing, back on Earth? Unless you have some direct information on that score, which would surprise me and gratify my curiosity, and make me change my mind in a heartbeat, yes, the interview is granted. What in hell do Freethinkers have to do with it all?"

"I don't know that they do. If I knew anything at this point, I assure you I'd say it, to prevent this. I'm very uneasy about your consent to this meeting."

Magdallen was uneasy, as if *Magdallen* had an opinion of his own that overrode his authority. Forget the Council, if he'd ever suspected it. Magdallen wasn't a Council spy. This was one of the CG's personal agents, one trying to find something very specific. Hell, *yes*, it was political. "Procyon is a trained observer with a good memory. An extraordinary memory. I will expect your support in protecting him, Agent Magdallen."

"I've said I wouldn't have recommended your agreement. I can't promise . . ."

I, I, and *I.* Deeper and deeper. And this wasn't a fool: Magdallen surely saw what the other side of the desk could read into it, the implication of a real authority backing him, on Apex. He *meant* to convey that impression.

"Frankly, Agent Magdallen, I can't see letting Gide leave this station without knowing what he represents and what he's going to report, and I can't see letting him draw more extravagant conclusions from what he wasn't allowed to see, to fester at distance. I say again, if you have more information on the precise reason he's here, if it has any connection to anything you know, my decision can be modified. The young man can break a leg. Develop acute heat rash. But talk fast, or stand back and keep quiet, and don't tell the CG that *I* was the stubborn one, holding back information that could have bearing, because I'm recording this session, and I'm not hesitant to bring it and you and *him* before the Council."

"I don't have more information," Magdallen said. "Clearly what Gide represents has force, transport, and finance at its disposal. That's *all* I can say."

Confront the man? Demand under threat of arrest to know what he was and what he was investigating?

He wasn't ready for that. This day's disaster had gathered passengers enough. "It's all I can judge by, either, and I take decisions as I can, with what information I have. Earth is Earth. It organizes itself, and then it fragments and shoots its own citizens for centuries on end. One last appeal to reason. Does this request of Gide's possibly, remotely agree with anything untoward that you know,

Agent Magdallen? Any scrap of a scrap of a rumor down on Blunt or even far off in Council halls on Apex that you really ought to tell me at this point?"

"I'm not convinced this arrival does involve Blunt—at this moment. About the other I'm not in a position to say."

Damn him. Damn him.

"So we have Gide. And the visible anomaly in Procyon is, as you say, his youth and his former affiliation . . . down on Blunt Street. Tell me, Agent Magdallen, might *you yourself* be an item of their interest?"

"I would very much doubt it, sir."

"Is smuggling illicits actually your concern down there? Or the Council's? Or do I draw conclusions that Council might somehow have foreseen this ambassador's arrival and sent you here? Might I hazard the remotest guess that your business here was *always* the chance something like Mr. Gide might show up?"

A moment of hesitation. Magdallen looked at his own hands. "I will confess that Mr. Gide has suddenly become a concern to me, sir. What motivates his interest, and who sent him, I do intend to learn if I can, since I'm here. I report to the Chairman General personally. I'm sure you know that by now. I'm sure if there are issues surfacing on Earth that we haven't picked up—I'd be very glad to pick them up, if I can, and I'm sure the CG would be grateful if I can. These I would report to you, if I knew them, but no, that isn't my mission here."

"Don't stir the broth, Agent Magdallen. Get your information on Gide directly from me and tell me what you hear from other sources. This business is delicate enough without your personal intervention to complicate my life. Let's minimize the number of vectors in this mess."

Eclipse of the remarkably green gaze, a downward glance. And glance up. "I'm a model of discretion. No one in my line of work ever wants to create issues, I assure you, Mr. Chairman. My job is simply to report them where I'm scheduled to report."

There. He'd thrown out a rational appeal for cooperation and Magdallen's answer was a standoff. He restrained his temper. "I'll share information with you as it becomes clear. Stay out of the collection business in Gide's vicinity." Conversation with Magdallen

had to be bounded by prudence—defense of the Project's preroga-
tives as independent from Apex governance, even while the general conduct of civil and international affairs he handled as
Chairman *was* answerable to the Council at Apex.

He was increasingly uneasy in his dual role. Second-guessing
said he might have made a mistake in his decision to allow Procyon to take the chance, that he ought to have hammered Magdallen for information before he ever agreed to send the boy into
either interview, little as he'd gotten from the Council ferret before
now or in this interview.

And still—still he hadn't learned anything he hadn't expected from
Magdallen. He hadn't yet had Magdallen's complete cooperation,
and he still very much wanted the benefit of knowing what Gide was
after . . . which might well be what Magdallen himself was after.

Sitting back, letting Earth affairs develop without learning what
was going on—Apex wouldn't thank him or respect his authority
for letting events slide on their own. Politically immune he might
be, at least as director, but revolutions on Earth and in the territories involved untidier and more dangerous situations than orderly
elections and quiet political cabals: assassinations had happened,
covert removals had happened. Untidy political actions notoriously annoyed the *ondat,* who were always an issue. He didn't intend to be removed—for the good of the Project and the health of
humanity he didn't intend to be removed.

Others, then, might have to be.

"I appreciate your full cooperation, Agent Magdallen." He rose
and held out his hand, ancient gesture, deliberate and provocative
gesture in a world of potential contaminants and infection. "Your cooperation and your reports, as you'll choose to give them to me. I
know you're not legally bound to report to me, but I shall very much
appreciate your opinions and your advice. And your alert obser-
vance on the street. I expect to have it, under present circumstances."

"I appreciate the warning, sir," Magdallen said, shook his hand,
and immediately left—taking himself and that extravagant shirt
back, the report of his own agents would suggest, to a certain
apartment on Blunt—to leave the coat in yet another apartment he
maintained in a very seedy neighborhood on 2nd Street.

It wasn't to say he didn't wipe down his hand thoroughly after Magdallen left, and he was confident Magdallen would hasten to do the same, probably going straight to a washroom. It remained a visceral comfort, the lemon-scented wipe washing off the memory of a foreign, off-station contact, not that he truly dreaded foreign contamination from Apex. The new scent, primeval cure, canceled the lingering presence that could convey viral intrusion or—in this hotbed of politics that Concord always was—things far more elaborate and damaging.

Being remote cousins of Earth, even knowing there were remediations, Outsiders had never quite cured themselves of fear. They didn't go so far as to use robot interface. Outsiders trafficked with other worlds, observing sheer bravado in their personal contacts—but still, for psychological reasons, scrubbed such contacts off, frequently kept packets of wipes or Sterilites in their pockets, quite, quite silly as the action was. If Magdallen had brought any engineered contagion aboard, the whole station was already at risk. Always was. Always had been. Always would be. Far more threat than a sensible, well-paid agent from the central authority, the station had its biocriminals and its active nethermonde, that element that had threatened, and acted, usually for petty profit, sometimes for political reasons, on numerous occasions that the Office of Biological Security had had to scramble into action.

As for their ambassador from Earth—forget any trivial threat of germs from them. Earth wasn't a threat: they feared biotech too much. Hence the containment unit.

One always, always, worried about one's internal security, however, when the likes of Magdallen showed up, as Magdallen had, two years ago, about the time Procyon had risen to his rank, about twice the time ago this ship from Earth would have launched. Or a complete cycle, if something had reached Earth and bounced back to them, in the form of Mr. Gide.

Right now he was more than worried: he and Magdallen had bumped spheres of authority, and the air still crackled with the static.

Handle this. Handle it well, they'd challenged each other.

Neither he nor Magdallen could afford a mistake in the next several days, and now they both knew it.

THE LAND GAVE ANOTHER SHIVER, sending little stones and slips of sand down the long face of the terraces, warning that massive slabs of Plateau Sandstone that had sat for millennia overhead might grow uneasy in their beds. Marak cast an anxious look up, as sand slid down to cross their intended path.

Wandering terraces a mile above the pans, the fugitives had stayed out of sight, now, behind the spires of rock. They might have delayed, eating the new growth that still grew atop old sand-slips, but a relentless series of tremors had spooked them onward, down and down toward the bitter water pans.

Water itself was not an attraction. A beshta carried water in its blood, and, well watered a few days ago, they were not that thirsty. But, free now of riders and burdens, they followed ancient instincts for reasons that no longer quite applied to their survival. And they would, being beshti, go down, and down, and likely easterly across the pans, heading toward their home range, the young bull increasingly anxious to keep his females well separate from Marak's old one, and maybe smelling him on the fitful wind. He was taking skittishness to the extreme.

"They made it down that slope," Marak said to Hati, seeing the evidence of unstable sand, where beshti had clearly fallen and wallowed getting up. "I distrust that slope. Let us go a little over."

Warmer wind whipped at them, swept up from the depths of the pans. A gust caught the tail of Hati's scarf and blew it straight up. It had been like that by turns, but this southerly wind brought, rather than sand, a clearing of the air, and the scent of growing things.

They turned about, which, with beshti in a narrow place, was best done slowly, letting the beshti fully voice their complaints and test the rein. A new shiver of the earth underfoot gave them no help in the matter.

"*Marak,*" Drusus said. "*Are you hearing me?*"

"I hear," he muttered, fully occupied at the moment.

"*We can confirm the Southern Wall has actually cracked, omi. The cold sea is pouring into the basin. Meteorology thinks your weather will change soon. The earliest flood will soak into the sand and much of it will evaporate and meet cold air aloft. Fog is certain. So is rain. A great deal of rain."*

"When?" Marak asked, overlooking the distance-hazed pans, and a drop off a sandstone ledge scarcely a handspan from his beshta's broad feet.

"They think the wind will shift, coming at first from the southwest, and meeting a front coming down off the Plateau—a great deal of evaporation as the seawater warms on the pans. There will be limited visibility, wind, and torrential rain, omi. We are watching that situation carefully. We are in contact with your camp. We have advised them to take extreme precautions. We urge you consider the possibility of thick fog and very poor visibility in planning your emergency route back. Above all, you should not go down onto the pans."

As the beshti completed their precarious turn.

"We are not on the pans," he said irritably, and to Hati, "The Southern Wall has indeed broken. The sea is coming in."

Hati frowned, vexed at their situation. "So let us find these silly beshti before they drown."

"Drusus forecasts rain and fog," he said. "As well as flood."

"Then the beshti may come up on their own," she said. Beshti from the Refuge had learned good sense about flood, if not about inconvenience to their riders. They had no particular liking for being cold, wet, and unfed, and he agreed: if cold rain came before the fog, the situation could work to their advantage.

"What does it look like?" Marak asked Drusus, aching with curiosity for the sight they had hoped to see themselves, from a safe distance, to be sure. "What can you see at Halfmoon?"

"The two thin waterfalls," Drusus said. *"Proceeding from the cliffs. Clearly seawater has won a passage of sorts through formerly solid rock. We can't see the source, which seems about midway up the escarpment, but clearly a crack has opened between the sea and the southern basin. As a direct result of the waterfalls, cloud is forming that blocks our clearest view from the heavens. We're having to go to other instruments, so our view is adequate, but not as good as we could wish. We believe the gap will rip much wider very quickly. The rock there may be the same basalt as that in the ridge. If it is, we fear it will not hold long against the rush*

of water. And if that happens faster than we think, weather calculations
will change. I cannot say strongly enough, omi, all calculations may
change without warning."

Without warning. The chance of their being at the right place to
see this wonder in person had, over all, been very small, unless
they had been willing to camp at Halfmoon for a few centuries and
wait for moving plates to move and geology to have its way. Ian
had argued it would be later, rather than sooner.

Other decisions—his, among them, a feeling that the frequency
of small quakes presaged something—had put them on this slope.
And by Drusus's report, they were all running short on luck. The
pans below them now looked entirely ominous, and fog and torrential rain was not good news. The descent after the fugitives
was a maze, difficult to navigate among the spires, and the slots in
the terraces hanging above their heads and the spires around
them had not gotten there by dryland erosion. Rain pouring onto
the bare surfaces up there would quickly find the best channels
down. Streams of water would come off those cliffs in their own
miniature waterfalls. He was bitterly frustrated to be in this
predicament.

But frustration meant that they were alive, and still had choices,
no matter they had missed the breaking of the Wall, which did not
look to be a long process after all.

In his long experience, survival was always preferable to a good
view of events.

No access to the tap, no contact, no information, nothing to do
but sit on his hands and avoid contact with everyone he reasonably wanted to have contact with. At very least, Procyon thought,
they could have rushed him off immediately to this meeting with
the all-important Mr. Gide and been done with it, but he supposed
Mr. Gide wanted to rest.

So he had to avoid contact with his ordinary associates, stay out
of his ordinary comfort places, all the while having indigestion
from sheer fright . . . and sit and wait until tomorrow, until Mr.
Gide was in the mood.

So he poured himself an uninspired fruit drink, settled down in front of his extravagantly expensive entertainment unit and scanned fourteen channels of Earther-managed news for information that very obviously wasn't going to be there, not in any degree of detail he wanted.

It was hell, he decided, being at the epicenter of information that the news itself didn't know—you couldn't learn a thing beyond what you knew, and you couldn't get any decent sleep on what you did know.

The ambassador's arrival—that was covered by cameras as the ambassador had left the ship. The usual trundling machine was gold, however, instead of silver. And it was different beyond that. The blue reflection on its surface seemed to have nothing to do with the lights of dockside, actually something to do with the metal itself, by the way it looked. It seemed to fume with cold.

Interesting effect. Even scary. But not at all informative in what the commentators had to say about it, except that one suggested it was some sort of new material. *New material* probably made customs nervous. But the news didn't manage an interview with anyone who had real knowledge, no, the news instead interviewed a shopkeeper down on Lucid, a shoemaker who thought the arrival was a strong signal to the government, a threat to get Concord to abandon the trade agreement with Orb.

Well, was it possibly that? Procyon wasn't convinced. The Orb agreement might be a hot topic with the import-export offices and the shops that dealt with goods. But the merchants saw every political sneeze lately as somehow part of a plot involving Orb, and the gullible news agency had either fallen into it, or took their orders from someone with money in those ventures. As if the Orb-Concord situation was a reason for an Earth mission of some kind to come all this way with a special ship. He didn't think so.

But was he a reason? He didn't think that, either.

Concord's merchants, the expert said, might go to Apex for backing if Earth tried to squelch that agreement with Orb. But Earth wouldn't give a hiccup. A merchant protest would only annoy the governor.

And ultimately Concord's trade with Orb would just burrow itself new accesses and get around whatever regulations existed, and the only ones to profit would be smugglers—who, if they got too wealthy, wouldn't stick at piracy, either, when authorities tried to shut them down. Hadn't they, at the end of the last Isolation? He'd read his history. That could be tolerably serious, given enough heat under the situation.

But if it was trade Earth came here to talk about, the ambassador didn't need to talk to a Project tap and annoy the Apex Council for starters. Even a junior tap could figure that out. Whatever Earth did want here wasn't to be found in a shopkeeper's worries. It was all in one confused junior tap and the mistake he'd made going to a few meetings.

He'd like nothing more than to go for a drink down at La Lune and call in his friends, who roundly loved an intellectual debate, to hear *their* opinion on the ambassador's mission here, and to ease the willies dancing in his stomach. But he was directly ordered not to do that.

The news, he decided, was hopeless. The alternatives he could find were chat, fashion, drippy drama, and, at last, at the very last, an intersectional ball game.

Which proved a no-contest, a 118–50 disappointment by the last quarter. He gave up on the massacre in disgust.

Last resort, he rented a highly recommended drama off the net, which engaged his attention no better than the ball game. Or he wasn't paying adequate attention tonight. He flatly forgot to watch the ending while he was getting himself an early supper—with cake and berries for dessert—and he didn't actually care when he got back and found the drama was over. He ate his dinner to the accompaniment of an astronomical documentary on the Betelgeuse anomaly, took things back to the kitchen, tidied up, and put the remnant of the cake back in the fridge.

It balked. The red light went on, and blinked, and it passed the cake back out.

That did it. He slammed his hand against the fridge—which set off his own intrusion alarm.

"Damn! Sam, kill that thing! Kill it! Alarm off!"

"Confirmation?" Sam asked.

He flung the closet door open to provide a finger-scan, to shut the alarm down, then tapped in to the agency—not an alarm company: *Project* Security—and informed them he'd set it off himself, like a fool.

After that he had a drink, two drinks, a third, and went upstairs, hours early to bed.

Long hiatus, brute alcohol-induced unconsciousness.

Then the burglar alarm sounded again and scared him out of the bedclothes, barefoot and confused, on his knees in bed. "Damn!" he shouted at the idiot alarm, and staggered out of bed, facing the red glowing display of the clock.

"Damn!" he said to the situation in general. "Sam?" He stormed down the stairs in full dark to deal with the malfunction.

Folds of cloth and a slim body blocked his way midstairs. He yelped, backed up a step and tried to convince his confused body to raise a proper self-defense.

"Procyon?"

Flicker of blue and gold lightnings grew on a face he'd seen transit from sister to someone half a stranger. His sister. Here. In the dark. Wrapped in enveloping black cloth that now acquired constellations of stars.

Fright only half ebbed. He'd yelped like a five-year-old and backed up his own stairs rather than use his hours of defense classes. That was vastly stupid.

Maybe she'd just smelled right. Maybe some hindbrain, primitive sense hadn't let him hit her.

Who didn't belong here. Who wasn't supposed to be here. Who could get him in a lot of difficulty.

And the damned alarm was still going off. Sam was asking, brilliant question, "Is there a problem?"

"Wait," he told Ardath, and slipped past her on the stairs to get down to the kitchen, where the physical cutoff was, apart from Sam's systems. "Sam," he said, at Sam's third or fourth inquiry, "shut up."

Then he tapped in to tell government security he was alive and well. "Same mistake," he said, acutely aware he wasn't supposed to be seeing friends and family and knowing the whole apartment was surely monitored. But he couldn't come out with the truth. Daren't. For Ardath's sake. "Sorry."

"*I'll have to report it, sir. Confirm your code.*"

They knew *who* he was. Tap didn't lie. This time they wanted a code to tell them he didn't have a gun to his head. He gave it, so as not to bring an armed team in on the situation, just to cap it all. Arrest on his doorstep wouldn't add glory to Ardath's résumé or his own reputation.

The last light quit blinking on the alarm console. He reached out distractedly for the physical light switch and moved it to half, a twilight in which his sister descended the last step of the stairs to join him, wrapped in stars, skin flickering with pale blue.

"I'm not sure I like the color," he said, irritated into a truth he'd never told her, and immediately wished he hadn't said that.

Blue flicker turned to gold and magenta pink. He liked it less. Pink wasn't Ardath at all. He doubly wished he hadn't said anything.

Meanwhile he found a cup and stuck it under the caff spigot, ordering a full cup. "Want one?"

"No."

"I do." Dammit, he was wide awake. Adrenaline was pumping. He couldn't drink another three vodkas to put himself back to bed or he'd have hell's own hangover when he had to be sharp. He didn't want to resort to pills because it was 0405h in the bleeding morning. He needed his sleep so he could get dressed in four hours and face the damned ambassador with his wits about him at 0900h.

His nerves were completely jangled. He took his cup to the small, two-seat table and sat down. "Go back to the blue and gold. It's pretty. I was being a toad. What are you doing here?"

6

"As if I'm not welcome," Ardath said.

"You set off the damned house alarm at four in the morning, for God's sake. I can think of nicer visits. I'm going to hear from the office about this. Believe me, believe me—tonight's really not a good time to do this."

"Why?"

"I can't tell you why." Procyon sipped at too-hot caff, found his sister towering over him. Her face and hands flickered blue and gold in the twilight, her body wrapped in constellations. "Sit down. If you want to talk, at least sit down. I'm getting a knot in my neck."

"You have one in your head." She didn't sit down. "What's this meeting with the governor? Are you suddenly looking for a job in *Reaux's* office?"

So the rumor had made the street. He wasn't all that surprised. "I can't talk about it."

"You can't talk about it, but everybody else is talking."

"That's not good." He really didn't like that idea. But he didn't know what to do about it.

"You're my *brother*! It's common knowledge you're in the Project."

How was *that* common knowledge? My God, he thought. "I don't know how it got to be common knowledge, since it's not true."

"Oh, come, brother. I know. Everyone knows, but I've always acknowledged you anyway and never, ever asked a question if you're not able to tell me, which I assume you're not, about where you work, and now you go and do something like this . . . which just makes us wonder if you're really a computer tech or into something else I really won't like. What do you actually do for the Project?"

So he worked for the Project. Whether it was in the civil or science wing was a fifty-fifty choice. Three-quarters of the people in government offices worked for the Project, at some remove.

"I just push keys, is all. I have no choice where I'm sent. I was just running an errand today, a favor for a supervisor."

"A keypusher runs errands to the governor? Who do you work for? For Brazis?"

"Believe me when I say you aren't supposed to be here. My apartment's being watched. You're into security systems you can't deal with."

"Then they already know I'm visiting my brother, don't they? *Who's* watching you? Is it Reaux, or is it Brazis? And you keep ducking the question. What do you *do* for the Project?"

She knew he was meeting with the governor. He couldn't exactly say he was "in computers" anymore. He couldn't say it was for any ordinary supervisor he'd undertaken that errand. "Ardath, please, if you mess with this, it's not going to be good." He weighed another question half a breath. And asked it. "What *have* you heard, and who told you this stuff?"

"I can't tell you who told me, if you're being spied on. That wouldn't be smart of me, would it?"

"It might well be smart of you to tell me. All right, all right, yes, I work for Brazis. I work pretty high up, for Brazis. My office wants to know where you got this information. Don't play games with them."

"You know what they say on the street? That you could even be a Project tap. That's what they say."

His blood ran cold. He didn't know how much he needed to tell her to distract her. As much, he decided, as was going to be common knowledge tomorrow, and hope the PO didn't think it became common knowledge only because he'd told his sister. "I'm meeting the Earth ambassador tomorrow morning. Did your sources say that to you?"

Ardath gathered her constellations around her and sat down in his

kitchen chair, eyes wide—glowing slightly as her color patterns retreated. Was that equivalent to pallor? Perhaps the same physiology?

"You're not!"

"Afraid I am. The same reason I went to the governor, I'm being
sent to the ambassador. It's secret. And it isn't any damned help
with my sister passing along the latest rumors as fast as people
come up with them."

"Is it some stupid politics that's the matter? Is it some fuss with
Earthers?"

"I can't say, and you don't want to know, either. That's why I
don't really recommend you stay for a cup of caff at this point, do
you understand me? Don't do me any favors. I have to do this.
That's not going to change. Just stay out of it before we both get
into trouble."

"Are you a tap-courier?"

Close. A reasonable guess. But a miss. "I can't say."

"You know what some people are saying on the street? That my
own brother is slinking for the Council. *Are* you a slink?"

"No."

"Then why won't you tell me the truth?"

"Ardath. I know this may all seem a personal inconvenience to
you . . ."

"An inconvenience! An inconvenience! You won't tell me the
truth, you go and do something like this when I've done all I've
done to make you a good reputation in the Trend—I've invested
in you!"

Sometimes his sister's focus was on her own navel. Not a clue
that events meant anything outside the Trend. And that short focus
was the one thing he really, truly detested in Arden as she'd become. "I really haven't any choice in the matter." He was on the
verge of real annoyance with her, and he didn't want that at this
hour, not counting the other troubles he had. The rumors she cited
were scary. "I'll breach security this far, just enough to tell you the
meeting with Reaux was because of the meeting with the ambassador, a simple briefing, which I conveyed where it had to go, and
don't you dare mention that fact anywhere. This is a test of what I
tell you, Ardath. I'm telling you, and if that information turns up
anywhere else before I actually have the meeting with the Earther,

I'm going to be way beyond mad, because I'll know who spilled it, and so will my office figure it out. It could be inconvenient for *me*, if you think about it for two seconds."

"How am I responsible, if your business is spilling all over the street? *Are* you a tap-courier?"

"*I* didn't spill any of my business on the street. That's why it's dangerous, idiot sister! People with bad motives are passing all this around from leaks in other offices. Just don't help them validate the rumors, if you have any sense. I'd far, far rather be on my regular job than what I'm doing tomorrow, but I didn't get that choice. I'm not supposed to go on the street for the next few days, and I'm not supposed to contact you or anybody else I care about, partly for your own protection. I don't slink for anybody. But listen to me, don't tell anybody what I just told you, not even the denial. Don't hedge answers with them. Don't try to defend me. It only creates more rumors. Just get out of here and stay out. It's a lot safer. I love you. I can't tell you any more than that."

"*Why* won't you tell me what you do for them?"

"I can't. If I'm any of the things you suspect, you know I can't. I assure you I won't do anything disgraceful. I won't do anything I don't believe in. I swear to you I want all this business over and out of my life as fast as possible. And if you dare spread it around the street what your personal guess is about what I do, you're going to ruin my life, Ardath—you're going to ruin my life and maybe cost me my job, just for starters."

"Oh, job, job, job. This is so déclassé, brother. Just swear to me you're not a slink."

"Far worse than the crystal egg. I know. I know. I swear I'm not a slink." Which dangerously narrowed the field of her suspicions, but pinned nothing down. He reached out and patted her hand. He knew everything had to revolve around Ardath when it came down to emotions. Everything had to, or Ardath refused to deal with it, or understand it, and he was the appointed family expert at dealing with Ardath. Scared—damned right he was scared at the moment, because she'd decided to be a fool. "I honestly I can't help it. I'm just running messages. So that's that. So I ask you, sister mine, sweet, intelligent sister, just go somewhere and don't get further involved, and above all don't assume you know anything about my business. I know, I know all this is all luscious gossip-fuel, and I know whoever's brought you this rumor is not your friend, and is trying to score on you, and you're all hot to defend us both; but I have absolutely no choice about going into this meeting if I want to keep my job, and I damned sure don't want what I do and where I go gossiped all over the street. My job isn't one where you ever want to be famous."

"Forget the damned job! You're my brother! You don't ever have to care what those people want! Only for what people think of you, out where it matters."

"The Trend isn't life and breath to me, Ardath. If you want the brutal truth, I don't ever intend to slip into the Trend, not even with the solid gold chance you could give me, and I couldn't live in the Style. Ever. I'm not that sort. So don't plot it for me."

"You could be. I could help you. You have the looks . . ."

"I'm telling you I don't have any interest in it, none. Absolutely none. What does interest me, what most interests me in my whole life is my job, which I assure you twice and three times isn't being a slink, so that leaves you your other guess, doesn't it? And your being here and telling me these things and me telling you isn't good. I could get in real, deep trouble, thanks to these gossips that aren't your friends. So *don't* repeat this. Don't repeat any of it and don't speculate even to your nearest and dearest. Be smart for me, be smarter than any of them, and keep what you know about me absolutely to yourself, no matter how the gossips annoy you. You can ignore them. This is my *life*, this is absolutely my life we're discussing here."

The simple case finally got through to his sister. Ardath sometimes, in little moments, became Arden, and Arden reached out her hands to him in a distress of her own. "Brother,—if you're really in this terrible deep secret, if you really are—"

"Beyond that," he said before she could work up momentum in her anguish, "more than that, I'm putting you in actual danger telling you as much as I have, and I insist, I want you to get out of here right now. Declare me anathema in the Trend if you have to. If the rumor gets too strange, I want you to create a fuss, make a protest of the scandal, make it clear you don't know anything or care to know—but keep insisting this business of me being a slink is just outrageous and stupid, and don't say *courier*. Say I'm sleeping with someone unsavory. I don't care. We can mend it later. The gossip all comes round again, forever. It's all just a game, isn't it?"

The patterns were back on her skin. Profuse and agitated. "Your reputation isn't a game! My life isn't a game!"

No, the Trend wasn't ever a game, to Ardath. The Trend was life and breath to her: what was visible, what was en vogue, defined all she valued, all she was. And the line was always a razor edge, that divided a designer from a grotesque, a divinity from failure and ruin. A brother gathering intel for the police as a slink or meeting with Earthers as a high-clearance tap-courier wasn't a reputation enhancement. He could do her real damage.

Well, so was the line of virtue a Project tap had to walk, a very fine line, one without compromise . . . without ties outside, and absolutely without publicity. Ardath was upset with what limited things she had now to guess. They were at a very difficult division of interests.

He touched her hand. "It may get much worse, I tell you. Be angry at me as long as you need to. Curse me as long as you need to. I'll still love you. And right now, do us all a favor. Just get the hell out of here."

"This is ridiculous. You can at least tell *me* what's really going on that everybody's so worried about, or why you, of all people!"

"If I knew, I still couldn't say, and the truth is, I don't know what's going on. Use your head, sister. My apartment's bugged. Possibly I am, in ways I don't know and can't even detect operating. Go. Do I have to throw you out? For God's sake don't discuss what we've just said."

"Don't talk like that!"

"I'm serious. Life is sometimes actually very serious. My job is. My career is. The enhancements that make you what you are aren't visible in me, but I can tell you they exist. They're as numerous, as expensive, and as irrevocable. I can't go back from what I am, I don't want to go back, and frankly I'm in a lot of trouble if I ever give my boss the notion I ought to be decommissioned. If my situation personally inconveniences you, I'm sorry, but that's all I can do."

"Dammit. That's not fair!" There was his sister. And she was sorry for what she'd said, and he was.

"I didn't mean that, Arden. I don't mean it."

She flung her arms around him, a hard hug.

He hugged her back, then disengaged. "Fine. Now go. Get as mad as you have to get at me and forget all the rest of it for all time."

"I can't forget it. What when they ask me?"

"*Who's* asking? Did you tell anybody you were going to ask me?" He didn't want his sister to end up the subject of an official query, but he had absolutely no compunction about setting the department slinks on certain ones on the street. "Is it Algol? If it is, I swear I'll shut him up."

"Everyone's asking, is all."

"I *asked* who's asking. Name names."

"Capricorn." That was another known bad actor, a prankster. "And Algol. Algol said he'd talked to you. That you were looking worried and wouldn't answer his questions."

"What did he say about me? I'm asking seriously, is he your source?"

"He was asking about you, if I'd seen you. He was upset about the curfew on Blunt."

"Stay away from Algol!"

"Why?"

"Because he's trouble, sister. Because he's affiliated in places so entirely déclassé you don't even want a whisper of his real affiliations. Trust me that I know. And if he's my trouble now, I swear I'm going to settle with him."

"Because you really *are* a slink for Brazis?"

"I haven't slinked for anybody. Ever. Forget it. I haven't reported Algol for what he is except as we're being overheard now— as I know we're being overheard because of the damned alarm you touched off and the names you named."

She hit his arm. "Stop it!"

"I can't stop it. Be angry as you like. I don't want any association with him or with Capricorn, and just watch—he'll try to get to you next, because he won't be able to get to me. I hope you're too clever for that. He's bad. He's extremely bad, and he deserves to go down. Believe me."

Flurry of blue flickers on his sister's face. Take it for a blush. Take it that his warning was late, and she was entirely defensive. It *was* Algol that had gotten to her. And maybe Capricorn, too.

"You don't trust him because he's a Freethinker?" Indignantly. "You used to be."

"Because *he's* the specific reason I got out of Michaelangelo's and got out of the group, because he's dangerous and he's gotten control of the Freethinkers, who don't half understand him. And yes, my bosses know about my time there, and they know about him. I'm not interested in Algol's politics and I'm not in his orbit, and never was, no matter what he thinks. He's anti-governor. He's anti-Brazis. He's interested in stirring up trouble at any opportunity, and he's a damned social leech who's got just enough glow about him to convince the young and desperately fashionless he's more in the current than he is. I say it, quite seriously, you're too bright a light to fall for him."

"He's much more interesting than some."

"He's *poison*, Ardath. Take it from someone who roomed with him. He keeps his digs like a stinking miner's dive, he deals with dealers who don't scruple to sting the gullible, he's a slime, in short, a glowing green slime with no redeeming uses, and I'm relatively sure he's got fingers in the black market and worse. He doesn't *attract* his close satellites. He buys them. He pays them in far more money and favors than he ought to have. I'm sure, and I can't prove, that he's killed one of them. Do I need to paint you any broader picture? I got as far as I could away from him long before I went to work for Brazis. Now he's snuggling up to my sister—now, of all times, with this ship doing what it's doing—and do you think his helpfulness to you is coincidence? You're not where you are and who you are by being stupid, or gullible. If you don't want to tar yourself with illicits and smugglers and attract the notice of the very déclassé police, get as far from him and Capricorn as you can get, and for God's sake, don't share a drink with them or their friends."

Ardath turned away, a rustle of cloth, a shifting of expensive stars, all gained gratis. She was leaving, and he had a last moment's uneasiness. He took her arm, delaying her, and she slipped free with a flip of a starry scarf over her shoulder. "Ah." A smile, slow and sweet and superior. "Now there's the brother I love to tease. So completely fast to flare. I take it by all this you really don't like him."

"Algol isn't a joke. Listen to me."

"Oh, do you think I'd ever socialize with him? You think so little of me. I can take a hint. I'm leaving. I'm going out where I get respect."

"Ardath, use your brain. You're in danger, coming here in the first place. Wake up and live in the . . ."

". . . real world?"

He winced. The family motto. Now he was saying what their father had said at the last disastrous family get-together. "I'm not quoting him. I'm asking my sensible sister . . ."

"To be all gray and sober like some we can name? To go to Earther church and work on the line in the plastic works until I get too old to be worth paying and station gives me a pension apartment? Or maybe I can just take a job with the government and lie to my friends. No! Where you are isn't the shaping works, but it's close, brother, it's all gray, and if it wasn't for me, you wouldn't have any reputation at all on the street."

She was getting under his skin. Way under his skin. She suspected enough to speculate in mutually dangerous directions, and he couldn't afford to defend himself. He was angry, and when she tried to make her grand exit on her terms, things he'd thought for years welled up into his mouth, things that needed saying, because he'd seen that look on Arden when she took out on a self-willed mission, to do exactly what she wasn't supposed to. "You wait. You listen to me until you get what I'm saying."

"You told me to go."

"Don't be a baby. You remember what you told the parentals when you left? *Try to get me to care.* Well, I cared about things then, and I still care, but I'm getting tired of caring all by myself. I patch things up while you make gestures, the way I did on their anniversary this year and last. I mop up, I handle the parents, I keep things in the family civilized, and even if they won't, *I'll* be there if you ever make a mistake with your mods and do yourself lasting harm. But *damn*, you're increasingly selfish!"

"*I'm* selfish, opinionated brother!"

"Selfish, self-centered, how do I say it? I've told you all this and all you can think about is your reputation and your ways of dealing with threats. Well, there's more to the universe than that. There's a world outside the Trend that keeps your world safe, and there's a world underneath it, and that second world's damned dangerous, sister. Don't tell me you have any real idea what Algol is, because I'm sure you *don't* know, and you *won't* know, not unless you get where I was, and I never, ever want you to go there. So shut up, go think about it, don't act, and don't do anything stupid."

"*Are* you a slink?"

"For the twentieth time, I'm not a slink."

"Not a slink. Maybe a courier. But very well paid. And you can't own up to what you do. What do I believe about you?"

"That the real universe is wider than the Trend. Wider, and far more dangerous."

"The *real* universe?" Bitterly. "We don't live in the real universe. We do live in the Trend. It's what matters. You're going to be notorious on the street before you're done, and I think I'm going to die of shame."

"Listen to me! Listen, for once in your life. The whole universe isn't out to embarrass you. Other people have lives. Other people have crises."

"They'd have fewer if they didn't tangle themselves up in silly secret jobs."

"Well, guess who pays the real bills at the restaurants that give you free food and drink, sister."

"Because you're stupid. If you just quit that silly job and came on the street I could tutor you. You could *be* someone."

"I have news for you. I'll say it a second time, in plain words. I'm not stupid and I love the job I do."

"It's a *job*."

"It earns money that supports you. Where do you think it all comes from?"

"From the gray people. The little people. What would they be, if they didn't have us to look at? What would there be to look at, at all, without the Trend? Would you want to live here, if there weren't the Trend?"

He knew where he'd want to live, if the microbes that lived in his body from birth wouldn't destroy that world and the peace that depended on its complete isolation. He lived outside and above one of those life-globes the Earthers favored. He protected, he observed, he did all he could to ensure life went on inside his precious sealed globe, but he never could touch it or reach inside.

That he didn't care that much about life in the larger globe he actually lived in—well, in that sense, maybe Ardath had a real point. That he didn't have a personal life because he'd never felt inspired to form a relationship inside the Project wasn't ultimately her fault. It wasn't her fault he worked where he did, so that every person potentially available to him had politics attached and every really attractive human being he met socially was off-limits.

All of which was a bad line of thought at 0400h in a morning when an intrusion alarm had blasted him out of bed, and when— he had the increasingly sickening realization—official ears were almost certainly monitoring their family quarrel. It was in the manual that they didn't, routinely, but he was never convinced they didn't just sample from time to time, or that key words wouldn't wake the system up, and if a burglar alarm at 0400h and a lengthy conversation with the burglar, contrary to the scenario he'd presented to security, didn't do it, he didn't know what would.

At least—at least the monitors must be used to windows into people's private lives, and wouldn't hold 0400h arguments with a relative too hard against him or her, per se. The fact he was meeting a family member against orders, and that there were rumors on the street, however—that was almost certainly going to send the transcript straight to Brazis's desk. That would likely get Ardath herself tailed for months.

"Get out of here," he said, thick-witted despite the strong caff, which by now was upsetting his stomach. "You've waked me up, I've got an early call, and now I'm not going to get any sleep and I'm likely to make stupid mistakes. Just go. We'll talk about this when we're not having a family argument."

"You aren't hearing what I'm saying. It's not as simple as my disowning you."

"I'm sorry about that. I can't do anything else. Go. Or do I have to get dressed and walk you back to the street?"

A sniff. Ardath drew her constellations about her. "Go back to sleep. It's clear you don't care at all about our reputations."

"Good night."

Ardath's eyes burned palest blue. "I am disowning you. I'm going to damn you to everyone for at least a week, and hope it works."

"Go do that." He could be kinder. "Shall I walk you downstairs?"

"No need." She walked to the lift floor.

"Sam," he said. "Down."

Ardath vanished into the floor and the shadows below. He didn't ask how she'd gotten in. Sam knew her voice. He'd identified her as family, as within certain long-established permissions. Unfortunately, Sam wasn't authorized to turn off the alarm system: *that* system wasn't under Sam's control.

He wished now he hadn't said such cutting things to Ardath, especially when there might be eavesdroppers. She was what she was. He was what he was. They weren't ever going to agree on lifestyles. She didn't know he forever gazed outside the globe they both lived in. And she *was* an artist, and a good one, an honest one. There was an importance, that the world have color, and movement, and controversy, for those who didn't have a view and an obsession outside that globe. What price on that? What price sanity?

Her world, the world she'd give him, if she could, held no attraction for him any longer. It didn't have the scale of the world below. And which of them lived in reality? He would give anything he had to turn up in Marak's path and say, to, he imagined, Marak's great surprise, "I'm Procyon. I've come down to stay."

That wasn't ever going to happen.

Though he might sincerely wish he could disappear down there, once information got to Brazis that his cover was halfway blown on the street. He'd tried to misdirect Ardath and her intimates even while counseling discretion, but he wasn't sure he'd been successful in either effort. If word did proliferate on the street that he was a government slink, he might have to say good-bye to where he lived and how he lived. And if they were speculating on possible jobs high up enough to be running messages for the government,

Project tap certainly had to be on the short list, and that wouldn't make him much safer. His career was at risk, and he'd put Ardath in danger, asking her to defuse the rumors. God, it was Brazis who'd made him more public, it was Brazis who'd sent him to Reaux—but who was going to get the axe if his cover was blown?

Damn it all.

When he did get called on the carpet, as he was sure he would be, he'd plead he'd been waked out of sleep and confronted with an already-formed suspicion that he'd tried to deal with. That his sister was smart and, if warned, wouldn't talk freely—that it was actually safer for her to know something, because she wasn't talking to the family and she served as a rumor clearinghouse for a certain influential element on the street.

God, he wanted his sister away from Algol, for reasons he should have told her plainly years ago, when he left the Freethinkers.

She *was* smart, however. She'd ask Spider and Isis what they thought about the accusations he'd made about Algol, and they wouldn't have a high opinion of Algol, either, if they were honest, and if they'd kept their eyes open. They were older, far more streetwise than Ardath, having grown up unsheltered. They'd talk sense to her. Maybe a hint from him that their little goddess was in danger would encourage them to take a mutual stand.

If word did get out in the Trend that Ardath and certain others highly disapproved of Algol, that would rob him at least of his better-funded prey. But that scenario also worried him. Algol was dangerous in physical ways, and had no scruples about violence.

Ardath was no fool, however. She knew the hazards of feuds in the Trend. That fear had run all underneath her arguments for him to shove the job and get out of it. The more he rethought it, the more he was convinced she'd come to warn him, in her little performance, her pretense of naïveté, signaling him as hard as she could—even after he'd warned her about the bugs. She'd been trying to tell him his cover was already seriously compromised and that what she'd heard wasn't just speculation from idle talkers. There already *was* a problem. He was the fool, not Ardath.

Brazis having gotten him into this, Brazis might be inclined to take the fact she'd warned him, and give Ardath some consideration—if he could do whatever he was sent to do tomorrow morning. If he could bring Brazis whatever it was he wanted, then Brazis might be a lot more sympathetic, working *with* his problem, rather than just dealing with it and sweeping him away.

And, always, there *was* Marak to deal with, Marak, who would back him, unless Marak thought he was a fool.

So he daren't, above all else, blow the assignment he had. He had to come back smelling of success and professional discretion so he could fix whatever Ardath had come to warn him about. Protect his life on the street. And protect Ardath, who would go to war for him, and who by no means should attempt it, against Algol and his ilk.

He looked at the cupboard clock. 0448h. He didn't dare oversleep.

But dammit, he had to calm his nerves.

He was going back to bed. Lie horizontal. Try to relax his mind.

THE NIGHT AIR was still. The dust had settled. The sky was clear, sparkling with stars, despite Drusus's warnings of fog and disaster. The ridges above them were shadow. The distant pans were ghost-white under the stars, a dizzy distance below their feet.

Marak stood at the starlit edge of the ledge and called out to the fugitive beshti—"*Hai, ye, ye, ye!*"

Lone voice in the night, provoking echoes. It was the call they gave out when the beshti were wandering. It reminded the fools of food, of sweet treats. On a good day it could call beshti in from the fields, for the rare sugar that could tempt the most recalcitrant old bull into reach of a halter.

He heard distant answers, likewise, lonely in the night, distinct from the echoes.

"By now they have no idea how to get back," Hati said glumly, from her perch on the rocks nearby, which he was sure was the truth. Far easier to slide down the yielding sand than climb back up it. Their own descent had its perils. They kept careful track of the trail they followed, to be able to find their way back up again, in what might become foul weather.

Their own beshti had heard and smelled the implied offer, and were on their feet. A wise man kept his promises, even overheard ones, and Marak was ready for them, a couple of sweets in hand, daintily picked off his hand by soft, clever lips.

Then he went to sit by Hati. Certainly the rascals were down there, in earshot, but it was too dark to try another descent until dawn. If they could find no way down, riding, fast enough to get close to them, he might try it afoot. If he could just get his hands on one of the leaders he could get the whole herd up. He didn't want to shoot the young bull. But he would. He had known that when he asked the boys for the pistol.

He had Auguste for a watcher, now, Auguste who told them nothing, who left them alone, for the most part.

Tonight, in the dark, suspended between the world above and the basin below, he was uneasy, and realized the unease was silly, an ancient fear of vermin, as if deadly surprises might skulk out of the dark places of the rocks. The thought of a foot trek had set off that thought. Vermin had lived in such places as this, before the world changed—

But not now. Tonight it was a foolish fear. The world seemed again what it had been. The hammer had never come down. The world had never broken.

But the vermin were gone. They themselves were the fiercest thing in the world now, he and Hati and the beshti and their kind. And not a thing moved or crawled, else, on the land, nor had for ages . . . one eerie silence, for all their lives since the Hammerfall, and the great storms. One great loneliness in the land.

And change that moved slowly, until this event Ian had long fore-told. The Hammerfall had cracked the world; and the pieces of it drifted on internal fires. And now the Wall had cracked, and the land went on shivering, settling into a new age. The place where they sat would be utterly changed—a seacoast, a sea to the south of the Refuge as well as to the west, across the great plateau. If he lied to his eyes, in that dim view below their feet, he could imagine dark, wind-driven water, water stretching out of sight across the horizon.

Someday, Ian was convinced, life would come crawling up out of that sea and take residence on the land.

Would they personally live that long? Ian said processes of change ran more rapidly than might have been predicted, that this fact itself caused unease in the heavens.

Lying warm in his embrace, looking above the eroded sandstone, Hati pointed out what might be a wisp of cloud on the dark western horizon, an absence of expected stars.

That, now, that was not good.

"SETHA. SETHA!"

Middle of the night and Judy was standing over the bed in hysterics. Setha Reaux lifted his head from the pillow, squinted, and put up an arm to shade his eyes as his wife ordered the light on.

"Setha, she's *gone.*"

"Who's gone?"

"I heard the outside door open. I got up and checked. And Kathy's *gone!*"

Reaux's heart started a moderately labored beat, enough to persuade him he had to fling back the covers, put his feet on the floor, and dutifully go to Kathy's room—for what, he had no idea—hardly a chance that she'd be hiding under the bed.

He walked. Meanwhile Judy was shouting something. He tended to screen Judy's voice out when it reached that frantic pitch, because sensible suggestions never happened when Judy hit that particular note. He just plodded down the hall barefoot at fair speed and looked in Kathy's room.

Kathy, it turned out, hadn't been shopping today. She'd said she'd go tomorrow. If she'd sneaked out, she had 500c on a card in her pocket, and a quick riffle through the closet didn't suggest she'd taken much else with her.

"She's worn the black pants," Judy said, making her own search. "Maybe a tee, I can't tell with those things. And her bag."

Now he'd reached his own state of incoherency. Black pants and a bag, and 500c on his credit card. He could call in right now and cancel the card's funds, but *that* was how they were going to know where Kathy had gone. He rather thought he was going to extend that credit infinitely. Every time she used that card, they had another chance to find out where Kathy was, and, knowing Kathy, she wouldn't do the simple addition until it occurred to her the card had held out far longer than she thought. Then she'd probably know they were tracking her and she'd try to be clever with it, but she still wouldn't throw it away. The need for money, and the sure conviction her softhearted papa would go on supplying it, would lead her to go on using it in emergencies—emergencies the nature of which he could only imagine.

"Ungrateful girl," Judy mourned.

He didn't say he counted the situation Judy's fault. Judy's fault, true; but maybe his genes. Unlike him, however, Kathy had never learned his trick of screening out Judy's tirades. Or maybe teen hormones just rose up in rebellion when Judy hit that particular note.

"I'm going to the office," he said.

"How can you?" Judy shouted at him. "Your daughter's run off and you leave me here with the situation?"

"I'm going to the office," he said calmly, "where I can engage my staff on a discreet search for our daughter. She has an account on one of my cards. If she buys a blouse or a soft drink on it, we'll find her. I have resources there I don't have here. It won't take that long."

"She's not doing this on her own!" Tears had started. After forty years of marriage, he had the rhythm of Judy's arguments down pat, and was neither surprised nor moved by them. "It's that Denny, and Mark!"

"Denny's fault. Mark's fault. Let's not forget Ippoleta Nazrani's fault."

"She could do worse than emulate Ippoleta!"

"*Nazrani*, for God's sake, Judy. And our Kathy has better taste." He hated the Nazranis, up and down, and found nothing to admire in their wispy blond daughter. "Denny Ord and Mark Andrews. Phone numbers."

"I don't have their phone numbers."

"Are the boys in Kathy's sessions?"

"I don't know. They're supposed to be in jail!"

"I don't guarantee they are. I don't sit on the courts. Give me some help here, Judy, for God's sake! I need to contact their parents. I need to find out where they are and where they go and get a tail on them."

"They live somewhere in the Meridian."

A district about ten blocks by ten. Thousands of people lived "in the Meridian." He walked out Kathy's door, bound back to his room, to find his personal phone, to rouse Ernst out of bed.

"I need two young men tracked," he said, when he reached Ernst on the house phone, and gave the particulars, the names, the recent arrest, and the Meridian district. Ernst, long-suffering fellow, didn't object, or protest he'd been waked out of a sound sleep, just said he'd do it. "I need their whereabouts confirmed. I need my daughter tracked. If they're out of detention, she may be with them. She's got a Concord Trust card with her with a 500c limit. I don't want that credit cut off. Extend the credit on it as far as it needs to go. Find out where she's using it, get somebody down there, and bring her home."

"Yes, sir," Ernst said.

While Judy alternately sobbed on their bed and paced the floor.

"Breakfast," he said, then. Judy just looked at him.

"How can you be so cold?"

"Because I've already done something," he said, not nicely, though he thought Judy probably didn't take it as personally as, at the moment, he meant it.

He wasn't pleasant when he waked to news like this. He was a slightly overweight, well-over-fifty, sedentary man, but he hadn't always been what he was now, and sometimes the combative instincts were twenty years old again. Sometimes he didn't have as perfect a rein on his temper at home as he had to have on the job. He tried not to let fly now, made an effort to pat his wife on the shoulder and take a conciliatory tone. "We'll find her, Judy. Just make me a bowl of cereal, will you?" Not that his arm was broken, but Judy needed to do something besides sob and wail, and *she* didn't have any friends she could call for help at 0500h. "No. I'll tell you what you can do to help: go through the clothes she had and if that tee had any figure on it, describe it."

"I'm sure I don't know what's on those wretched black things. I try not to look!"

"Do you know where she'd shop?"

"Decent shops are closed at this hour!"

"Judy, she's not going to go to Hampton's, for God's sake. Do you know any of the shops the kids go to?"

"*No*, I don't know those places!"

"I want my breakfast," he concluded, putting his temper on autopilot, just a steady low-key response she couldn't ruffle. "In an hour, Ernst may have found something. At least he'll be at the office. Meanwhile we'll find out what she's buying. She's in a finite number of places. It's not the apocalypse."

He made his own breakfast while Judy hiked upstairs and went through the closet. As best she could figure, when she came down, it was a gray plain shirt and her makeup kit. Black pants, underwear, black three-strap shoes. Wonderfully descriptive. But Ernst had Kathy's picture, by now, in the hands of every agency on the station, and the card number set to report to security on every use.

He hoped the Earth ship wasn't tapping into station communications, and he feared it was. It wasn't going to look good for him, with a daughter running wild in questionable areas of Outsider fringe society. But it couldn't be helped what they heard.

He had half a cup of caff more. Judy was calling her mother, and the tears had started again. It was 0548h, and he decided it was a good time to go to the office. There was a chance, if Kathy was on the outs with her mother, she might call there to complain. He hoped she would.

"Stay here," he said to Judy, putting on his coat. "In case she calls."

"Where are you going?"

"I told you. To the office."

She wasn't happy. He didn't listen to it. He headed for the door.

"I need you!" Judy yelled at him, and cried.

He couldn't afford to listen. He left, wishing, not for the first time, that he dared actively shut down the ship's probing into station's communications, Earth sipping delicately and routinely at this and that tidbit of people's lives whenever one of their ships docked. He didn't dare prevent it, beyond the fact that the station's automatic defenses and a battery of technicians routinely defended them against some of the best crackers working.

Dammit, this scandal would be a nice mouthful for station gossip.

But what could the Earth ambassador say about it to damn him with authorities on Earth? The governor has domestic troubles with his teenaged daughter? He wasn't the first and wouldn't be the last father in that situation.

He went to the office, not letting himself be distracted, confident that Kathy would use that card, sooner or later—as fast as she could get to a shop.

He didn't use the phone. He reached the office. Ernst had made it in first.

"Any card use?"

"Not yet."

"She's still shopping, then. She goes by Mignette on the street. That's M-i-g-n-e-t-t-e, I have no idea why Mignette and not Katherine, but she likes it." He watched Ernst take notes. "Any news on Denny Ord and Mark Andrews?"

"Denny's in jail for petty theft, still awaiting arraignment. The Andrews boy was sent home."

"Marvelous! Theft? What in hell? No, don't tell me. Let Ord loose and track both of them. I don't care how. Hold it. Are they tapped?"

Ernst called up a record. "Yes."

"Damn." By no means respectable Earther boys. And tap traffic was a lot harder to follow. "Physical tail, then. Go ahead and let them go. Mark their ID cards and get a trace on them. If we're unlucky they'll reform and stay at home. But let's just do this practically. She'll turn up. Have we heard this morning from Mr. Gide?"

"Sleeping, we suppose. Dortland reports no output from that source for the last six hours."

"Good. At least someone's having a quiet night."

"That reminds me. Young Mr. Stafford had a visitor last night. His sister, highly respected in the Trend. We were not able to monitor the conversation. We only observed the arrival and the departure. We're sure the Chairman has other resources."

"Probably actually none of our business, if he hasn't run amok since. Make a note to ask Brazis if the sister is a security concern. Do we have a file on her?"

"She has associates with extremely troublesome contacts in petty crime and among the radicals, but that covers most of the Trend *and* Mr. Stafford. She's a Stylist, no less, very well respected."

"I'm not concerned with Mr. Stafford until 0900h. If my daughter calls, put her straight through. Cup of caff. A sweet roll. Two. I need the energy. Get one for yourself."

"Yes, sir."

He walked into his office, and the office systems powered up. The anoles scrambled, startled by a sudden blaze of light. Their morning was starting early and the gods were annoyed.

Reaux sat down at his desk, head against his hands, eyes pressed against his palms. God, he hoped Brazis didn't pull anything beyond what they'd agreed on.

He hoped Stafford was reliable. Considering what he was, he ought to be. But he didn't like to hear he'd had a clandestine contact last night, when everything else was going wrong.

Ernst came in with the cup of caff and the rolls.

"Dortland is on the case himself," Ernst said.

"Hell, no, I don't want to divert Dortland. Tell him pay attention to Gide and delegate my daughter's case. A teenaged girl, for God's sake. Does it take the top end of station security a whole hour to find her?"

"I'll tell him that, sir. Mark Andrews has supposedly gone home. We're moving to verify that. Denny Ord is released. He's bolted off to the lower levels, toward the Trend."

Andrews had gotten cold feet. Ord had dived for cover in his chosen element. Had Kathy any way of getting that information? She had her phone. He *knew* his daughter wasn't tapped. And her phone would leave a record. But if she was with anyone, and he almost hoped she *was* with someone who knew the district, it didn't seem to be Andrews *or* Ord.

That was a new worry, all on its own.

Ernst left. He sipped a better cup of caff than he had at home. Judy's damn dark roast.

They couldn't afford Dortland distracted. If there was any question about Gide's own legitimacy, they needed to know as much as they could find out. So did the Outsider government, which, if it wasn't in on the matter from the beginning, could become difficult, with any hint of facts hidden from view.

He riffled through reports, chewing sweet roll, washing it down with caff. He had yet to hear anything that could justify Gide's insinuations about the Project taps. And he reminded himself that this whole business of meeting with the youngest tap was Gide's idea, not his, not Brazis's.

So he at least was blameless in any confusion. He hoped he was.

Could some future mission fault him, when Earth missions routinely declined to divulge the reasons for their inquiries?

There was nothing in the reports to create a governmental crisis.

On the other hand, if some utter fool back on Earth was trying to provoke a *casus belli* . . .

0714h.

"We have a credit card use," Ernst came in to report, "and security is moving."

"On?"

"Blunt," Ernst said, not happily.

"Ord?"

"Heading in that direction. The credit card use was a public phone."

She damned sure wasn't phoning home. And she didn't use her phone, clever girl. That she would call Ord, or someone who could contact Ord, wasn't at all surprising.

"If we find her, sir?"

That was a leap of procedures he hadn't made yet. What did he do with his daughter? Talk to her?

Talk wasn't enough at the present juncture of events.

"Take her into physical custody and bring her back to my residence when you find her. Put her under house arrest, and watch the door." He could only imagine what Judy would say about agents out front. And he was afraid Kathy wouldn't go quietly. He flinched at the thought of handcuffs or taser. He didn't want to ruin his relationship with his daughter. He didn't want her hurt. But he didn't want to expose his daughter's youthful follies to Gide's snoopery, or have them made an issue at a level of politics Kathy wasn't ready to imagine.

He sipped the cooling caff and watched the anoles creep about the foliage in quest of the small nuisances that lived below them on the food chain. Top predators in a bubble world. They, like Kathy, were not fierce, on other scales. Like Kathy, they conceived no higher threat in the universe than themselves.

He still loved his daughter. He wasn't sure about Judy this morning. He hadn't been that confident about that transaction for quite a long while. He suddenly reached that conclusion, curiously, without overmuch pain. Like Kathy, Judy had her bubble. It wasn't his. Unlike Kathy's, he knew what Judy's looked like, and he'd been reluctant to live there, from long before he married her.

A governor needed a spouse. Absolutely needed one. That had been the transaction. Earth believed in traditional values. It might be a reconstructed reality, crashed, oh, so many times during the long hegemony, but if it was anything, it was traditional, and it was what people wanted to feel safe.

Damn Gide anyway. Him and *his* traveling environment, as if anything out here was going to wreck Earth's purity. As if the taps were spreading formulae and processes for deadly nanoceles that were going to spread throughout humanity.

"Listen," he'd say, if Gide could possibly listen, "let's just go to the club and have a drink. Let's solve whatever you came here to fix or find. I can tell you nobody's going to do a thing like that. It can't make anybody any money, and money's what drives the smuggling operations.

"Believe me," he'd say, further, if Gide would believe anything he hadn't, himself, experienced, "Concord's still here. Earth's ages come and go, in all this fear of contamination. And we've lived for ages out here, right above the source—we've lived with every fault and failure of the system. We've lived with *ondat* accidents and Movement sabotage, way back in our history, and we survive very handily, still human after ages of exposure, no side effects . . ."

Well, he'd tried to make that point, regarding the gardens. And to keep him out of view of an Outsider populace that experimented on itself in its long personal progress toward remediation. An Outsider populace that was, in general, colorful and in damned good physical shape, give or take the grotesques' bad judgment or bad taste. Illicits *didn't* run rampant on Concord Station, thank you, as much because the populace was educated about their hazards as because station police chased down each and every outbreak. Outsiders weren't a splinter of humanity, some artificial second species. They were healthy, trim, fit, and they still bred true from station to station, or with Earthers, if one was foolish enough. They were in such fit shape it made an honest governor who'd had one too many desserts wish he dared take on a few long-term nanisms to sculpt his own youth back, but never say that to the ambassador. Never admit any such thoughts.

He *had* used short-term nanotech for approved medical reasons. He'd taken the viral treatment to retain his thinning hair. Earth allowed that much for its own citizens.

But those extra desserts were their own protection, weren't they? A Concord governor couldn't afford to look *too* good when one of these types came calling. Unexpected attractiveness, a good-looking middle age, who knew? It might end up as a sin in some secret report.

Three more days. They'd pack Mr. Gide onto his ship and wave him a fond good-bye. And there *wouldn't* be any proof that Project taps were passing technological secrets. The Outsiders weren't fools.

He hoped Dortland moved fast. He hoped they found Kathy before she made a misjudgment that wouldn't *let* him take her back under his roof—before she landed in a hospital bed. If it weren't for Gide, damn him, he'd be personally on Kathy's case. Give him one address where she'd just used that card, and he'd be there. He'd talk to her. He'd take her shopping for some look she could live with, he'd buy her an ice cream the way he'd used to, and they'd reach an understanding about her mother, and her sessions, and so many things, so many issues he'd postponed dealing with, all because he'd tried to take Judy's side and not Kathy's for years.

That had been a terrible mistake. He saw that, now, clear as clear. And he knew what he had to do about it now to preserve the peace. Not a divorce. It was late in his life to create a scandal. But a very different understanding was going to exist in his household.

In three more days, when Mr. Gide's ship was a blip outbound and out of his life.

7

0837H. Procyon dressed in the sober shirt, the solemn coat. Break-fast wasn't sitting any better on his stomach than the 0400h caff had done, and he tried not to think further ahead than he had to.

0842h. He checked the mirror in the bath and had a wild mo-ment's fantasy, as the Old Man had suggested, of calling in sick—sick with something disgusting and of at least a week's duration. The way he felt, he could almost qualify. His head felt fuzzy. He wanted to go back to bed and try for the several hours' sleep he hadn't gotten. But he wouldn't sleep if he did, and he was in it too deep to try to dodge it now.

On the other hand, he promised his bleary-eyed reflection, if he got through early with this interview, he could take this one day, maybe tomorrow, satisfy everybody, make the Director very pleased with him, try to settle the mess with Ardath, and maybe be back where he wanted to be, in his own downstairs office, by the time this ship left port—maybe even late-shift tomorrow if the re-port was what they wanted and if he could keep his eyes open. If he just got through this one day without knocking into politics he didn't want to know about, and lived through the debriefing, then he could tell Brazis all about his sister's visit before Brazis told him. He could put it in the best light, and come out clean. It was all he asked. Just back to the job and no blowup.

He was about to go down to the door when he noticed a blink-ing light on the entertainment unit.

Messages. Physical line. He didn't have Sam report on them—usually they were social messages coming in from that source. He'd get the list when he had time to handle it, see if it was anyone he wanted to talk to. His friends all accepted that he was rotten about messages. It wouldn't be anything.

No. He couldn't stand it. This morning, of all mornings, he had to be sure. He punched the button to get the ID.

His mother.

The anniversary call had ricocheted. The crystal egg and his excuses had, two of them, and nothing had dissuaded her.

Or it could be an emergency. A problem. A health problem. He punched in.

"Jeremy, dear, thank you so much. I know you're busy, but you have to eat. You don't have to bring anything. Aunt Melody is bringing that fruit salad.

"Do you suppose you can get your sister to come? . . ."

God. It was 0858. He had two minutes to get to the lift station. He left the message still playing.

"Down, Sam."

He descended. He walked out his door and lit out of the close at high speed, down Grozny and up Lebeau. He didn't need to run, quite. But he couldn't slow down.

He was out of breath when he arrived at the lift station, so out of breath he leaned a hand against the wall beside the lift call, in among half a dozen others waiting for a car.

One of the crowd was an Earther, in a plain gray suit.

"Mr. Jones?"

"Yes," he said, appalled that the man going through this clandestine charade of code words hadn't bothered to look other than what he was—Earther to the core, and near the Trend.

"We can take the number 4," the man said, punching in a code on the nearest bank. And said, blocking with his hand an annoyed woman who tried to input her own destination, "Sorry. This car is locked. Maintenance."

Damned sure the Earther didn't look like maintenance. He was as conspicuous as a missionary in a Blunt Street bar. Procyon looked a mortified apology at the woman, at two others watching the embarrassing little scene.

The car came. The escort waved him inside. He went, and the escort followed.

The door shut. The car moved.

"I want to see the badge," Procyon said, furious, and the agent reached to his pocket and flashed it. "Up close, please."

The man gave him a slower look at it. The badge had a number, a photo ID, and the governor's seal. James Peter Fordham was the name. The number was 980S. Procyon logged that to memory, leadoff to a day he was sure was going to be excruciating. The Old Man would want detail. He logged every detail to memory, including that number, in case even getting there went wrong.

"Why don't you walk on ahead down the street when we get out and I'll follow you?" he suggested to the cop.

Fordham wasn't, surely, entirely unaware of his appearance. "I'm supposed to take you to an address."

"Just head right, and I'll follow you," he said. "I've no interest in losing you. I'm clearly not Earther. You clearly are. I'm afraid there are already questions." His sister's visit last night loomed like a bad dream. He'd been public, getting into the lift. Someone in the crowd might, worse, know his face. He hadn't been looking around. But he wasn't exactly incognito on the street, and when Earthers came throwing police authority around to get a lift car, it made noise. If anyone had noticed him, gossip would say Procyon had been in a suit a second day in a row and that a government slink had put him in a lift car. And he was going to have to live with it.

Ardath would get up to face her own day, usually noonish. Everybody in her circle might know about his doings by then. If they did, they'd tell her. And damn it, then there'd be another round of chatter and gossip.

She'd follow through with the program they'd agreed on. She'd say he'd been stupid, and that he'd gotten himself in trouble.

But if the governor wasn't more careful than he had been, then the rumor would get out that he'd met with Gide. He hadn't even thought of the timing involved. His sister denied everything, and then the governor's handling of this whole affair let the big news hit the street. He'd be notorious by suppertime. Ardath would have to disown him for real. He might not be able to venture onto the Trend for weeks without drawing comments behind hands, and catcalls in some of his old haunts. It was more than inconvenient. It was a disaster, before the day even started.

And given the meeting with Algol, and Algol's going to his sister with gossip—hell, he didn't know what to do.

The lift took a turn, dived, and zipped along. Probably it would have been common sense to sit down during the gyrations. Fordham didn't, so he didn't.

The blue panel light flashed imminent arrival at their destination. The car slowed to a stop, and Fordham keyed the door open on one of the really high-priced locales—up in the official residencies, near where the governor lived, Procyon guessed, if not in the same neighborhood. He doggedly didn't gawk at the decor, just took in the fancy windowed balconies, every one jutting out further toward the street than the one below, until the green and white hanging plants dripping off those balconies closed in the overhead. He'd seen this place in vids, he realized. It was Concord Street, the heart of the Earther sections. Lights embedded in the tiles came up from the centerline of the deck to make the plants grow. You could walk on those light-circles, and they did, crossing the street, a moment of intense warmth and illumination that came and went, in the heat-budget of this sector. Foot traffic moved slowly along these streets, sparse, concentrated around a handful of corners. No shops. No eateries. Just a handful of clustered gardens and fountains.

They turned down a side street where balconies were slanted in the other direction, and brilliant sim-sun filtered down from above, past rising curtains of vines, sheets of flowers. The plants shed a few leaves and dead petals onto the walk, and a small dome-shaped cleaner-bot idled along, nabbing the recently fallen detritus as prey and reward.

Another turn, to a nook not that different from Grozny Close, except the garden enclosed here held sizable trees. What was truly remarkable to his eye—there was only one door in this whole close, with numerous off-ground windows.

Ultimate luxury, Procyon said to himself. Real privacy. Huge premises and a private courtyard. Could anybody have more than that?

Fordham led him up to the door in question and punched the button. "Mr. Stafford to see Ambassador Gide."

"Alone," the door speaker said ominously. And the door opened.

Fordham, duly advised, stayed back. Procyon took a deep breath and walked into an inside foyer decorated in plants, glass, and polished stone.

The door immediately hissed shut behind him. He hadn't been that worried about his physical safety until he heard that door seal. The governor's man was outside, but he was completely on his own in here. And his heartbeat raced.

He walked forward a few steps, where the foyer gave a view of two side rooms and a hall ahead. He looked to the left. Fancy cream-colored furniture, pale arabesque tilework. Potted palms, each with a growth light.

Machinery whirred behind him. He looked back toward that other room, and met the gold, tear-shaped containment that he'd seen on the news.

"Mr. Ambassador?" Trembling with fear never helped. He took a deep breath and tried a deeper, steadier voice. "I'm Procyon. I'm told you want to see me."

"I do see you." The voice came from the containment, deep and rich in proximity. The machine trundled forward with a soft whirr of gears. So positioned, it occupied the foyer and blocked the way out. "Mr. Jeremy Stafford. Young. Outsider. And of course highly modified."

"Yes, sir." A little nod. He felt a cold regard all over his skin. "That's who I am."

"You certainly look human."

"I am human, sir."

"A point of controversy, where I come from. But all the same, you present a decent appearance." The gleaming gold surface fumed, condensing a fog around it, and acquired blue tones. It deformed, and astonishingly extruded a bubble that became a face, a head and shoulders as large as life.

And it thought *he* was an oddity.

"Procyon. That's the name you prefer, Mr. Stafford?"

"Yes, sir. I rarely use my registry name."

The machine rolled closer. The head was eye to eye with him, now, and he didn't like it.

"You work with Marak. You're his personal observer."

Attack. Straight to the issue. "I can't discuss my work, sir. I'm sorry."

"Well, well, and also working closely with Chairman Brazis."

"I can't discuss my work, sir. I truly can't. I'd like to help you, but there's no way I can talk about that."

"You know the Chairman, and you work directly with Marak. No need to discuss it. We know. We know, for instance, that Marak is in some immediate danger down on the planet. A sea is pouring into a very large basin and he's on a rather precarious neck of land chasing after his missing transportation."

He was disturbed that this creature knew things he didn't—the ship must have gotten into ordinary communication flow, likely from Earther sources—and he was even more disturbed that Marak might be in danger he hadn't known, but he tried not to react.

"I'm sure I have no idea what's going on there at the moment."

"Odd. I do."

The Earther ship was definitely monitoring conversations.

And this Mr. Gide sounded primarily interested in Marak. Why? was the salient question, beyond the obvious, that Marak always had that kind of importance to Earthers, to Outsiders and *ondat* alike.

But for what purpose?

"He's in a difficult position, at the moment," Gide said, "while the land is shaking itself apart. The Refuge would like him to return to camp and wait for rescue. He refuses and seems intent on risking his life. Do you think if you were on duty, you could persuade him to return to camp and accept rescue?"

"I can't discuss my work, sir." He had to use his head, get something *out* of this Gide, and not give anything away. "You haven't created this situation, have you, sir?"

"Cause an earthquake? Split a continent? Hardly."

"I have to take your word."

"Impertinent fellow."

"Not intentionally, sir. If you can do it, if you did do it, I'm curious to know how."

"Are you tapped in? Is that how you say it? Are you tapped in right now, spying for Brazis? Are you asking his question?"

"Not at the moment, no, sir."

The shell moved, a whirr of gears. A hand extruded and gestured toward the elegant reception room, beyond two broad, white-columned arches. "A chair. Do sit down. Make yourself comfortable. Let's talk frankly about the situation down there."

He didn't budge from the hallway, maintaining his avenue of escape. "No, sir. I've said as clearly as I can that I can't talk about it. I know you're comfortable. And I'm comfortable standing."

"Obstructionism can't improve relations."

"I'm not obstructive, sir." He remembered his instructions. "I'd be quite happy to take all your questions and see if I can get permission to answer."

"Permission from the Chairman."

"Yes."

"Not from the governor?"

"I take orders only from the Chairman, sir. Chain of command. I'm here as a courtesy. An offer of good faith."

The arm and hand retracted, resorbed. The face frowned. "Well, let me be honest, and you can relay this to your Chairman. We've heard claims the remediation is actually making progress, that this prospective sea will issue forth new changes, a shallow sea, where life can breed in abundance, flowing out onto the land. That global weather will change, bringing rains to the arid midcontinent."

"I can't talk about that, sir."

"Oh, but I'm sure you've heard such speculations."

"That falls under the job prohibition, sir. I can't discuss it."

"Changing the world. But it might allow nanoceles that may have survived the hammerfall to proliferate and modify themselves again."

"I couldn't predict, sir, but again, I'm not—"

"Yet such nanoceles remain in the environment down there. And up here. Even in you, for instance."

"I don't understand the biology of it, sir. But I'm not like Marak."

"Not immortal."

"Far from it, sir."

"Yet Marak himself and his generation . . . are immortal."

"So far, the nanoceles just keep repairing them, whatever goes wrong. But that's what I hear. I don't know."

"So Marak and his generation now pose one of the chief sources of recontamination in this new remediated world, don't they? Yet we understand the plan is never to do away with them. Is this true?"

"I have no idea about that, sir." All that was, in fact, way over his head. There was no way to scrub out a nanocele. None that he knew about. And terminate Marak, and Ian, and the rest? Unthinkable. "Immortals do die of accident. I understand no few have died."

"Mostly by mental collapse, so I hear. Suicide." The shell moved, started forward, went through that arch between the columns, spun about. "But even given that slow purge of the world, a written archive remains. And a living example of that technology, even beyond Marak and his relatives, in the person of a First Movement survivor with no motive to love her containment. A treasure-house of survivals, and a library with the informational key to its data, all of it in reach of Outsider researchers who *themselves* contain those pre-Hammerfall nanoceles. Is that a good situation? Has that ever been a good situation?"

"I have no idea about such matters, sir." Not a brilliant answer, but it was all he had.

"Listen to me, boy."

"I assure you I'm listening very closely, sir."

"You know it's against the Treaty to lift that technology off the planet. Don't you?"

"I'm very sure it's against the law, sir. I can't imagine anyone doing it."

"What if I were to tell you I can prove your associates in the Project have illegal information? That data of that kind *is* being rescued, illicitly, from the planet?"

"I don't know any such thing, sir." He was cold clear through, half understanding what the man was talking about, as if all the words were there, hanging in the air, but they just wouldn't make sense in the real world. "I don't know about any such thing, but if there is proof, I'm sure the Chairman would like to hear it."

"Are you sure he would? Are you in any position to be sure?"

"Only the position of someone who's grown up here, who can't imagine anybody doing that or wanting to do that for any sane reason. I never heard of anybody smuggling data, sir. I don't think they could, physically."

"Unless it were officially sanctioned."

"I'm sure *not*, sir. Work is monitored to the hilt. I can't think how anything of that sort could ever go on without somebody knowing. Management wouldn't. They wouldn't. There's just too much at stake."

"Oh, a great deal is at stake. You're quite right in that. But we're not necessarily dealing with you and me, are we? Marak dates from the foundations of modern civilization. How do we possibly say we understand him?"

"I can't say anything I know, sir. It's a restricted area."

"Come now, how sane can one remain, in that kind of age? How can memory function? And, older than Marak, the Ila. An individual of questionable sanity and absolutely certain motives for getting her contamination off the planet and back into the universe."

"I don't know that. I don't know any such thing. Marak's sanity is absolutely solid. And I don't deal with the Ila, but she's just—perfectly fine. I've never heard there's any question of her well-being."

"Sane, and immortal. You maintain so, on your personal observation. Do sane, and immortal, possibly go together in any mind?"

He was being backed into a corner. Harried. Distracted. "The *church* says it does. Doesn't it, sir?"

"Blasphemy, Mr. Stafford?"

It was like talking to his father. But you didn't get anywhere with him by backing up and backing up until you had no room at all. "No, sir, I *believe* immortality and sanity can coexist. I'm the one that believes that. Personally."

"You think of Marak as a god?"

"I can't talk about the job, sir. Sorry."

"Nonsense. You've been discussing it. No reason to back off now. You have an intimate, personal acquaintance with one of the most unusual minds alive, and I ask you, *does* he impress you as sane?"

Small breath. "As sane as anyone I know."

"Ah, so you can talk about the job."

"I don't want you to take a misconception away from this interview. I'm sure that wouldn't be useful to you or to the Director, sir."

"So." The face smiled. "Do you like Marak?"

Deeper and deeper. This man was doing exactly what Brazis had warned him about, gathering data by his silences as well as his statements, by the readout of truthers inside that shell. He wanted out of here.

"I'm not appointed to like or dislike anyone, sir. I just do my job."

"New to that job, as I understand."

The predicted direction. The pressure went off. And he didn't dare trust it. "A year or so."

"Two years, precisely."

"Yes, sir, not precisely, but close to two."

"Two years, three months, five days."

"That could be right." God, now it was his life under the microscope. He'd gotten cocky for a moment, and wished now he hadn't.

"I understand Marak himself chooses his contacts. And he chose you. Why choose an absolute novice, do you suppose?"

"That falls under the job classification, sir, and again, I can't say, even if I knew, which I can't say I do."

The machine rolled close to him, the simulacrum maintained at eye level. "So tell me about yourself, if that's more comfortable. A Freethinker, so I hear."

Truthers, he reminded himself, and tried to keep his bodily reaction down. "A teenage curiosity. I quit them after a few meetings. They're fools."

"And Brazis accepted you, with such a background."

"A teenaged notion I rejected. The department put me through all sorts of truthers, and I cleared."

"Did your sister make that personal decision, too?"

His heart rate spiked. He couldn't help it. "She has nothing to do with Freethinkers. They're not in her social circle. I'm frankly amazed, sir, amazed and a little offended that you've researched my family."

"She visited you last night. A sisterly visit?"

"That falls under personal, sir."

"But she did."

"It's my parents' anniversary. There's a family dispute in progress. About a crystal egg."

"I know when you're lying. I know when you're evading me. I know far more overall than you might expect. Tell me—an element of personal curiosity—why Procyon? Why that particular name?"

"I just liked the sound of it."

"Sirius would have been more ambitious."

The greater dog star, Procyon being the lesser, the follower. "Procyon suits me, sir. I never have been an ambitious sort."

"And you live very expensively on the Trend, a young man in such a responsible position, exposed to all sorts of questionable elements that come and go in that district."

"*In* the Trend, sir, that's the term. I live in the fashionable district. You can tell by my clothing that I'm not *in* the Trend. And I haven't talked to anyone about what I do. Even my sister has no idea what my job is."

"Come, come, Procyon. I've come all this way to talk to you. Specifically to talk to you."

"To me, personally, sir, I doubt it. Maybe to the person you think I am, but I'm pretty sure he doesn't exist."

The face smiled benevolently. "Clever young man . . . very quick-witted for your years. I say I know who and what you are. A Freethinker. Ah, pardon me: a former Freethinker. Marak's personal contact. And what more?"

"A former Freethinker. That's all. Long past. Dead issue."

"You say you have no more contact with those people. Yet your sister lives quite intimately with them."

"No one actually *in* the Trend is a Freethinker, sir, that's absolutely contradictory in terms. The Trend is everything the Freethinkers despise, and I assure you, my sister wouldn't touch them with tongs."

"No? I could have possibly mistaken this notion. Inform me how this is."

"I *have* informed you, sir. The Freethinkers are yesterday's items. Last year. They're not well-thought-of these days in the Trend. They've blown whatever cachet they used to have."

"I thought time never changed in this place."

"The Trend changes constantly, sir, it changes by the hour. You've affected it yourself. Believe me, gold and blue will be all the fashion for weeks after you're here. Then those colors will turn utterly déclassé, just that fast, and my sister will probably change her personal color scheme. Everything passes."

"You speak a dead language. Your education, your culture replicate the past, endlessly—Concord in every respect is a living museum. But I forget. An Outsider's personal genetic information is as fickle as his fashion, dare I say? Without change yourselves, does Concord not perpetually traffic in change . . . to Orb, to Arc, to Apex?"

"Concord trades licit change. Not illicits."

"Do you like being modified?"

"It's useful. It's convenient. I'd do it twice."

"And you don't mind being contaminated?"

"I'm not contaminated. They don't pass on."

"Enlighten me. I'm told nanoceles can pass quite easily."

"A mod isn't a nanocele. I'm sure you're aware of that distinction, sir."

"No, no, go on. I'm sure you're going to tell me any moment that you're as human as I am, and that what makes you part of the Project is an ordinary modification."

He confronted a monster, blue and gold and fuming with a cold he could feel, challenging *his* humanity. "About the Project, not a word, sir. But we're all human, if we're not stupid, and if we don't play with illicits. Which no one sane ever does, and those that do end up in hospital to have it cleaned out of them. I promise you, you could set any Concorder down on Earth and your geneticists could never pick us out of a crowd."

"Not true. Concorders are genetically unique."

"Only statistically, sir. Only statistically. Scatter us all across space, and you couldn't pick us out."

"You know that for a fact, do you?"

"It's what I understand to be true, sir."

"And the Freethinkers? Where do they fit in your statistical theory of the universe?"

"The same as the rest of us, if they're not fool enough to take illicits. Some do. Some have. Some are dead. But there's never been a runaway that I've seen, just some bad personal outcomes."

"Freethinkers. Free thinkers. What do they think freely about, young Procyon?"

"Is that a question, sir?"

"It's a question. What did you hear them talking about?"

"Supposedly about issues. Dislike of regulations. Opposition to surveillance. Freethinkers supposedly think for themselves. But they keep electing fools to run them."

"Tell me, what attracted you to them in the first place—back in this forgotten past—if they're such absolute fools?"

"I was sixteen, easily impressed. I didn't know what they were when I walked in. I thought they were, like you said, really free thinkers. They aren't. They don't like certain ideas. Like a job. Like doing anything constructive about a problem. They just sit and talk. I've no respect left for them."

"What did you want them to talk about? What great change would you make in the universe, if you ran things?"

"Not in the universe. Much more modest than that, sir."

"What great plan did you have?"

"Oh, I'd like more libraries. Better free schools. I'd like more free clinics. Better maintenance for the people spinward of Blunt. Then I found out someone actually has to pay for all that happening. So I vote for station improvements whenever there's a referendum, and I pay my taxes fair and square so what I vote for gets funded. That's what I do for civilization. It's slow, but it's more than they're doing."

"Relaxation of import restrictions. How do you feel about that one?"

The eternal Earther worry. "Tax on books and news? No. No tax on creators. No tax on food."

"You're not a free-tax advocate, are you?"

"No. I said I pay my taxes. I believe in taxes." God, he hadn't argued that particular politics since he *was* a Freethinker. It wasn't comfortable ground anymore.

"Illicits do exist here, you say, in the tax-free underbelly of the economy."

He feared he was sweating. He knew his pulse had jumped. "You should ask the police. I don't know about things like that."

"But you live down there. Personally, financially, you can get anything you want."

"I have no idea if I could, but I'm not fool enough to want any illicits."

"What would a fool do, if he did want any?"

"Oh, go shopping among the freelancers, if you want to die young. You can see a few fools walking around on Blunt. Too many lethals. Unintended results. People with common sense don't take just anything they can buy on the street."

"These illicits don't . . . spread."

Naive point. A laugh, from real relief. "Well, they'd be useless if they did. If you didn't have to pay to get killed, there'd be no profit in them. And if you got killed every time, the labs would all go broke."

"Labs here?"

"None that I know of." The honest truth. "I don't think there are any."

"Genetic illegals—as well as illegal nanisms?"

"Both are out there. Biostuff and mechanicals. But nothing originating here."

"Any talk, for instance, of Movement nanisms among these illegals?"

"No." Another pulse jump. Were they back to that? "Absolutely none such."

"Nanoceles?"

"No. Nothing of that nature that I know about. Absolutely nothing."

"You don't know of any leakage coming off the planet."

"Can't. Can't happen."

"They have rockets down there, don't they?"

"Nothing but surface-to-surface. Landing vehicles go down. Nothing comes up. I don't really think I'm qualified even to talk about this, sir."

"Not qualified to tell me about information passed down and up by tap, little secrets committed to record utterly in soft tissue, no eavesdropping possible."

"There's no way," he said, absolutely convinced, though rattled. Surely the truthers wouldn't misread his disturbance as guilt. "No way that's true."

"You do doubt it, then."

"The system isn't like that. I'm appalled anybody would even think it. I don't think you could do it at all. And if you pick up that I'm nervous, sir, I am. You're asking me things I don't know anything about, and I shouldn't have tried to answer you on this topic at all."

"Marak still doesn't get on well with the Ila, does he?"

"I can't say, sir."

"So . . . by what I'm told is current fact . . . Ian risked the second most important person on the planet to go months out into hazardous terrain to set up a relay that one of your surface-to-surface rockets could have landed in a day. Why? Because Marak had rather take a long trip into the wilderness at this precise moment?"

On this he felt far more confident. "Marak does what he wants. If you know anything about him, you know that."

"Is he dodging the Ila this year, perhaps? Is something afoot he'd rather not countenance?"

"I have no idea."

"Mmm. So."

"He took the relays out by caravan, as you seem to know, sir. There was no particular hurry about it. He does this sort of thing. He's done it every few years. We had no way of knowing there'd be an earthquake of this magnitude."

"Yet you knew that there would be, eventually."

"Fairly soon. We knew that. And maybe he hoped to watch the Wall go. I don't know."

"Dangerous, would it not be?"

"It seems it turned out to be."

"Tell me: if there were ever a resurgence of the Movement—where, logically, would they like to be to start with, and what would they like to do?"

"I absolutely have no idea, sir. Movement and Freethinkers aren't the same thing."

"They were once."

"Now they're not."

"Oh, come, now, Mr. . . . Procyon. The Ila is still alive. Memnanan her captain is still alive. All these people of that age are still alive. Therefore—so is the Movement, here, on the planet Concord watches."

Spooked. Spooked and sweating. He couldn't find a reasonable way out of this debate.

Flash of light. Of sound. A tap had gone active. A relay had turned on . . . nothing in the apartment, but maybe in Gide's rig.

Something had just reached out and touched him. Electronically.

He immediately maneuvered to the side, dodging a potted plant, putting distance between himself and Gide.

The machine zipped forward, between him and the door.

"Mr. Stafford. Whatever's the matter?"

"Don't do that," he said. He was shaking, hands trembling, but he stood his ground momentarily, trying to salvage this interview.

"Do what?" Gide asked.

Now he was leaving. No question. He hadn't been Marak's tap for nothing. He knew a dead-end debate when he heard one. He'd heard Marak talking about the Ila, and about Ian. He knew he skirted continually on a volatile relationship that held civilization together, and he knew another determined power when he met it. He was in direct danger. Likely he was being recorded right now on a dozen levels— even the tap was being probed. They'd already gotten way too much from him. Get out, Brazis had told him, if that happened.

"I can't stay here," he said, trying not to show his agitation. "Not when you do that, sir, I'm sorry, and especially not when you deny it." He remembered his instructions, what he had to do. "I'll report to my office, and if you want me to come back, maybe, but only if they say so. I'll get clearance for your questions before I say anything else."

"I won't wish you good-bye," Gide said. "Tell them, among other things, that they *want* me to ask my questions. If I don't get answers, it could be the worse for this place. Tonight. Tonight at 1800h, you'll come back."

"I'll tell them," he said, and headed past Gide, for the door.

The shell trundled close behind him. He hit the door switch frantically to get out.

"The door's on *my* lock," Gide said. "Do you want out, Mr. Stafford?"

He didn't answer. Didn't trust himself to answer.

He heard the lock click. He hit the switch again and the door opened.

An explosion slammed him back, off his feet, skidding on his back on the polished tiles. Shock had hit all the way to bone and brain even before he slammed into one of the pillars.

Smell of burning metal. Absence of sound. Hazed view of blinking lights and something gold moving. Gide had shot him, he thought in shock, scrabbling after leverage to escape. The outside door was still open, past his feet. He scrambled to get his knees under him, and his hands slipped on the tiles, something fluid soaking his knee. Acrid fumes stung his nose and eyes. His hand came down on something sharp, and he felt the pain.

Sharp metal. A few feet away, Gide was over on his side, a living human body wriggling out of its gold shell and bleeding onto the tiles.

Gide hadn't shot him. Gide himself was shot, struggling to get out of his confinement, injured, mouthing soundless words. Procyon stumbled up, dragged the man clear of the fuming plastics and torn metal of the shell.

Gide writhed around and struck at him, wildly shouting something that had no sound, no sound at all.

Angry at him. Blaming him. But he couldn't hear anything the man said. Just the ringing in his ears.

He couldn't stand here. He couldn't be swept up by the police. He didn't know what he decided in the next few seconds, but he found himself out in the garden. And after that he was running down the street outside, past scattered shocked onlookers in this exclusive district. He tried to tap in to reach Project offices, but when he tried a pain lanced through his eyes, and he stumbled half to a stop.

Couldn't do it. Couldn't call for help. He just ran after that, and Earthers being Earthers, people just stared at him without trying to stop him.

He reached a lift station and called a car, and the woman who arrived in it got out in a hurry and let him have it to himself. He programmed it for the Project offices and didn't sit down, just hung on to the bar and hoped the police wouldn't be fast enough to stop it.

The next thing he knew, he was walking sedately down a street nowhere near Project offices. He was outside Caprice's, and why he was there, he couldn't figure. His coat looked like hell. He brushed flecks of spattered plastic and white ash off his sleeve, but it smeared, and he took the coat off and dropped it on a bench along the frontage.

This wasn't at all where he'd tried to go. There were blank spots in his mind. He couldn't remember how he'd gotten here from the lift, but he saw his reflection in the shop windows. He looked like hell, and he kept walking, thinking vaguely he had to get home, and he was supposed to buy a present, and call his parents, and keep Ardath happy. But he couldn't be conspicuous, walking around like this, deaf to the whole street.

There was one route safer than the rest, for somebody who looked this bad, duck out of public view down the service alley, beyond Caprice's frontage. That was safe. That led back—wherever he had to go.

To his neighborhood, at least, eventually.

He had a splitting headache. He took his hair loose as he walked, hitting one elbow and then the other against the narrow walls of the service slot, but undoing the clip didn't help his head.

He heard a buzzing on the tap, first sound he'd heard since . . . since he couldn't remember. The office, he thought. He tried to tap in, but he couldn't sustain the contact. He knew he'd done something wrong. That he shouldn't be here. Whatever had hit him, he didn't belong in the service alley.

Headache stabbed behind his eyes and made his nose run. He wiped his face, forgetful where he was going, at the moment, but he was sure if he kept walking he'd come out in familiar surroundings, and if he got home he could sit down, and if he could just sit down a minute, then he'd remember what he was supposed to do.

EARTH WOULDN'T BE AMUSED, Reaux well knew, to find out that the governor's daughter was skipping from shop to shop in the Trend, growing less and less like Judy's daughter in the process. He knew that she'd had lunch for two at La Lune Noir, where Dortland's agents had just missed her—that fact had Reaux's blood pressure already at max. Highest security in the universe, that at Concord, and a fifteen-year-old with a hot credit card gave Dortland's best operatives the slip on a shopping binge.

And she'd, yes, been *with* someone, God help him. He hoped it was no worse than Denny Ord, who was only amateur trouble. At least she wasn't alone.

But he couldn't take time to stay with the succession of reports until they actually turned up something. He'd taken one anguished call from Judy in the hours since he'd gotten to the office, and since then claimed to be in a chain of meetings, when, in fact there was only one meeting the outcome of which he ached to know, that between Procyon Stafford and Mr. Andreas Gide.

So long as Gide's ship was attached to the station, he had to assume his office phone was tapped. He'd asked Judy to keep off the phone with the family crisis, so Judy had wanted to go to her mother's. That meant her mother would be on the phone, what time she wasn't listening to Judy. And the media was still lurking.

No, he'd said. Stay put. If Kathy comes home, be there.

And did Judy do what he asked? No.

He'd told Ernst, long since: "If Kathy calls, put her through immediately."

Dortland's reports said at least two off-station interests and the local Freethinkers had attempted to hack the physical lines in the last twelve hours—but Gide's ship had actually succeeded, and succeeded with more than the phones, delving into things Earth government had no business meddling with, before bumping up against the separate system that was the Outsider network.

There was, Dortland had reminded him, a Council agent on the station, who'd been reporting to Brazis, but who might be independent and without Brazis's knowledge. Did they think now, with this ship here, that this presence was coincidence? Maybe that was what Gide was really after.

And Judy called him, crying that *she* was suffering stress.

"Sir." Ernst opened the door in person—rare he did that. His face was white. "Sir. The ambassador's been attacked. Shot, along with the security team. Our two men are dead."

Shot? My God.

While Ernst stood there awaiting a sane directive from him, and he didn't have a clear thought, not for half a dozen heartbeats.

"Gide's alive?"

"He's alive, sir. Headed for Bonaventure Hospital, as the nearest. Mr. Dortland's going up there right now."

"I'm going." It was the worst imaginable disaster. It was political, personal ruin. He couldn't think straight. "Brazis's man? Stafford. Where is he?"

"He wasn't named in the report, sir. He may have been there at the time. Or not. That's all I know."

"Call Brazis. Tell him what's happened. Tell him—hell. Tell him I'll talk to him when I know something. Ask *him* where his man is. Get a search out for anybody out of district."

"That's under way, sir. I'll call an escort for you."

"Armed escort didn't protect the ambassador, did it?" He was putting on his coat, and Ernst dived back to his desk, to call the security office. He was going to have his escort, like it or not.

If things were going to hell, rule one, the government had to stay functioning. He couldn't abdicate the investigation to that ship out there or they'd start grabbing more and more power. The tripartite authority on Concord demanded that not happen, for the sake of the peace they maintained.

He walked through Ernst's office, on his way out. "Call the advisory board into session. All police to duty."

"Yes, sir," Ernst said. "Escort is on the way, sir."

"Call the *Southern Cross*. Advise them there's been an unexplained incident, connect them to my handheld if they want to talk to me, personally, isolate the crime scene, and tell them we're doing everything we can for the ambassador. Tell Dortland I'm coming. No. Cancel that last. Phone lines aren't secure. Just call the ship. Get the translation staff all to duty: tell them prepare something, some explanation for Kekellen, fast, before he hears about this, do you hear?"

"Yes, sir."

He fastened his coat and walked out through the outer foyer, not surprised when four plainclothes security agents turned up somewhat breathlessly in his path and fell in with him.

"Bonaventure Hospital," he told them. "Get me a priority through the lifts."

"All secure, sir," the senior said.

It might be the only thing on Concord that was.

PROCYON WAS OFF visiting some lord and had not returned. Three quakes had shaken the rocks in the last short while and sent pebbles and sand-slips cascading off the plateau.

Auguste, meanwhile, reported a panorama Marak ached to see—the two streams spurting out of the Halfmoon cliffs had joined, ripping out rock, forming one great waterfall in the midst of the Southern Wall, and a deepening pool at the bottom. A cloud of spray obscured the lower view from the heavens. But Auguste said it was a great deal of water coming in . . . and when the rock above it failed, as it was likely to at any moment, it would be a sudden, cataclysmic flood.

So here they were, he and Hati, patiently negotiating the alternate descent of their terrace, with a sea forcing its fingers through a barrier to the west, threatening to become a waterfall of unimaginable proportions.

Right now their new sea, so Auguste assured them, was only a spreading line of damp going out from that pool, saturating sand dry for millions of years. The pans would soak up a great deal of salt water and battered sea life as that shallow pool spread. The volume of inflowing water had tripled in one day. It could magnify a thousand-fold without much warning, that was the worse problem, and if the worst happened, *then* how fast did they need to climb the terraces?

Auguste said he would get back to him with that answer.

The eyes in heaven had other, more pragmatic uses. The watchers on high had spotted their runaways down midway, stopped on what might be a plateau with no safe way further down. That might be good news. Topologists in the heavens were trying to plot a reliable route for them to reach that site, as well as mapping a safe path up, and meanwhile the beshti were busy eating the green growth down there. The young bull might try even an impossible slope, if he spooked; but he would delay to move the females, and the females, already run hard, would grow less and less inclined to move from lush graze and run again.

Their base camp, up on the spine, Auguste had reported, luxuriated in hot tea and a leisurely morning. Their radio link had Fashti in contact with the Refuge, now that the relay was up and working. Meziq was in less pain today, and had nothing to do but sit, be waited upon, and heal, in their enforced wait. Fashti sent regards and wished them success, saying that they were all eating well.

"The rascal," Hati said, when Marak told her that. She had banished her own watcher's chatter in frustration, during the last shiver of the land. Ian himself was proving a nuisance, this morning, arguing with Auguste that the heavens should not spend any effort to offer them a path to the beshti, which only encouraged their adventure. They should not go down farther, Ian argued. Auguste, however, agreed with them, that there might be time, even yet, to get the beshti back and give them a fast route off the spine, which—Auguste hinted—might not be that stable, once the flood reached it.

Auguste had said meanwhile that Procyon was still engaged, that he, Auguste, intended to stay on duty through this shift and half of Drusus's. That Brazis would give his watchers both a few hours' sleep, leaving only Hati's watcher on duty during the coming night.

Another shaking began. The beshti stopped where they were, and their riders bent down low to the saddles, to lessen the strain of a high load on the long-legged beshti's balance.

"Husband!" Hati exclaimed, pointing straight ahead, as—at first silent, hazy in the distance—a section of the towering cliff face gave way, an immense promontory splitting from the ridge above and falling, falling down to the next terraces, where its ruin provoked a tremendous landslide and carried a plume of dust all along its course.

That might have been above their heads. They were lucky.

On the other hand, it might have spooked the beshti below them into another run.

Marak stole a look up, not his first, as he had watched for cracks and flaws in the rocks of the cliffs above them. They had avoided one easy-looking descent as unstable. Harder, however, to judge the terrace directly underfoot. Hati was curt with her watcher's renewed attempt to question her, in no mood to give a detailed description.

He, himself, had far rather Procyon's modest silence, at the moment, than Auguste's worried questions. And if, on the other hand, he ever wanted information from Auguste, that cautious watcher always said wait, he would find out. What he knew was never enough: he always wanted to ask the absolute latest before telling him a damned thing.

"*Do you judge it safe to continue?*" Auguste asked of him, however, wavering in his support.

"Safe? Do we seem to be fools? It is by no means safe with the cliffs coming down, but our other choice is no better."

Not wise to berate Auguste into silence. He was usually more patient than that. He was running out of resources, he was down to two watchers. And he had no wish to drive Auguste and Drusus toward Ian's side of the argument.

"Forgive me." He wanted a favor from Auguste and decided not to antagonize the man. "No, we are not in a safe place at the moment." They urged their nervous beshti into a judicious descent down a sandy stretch. Beneath his left foot, in the crook-legged posture in which one sat a saddle, he had empty air. A cloud of dust still lingered where the section of cliff had come down, the last of the ruin just now reaching the basin floor.

Let the oncoming flood begin to saturate the ground, however slow its advance, then more of the cliff might come down. He foresaw that event, looking very differently at the ridge above and around them. The watchers aloft could not see the rocks as they were, split with ancient cracks, sandstone that had resisted wind and rain, but which might not resist saturation, basalt layers which occurred in natural pillars, already fractured, that strong current could carry apart. Seawater rising and lapping about the base of these cliffs could seep through cracks, eating toward the spine to the layered rock of the Needle Gorge itself, so that this might not be the future shore—only a half-drowned island.

The rock fall and its earthshaking thunder played over and over in memory. He felt an unaccustomed fear, and thought that, on this occasion, Ian could have been right about the rocket, but Ian was not right now. Ian and his trucks or an arriving column of riders could not be fast enough to rescue them.

And knowing that Ian and Auguste were likely engaged in debate on his case, he did what he rarely did: he tapped into the dialogue.

"*Marak,*" Ian said, recognizing his arrival. "*Where are you now?*"

"I thought you knew."

"*In general, yes, well down off the ridge, not taking advice from anyone. Give up this chase, Marak, in all friendship. Your position is growing far too precarious.*"

"Once the sea arrives, very much too precarious. This whole expanse of cliffs is fissured and apt to give passage to water going toward the gorge, Ian. A section of the cliffs just gave way in the last quake. All our arguments aside, we are not safe here. We need the beshti now to get ourselves and the boys out of here, back toward the Plateau."

A small silence. Ian was considering his argument. "*If it's that dire, go down now, do you hear me? I can send a plane to the basin.*"

"I have young men waiting up on the rim."

"*If you need rescue that badly, Marak, you and Hati. I can save you. If it comes to that. Don't refuse the thought. I can get you out, if you don't wait too long . . . or divert yourselves in a useless chase. Go straight down now. I'll send a caravan after the others. But get yourself and Hati out.*"

Hati's danger was, Ian knew damned well, the thought hardest for him to bear. He was hardly subtle.

"Save your plane, Ian. We shall find the beshti and get us all off the ridge, quite handily. Auguste has promised us a safe trail along the terrace. It saved us being in the path of a landslide just now."

"*A rocket is going out within the next hour to deliver our reserve relay to Halfmoon.*"

Doing what they had failed to do. What he had argued against, months ago. "I truly wish it luck."

Luck, which a soft-landing in that place certainly needed. They had as well drop it from a height.

"*It's a spectacle out there, Marak, a long, long waterfall that ends in a plume of spray. I have the transmissions from Concord and the satellite. I hate to say, if you had stayed here and gone by plane in the first place, you might have both seen it and gotten pictures.*"

Ian tormented him. Ian had to make his point, even now, while he had empty space beneath his left foot and little sand-slips sliding down from every step the beshti made.

"Send out your rocket," Marak retorted, and let fly his own annoyance. "Send your plane to the Wall and get your pictures. You were right, Ian, I entirely admit it. We shall not be there to see it. We are here, on the face of this cliff, which is our just reward. But we deserve more help than we have gotten from the heavens in the last two days, do you hear me, Ian-omi? Now Brazis is saying Hati's watchers will give Drusus relief tonight. By noon, tell Brazis so, I wish all my watchers back as they were. This is not a moment to indulge some foreign lord's whims, and the threat to our camp does not take the night off because two men are tired. I ask you make this clear to him, Ian."

"*Marak, be patient.*"

"Is there reward for us in patience? We had little warning of this event. Where was my warning, Ian? Was all-seeing heaven perhaps distracted from watching us, while it was watching this foreign lord?"

"*You know the difficulties of prediction. Your position is between us and the epicenter.*"

"Excuses, Ian."

"*You cannot argue with physics.*"

"I *can* argue with distraction and delay of information." He grew angry much more slowly than Hati. He took far longer to let it build, but here, on this slope, after the ruin that had cascaded down to the basin, and with the gnawing thought that if he had managed better, and used Ian's damnable wire-cored rope, he would not be chasing the beshti, his temper was very near the boiling point. "I find it remarkable that when we should have had some slight warning, Brazis was busy reassigning my watcher to this foreign lord, and he either has not explained to Drusus why this is, or has told Drusus to lie to me, promising me Procyon's return soon, soon, soon, which has not happened yet.—Are you listening, Auguste? Ask Brazis when we will have his full attention."

"*Sir,*" Auguste protested.

"Do you wonder the same, Ian? Or do you by any chance *know* what Brazis is up to?"

"This is a major event at Halfmoon. A great many people have been distracted from routine. A great many people have changed shift."

"Give me no excuses. I have every confidence in Drusus and Auguste and Procyon. But less now in Brazis, who seems to believe earthquake and flood will not happen once the sun goes down. Tell him what I say, Ian. Ask him why the heavens were sleeping when the quake came. Five seconds' warning would have averted this. Heaven has eyes and ears to see an event as it happens, anywhere in the world. The beshti foreknew it. Where were the watchers? Why were we caught by surprise?"

"Because they have no ground sensors at Halfmoon. They relied on us to get them there."

That stung. It was even possibly right. But he was not willing to back off his argument. "They have their lasers. They measure the earth. They keep their watch. I want better information."

"They will have better information soon. Our warning margin has greatly improved with the new relay. It will become much better with the next."

"Granted your rocket survives."

"I have a greater concern for your survival, Marak. You and Hati are far too valuable to risk. Give up this folly. The beasts may come up to the camp on their own once they see the water advance."

"The forecast, have you heard, is fog and rain. The terraces are a maze. The water is coming, the cliffs are apt to give way, and if the beshti have any sense, they will take out running, away from the flood and away from us, across the pans. They may even make it, but we may not, without them. I do not choose to go up to camp without trying and hope for the cliffs not to fall down, Ian. I do not, to be honest, trust your planes. Sometimes they fail to take off, once they land in that much dust. And never suggest to me that we abandon those boys in camp and get ourselves to safety."

"As a last resort, Marak. If you should be trapped. I shall send a plane out, when the flood comes nearer, as a last resort."

"We are not that far from the beshti." This was not quite admitting that their fugitives were well down on the next series of terraces and out of sight. "Another day, Ian. No need of your airplane or the risk to the pilot. The water is coming, but it is not coming that fast."

"Not coming that fast yet, Marak-omi."

"Only give me heaven's undivided attention and all my watchers, Ian!"

"I promise you, I promise you I shall talk to Brazis about the situation. Do what you can."

"Do this. Call my camp. Advise the boys leave the other relay, pack up only essentials and short canvas, and move back down the ridge. Tell them move day and night, by what stages they can, and stay in touch by hand radio. If we have to overtake them well to the east, so much the better."

"You agree you will not attempt to continue this mission to the Wall."

"I admit it. I admit it, Ian. I know it pleases you greatly. I shall gather the boys and retreat to the Plateau."

"I'll call them with that instruction. Meanwhile, Marak, in all good regard—take care. Don't take chances. And remember the airplane."

"I hear." Broken sandstone from the edge rolled down the sandy face below him. But the footing looked solid, and led out onto unfissured rock. His temper improved, the ledge proving solid. He had made provision to get the boys to safety. He had admitted to himself and to Ian that they were not going on from here, no matter if he recovered the beshti in the next hour. "Keep me advised, Ian. And, mind, tell Brazis, in the strongest terms, better warning, and no more excuses."

HAIR, NAILS—Mignette wanted a makeup tattoo, but she couldn't make up her mind about the style or the shade, so she tried out a look instead, glowy green cat-eyes—she'd gotten cosmetic contacts—and a slinky black bareback blouse with fringe that sparkled. Soft boots that matched the blouse. Deep red hair with blazing coppery highlights.

And she felt good. She felt *good* and alive for the first time in her whole life. Noble liked what he saw, no question, and they linked hands and walked down the Trend, part of the scene.

They were quiet, compared to some. She studied the nodding plumes she saw, wondering how much, and where, and if she dared be that extravagant immediately. The Trend could be cruel. Though there was something to be said for daring.

But they passed for Fashionables, now, she and Noble, and she was really, truly, classy Mignette, who didn't overdress, who, if anything, kept it understated and dark, except the dramatic eyes, the shagged hair with the V-cut bangs. She'd tentatively begun a Look of her own, and she was increasingly sure it would be black, with green eyes. Maybe she'd do the hair deepest black, then. She hadn't decided. She was Mignette, but when she became a Stylist she might become Minuit, *midnight*, with pale skin—she'd change her complexion—and deep black dress, because most of the Trend didn't have her looks, and simple was best. Her face was pretty enough not to need the shapers that turned so many people just too pretty and too regular to really carry a Style. Black was inexpensive, compared to matching colors. She'd learned that from the education she'd gotten. So she could have quality on not too extravagant a budget. She'd be Minuit. As for Noble, he was trying to afford a treatment to get rid of all his freckles. He'd be far different without them, and maybe not better. She couldn't imagine Noble without freckles, but that was what he wanted most, aside from fixing his nose and his chin and getting a fancy tap. He'd be creamy-pale, kind of an interesting face, if he got what he wanted, because his forehead was low, and his natural eyes were pale blue. That meant he could wear all kinds of contacts, down to dark, which he had on at the moment. He had on sexy black pants that showed off really good legs. A good silk shirt. He had nice, high cheekbones, from the start. If he went on, he wouldn't be just Noble. He'd become Somebody, if he could maintain a good, clear imagination of what the shapers could do, and stuck to it, with real quality, no matter how he had to piece-meal the work.

Meanwhile they walked to the same music and watched the traffic where they walked, awed by the occasional Stylist, amused by those who tried to manage a Look, not that successfully.

A gang of juvvie sessions-dodgers watched them pass, wide-eyed. "Look at that," one said. And, in awe: "Look at the *eyes*."

They talked about *her*, not about Noble, who'd had far more practice down here, shaping a Look. Her first venture, and they talked about her, as if they might want to go buy the same item, even if it would be a disaster on their scrawny pale faces. They'd do better to buy mods to fix their blotchy complexions and give up greasy snacks.

But she was *born* with good genes. She could get away with things. Her mother always said so.

And people down here who didn't know she was her father's daughter and important for who she was born to be—they just liked what they saw of Mignette, who was all on her own, with Noble, who was looking for Random, who was Mark, who'd phoned that he'd dodged out again, Tink, who was Denny, still being with the youth authorities, Random supposed, though incorrectly—they'd had one contact with Denny, who was lying low.

But at the moment Random was living up to his name, and they hadn't found him, constantly just missing him, so the phone calls indicated. They were afraid to stay on too long. She was sure her parents were having the phones traced, so they used Noble's card, but they didn't press their luck.

They turned up Blunt Street, which they'd searched before on their intermittent quest. When they found Random, Noble said he would know him, being pretty sure at least what his Look would be, and Random could recognize Noble and probably even recognize her, expecting at least something different.

So they just walked the street, still flush with finance. She had her card, and, just the way she'd figured her father, he'd gone all softhearted and extended credit bit by bit to his one and only daughter, worrying how she'd get along. He'd go on extending it. He'd hope she'd call. She would, tomorrow.

Papa needn't worry. Noble said he had a friend who'd let them sleep over in a safe place, upstairs of Michaelangelo's.

She was going to do it with Noble tonight, if they didn't find Random. With Noble, who was older than she was. She really was going to do it, if they turned up alone in a room in Michaelangelo's, and she thought maybe Noble wasn't *that* anxious to find Random, having ideas of his own. She knew just how it would play out. She'd made a few decisions for herself. Finally. And her mother couldn't stop her.

8

BLOODY HELL, was Brazis's opinion of the entire damnable situation. He sat at his desk and punched physical keys on one of two secure consoles that could direct and redirect the taps. He more than canceled the security hold on Procyon's tap code: he keyed through a general permission, any relay, any contact, anybody that could possibly get hold of him, all over the station, was open to Procyon's code.

They had a complete blowup on the Gide affair. Gide was in hospital by now, and Procyon, who'd been an eyewitness, hadn't answered since the incident.

In desperation he tapped in on Drusus, waking him from off-schedule sleep. "Drusus. Procyon's in trouble. I need someone who can physically recognize him to get out on the street right now, find him, and walk him home."

"Yes, sir," Drusus answered muzzily. *"But I'm supposed to go on at noon."*

"Don't quibble. Auguste can handle it. Just go. Fast. Procyon may be injured. Fifth level, sector 4, section 15, headed toward Blunt, for a start. He's not answering his tap. The finder works only intermittently. He's taken some sort of damage. There was apparently an explosion."

"Explosion, sir?"

"Don't ask. Just go."

The whole Project stood on its ear. Interfering with Marak's taps wasn't what he'd like to do, especially now, and he knew Marak was outraged and they would have to calm that situation down, but Drusus knew Procyon socially: Auguste didn't. Drusus knew Procyon's body language—stood a chance of finding him on a crowded walk, which his other sources hadn't done in half an hour of trying. He had three reliable men out looking, now contacting Procyon's sister, Procyon's parents, Procyon's known friends, to advise them where to call if he needed help and contacted them—but Procyon didn't know any of those agents, and neither did the sister, who might deliberately misdirect them, thinking to protect her brother.

His best hope now was that Procyon might not run from Drusus.

"Sir."

He read the incoming signal. Jewel. Tap-courier, assigned to tail Governor Reaux. He'd just asked her to approach Reaux, who'd gone to the hospital where they'd taken Gide.

"I'm with Governor Reaux now, sir."

Shift of mind. Fast. "Are you secure?"

"Yes, sir. I'm at the hospital, in a secure area. He's anxious to talk to you."

"Good. How is Gide?"

"Alive." Jewel had amped, at the risk of a painful whiteout. Reaux's living voice came through at near ordinary volume. *"Where's Stafford? Have you got him?"*

"I'm trying to find him at this very minute. He didn't have anything to do with this attack. We're afraid he's injured or worse, that he's been snatched."

"Who did it? Who attacked the ambassador?"

"It assuredly wasn't us, Governor."

"It assuredly wasn't my office. And I'm sure Earth didn't try to assassinate its own representative."

"Stranger things have happened, Governor, in recorded history. But let's assume mutual innocence. That leaves us dealing with radical groups, yours or mine. My office is scrambling to find out about the ones on our list. In the meantime, I have a physical search out after Mr. Stafford, in case he's gotten away on the street. He may be injured, and it's possible your police search is spooking him to run. Call off your dogs. Let me find him. I have various people searching."

"I have an armed ship out there asking questions I can't answer. I have inquiries from Kekellen."

"I have no doubt. Count this office a third alarmed source, equally perplexed. What's Mr. Gide's condition?"

"A glancing wound to the ribs. Shock. Hysteria. Some inhalation damage. It's not the physical wound, understand. That's relatively minor. But his containment was breached. He can't go back to his ship. Ever. He insists Stafford set up the attack. The security guards are both dead—hit with neuronics, I'm told. They didn't have a chance."

"Stafford has no weapon. Penetrating the mobile unit can't be a handheld proposition. Neuronics isn't a street weapon. We're climbing the ladder to more than the usual criminal element, Governor."

"An armor-piercing shell. We found its launcher in the bushes, no prints, bioerase strong in the area, no trace left for the sniffers."

"All professional skills. Well-financed skills."

"How can I be sure they weren't yours?"

"Not mine. Not Procyon's, I assure you. I have no interest at all in blowing up the ambassador. Procyon doesn't even know how to fire a gun, let alone a launcher. Any evidence within the mobile unit?"

"Slagged. Slagged, completely, likely a command from the ship. If Gide hadn't gotten out of it—"

"Kind of them, though I can understand it. So they'd have killed him if he were still lying there unconscious. Neat and tidy, isn't it?"

"I don't like this. I don't like it at all."

"I'm not fond of it either, let me assure you. His shell was breached, and they didn't give a damn whether he lived or died. Can my people get access to that unit, slagged as it is?"

"I don't know. I don't know its status at the moment." Reaux sounded completely rattled. Likely he wasn't lying about his being out of touch with elements of the situation, not having the advantage of a tap, and had no idea what disposition his police had made of the unit. *"I'll try to find out."*

"I'll try to find Stafford in the meanwhile."

"While I have a ship out there questioning whether it can believe my office in any particular."

"That ship has no choice but take your word for what happens here, since its precious occupants won't come on board station, will they? They can threaten. But they won't use the ship's guns on Concord with the *ondat* sitting here, assuming they're not stark raving crazy."

"No, but they can use agents embedded in the population."

Threatening Reaux's life. "So can we, if they try. We can defend ourselves, and we extend our protection to our governor. Breathe easy. They don't want that kind of trouble. We're not an easy target."

"Antonio—" Quieter. Realizing, perhaps, the enormity of the promise he'd just extended. So law-abiding. So careful, this governor. Reaux would never think of defying assassins sent after him . . . not to the extent of having them shot on strong suspicion.

His agents certainly would take care of such a problem, if he spotted it. "Is Mr. Gide conscious at the moment?"

"I think he's under sedation."

"Get to him. Wake him up. Talk to him. Convey my extreme sympathy for his situation and make him believe it. Suggest it was some underworld agency, hitherto unsuspected, which probably covers the situation entirely. I'll send a personal letter to him and another to the ship out there, expressing my outrage at this situation, my intent to cooperate with them through your office, my intention to preserve peace and tranquillity on the station, all the appropriate phrases. Which also happen to be the truth, if they're listening. Find out what the ambassador's really been tracking. Why he came here. Our key to what we're facing is very likely in that."

A small silence. Then: *"Antonio. Antonio, I confess I may already have your answer. Gide said—Gide told me he was tracking the possibility of banned information escaping the planet. Via the taps."*

Brazis drew a deep breath. The universe reconfigured itself. "Well, that's an old one. What makes him suspect so? What information does he have?"

"Apparently something about First Movement tech and the Ila, something about nanoceles getting off the planet."

"Not the case, I can tell you." He was disappointed. Frustrated. "You knew this was the nature of it? And didn't say? Setha, Setha, I'd hoped for more honesty."

"I knew it only after I led Gide to his apartment. I didn't count on it becoming critical information, at least . . . at least yet, and by no means after this fashion. I believed your young man could get through the interview if he was innocent. A misjudgment on my part. A complete misjudgment. I hope you can understand, Antonio. I thought we had time to work this out. At this point—I can only apologize for the situation."

He could understand Reaux's holding back information at Gide's request. A man with a constituency to protect was honorbound to protect those core interests against his allies as well as his enemies. Reaux had believed if he kept things quiet, he might find out something, and have a chance to sort this out.

But now he had a crime on his doorstep and the real possibility of a major blowup in international politics.

Maybe it was an intended outcome. Gide wasn't the only Earth-based interest that might have an agent or two loose in the governor's territory. He hesitated to suggest Earth as the culprit in assassinating its own representative, but the high-priced tech involved suggested very ample funding and concealment, far beyond the usual underworld operation.

"Setha, my friend, I understand your reticence. But now that we're in this very delicate situation, believe me absolutely on this one: there is no First Movement tech, informational or otherwise, that has ever escaped the planet—not to my knowledge, and I sit on all the conduits. If there is anything loose, I don't think it originated here. *Why* did Gide pick this particular tap to interview about this problem? Does Earth particularly suspect him of passing information?"

"The Freethinker connection. He was a Freethinker. They don't like that."

"Is that where they think the problem has its base? Among the Freethinkers?"

"You know his sister visited him last night. Clandestinely. I think Gide could have found that out. I know that contact would be suspect."

"I knew. You know. They know. I'm sure any interested party alive knows by now she went there. It wasn't the brightest damned thing Procyon's ever done, but it didn't seem to be his idea. He threw her out and kept his conversation more or less honest, and I know precisely what they said. Do you?"

A pause. *"My intel isn't that specific."*

"Mine is, I assure you. I'll go over that transcript again, but I don't recall any part of it that could implicate him or her in any nonsense among the taps. Gide could have asked for the *Ila's* taps if they'd thought something underhanded was going on."

"I don't think they'd want to touch her off."

"Touch off is a fair description. But do they think bothering *Marak's* is without consequence? Tell Gide that the Outsider Chairman is as interested as they are, if they've got any solid information about a breach of security regarding First Movement tech. But I doubt it. It's the oldest crock in the book. It surfaces periodically. I strongly doubt it."

"I'll relay that if I can. If I can find a politic way."

"You say you've heard from Kekellen this morning?"

"He's asking what Gide wants and about activity in the systems."

"Their damned probes." He wiped his face, trying to think. Dealing with Kekellen required an extreme mental shift, a maze of do's and don'ts, and consequences far more alarming than an ambassador in a hospital bed. "I trust you to handle it. You're the associated party." Coldly put, meaning he didn't want his own administration in any way dragged into question. Let Earther authorities answer Kekellen's queries about these goings-on. "Meanwhile, get all your people off my man's trail. He's got orders to report to me to debrief. He will as soon as he can. But it's very likely he's going to run if you're behind him. And, not to cast a pall on our working partnership, but I have to assure you, just for the record, that you don't want the trouble that will follow if you do lay hands on him and don't tell me. That's not a threat. It's a fact of my administration. I can't stress enough how serious that is. If anyone has laid hands on him, I *will* take action."

"The law moves under its own direction. He's a material witness, at very least, in something that impinges on our constitutional authority. He has to give us at least a statement to satisfy procedures. That ship out there—"

"That's all well and good, you and your constitution. But don't arrest him. We'll get the truth out of him. We'll share it, and you'll get your statement. Chasing him is a waste of your police time, while the actual perpetrators may be running loose up there in your areas, armed. If they're not our domestic sort, I'll be frank about it, I'm concerned you're the next likely target on their list."

"*I take that as a friendly wish.*"

"It is. I assure you, we did not do this. We would never put a tap in reach of your authority if we had arranged this. There are people we would risk. *Not* a Project tap. That's a fact you can rely on."

A pause. "*Antonio? I think I know what Gide is. A theory . . . a theory that I can't support. I think Gide is from the Treaty Board.*"

"The Treaty Board?" That ancient body, bestir itself out of its torpor?

Credible, though, if there actually was a security breach, and there actually were First Movement tech in question.

Reaux had reason for his hesitance to breach Gide's confidence.

"Setha, fear of data transmission from the planet—that crock's as old as Concord itself. I admit the Treaty Board's not going to involve itself on a whim, but whatever Gide came here for didn't come up through the taps, I'll just about swear to it." He trusted Jewel to assure her surroundings, not to tap in where she hadn't checked for bugs or eavesdroppers, but he didn't want to lean that hard on Jewel's ability. "This discussion in depth isn't appropriate for your present location. Just take extreme care for your own safety. I'm ending, now."

"*I'll get back to you. I'll try to talk to Gide in the next few minutes. Can this lady stay available to me?*"

Meaning Jewel.

"Jewel, stay with him, wherever he wants you to be. I'm going out."

"*Yes, sir.*" Jewel herself tapped out.

So Reaux wanted the tap-courier with him. He likely realized she might have other mods, too, mods in Jewel's instance that gave her extraordinary hearing and other perceptions. Reaux wasn't that worried about what Outsiders might overhear. He *was* worried about what the ship would hear.

That said comforting volumes about Reaux's straight dealings with him.

He'd reached the end of what he himself was willing to say. They had a geologic cataclysm in progress down on the planet, a Project tap had possibly fallen into the hands of whoever had hit

Gide, Kekellen was upset, and the Earth ship was sitting out there watching it all, blaming Reaux, and writing reports that were going to racket all the way to Earth and Apex.

Bloody hell.

THE LITTLE CONFERENCE ROOM, Reaux having disposed his own security outside, was at the end of the emergency corridor, a special corridor isolated from the run-of-the-mill traffic of a sectional hospital—some kid who'd fallen off a third tier balcony while climbing in the flower gardens, a man who'd developed gastric distress at a restaurant: those patients didn't get near this section.

The hospital, citing its own regulations, had objected to admitting Mr. Gide because he had a penetrating wound of unknown origin. They'd delayed half an hour admitting him, until Dortland prevailed. Then they'd hurried him into the isolation ward, ironically treating the Earth ambassador as a contamination case—the sort of case they'd have preferred to shunt down to the 5th level emergency room at the Institute. Outsider hospitals had special resources to deal with bleeding wounds and clean out illicits if they were in question.

Terrifying. A cut was all it took to endanger a life, or ruin one: a sore, a cut, even a drink of water, a risk stupid kids continually brushed up against, if they went down on 5th, where he had it on good authority his own foolish daughter was at this very moment. Suspicion, motive, and an open wound combined to get even a man of Gide's importance surrounded in plastic containment, every swab and piece of bandage contained and sent off to a lab for analysis. Gide was bleeding and he was not from Concord, and that meant, no matter his status, that the medical system handled him as a contagion, with a biosquad swabbing down the apartment and the area of the incident, not letting even investigators in until more was cleaned up than was going to help any investigation—but for the station's safety, that had to be the priority. The hospital authorities were trying in vain to find the elusive Mr. Stafford, who might also have been contaminated and now he had to pry Biohazard off Stafford's trail, far harder than calling back the police chase.

But he tried. He made the call to Ernst, to let Ernst argue with the police and Biohazard alike.

Then he explained to the supervising nurse that he intended, was absolutely determined, to visit Mr. Gide.

Regulations insisted Gide's doctors and nurses wear full suits. Regulations made his visitor, even the governor of Concord, sign a waiver before they let him and two of his bodyguard suit up in ridiculous-looking clear plastic affairs with flimsy filter masks. Jewel Sanduski stayed at the entry station: to bring her in would leave a record of her presence and who had brought her, not to mention that she would tacitly convey everything they said straight to Brazis, and Reaux shuddered to think of the fallout if news of her presence got to the ship. She had heard and likely re-layed all the conversation he'd had with the nurses about Gide's condition. What else she might hear, waiting back near the nurses' station, he had no idea, but with the ship on its own agenda, Brazis warning him of threats against his life, and Stafford having gone God knew where, he wanted a pipeline to Brazis, one that couldn't be recorded by any snoopery, and she re-mained that conduit.

With his two bodyguards trailing, he cycled through the airlock barrier of the isolation ward and walked, rustling with plastic, down to number 10. Suited attendants were on watch there, unad-vised, and they had to get permission to open that door.

Until the lab reports came back, the physician of record had said, Gide was stuck here. Gide had been belligerent about being put in isolation. Consequently the doctors had tranked him, re-portedly with enough juice to fell a dockworker. It was not, the doctor assured him, going to be a productive interview. No, they could not just give him a restorative, not until the lab work came back, not until they had done a thorough health workup. But yes, if the governor insisted, on his own responsibility, he could go in and try to talk to Mr. Gide.

The attendants opened the door. It was the sphinx-face Reaux saw lying against the pillows, the sphinx, but human now, with white hair standing up in two odd-angled spikes, a pasty-pale complexion that held a faint blotchiness. Though tranked, Gide re-garded him, slit-eyed.

"Mr. Ambassador?"

A blink. "Get me the hell out of this room."

"As soon as the external wound heals over, Mr. Ambassador. A few cracked ribs and a shallow shrapnel wound—it's only the possibility of contamination they're worried about. There's a rule about bleeding wounds . . ."

"Only the contamination! As if spit and piss couldn't carry a contamination." Another blink. Several more. Tranked or not, Gide was waking up, and angry. "Where's Stafford?"

"We don't know at the moment."

"I'm not surprised." Gide moved, thin-lipped with pain, actually moved in a coordinated way, and jammed the pillow double beneath his head, fighting to keep his eyes open.

"Stafford may be another casualty."

"Dead?"

"A possibility. I can only apologize—"

"Apologize! I'm *banned*, do you understand?" Rage got past the sedation, justified rage. "I'm banned for life, thanks to your so-called security! My God!"

"I can only express regret . . ."

"I can never see my family again! I can never so much as approach Earth!"

"For them, emigration is a—"

"Emigration! The hell! The *hell*, sir! I'm not bringing my family out to this hellhole! God knows what damned thing they sent inside my containment with that shell!"

"I'm terribly sorry. But I can assure, for what it's worth, there's nothing lethal on Concord. Nothing of that sort."

"You're a damned fool."

The man was distraught—small wonder; and drugged, and apt to say things he wouldn't, but Reaux found it more and more difficult to keep his equanimity.

"Have you been in contact with your ship at all, since, Mr. Ambassador?"

"Only to be apologized to. A message relayed from the doctor. They can't take me back. Is that news?"

"Well, if it's any comfort at all, every governor and every trade representative out here understands your distress. I was voluntary, of course, but no few enter the system accidentally, in your situation. Hardly with an explosive shell being the agent, but—"

"Fool, I say!"

His own patience was running thinner by the second. He thought of Kathy, and the risks she was running—voluntarily, down on 5th level—and this man lay here whining because he was damned to live on Concord in luxury, a future thorn in his side, no doubt politicking against him, only because his injury had happened on his watch, on his station, on his doorstep.

Depend on it, if his suspicion was right and this man was from the Treaty Board, this was not only a full-blown diplomatic disaster, this man could be a long-term resident problem, right on his station, and he could only make matters worse by antagonizing the man while he was half-aware.

"I can assure you we're actively tracking Mr. Stafford and tracing the weapon we found outside the apartment. The attack came through the open door. Was Mr. Stafford just arriving, or just leaving?"

"Leaving." Out of breath, Gide recovered angry rationality. Eyes rolled, an attempt to gather resources. "He took exception to a body scan and opened the door. At that point, the world blew up. Next I was aware, I was on my side and that damned Outsider had his hands on me." A breath and a shudder. "Then your police came blundering in, exposing themselves to whatever might be there— if they're not in quarantine, why do they have me here? And Stafford is loose in the station, and you can't find him. But I'm in quarantine!"

"His own authority is looking for him. We're pursuing every possibility . . . including the chance that some Earth-based entity with an agent here is your enemy. But there is the fact they didn't kill you. They didn't use force enough to kill you *or* Mr. Stafford, who was far less protected."

"What are you saying?"

"That it's possible they didn't intend to kill you."

"Idiocy!"

"You are, however, alive."

"I doubt my welfare was anywhere in their consideration."

"In my personal experience of assassination attempts, sir, which has been several, the usual suspect is either some local disturbed soul with a direct line to God, or someone *within* the same system as the intended victim, who has a motive and a plan. If you're not crazy, you don't assassinate someone who can't be an inconvenience to you. And you try not to botch the job. So why do you think someone would pick you in particular for a target, out of all the Earthborn officials that have ever come and gone here on a regular basis? It makes sense the motive lies in your specific business here. Though it's possible they didn't need to kill you, but to prevent you going further with that ship. Would there be any profit in that?"

Gide was paying attention now. "What are you getting at?"

"That's all I can possibly guess. Our investigation is necessarily hampered by not having the least idea what authority you represent or what your future plans are."

"I have the legislative seal. You accepted the documents. That's all you need know. You can damned well take my word when I give it. Find Stafford. That's your start."

"Very well and good, Mr. Gide, if that's the course you choose. But I'm sure Stafford, involved or not, didn't pull the trigger. And assuming they made a serious try at killing you, I'm also sure it's in your interest for us to find the agency responsible before you leave this hospital. You'll have to walk our streets as a private citizen for the rest of your life." He took a chance. "Or are you counting on being very much safer as soon as your own ship leaves?"

"That's ridiculous!"

"Whoever did this had resources much beyond a local lunatic or the average dissident. That shell was not easy to get, to hide, or to set up to use."

"The *Southern Cross* didn't order this attack! Damn you, sir. Damn you for a complete incompetent!"

Temper. A deep breath. "Then you need to tell me the truth of what you represent, Mr. Gide, and don't expect to set up and give orders on the basis of the documents you carry. If you're banned and abandoned here, you become one of my citizens who I have to presume is in possession of some very touchy state secrets, and you become *my* responsibility, both to protect you and to prevent any illicit use or compromise of those secrets. In that light, Mr.

Gide, I suggest you make it clear to me what I'm protecting, or I'll have to assume the worst case possible."

Gide blinked, blinked twice, as if to question what he'd just heard—perhaps too much for the heavy sedation. But depend on it, Gide was not a stupid man—one didn't get to the position Gide held by being a stupid man.

"Point," Gide said, close-lipped. "Get these two idiots out of here. This is for your ears only."

"Gentlemen." Reaux motioned at his escort.

They withdrew. The door shut itself.

"I'm with the Treaty Board," Gide said, and shifted up among his pillows—a move that occasioned a wince. "Career diplomat, specialty in the arrangements at Concord."

"Hence the fluency in our language."

"I never intended it to be this useful." Gide had a sense of humor, it seemed, however deeply buried. "You say you have a working relationship with the local Outsider Chairman. Is that true?"

He had an Outsider tap-courier in the outside office. Which he didn't intend to admit. "An operating relationship, to smooth jurisdictional boundaries. That's all. I assure you I *don't* leak restricted information in that direction."

Gide stared at him. A clammy sweat had broken out with his slight exertion in shifting more upright, and it might be pain that drew down the corners of his mouth. Or distaste. Or a battle against the tranquilizer, which didn't seem to be as heavy as the doctor indicated. The eyes were very sharp, very focused at the moment. "You and I have no choice but to get along, governor, or it might go very badly for your administration. We clearly have a mutual problem."

"I'm listening."

"I may be banned, but I *am* still an agent of the Treaty Board. I become, in fact, your local agent, in a local office, whether either of us likes it or not. As to the reason for my presence here—finance is moving here to fund activities and recruitment for a First Movement cell."

"Here?"

"Your Freethinkers, sir. Your tame Freethinkers."

"In the absence of exact evidence, Mr. Gide—"

"The black market in illicits is involved in the finance of this cell, and we rather think it's on Orb that the actual manufacturing facility exists, labs we're watching very closely, labs capable of producing very sophisticated illicits. *Leadership* is what Concord has to offer the Movement. Leadership that has existed since the last days of the War—leadership operating right under the noses of the *ondat* observer as well as ours."

"*Here?*" He had had a lifelong penchant for questions that made him sound like a fool. But Gide was talking all around the critical point, deliberately, and deliberately obscuring as much as he gave out. Leadership? "Are you talking about the Ila herself, sir?"

"It's either a good time or a bad time for you to have close associations with the Outsider authority. It all depends on what you do with that situation, Governor Reaux."

Him, with Jewel Sanduski in the outer office.

And from, an instant ago, him asserting authority over Gide, now Gide seemed prepared to unfold his tent and camp right in the heart of his authority, an entity outside local law, and impossible to get rid of. He didn't know what to do.

"Let me have it clear, Mr. Gide. You think the Ila is in indirect contact with the Freethinker movement, passing information to them via the taps? And that some rogue lab on Orb is financing a cell here?"

"Yes."

It was too incredible.

"I'm assured," Reaux said, "that such information absolutely does not get out of Planetary Observations, sir. The Project Director reminds us this theory has surfaced every few generations, never substantiated in fact. Whatever you think of our information-gathering abilities, we're constantly on the alert for such a move, however it would come, by some such technology as that pot you questioned, by any other means. We would be aware of any such breach of security."

"You can't even find Stafford after a thundering great explosion. Do I think you couldn't be unaware of something clandestine operating under your nose? I want out of this place. I want office facilities and staff . . ."

"Staff, Mr. Gide?"

"You are required to cooperate, sir. My authority and my credentials haven't terminated. It wasn't my intent to establish an office of the Treaty Board here, but, de facto, it now exists, as a result of this attack on me." Gide's tone was brittle, his jaw alternately trembling and set hard among several chins. "I assure you, Governor, my credentials give me sufficient authority to form such an office, to engage security, to arrest and to bind for trial, in equal legal standing with the local governments and treaty-mandated offices, *including* Mr. Antonio Brazis, including you, sir. I'll require a residency—the one you afford me is adequate. Office space—*I'll* choose my own personnel, thank you, starting with my own security, in an office near yours. I'll expect . . . Mr. Dortland, is it . . . ?"

"Yes."

". . . Mr. Dortland to present me a list of possible hires, perhaps some from your staff, but by no means entirely. I'll want clericals . . . I assure you, sir, my authority does not depend on the ship's being at my disposal, and they may bar me from entering, but by damn, I can hold the ship here indefinitely or require they take enforcement action, if I'm not satisfied with the level of cooperation I'm receiving from your administration or from Mr. Antonio Brazis's various imperial domains. You'll respect those credentials, sir, or there will be consequences."

In an inner, mostly numb spot, Reaux began to be afraid as well as outraged, while he tried to keep his expression neutral and his mind on track. This was a dangerous, intelligent man. Tranked as he was, unkempt as a drugout in a gutter on Blunt, he still tracked, still reasoned . . . still mounted a terrifying threat. What did it take to knock this man out? "I'll make initial arrangements for office space, if you like. I understand your injuries will let you out of here in fairly short order."

"I expect it."

"I'll relay your requests to Mr. Dortland." He was scrambling, mentally, to find a pocket to drop Mr. Gide into—preferably a deep, dark one. And hit on a reassuring objection. "There is an operational precedent for cooperative administrative operations, in the Medical Authority itself, limited by the Treaty on this particular station, but having absolute powers in its sphere. And there is the PO. There's always the PO, on Concord." And my relations with it, he thought, doggedly, which weren't going to change. "And the *ondat,* who have their own voice. Not to mention the planet itself. All of which I'm charged to keep in equilibrium. The Treaty Board has its powers, but, I'm constrained to point out, sir, the Treaty Board's authority regulates Treaty compliance, not the planet, *or* the PO, and certainly not the *ondat,* so I must dispute your interpretation of equal standing."

"You have no authority over my office."

"You propose to open an office to make yet one *more* authority on Concord, which only makes one of half a dozen, Mr. Gide, and you do *not* outrank the Earth Authority, which appointed me, or the Apex Council, which appointed the local Chairman, nor yet, I assure you, the *ondat* authority, in whose territory, let me recall to you, we actually sit. You don't even outrank the Medical Author-ity, which I assure you is very potent within its own sphere. As governor, it's my job to keep all these jurisdictions in balance and keep relations with the *ondat* and Apex in good order. Your inves-tigation of any breach of containment crosses all these jurisdic-tions, but most of them are foreign, and that boils down to the fact that you can't order these other jurisdictions to act, you can only request. Close cooperation, sir, close cooperation between your of-fice and mine is essential, and I assure you that, whatever your cre-dentials, you and your office cannot superimpose any authority over mine. On any other station, perhaps. But try to get me re-placed, and discover that you'll disturb all the alliances and work-ing agreements extant here, in a way very disagreeable to Earth itself. You may be the advocate for the Treaty, but you exist in a constellation of authorities on this station, and you will exist coop-eratively within that framework, or you will not function with any power at all. Now let me not be rude. Let me assure you you'll re-ceive very good cooperation from my office. But not obedience. You likewise need Brazis's cooperation, to make headway in his sphere. I suggest diplomacy, Mr. Ambassador."

It was the best speech of his life. It was absolutely his most elo-quent, and after he'd delivered it he found he'd scared hell out of himself, but he meant it. And the one witness to his moment was the victim of an adrenaline load clearly running out, apparent in the droop of eyelids, the lines of pain and anger in a pasty-pale face. "Meanwhile my would-be assassin is loose on your well-run station, Governor, and you've conveniently misplaced Stafford."

"We'll find both, at high priority, I assure you. Meanwhile—" Reaux started foolishly to reach for a pocket and couldn't, through the isolation suit. "Meanwhile the hospital staff can reach my office at any moment. Call me if you recall any further details, anything you may have noted and failed to state in the report."

"Quite a blank at the moment," Gide said muzzily. He reached for a water glass on the table. It escaped his hands. It fell, spilling its contents.

A cleaner-bot zipped out of its housing in the baseboard and sucked up glass and water both.

"Do you want me to call the nurse?" Reaux asked. "I'll get you some more water."

"The hell with it. I'm tired."

"I'll be in contact," Reaux said. "Rest."

Gide, falling back, shut his eyes, looking like a corpse.

Reaux walked out, earnestly wishing Gide were one.

9

Down on Blunt . . . down in a maze he couldn't remember how he'd gotten into—Procyon walked somewhere among the warehouses that supplied the fancy shops on Grozny, somewhere near a bar he thought he recognized.

But that would mean he'd been going the wrong way.

He'd lost his coat somewhere. Stupid of him. He couldn't remember how. He knew he was in trouble with Brazis, and he'd folded on his assignment, and the man from Earth wasn't dead, but good as, with the suit breached. The explosion came back to him. The situation began to reassemble itself, in shattered bits, like glass, each one containing an image, and all out of order.

He did know he shouldn't be where he was. It was a bad neighborhood. He'd thought sure he was headed right, and after a blank, he turned up here, disoriented, not even sure of the cross street. Bars and frontages changed on Blunt. They moved, sometimes color-shifted overnight without warning, and sometimes the owners just stripped the facade and glued it up somewhere else down the block, which wasn't guaranteed to be at all where you remembered it being. Cops hated the zone. He wasn't fond of it, himself, at the moment. He wanted to get home, was all, and he made repeated attempts to tap into the office directly from where he was, that only gave him headache.

He tried again. "Sir?"

Blood shunt and pain behind the eyes.

Bad pain. Really bad pain, right to the roots of his teeth.

"*Procyon.*"

The tap came crystal clear for a second.

It was a woman's voice. Downworld accent. He figured it must be somebody really senior in the offices, somebody senior like Drusus, a tap so used to dealing with the Old Ones it just crept into ordinary speech.

"*Where are you, Procyon?*"

Pain ebbed. He could think. "In public, ma'am. Can you ease back? You're coming through very high. It's painful." Tears blurred his eyes. But the tap was working. He wasn't cut off. He didn't care about the pain. It was all relief. "Tell Brazis I'm sorry . . ."

"*What are they doing? What is Brazis doing?*"

Then, sharply: "*This is Luz. Answer me.*"

It so confused him he stopped cold, out of breath and leaning against a building frontage, ducking slightly into a nook between frontages. He tried to form an answer. A coherent thought.

Luz? There was only one Luz that could be reaching him on that tap.

And she was downworld. Was he hallucinating?

"*Answer, Procyon.*"

"I don't know, ma'am."

"*What happened?*"

"Something exploded. Something blew up when I was talking to the ambassador. I think—I think I couldn't hear for a while. I think the tap is damaged. My ears are still ringing. Tell Brazis."

"*Where are you?*"

"On the street. I'm confused. I think I'm on Blunt. But I don't know for sure where I am."

"*Are you badly injured?*"

He looked down at himself. Except for losing his coat, except for the dizziness and the memory lapse, he didn't look hurt. A little dust. He thought he might be bleeding here and there, but it was a dark shirt. "I don't see anything physical. I'm just shaky. My ears hurt. I can still hardly hear the street. Like everything's down a deep pipe. Can you help me reach the Chairman?"

"*What blew up?*"

"I think somebody shot through the door. I tried to help the ambassador. His machine was over on its side, but I don't think he's dead. Somebody needs to get to him . . ." The pain in his head ebbed a little. Someone in charge of the taps had detected something way out of parameters . . . he didn't know: he didn't understand all that went on in Central. He only used what he was given. Discreetly. Which this wasn't, standing here, leaning on a frontage like a drunk. He was in deep trouble with Brazis, who wouldn't like him talking here in public. And Luz was involved. God help him. "Can somebody please get me to the office? I'm a little dizzy."

Sharp stab of pain. *"Marak is concerned,"* another voice said, likewise female, and in old, old downworld accents. *"Now we know you're alive. Good. Ignore Brazis's orders. Marak demands your attention. He trusts everyone in this affair less than he needs do, until he hears from you, and he refuses common sense. Speak to him! Do you hear us, boy?"*

Female. He didn't know who. But he had a sudden, dire suspicion who it was, besides Luz, and shivered, whispering, "Yes, ma'am."

A third female voice interposed: *"Ila, he's not permitted."* Station accent. Maybe one of the taps.

"But we are permitted," that second voice said, autocratic and absolute. And he tried to shut it out and not to answer, but an off signal didn't work. Nothing he did worked to protect him from that contact, loud as it wanted to be, as nothing he had done had summoned it. He leaned against the wall, unable to control the tremor in his hands, unable to see anything but black, now, and flashes of light in his eyes that tried to form patterns. And he kept thinking what that voice had said, that Marak needed to hear from him, but he couldn't tap through.

"Where have you been?" the female voice demanded of him. *"Some Earth lord arrives, expecting to gain satisfaction from our servants? And local authority permits this? Brazis is mistaken in that estimation of protocols and priorities, let me assure you."*

Silence. Silence so deep and so sudden after that storm in the tap that he felt deaf and blind in its departure. His heart pounded as if he had run the length of the Trend.

Vision returned, hazily so. The lights had stopped flashing.

He tried to reach Brazis. Tried to tap into the system, but pain shot through his skull, his pulse raced, and his control was gone.

Passersby on the street surreptitiously stared at him, pretending to continue their own business, but noticing, some sizing him up. Perhaps he had gotten bad news in a tap message. Perhaps he had become ill. In this neighborhood, no one asked. Nobody would intervene—except the predators.

Flash of light. Gentler, this time.

Quieter voice. *"Procyon."*

"Sir." *Brazis.* With ineffable relief, he turned his face toward the cold wall—not that people on the street weren't accustomed to drunk people talking to their disembodied taps, or singing or dancing to them, but he had his wits about him now enough to remember some people read lips. "Sir, somebody shot the ambassador."

"I know."

"Downworld just tapped in."

"The Ila, piggybacking on Luz. We know that, too."

"She can do that?"

"She's done it before, which you unfortunately now know, and we don't know what else she's gotten her hands on. Don't discuss that where you are. Just listen. Where are you?"

"Don't know, sir. On Blunt, somewhere. On Blunt. A Brant's Drug. Across the street." He leaned against the wall and craned to see the adjacent frontage. "Mullan's Delivery."

"Drusus is coming to get you. Physically coming to get you. Stay off the tap right now, if you can. I know everything that's happened. The ambassador is not dead. We need you back in the office. Immediately."

"Yes, sir." He leaned back, shivering. Relieved at that news, though the tap had given him a horrid headache that shot from ears to eyes, blinding light, right at the seat of his personal universe. He tried to think past it, tried to remember all that Brazis had just said. And what Luz and the Ila had said about Marak, which alarmed him.

Brazis opposing Luz and the Ila. That wasn't good. If Brazis was taking a course contrary to Luz, it wasn't good, and the Ila herself was saying Marak was in trouble.

Drusus was coming to get him? Drusus was supposed to be with Marak, wasn't he? Or was he wrong about the time of day?

Don't use the tap, Brazis said. Don't use the tap.

He walked a few steps, then tried to remember whether Brazis had said stay put, or whether he should try to get out to Grozny, where he was easier to see. Method wasn't clear to him. He didn't know where Drusus was.

Flash of light. Blinding. Roar in his ears. He found himself sitting down on the street, conspicuous, not remembering the last few minutes, and tried shakily to get up, dusting himself off.

A knee-high cleaner-bot had come out of the adjacent service nook to see about him, mistaking him for refuse. A half dome, it hummed and flashed across its surface with, he imagined, reproach.

"Come," it said.

He thought it was Drusus who was supposed to find him. And here he was hearing voices from a cleaner-bot.

"Come." It butted him in the ankle. Hard. And moved off.

What was he supposed to do? Was this thing under someone's personal control? He tried hard to tap in.

Senses exploded, a flare of light that hit his aching head right behind the eyes, sound that buzzed in his ears. He crouched down on the street, making himself a human ball, trying to shut it out. He pressed his hands hard against his eyes, trying to stop the flashes, trying to order his blood flow past the headache to send a clear signal on the tap, before his head exploded.

Cleaner-bots were all around him. If a man went down the bots were supposed to call the hospital. But these seized on him, gripped his clothing, gripped his arms painfully, and extruded lift-arms under him.

"Let me go!" he cried. But they dragged him away into the adjacent service nook, rapidly, rapidly. He couldn't kick, he couldn't move his arms. A clicking of wheels on tiles marked their passage, and tugs at his limbs indicated a certain AI randomness in their movement—autonomous units cooperating, robots deaf to his protests.

He was swept up with the damn garbage, was what. He couldn't break free. He yelled for help, and no one on Blunt gave it.

A low metal gate gaped ahead, affording scant clearance for the machines dragging at his limbs. It was dark inside. He tried desperately to free a hand or bend a knee and catch the edge of the opening, but with a concerted whirr and a buzzing of wheels, they dragged him painfully past the gate.

They were in a cleaning chute. He was headed straight for disposal.

"Help!" he yelled, in total darkness, and the tap got only wild signal, flashes of white shock.

"Help!"

Down and down. He didn't know whether they combusted the trash or chopped it to bits or compacted it before they did any of that. He fought, he yelled, he tried to kick. He felt joints in the metal passage as they dragged him along, faster and faster. His skull banged over the seams until the small impacts began to distract him, a misery unto themselves.

They took a turn, and another turn, clattering along in absolute dark, where bots obeyed impulses that had nothing at all to do with sight or human senses, and the only measure of it was the seams in the chute. He yelled. He fought as hard as he could in the narrow chute, until the pain in his skull overpowered his coordination.

Then they were free of the chute, wide enough to bend his knees, to try to roll over. The air was choked with ammonia. His eyes began to water with it, and he made out a dim green light, illusory, like phosphor glow. He tried to tear free and turn and get a knee or a foot on the surface.

Something dark and insubstantial wisped over his face, a horrid contact. The robots froze, holding him in their unbreakable grip as that presence loomed over him.

Something spidery and soft and alive touched his face. He heard a sound, muttering, clicking.

"Let me go!" he yelled. Reason began to tell him where he was, what he felt, was real. That he had met the *ondat*. "Let me go. Human. Let go. *Let go!*"

It muttered and clicked. That wispy touch pressed down on his skull, on his forehead, with increasing force.

Pain, then. Sharp pain. He yelled at it to make it let him go, before his skull broke.

He couldn't breathe. His skull was bursting. He couldn't yell any longer. Couldn't move. Couldn't ask it to let him go. It just did. Finally.

It said something. He didn't know what. Something huge drifted past the source of the glow, something that moved, away from him, and blotted out all light, all sound.

MAGDALLEN HAD REACTED to that unexpected intrusion in the tap system—Magdallen had been talking to Dianne, in fact, and fallen quite ill in the outer office. Dianne had gotten him a cup of water and a shot of vasodilator. Luz's call and the Ila's pirating of the contact had blasted through the entire system like a nuclear device.

Brazis hadn't personally felt the attack. He'd had channels opened up all over the station trying to make contact with Procyon, and left them open for Drusus. That had possibly widened the disaster. *He* wasn't regularly on that channel, but the Project taps who happened to be on the system were all affected. One of the Ila's senior taps had suffered a stroke, and was in medical right now, at risk of her life and future health—

Not that the Ila gave an effective damn.

Luz had started it—Luz had had a long and uneasy relationship with Concord, being inclined to push a situation and push it hard. Ian was the reasonable voice. But then the Ila had gotten into it, and *had* gotten Procyon's attention—the one benefit: so had he, though without being able to pinpoint Procyon's whereabouts.

But now he couldn't get Drusus, who would have been wide open to that blast through the tap system, if he had been trying to contact Procyon. Drusus could be lying unconscious on the street, for all he knew. Could have gone down like the Ila's tap.

He'd called Council into emergency session, under the vice chairman, while he stayed in his office. He'd just sent agents out looking for Drusus . . . and now he wanted to see Magdallen, as soon as Magdallen got out of the restroom.

Meanwhile he tended his orchids, which had received an inordinate amount of care in the last couple of days. He let his mind concentrate utterly on the gloss of the common phalaenopsis and its new growth: its bloom stem had yellowed, and he had soon to take the critical step of separating the parent and the offshoot on that yellowing stem. Those two lovely leaves were doomed. It was about to suffer stress, and those leaves, too, would yellow, as new growth appeared. Depend on it, he had far rather think about that than about Magdallen—or the Council at Apex, which, yes, he now knew, and not too remarkably so, had kept alive its own store of the highly classified nanisms, the biological base of the downworld taps, that never should have left Concord, nanoceles that were supposed to be confined to the Project from the making of the Treaty onward. *Magdallen* had been affected by the Ila's intrusion. Therefore Apex had inserted Project nanoceles into one of its agents and sent him here to spy on the Project—a plan more than a year in the making, since learning to interpret the taps was not instantaneous.

So if Concord should be taken out, if some utter disaster should happen here, some hiccup of the sun or some hostile action that destroyed the station, yes, it was only prudent, he conceded it, that the Council at Apex keep the Project nanoceles secretly in reserve, a means to reconstitute this last spaceborne link to Movement technology and the downworld team of Ian and Luz. The Project tap *was* Movement technology, all told.

And that highly classified knowledge had always worried Earth.

Was it *Magdallen* Earth had heard about? Had it sent its ill-timed investigation in to find an illicit use of Project technology?

That Apex had let someone carrying that technology loose on Concord, to eavesdrop on official taps without telling him . . . that, as far as he knew, was unprecedented. That he had only now found it out, when a burst through the system had dropped their previously covert agent on his ass along with the rest of the taps, made him madder than hell. *Gide* might be from the Treaty Board, and they were likely stuck with him, a situation that also made him madder than hell. That was a problem they would have to handle. And *Gide* was convinced they had unregulated First Movement operating on the station, which he had denied, while someone tried to blow up Mr. Gide.

So now, in this very hour, they had had the Ila walking roughshod over their security systems, a flaming advertisement to all who could possibly touch those systems that First Movement tech wasn't always under control. Marak was refusing to abandon his chase after their transportation, was refusing just to go straight down to be picked up, had his own plan, which he was following to the edge of perdition, and now Luz and the Ila were irate about the disturbance that had pulled Marak's taps out of sequence and so irritated *him* that he wasn't taking their advice. Luz was angry with Ian, the Ila was angry and broke into the system he'd left wide open . . .

And it all happened with an Earth ship to witness, while the ambassador was lying in hospital. The whole damned fiasco sent him incandescent, and he would soon have to explain it all to involved parties, including the *ondat*.

To cap it all, Marak himself might have been affected by the latest outburst, since he had been in contact with Auguste, as best he gathered, who was in his own apartment's lavatory puking his guts out.

He wanted answers. He wanted them now.

"Magdallen is mostly recovered at this moment," Dianne reported, *"but pleads intense headache. He wishes to go back to his apartment."*

"The hell he will," he said. Damned right Magdallen had suddenly changed his mind about wanting to see him. Likely Magdallen never wanted to visit his office again, and wished he were safe back on Apex. But it was far too late for Magdallen to pretend he didn't have that tap. "Send him in," he told Dianne. Hell, he supposed he could tap in and *call* the damned snoop in, if he knew his tap code.

Which he didn't. Which he meant to get forthwith, and not have to hunt noisily through the system.

With a careful fingertip, he wiped a fleck of shed plant matter from the spotless lighted shelf, then stalked to his desk and sat down behind that solid fortification before the door opened and Magdallen walked in.

White-faced, Magdallen dropped into the interview chair.

"Feeling better?" he asked Magdallen.

"Yes, sir. A little indigestion."

"There's a damper in place to cut the top off the spike, or I can guarantee your indigestion would have been much worse." Brazis made up his mind to level with Magdallen to a certain degree:

truthers could only get so much. He hoped to shake the truth out of an already-shaken man. "We moved a particular agent off the tap, and *Luz* is mildly annoyed. More, the *Ila* is annoyed. Marak, who is out there in a situation, short of his mission goal, I'm sure is beyond annoyed at this point, if not injured, and his sole remaining tap is, at this very moment, in his own bathroom, trying to get back on duty and communicate with him despite the shock to his nervous system. Gide is in hospital, madder than hell, and we know his opinion of all of us before this even started. I've carefully explained to Ian that there's an Earth envoy up here, and Ian said that *they* weren't pleased about having this ambassador talk to Marak's tap, but he did agree that we've done as well as we could under the circumstances. Patently we don't have Luz on our side in this business, however, and a little two-person cabal we've had concern us before may have just re-created itself: two women I assure you it isn't good to argue with have now formed a society of mutual reinforcement. The Ila and Luz are irritated extremely at Earth's interference, and probably at me. So, bluntly asked, Agent Magdallen, what was Apex intending to do? Why in hell are you on my station? What *lunacy* let loose someone who can eavesdrop on the Project and involve himself with Marak's World without clearance from me, and why do you just happen to coincide with Mr. Gide's arriving from the other end of space? And while we're at it, give me your tap code. I won't have taps wandering around the station without their codes in my system."

Sweat stood on Magdallen's face. "You forgot the cracking of the Southern Wall, to lay to my account."

He ordinarily admired humor under fire. Not at this precise moment. He fixed Magdallen with a cold stare.

"I assure you," Magdallen said, "that's far beyond my abilities."

"Nothing else seems to be. Your hidden tap code. If you please."

"Three space two-one-four."

He wrote it down. The deliberate act calmed him, let him think twice about simply tapping in and blasting hell out of the man.

"Thank you, Agent Magdallen."

"Yes, sir." Much more meekly.

"So spill it. Why are you here? The truth this time. I can tell you if the Ila thinks *she's* been spied on, or that you're responsible for her being spied on, you may be dead before next shift. Or worse. Her on-shift tap's in hospital, fried. She may never recover. Do you understand me? In fact—you may have gotten her *and* Luz on your neck, in which case you won't be safe again, waking or sleeping."

Magdallen stared at him, absorbing that information.

In silence.

Brazis's carefully cultivated patience ran out. "Talk, damn you."

"I assure you we're on the same side in this affair, Mr. Chairman."

"Then you'd better figure from here on to cooperate with me, to hell with your orders. The situation is mutating by the hour. You can't communicate with Apex fast enough, so start communicating with me. I *am* protecting you from the Ila. I have all the taps damped down, way down, to the detriment of our supporting Marak, who's currently in a nasty situation. I'm not sure how long our damp-down is going to resist a skilled hack from downworld. So for starters, I'd suggest you tap completely out."

"I have."

"So what brought Gide here? What have you got to do with it? And why am *I* having to get my information from an Earthborn governor, who seems far more informed on this business than anybody else?"

A frown knit Magdallen's brows. "The information can put you and me both in jeopardy with Council."

"Right now, let me tell you, the Council is in dire jeopardy with *me*. And I *will* spill what I know to Ian and Luz and let them use their judgment how far to take it to the Ila and to Marak, because right now, this could look like an attempt by Earth to get their hands on one of Marak's taps for no friendly purposes, and they may still be trying. I'll tell you another tidbit of information. We don't have readout from Marak at the moment. He's either shut down to protect himself or he's lying unconscious or dead somewhere in chancy terrain. Hati, thank our lucky stars, had lost patience with us and tapped out well before this happened. But in the general damp-down, we can't get to her to find out. We daren't reestablish contact until we know what Luz and the Ila have gotten up to and until we're assured they're not going to blast through again. So the Council's displeasure looms small in my path, Agent Magdallen. Talk, and talk in depth and detail."

"All right, all right, sir. The theory is, there is First Movement on the station. That's why I think Earth's come in. They theorize—they theorize the Ila has been passing tech up here via one or more of the taps. The Treaty Board on Earth contacted Apex, advising Apex they were sending a mission here. Apex sent me. I was under orders to burrow deep in advance and not to say what I know."

"Did you attack the ambassador?"

"No. I didn't."

Truthers still greenlighted on the desk rim said that was the truth. But a little yellow also flickered there. Magdallen was hedging, or nervous about that question.

"You know who did hit him?"

"I don't. By all evidence and circumstances, it could have been the black market."

"The smugglers? That would be a damned fool thing, way too much public notice."

"On one level, yes. But creating confusion, government hearings, a lot of finger-pointing . . . we go into hysterics, so does Earth, the politicians are busy creating greater security, and they cover their tracks and explore whatever protective system we devise to detect them."

"If they were that bright, they'd be running the station."

"That's the point, sir. They may have very good direction. They may have tap communications they shouldn't have, not downworld, but at least office-level."

"The system has safeguards."

"You didn't find me before I blew my own cover out there in the outer office. You didn't find the Ila until she blew through like a solar flare. Your alarms aren't working, sir, have you figured that?"

The burglary alarm hacked. Undetected. A leaden cold settled in Brazis's gut—and a sense of profound embarrassment chased after it.

Not that Magdallen seemed to be enjoying his moment: sweat still glistened on his face.

"All right, Agent Magdallen. Points to your side. So you damn well *knew* we hadn't picked you up in the system. You were operating in that shadow. It would have been civilized and prudent to warn us there was a problem with our alarm system."

"I wasn't sure whether you hadn't detected the breach, or whether you'd consented to it. I wasn't sure, sir, that you weren't in collusion."

Infuriating on the surface. But logical. He had to ask the next question. "Have you reason to be sure now, that I'm not in collusion, as is?"

"I think I know who hacked the system. The Ila did, no telling how long ago. I believe you didn't know. Whether she knows about me at this moment is another matter. If she finds out—she may try to kill me. And I'm not that confident your systems can take the top off the spike if she decides to take the taps out entirely."

"Go on."

"There is a lab on Orb working on a medical illicit of a very worrisome nature, that may be an advanced tap, or at least something complex. Apex is extremely concerned. But nothing is going to leave Orb. Someone will see to that. There may have been a fire at that lab already. When there is, there will be arson arrests—on the lab staff."

"And Earth is aware this is going on?"

"I believe so. Gide wasn't discreet, coming in here. I can only hope if Earth's agents have come in at Orb, that they'll be quieter, or we'll see our operation there blown. I hoped Gide's protection would be stiffer. It wasn't."

"Damn." Nanisms. Illicits. Smuggling. All the versions of the Movement had that particular focus, the hope of getting some magic bullet, a tap to enable their members to communicate unheard—more, a magic pill to make their members as immortal as the few down on the planet. "A medical nanism . . . not the immortality nanocele, nothing like that."

"Not that we know," Magdallen agreed. "Theoretically the Ila has her own reasons to keep that nanocele exactly where it is, so her enemies eventually die and she doesn't, and none of them can get what's her trump card. She's been very careful where she's bestowed it."

"That's the thinking."

"An adaptive nanism, however, that could be weaponized . . . that could be in question at that lab on Orb. Earth is clearly scared. Apex isn't happy."

Scared? Adaptive nanisms, let loose in a population, let loose on Concord, of all sensitive places in the universe, where it could prove to the *ondat* that remediation never had been the goal?

Kiss civilized understanding good-bye. Kiss containment good-bye. The genie could break the bottle for good and all. Ilia Lindstrom, the sole surviving member of the First Movement, sitting in a shelter that had withstood the planet-breakers, would just have to sit it out and wait for her ticket off planet, to take up the war where the Movement had left off.

They'd always known what the potential game was, in that woman's survival.

"The lab fire has likely already taken place on Orb," Magdallen said. "If Gide is here, they've probably already moved."

"So Gide comes here looking for Movement contacts inside *my* offices. Comes here forearmed with information on Procyon Stafford, so sure he's to blame. If I can be sure of anything, that kid is innocent of any conspiracy."

"I'm sure so, too, sir. They have dossiers on every tap. I think it was the Freethinker connection that attracted their attention. Mistakenly so, in his case, but right on target in certain facts."

"And why in hell, Agent Magdallen, didn't you advise me of those facts before I sent that kid in there to investigate Gide?"

"I'd no way to do that without blowing my cover, which I was under orders not to do. Unfortunately—someone was aware of the Gide situation. Someone disposed of the guards and sat outside waiting there for the door to open, for Gide to be in view. If he hadn't been, they'd have gone in after him. They didn't snatch your tap. I don't think they wanted to. They didn't want him."

"Why not?"

"Perhaps because they didn't want you to invoke the police powers you have. They didn't want Project law to activate, and it wouldn't, so long as Procyon got back to us. I don't know, sir. I only conclude that because they *didn't* take him. They didn't want that train of events to take place."

"Meanwhile the Project tap has been hacked from down on the world. The alarm system hasn't been functioning for months. Years."

"The Ila could indeed have passed critical information. Or orders, to persons on this station. Yes."

The Ila herself could have been behind the attack on Procyon. He weighed the notion. Weighed it twice, and it came up far short. "The Ila doesn't botch her moves. Whoever did this missed killing the ambassador. Possibly the agents panicked. Possibly the result was what they wanted. But if at any moment she'd wanted to kill Procyon, she could have done it outright. Ask her current tap— who can't be asked anything."

"You say she doesn't make mistakes. Possibly her hands up here did. But as you say, sir, the result fell short of murder. Maybe the result was exactly what someone wanted. Not to kill either of them."

"Only to penetrate the containment? To strand the man here? To create disturbance between our office and the governor?"

Magdallen shrugged.

"You think the Movement wants Gide stranded here?" Brazis asked him. "For what bloody reason? Gide is Treaty Board, almost certainly. And survives, now, as a permanent resident of this station? What possible advantage to the Movement?"

"I can say *I* didn't attack Gide. Did you, sir?"

"No."

"Because?"

"Because it would be stupid."

"Exactly," Magdallen said. "Exactly. Why would the Movement want Gide here? *Cui bono?* To whom the advantage—in this attack that doesn't kill Mr. Gide?"

Not to the governor. Not to the Ila. Not to the Project or to Apex. "To his own authority." He didn't like being led. But he followed the logic. Some Earth faction. It made uncomfortably thorough sense.

"To strand Mr. Gide here. To set him up here, an establishment without the trouble of negotiation against the provisions of the Treaty—negotiations that might take decades, provoke problems, and still be refused."

It made disturbing sense. Negotiations would be refused. A Treaty Board officer, stranded here, alive, was still a Treaty Board officer. They might not have told Gide what they were going to do. Gide might have been sandbagged by his own authority.

"Earth does have agents here," Magdallen said, which was an of-course. Then: "Highly placed agents."

"Specifically?"

"*Dortland*, sir, to be precise."

Dortland. Reaux's security director, in command of all the special agents and all the Earther police on the station.

"Are you entirely sure of that?"

"Apex is sure of that."

"What agency is he?"

"That, we're not sure. But by the direction things are taking, someone who wants the Treaty Board to have an office here."

"Damned little use if Dortland already is a Treaty Board officer."

"If he can preserve his clandestine nature, that would be useful. And he may not be of Mr. Gide's intellectual level. But I'm relatively certain Apex's suspicions are correct. It's suspected in certain underworld quarters that Dortland is slinking for some agency or another, that he's just too well networked to be the usual governor's security appointee. He's suspected of having his fingers on the pulse of Blunt—having contact with persons who, if picked up for any reason, don't stay arrested. Persons that don't form part of the ordinary criminal element, persons that make the criminal element very nervous. I personally wonder," Magdallen said, "if he's been not chasing the same thing Gide is chasing."

"And then attacks Gide, establishing him here?"

"There are rival agencies," Magdallen said.

"None that would *want* a Treaty Board office here, none except the Treaty Board itself."

"There is that point."

"And the governor?" Brazis dreaded to learn. He had come to *like* Setha Reaux, in a limited way. "Is he in on this notion?"

"Certainly due to be watched by this organization, which holds a power quite outside the authority that appoints governors—an organization that doesn't accept policy directives from the Earth Authority. Possibly they're ambitious to expand their office. Gide will run an aboveboard operation. And Dortland will remain in the shadows as a countercheck on Gide, never informing him that he was the one to strand him here."

That theory was worth examining. It wasn't the first time he'd wondered about Reaux's staff. "His secretary, Ernst Albers?"

"Loyal, as far as I know, but Albers moves outside my circle. There's another point, however. Reaux's daughter. Her friends have friends on Blunt. Her situation is worrisome. She's run away to Blunt. She's certainly vulnerable. Therefore, so is the governor, who may be asked directly for favors."

"I doubt Reaux is part of this. He predates this mess."

"I happen to concur, sir, for what it's worth. But Earth may know about the contact you have with him and take a dim view of it, to Reaux's great detriment."

Damn. *Damn.* Warn Reaux about Dortland? Or not? Ask Magdallen's opinion on the matter? Or not?

"You do have heightened security, sir," Magdallen informed him. "Also from Apex. Word's come down, through channels not unrelated to my presence here, that your personal security should take every precaution against your untimely demise. Don't leave the offices unguarded. Don't meet personally with Reaux. Apex had rather Reaux than, for instance, the governor's opposition. Lyle Nazrani, the financier, isn't personally eligible for the office, not being Earthborn, but he's certainly apt to be a prime source of information for this new Treaty Board installation, much of it aimed at Governor Reaux. Most significantly, Apex had rather have you over the PO, rather than wasting your time with the civil politics of the Council at this point. They wish you would resign the Council chairmanship forthwith in favor of your proxy and concentrate entirely on the PO. They assure you of their protection should you do so."

For a moment it was not Magdallen speaking. It was a set of voices he knew, and little liked. An old argument, that he should remove himself farther from politics and controversy. But Magdallen managed to raise it not offensively, but as a matter of logic.

The Chairman General would love to have him out of the political arena.

But this time, in such grave circumstances, he found himself actually listening to the proposal and considering the step that would set his proxy in the station administrative post for good and all. His hitherto placid PO domain had several major crosscurrents he hadn't been able to monitor—one of which, the condition of the alarm system, might well have predated his administration. That had to be fixed. That was going to take some serious attention in the process.

But protection? *Damned* if he liked Apex meddling with his security. He had to accept the security arrangements that both watched the Project and protected *him*, but he didn't want them triggered from Apex without warning, and he certainly didn't like clandestine operations that came tramping through here, provoking reactions—knowledge that a stranger was on the tap system could itself have triggered the Ila to act.

And at the same time, Magdallen had failed to pass vital information to him. Advance information might have preserved the Ila's tap, the one person who could have informed them on the Ila's guilt or innocence. But that person was now in hospital and not likely to recover.

Magdallen had been investigating *him*, to top it off, and very embarrassingly finding holes in Project security.

A fool would get mad about that situation and not listen to the information that came from the investigation. A fool would react more to his own embarrassment at being outmaneuvered than to the fact of who had actually bypassed the alarms and what it meant.

"I'm going to warn Reaux about Dortland. I see no benefit in keeping him in the dark. The governor may become more valuable, given the situation you project. Do you have any advice about that move?"

"No, sir. That's entirely within your discretion to do. I'm not qualified to make that decision."

"I've done your kind of work. I've been in your position, Agent Magdallen, as you may have learned. It's a lot easier to find out things than to know that things are found out. I know the uncertainties in your job, and I know our own limitations in security. Some classified data may have gotten out under our noses. Now we know. If the Ila's involved, I assure you this present affair's not a life's work for her, but an hour's amusement. Her senior tap is not likely to survive in any conscious way. The woman will not likely be able to answer the questions we'd like to ask—ever. So we have the ambassador about to set up a subversive office here to watch us, the governor's daughter has gone missing, Dortland's doubled, every tap working has a headache, and Procyon is wandering somewhere on Blunt with minimal awareness where he is. Is there any other piece of bad news you'd like to tell me?"

"No, sir, to my knowledge, no."

"Can you lay hands on this stray daughter?"

"I can try. I have limited physical resources."

"Just get the daughter off the list."

"Her street name," Magdallen said, "is Mignette."

He was forming a new category for Magdallen—not trusted, but possibly an asset. He'd just laded Magdallen with various tidbits of information the future vector of which he wanted to test . . . a trick which Magdallen might see through. Or not. There was no way to query Apex about Magdallen's credentials: he had to find out for himself whether Magdallen had been feeding him a string of lies—or not.

Clearly Magdallen was wishing he were somewhere not laced with tap relays and in proximity to the Ila.

So was he. But that was where they all lived.

He had to pull Drusus back off the search for Procyon, if he could find Drusus, no matter if he had promised Procyon Drusus would find him. They need him in contact with Marak to prevent that situation blowing up. Time to get every tap they had off the street. The chance that Earth might have meant to kidnap Procyon was nil. If they didn't want Gide back aboard, no chance they'd want a kid with mods shedding skin cells and breathing into their systems. Earth's agents getting their hands on him, here on Concord—that was, operationally speaking—entirely possible; but if they hadn't done it by now, they likely didn't want to do it. If Procyon could just get off the street, get to somewhere safe, where some unlucky cop might nab him and create a real mess—

He was hesitant to make a committed move in any direction. He had too little sure information. But the consequences of inaction were as dire as those of a mistaken trust.

"The daughter's safety," he said to Magdallen, "the particular people you're watching—all these things I lay in your lap, since you've clearly formed an informational network of some useful sort. But let me warn you—look at me, Agent Magdallen; *look* at me for a moment, and know very clearly that there is *one* authority on Concord, and only one, bottom line. If the Ila is acting in her own interests, those interests include infiltrating the PO and taking over this administration by remote, which will touch off the *ondat*. The only defense against politics erupting down on the planet is *not* to alienate Marak. I can tell you he's the one true moderating influence down there, where Ian and Luz have their differences. He's one human influence even the *ondat* regard as honest, for whatever reason proceeds through their alien brains, and if we lose him—if he's been harmed by this venture of the Ila's, which has affected *his* taps—or if he just gets mad enough to go walkabout and damn them all for the next hundred years—we'll have to come to him confessing everything that's going on, abjectly begging him to straighten things out and only hoping the Treaty with the *ondat* survives the incident. Treaty law, Agent Magdallen—as we have it fairly well established that's what Gide represents—offended Treaty law is a danger I don't want to risk. I want Procyon back, sane and in one piece, and I want him soon, without their hands on him. So if you see him, get him here alive and whole. That's number one on the list. The daughter's number two."

"I'll try," Magdallen said somberly—indeed, looking him full in the eye for at least five seconds. "The daughter and your missing tap both. It's a difficult order. But I'll do my best."

Brazis stared back at him. Magdallen's stare back was a window into flat dark. There might be one loyalty for this man, but it wasn't to him.

Mark down a heavy score against the Chairman General at Apex. There were so many.

It might finally be time to call in old favors at Apex. He hated like poison to involve himself in Apex politics, which he foresaw would take years to evolve and dangerously distract him at a time when he most needed to repair damage to Project systems.

But if even a fraction of what Magdallen had spun for him was the absolute truth, he might have erred dangerously in letting the situation with the Chairman General ride all these years. The CG had launched a major investigation to participate in a question

Earth also was investigating, instead of just posing the question and asking him for a response, as the Apex authority on scene; and in doubt of *him,* and evidently believing Earth's suspicions, the CG had let a delicate matter reach a white heat, let the Ila blindside them all and destroy the evidence, then sit smugly by and watch the pieces fall.

The CG didn't personally like him. So the CG had primed Magdallen not to trust him. And Magdallen, if honest, still wasn't sure what he was dealing with.

"Yes, sir," Magdallen said.

"Good. Go."

The CG might indeed have overstepped his limits this time, he thought, staring at Magdallen's black-coated back. This man was not stupid. This man was going to think, and think for himself.

A blink as the door shut. He activated his tap cautiously, contacted security, asked:

"Can the Ila's tap be questioned?"

"Brain-dead, sir. They're attempting restoration. They say the outlook isn't at all good."

"Understood." He tapped out in disgust.

For the rest . . . he punched physical keys, glossed through the med reports that flitted across the desk, one in front of the other. Every tap on duty had been affected, and that included Auguste, who was suffering blinding migraine and who, despite valiant efforts, couldn't find Marak. Or Drusus.

Lovely.

He *didn't* tap down to the planet to investigate Luz or the Ila, and he didn't contact Ian, who was very likely furious with Luz over the incident and probably had a headache to match his. He didn't want another of the Ila's messages blasting through the system—not at the risk of the taps.

The Ila had managed to set the whole system on its ear.

And the new rift in the Southern Wall, meanwhile, which was the slow tumble of a house of cards, *ondat* revenge, long postponed . . . that cataclysm just casually proceeded on its way like a juggernaut, as the plates had been moving for ages.

Did he half suspect that the Ila had timed her efforts up here to coincide with an era of maximum attention on a planet-changing event? He had his strong suspicions. His very strong suspicions. The whole Project had been concentrating on a narrow section of planetary crust—and never even thinking the tap system had become a sieve, coinciding with actions attracting Earth's passionate disapproval.

Instruments could, however imperfectly, see beneath the clouds of condensation down there, and it was truly spectacular now, that waterfall.

Damned lucky that Marak hadn't had a closer view of it. *He* was diverted, Ian was diverted. Everyone was busy and a little desperate. And no matter how involved Ian might like to be now in the Luz-Ila matter, quakes down at Halfmoon would likely continue to be a priority, getting Marak and his people out alive.

The Ila had appeared to reform, abandoning her usual diversion of making a director's life interesting. She had been so nicely cooperative lately. God.

What was this new sea about to bring the universe at large? The long-sought remediation? Proof that life on Marak's World was unlikely to infect *ondat*? Proof that Movement technology, running down its own evolutionary track, could devolve into simple, nonaggressive biology, ultimately capable of working only in its own limited environment?

The Ila was dead set, as always, on blowing that happy outcome to hell.

So Apex would check her move at Orb, and if they were lucky, on Concord itself. The Treaty Board had settled an agent here in the mistaken theory they were going to overturn a conspiracy and get their fingers into all sorts of business, while Earth's more conservative public, convinced by agelong propaganda that one simple mod was damnation, would view an assassination attempt on Concord and a lab raid on Orb as armageddon in full career. Concord and Earth were in for a period of unhappy and dangerous relations, while the Ila sat and watched, ever so pleased.

God, he'd like to ask the Ila's tap some critical questions. But that was never going to happen.

And he had a meeting of the Council in less than an hour, in which time he now had to decide how much of Magdallen's claim to let out to that body for debate. He decided that, no, he *wouldn't* attend. But he did have to instruct his proxy. And he had to consider what Magdallen had said, that it might be time to turn over that office.

"Sir." Dianne. "Drusus is reporting in, on one."

Physical line. He punched a button on common com. "Drusus. Are you all right?"

"Not so good, sir. I'm at a public phone. But I'm on my feet. I heard it. Shall I go on?"

Drusus, veteran Drusus, didn't ask what had happened to cause that blowup on the tap. Didn't sit down and quit. But he'd been hit, wide open.

"Do you need medical?"

"I don't think so, sir. I'm functional. Bad headache, but not so I can't continue. I've talked with several people who know our man. They claim they haven't seen him. That they're concerned and looking for him. Which probably means he's found a dark hole somewhere, if his head is like mine, right now."

Brave Drusus. "Get home right now and relieve Auguste. Auguste was hit hard. We don't know about his contact."

"Yes, sir," was all Drusus said, the public line being no place to discuss department business, and depend on it, Drusus was on his way at all possible speed, to take up a duty, bottom line, more important than Procyon's survival. The man deserved a medal. And his reporting in meant the PO had one less worry on the streets.

He didn't think the Ila had meant to kill Marak's taps. Antagonizing Earth, threatening civilization, yes—on their scale a disaster; on hers, a maneuver that might or might not pay what she hoped. But a war with Marak, an antagonism that could keep an anger alive as long as Marak's memory, he very much doubted was anywhere on her agenda. In their way, the oldest immortals stuck together in a dynamic of touchy personalities, and what Luz currently wanted, which was to find Procyon, the Ila seemed to want. She had told Procyon to get home. Her help was intended to win leverage, maybe, inside downworld's ongoing politics . . . because Marak was going to be damned mad if he gathered the scattered pieces of this business and put them together, to find out that the Ila had harmed his watcher.

He had one more call to make before he briefed his proxy for the

Council meeting: he wanted to find out what Reaux had learned from Gide, and simultaneously to drop a piece of information in the governor's lap.

"GOVERNOR." Jewel Sanduski hastened her pace to overtake Reaux in the hospital corridor right by the front doors. "The Chairman wants to talk to you. Where?"

There wasn't a convenient place. "Take station there," Reaux said to his bodyguard, pointing to a public restroom back down the hospital corridor. He walked back, ascertained it was empty, set them on watch to keep people out, and took Jewel inside the restroom foyer with him.

"Antonio?" he asked, over by the mirror and away from the door where his guards were. "We're as secure now as we're going to be."

"We've had several problems just come to light. How's Gide?"

"Not that bad. Angry. Very angry. He has credentials, and he's threatening to establish an office of his own on station, which I don't think I can prevent, but I can limit, by the Treaty itself. I'm headed back to my office at the moment. You caught me on my way out of the hospital."

"Have you any word on your daughter?"

How in hell did Brazis know about Kathy? His face heated. His heart skipped a beat. But he kept his equilibrium. "No, I haven't. Agents are out searching. No word on Mr. Stafford at the moment. No word from the ship out there. My staff's monitoring the situation, but no one's talking to us."

"Someone was talking, unfortunately. The Ila pirated her way onto the tap network looking for Mr. Stafford and completely fried her senior tap in the process."

"God!"

"Every tap we had working is affected—migraines, nausea—and the one they're trying to resuscitate, but they hold out very little hope she'll ever function."

"This is intolerable!" He wasn't sure whether he meant this unnerving mode of conversation, through a tap-courier's unexpressive mouth, or the fact the devil incarnate had breached station security while Earth was minutely scrutinizing every move he made.

"I did get brief contact with Procyon, in the process, but I couldn't ascertain location. He is alive, and there are a lot of holes he could duck into. We're trying to find him. Apex is upset. They have an agent here, who's just presented himself to hear my strong complaints, and he's likewise interested in what your Mr. Gide came here for—the notion of illicits getting up off the planet. He's here to counter Mr. Gide's presence. So we have a problem, Setha, a big problem. The Ila is involved, to the hilt."

"She can get in on your system anytime she wants?"

"Unfortunately that's turned out to be true. Worse, I fear she can do it with far less commotion than she just created. She's had the Project tap for a very long time, which we did of course know: she acquired it from Ian. And now we know she's breached our codes to reach us as noisily as possible, doing a great deal of damage. I wouldn't put it past her to be involved with data-smuggling, if she had the means, and quite frankly, she may have found a way in. Why she blew through so publicly—the motive may have been to silence her own tap contact, who may have been passing information as Gide thought—or maybe to try to convince me she's necessarily that noisy when she does it, and I don't believe that for a moment. I think she's been into our system many times without being detected. I'm ready to believe Gide's suspicions may actually be valid."

A deep breath. Second thoughts. And a desperate commitment. Give information and get information. "Listen, Antonio: Gide is definitely Treaty Board. He's setting up an office here. I can't prevent that. He insists there's First Movement operating on the station, among the Freethinkers, of all places. What you've turned up, then . . . that makes you think he's not mistaken in his suspicion. Something *has* gotten off the planet."

"Not necessarily the things we would most fear. We doubt she would start with her most valuable commodities. We take it seriously enough. Council is going into session." It was always Jewel's voice, incongruously so, Jewel's eyes that assessed his reactions. "I'm going to be hard to find for the next hour, but my proxy will be handling Council, informing them of what they have to know to deal with Mr. Gide. I have other business, which I can't talk about. No matter where I am, Jewel can reach me at any time. She'll stay in your vicinity. I say again, stay entirely away from Stafford. Let me bring him in. We have strong evidence

*that your chief of security is secretly reporting to the ship, that he's an
agent of some party on Earth, or of the Treaty Board itself. We think* Dortland *may have deliberately cracked Gide's containment and stranded
him, on orders Gide knew nothing about. This would mean an overt and
a covert operation of the Treaty Board here at Concord simultaneously.
Does this alarm you?"*

Reaux's heart accelerated its already rapid beat. Dortland, a
spy? It might be a clever lie. It might be a deliberate attempt to isolate him from his own staff, and make him get his information
from Outsider sources at the very moment Brazis had just confessed how compromised those sources were.

But exotic equipment, a short-range missile, for God's sake,
smuggled into an exclusive garden court, past tight security—

Two of Dortland's men had died, in that garden, of neuronics, a
close-up kind of weapon, and not one the average criminal could get.

Would Dortland do a thing like that? His own men? Men he
could just walk up and touch? Take utterly by surprise?

"What evidence do you have of that?"

*"I tell you the barest, unproven information I have. I have yet to con-
firm it from another source. But I value you as a stable influence in office,
and I have no wish to see you replaced or in any way subordinated to the
Treaty Board. That would be an unacceptable change in the status quo.
Don't trust Dortland. Above all, I ask you* don't *let him near Stafford. I
want you to get Dortland off that case. If he snatches a Project tap, you
know what hell is going to break loose, with my government and, for that
matter, with the* ondat. *Let's never forget them, if the peace is violated."*

Where was he going to get a distraction to take Dortland off the
hunt for Stafford?

Send him hunting for his own daughter?

That was all the distraction he had to offer. Damn it all to hell, if
he couldn't trust Dortland, he couldn't trust anybody Dortland
had hired. He was utterly isolated, except for Ernst. Except for his
Outsider contacts.

And could he use Kathy that cold-bloodedly, even put her in
harm's way, supposing Dortland might have motives to bring him
down?

He didn't know what viable alternative he had. He didn't know
who he had left that he could trust.

He signed off with Jewel and exited their impromptu conference room, gathering up his escort, two of Dortland's men, as Jewel tagged behind them. He made a phone call as he walked. "Ernst?"

"Sir?"

"I've received very alarming news. Call Dortland. I want him to go down to Blunt himself, I want him to find Kathy. Highest priority."

10

"NOTHING," Marak reported to Hati, who begged him to silence all the voices and not to attempt the contact again—but he was more than annoyed, now, beyond the fact of a brutal headache. He rode, still, patiently along a sandstone ledge, Hati behind him. There was silence in heavens and the earth alike—the chatter was all hushed, now, everyone lying low.

No response from Luz, none from Ian. Auguste was ill, incapable of coherent answers if he had any beyond, *"I swear I have no idea, omi."*

Now the system had blown up. By all he could determine, the Ila had broken into the system for a momentary contact with Procyon, which he had not managed to join quickly enough. Auguste, close to a relay, had fallen ill, and Ian and Luz were probably still arguing age-old grievances with one another. It was one of those times when the width of the desert was probably a good distance.

It would have been a good thing, except the haze in the west, that they had watched grow and grow—a cloud now towering into the heavens and spreading.

More, the wind had acquired a strange smell, a dank, rotten smell compounded with the tang of wet sand as the wind swept upward from the basin floor. There was no sight of the distant calamity. At any moment the gap might break wide. The sands nearest Halfmoon were being deluged with sea water, a widening pool, by now, churned deeper and deeper by falling water. The heavens failed to advise them how the catastrophe was progressing. Auguste, who had been advising him on his route, and who had promised him a way back no matter the weather, was afflicted and silent.

If the whole of the Wall at Halfmoon should go—suddenly—in one of the frequent aftershocks—what might they see on that horizon?

Much more than a cloud, he was sure, and meanwhile the silly beshti kept zigzagging their way down and down as if they had all the time in the world, ultimately headed to the pans, the sort of terrain that had made their ancestors lords of the desert. Down there was graze. And water. Could they not smell water on the wind?

The fools had no idea what they smelled. That it was all the water in the world threatening to thunder down in a kind of flood no beshta's instinct could imagine; these beshti had no idea.

In the scales of the worlds above the world, this handful of recalcitrant beshti had become a dire problem. There might well be siege in the heavens. The long peace with the *ondat* might be ending. The earth still shuddered from the last cataclysm, the broken pieces of its crust drifting across the heat of hell, and now the heavens threatened to go to war over an Earth lord's whim and a feud breaking out between the Ila and Ian, one he had wanted no part of in its early stages. Let them shout and threaten, he had said, when it started. Let them spend the first wind of their anger.

He had in mind to spend a great deal of time in the desert. After that he might mediate. He had not planned on being the center of the argument.

They came easily down to the next terrace, he and Hati, following the still recent passage of soft pads on old dust. Beshti hardly went without a trace—but if that cloud went on spreading across the horizon and a deluge came down, adding to their hazards, the tracks would vanish, too. The young bull kept his stolen herd moving just enough. But let him get a head start, let the thunder and the rain add panic to earthquake, and the females, however reluctant now, might take out for the pans for good and all.

The beshti under them smelled change in the wind, too, and there was this about beshti: they stuck tighter together when things went badly. Their own pair sniffed the tracks and smelled the rocks, aware what they were tracking, uneasy in this shift of the wind, Hati's female seeking others of her kind and his own old bull, smelling the scent of the young rebel, gaining a darker, more combative intent.

The terrace they reached was vast, having its own horizon, having piles of rock and growth of vegetation, some of which, greasewood, grew taller here than it had on the unprotected plateau or the ridge above.

Their fugitives might be somewhere on this very level, somewhere beyond the spires of sandstone, the irregular ins and outs of the shelf and the obscuring growth of tall brush. The terraces and ledges that seemed from above to offer easy passage down to the pans proved, not unexpectedly, a constant frustration of dead ends and precarious edges, the most promising ways as apt to strand the herd with no way out but a long trek back the way they had come—toward them. At all disadvantage, they were still gaining on their quarry, and if the heavens could settle down and pay attention again, he still might get his needed information on their route.

But he could not wait for that help. Night was coming on, when the young rascal might not rest. The Ila had made a disastrous move. Now the sullen and strange tribes of Earth were making demands on Brazis that for some reason Brazis could not resist, and the whole untidy intersection of interests was increasingly threatening.

The Ila had had one of her notions go extremely wrong, in his best guess. He could sometimes prevail with the Ila: they shared certain views. They both knew the world as Luz and Ian had never seen it, and shared opinions Luz and Ian did not understand. He knew her ways and her attitudes, and he would offer to intercede, if anyone could listen. Luz was alone with the situation, alone with the Ila in the Refuge, he was aware of that, and knew the two of them had been entirely too friendly lately. Luz was in the Refuge, and Ian—Ian was likely off at the far end of the lake, in the town that had grown there. Ian, who had been Luz's lover off and on for as long as the Refuge had stood, was currently not Luz's lover, and a feud had simmered between Ian and Luz with varying heat for most of the last hundred years. It had started over Ian's insistence on autonomy in his own work, unease in a relationship that had grown with Luz's dislike and Ian's support of the previous director in the heavens, who had had ideas coinciding with Ian's, on the apportionment of scarce metals.

And now, it seemed, that old rift had led to uneasy relations with the director's successor, Brazis, and Luz, of course, had found a sympathetic ear in the Ila. The two of them, disliking Brazis, complained of his continuation of the old director's programs. Luz clung close to the Refuge, which the Ila never left, while, tired of the disagreement, Ian lately lived with Nai'ib, a mortal woman from the tribes, out on the Paradise shore.

Ian sulked, working on his rockets, his robots, machines that supported certain of his desert roads, and occasionally made his own forays into the eastern desert. Ian was consequently in closer contact and sympathy with the tribes than Luz had ever been willing to be, herself. The tribeswoman living with Ian was only one cause of the rift between them.

"Wasting his time," Luz had complained to Marak two years ago, and asked if he had a better understanding than she did of Ian, the man who had been her lifelong partner. "What in all reason does he do out there?"

"He receives reports from the riders," had been his observation. "He does the same as always. He tests his machines."

Biology and mechanics, life and cold, scarce metal, which Ian hoarded for his projects and sought in the wreckage of villages and the Holy City itself, up on the Plateau. Such were Ian's consuming passions. Luz was the theoretician, the planner, the builder—and oh, the Ila was a builder and a planner, herself, no question of that.

Now he feared they would see the result of all this diverse planning, disturbance in the heavens and this ill-timed schism in the Refuge—or a very well timed one, chosen to break out just now, when he was not at hand, when the heavens were besieged by angry allies.

But if Auguste was hurt in this assault, Ian had been quick to protect all of them whose watchers might be affected. Luz, who might well have figured by now that she had been deceived, would be busy reasoning with the Ila and trying to protect the relays themselves: that would be her first thought. Luz would banish until later, in her realization, the thought that flesh and blood might be in danger, might feel pain, might die. That was the way they were, Ian and Luz. It was why he attached himself more to Ian.

But now he asked himself if Ian drifting away to the Paradise shore with Nai'ib might be why Luz continued lonely and upset, and why she had fallen more and more into the Ila's company.

That association had its inevitable outcome. Luz was betrayed, now, it seemed, by an expert at betrayal. And would she learn? For a century or two. Maybe.

But there was nothing he and Hati could do now but go on as they were and keep careful track of their lacework of escape routes, making sure no shortcut brought them back up to a dead end, if the worst suddenly happened at Halfmoon. Negotiate with the Ila, he might, but not with the earthquake.

And once they had the beshti back, if the heavens and earth wanted to quarrel for a century or two, they would still have the beshti, and the boys, and the canvas. Let them all do what they liked, Brazis and the Ila, Ian, Luz, and the rest. They were untouchable out here, give or take another hammerfall, once they got back to safety. There had been quarrels before. There had been long silences in the heavens. The *ondat* were the problem. The one uncertainty. The threat none of them wanted to wake.

"We shall be soaked before nightfall," Hati estimated. She tapped her beshta with her heel as it showed interest in a thornbush, and shortened up on the rein.

The beshta squalled a protest at this injustice, swayed from side to side under the taut rein and kept squalling to the heavens. The cliffs above echoed with her indignation.

And found a new source not so far distant. Beshti called to beshti, in the uneasy smell of the wind.

Then the old bull bellowed out, throwing up his head.

That brought a second distant answer, three, four voices, female. And a raucous challenge.

"Aha," Hati said. "The young bull out there is worried now. We may get them yet."

"*Marak.*"

A quiet voice from the tap, this. Ian's. He was by no means

sure he wanted to listen. His headache persuaded him it might not be safe.

"*Marak, do you hear me?*"

"Ian. We have very little patience for this."

"*Marak-omi, there's trouble in the Refuge. The Ila has invaded systems aloft and killed her oldest watcher. She has demanded Procyon's return to duty in your name. Luz has now entered her apartments and attempted to reason with her. The force of the Ila's action has done damage to all the watchers.*"

Forgotten, the beshti, everything, in the vivid imagination of the Ila's establishment in the Refuge, the Ila and her aau'it and her guards, Memnanan still among them. Memnanan would be put in a very difficult position if the Ila bade him bar Luz from her premises.

Without hesitation, headache and all, he reached out for the Ila himself, the system being open for the moment. He did not do it as he wished, like a thunderbolt, but reasonably, quietly, well under control. "Ila. What have you done?"

"*There you are, Marak Trin Tain. And how do you fare?*"

"Well enough, until I hear earth and heavens are in an uproar. Why should you kill your watcher?"

"*Why? Why not?*"

Temper. High temper. "Ila, favor me with an answer. Why would you harm an innocent?"

"*For your safety! For the safety of the world, with traitors in the heavens and the ambitions of the small, stupid men who protect them, now let loose to cause all of us grief! Be silent, Luz! We will tell him! Listen, Marak. Are you listening now?*"

"I am listening, Ila."

"*This watcher of ours, this long-trusted watcher, this innocent, requested information of us regarding the watcher nanoceles. She said this was the request of the director, to investigate suspect development at another station. With this answer, she evidently, and on her own mischief, misdirected what details we told her to the very culprits at issue, who are complete fools, and who have now been detected, not only by every authority in their vicinity, but by Earth, which should have never been involved at all. The director's establishment has lied to us, Marak Trin Tain. A watcher has misrepresented her authority and betrayed us to fools.*"

Compton *installed this treacherous woman when he was director, and that fool Brazis has allowed this liar to continue in her office for a decade, in a trusted post, when by now even remote Earth had gotten wind of her actions. How were we to know? Wherein are we at fault? Now they dare accuse us—us!—as if this were our initiation and our doing. Damn them, we say! We are outraged!"*

As if she were the most innocent of parties. And who was to know the truth of it, once the watcher in question was dead?

"Ila." That was Ian. *"You should have told us the moment there was such a request made of you. Why should you keep it secret?"*

"This person claimed it was investigatory, and that you were not to be brought in. How were we to know if your own watchers were in question? You, honest Ian, we did not doubt. But the watchers, who can ever know?"

Hati looked at him, that long-eyed sidelong look. She had heard. Hati had never trusted Luz, and least of all trusted the Ila at any time. It was a plausible story . . . if there had not been ages of history behind it.

"Now," the Ila said, *"someone has attempted to kill this Earth lord. We have not breached the Treaty. Their notion of our deception is utterly false; and they have attempted to blame this innocent boy of yours, while Brazis has done nothing to find him or protect him from these rival authorities. We, mind you, we have located Procyon with no trouble. He was injured in the attack on the Earth lord. He is attempting to get to safety with no help at all from Brazis, even in Brazis's own territory, and now, now, of course, just as we locate him, Brazis leaps in and disturbs the contact. Ask what hope this boy has while the powers that rule him maneuver for advantage. Ask where he may be now, in whose hands, asked what questions. Brazis wishes to divert all our attention to a dead traitor. But where is the danger? In a dead watcher? We think not. We have all been lied to. We answered a watcher's questions to control a breach in security; and now that Earth is offended, Brazis makes diversionary attacks on your watchers. Ask yourself, Marak, what does Brazis intend? Why did he give you no warning that this great quake was coming, when he has accurately predicted others? One might think Brazis was a fool and too compliant; but we, at least, have never thought he was a fool, or compliant in anything."*

Marak listened, and met Hati's burning gaze the while. There was a small silence from Ian and Luz.

"I will find Procyon," Marak said. The beshta under him, at a standstill, shifted uneasily, as, far distant, he heard a stone roll and saw it make a track down a sandy slope.

A very minor quake. But the minor shiftings of the earth no longer alarmed them, in the scale of things. The Ila and what was happening back at the Refuge had sent out tremors of their own. And a hapless boy was involved in things far, far older than his knowledge, where it was likely those in power had set him far down the list of their concerns.

"*Ian,*" Luz said urgently. "*Come home. Come home,* now. *I need you.*"

"*I would, I assure you. But I'm trying to put together a mission to get Marak back.*"

"I shall deal with my own situation," Marak said. "Go home, Ian." If Luz forgot she was angry at Ian, if she forgot about the tribeswoman, then she was truly alarmed, whether by what the Ila had just said, or by what she feared the Ila might have done without her knowledge, or at the situation she herself was in. If the makers were indeed loose in the heavens, with the *ondat* and the rest of the powers alarmed, there was ample reason for Luz to reconsider her quarrel with Ian and question her alliance with the Ila before everything slid to perdition.

"*We are quite enough to deal with this,*" the Ila said. "*If we approach Brazis, we can settle matters without Ian.*"

That might be, but Ian had heard that. "*I'm on my way.*"

"*Nonsense,*" the Ila said, irate, and pain lanced through Marak's head.

He fired back, spiked the contact as high as he could, and gave the Ila as good as he got, reckless, for the moment, of Hati on the system.

He was as near a relay station as the Ila was near the center at the Refuge. *He* threaded his way through Ian's contact and into the main systems.

And having done that, he broke through all the relays and onto the uplink. Auguste was not his target. Not at all. He used a different code, one he had known a long, long time ago.

"Brazis," he said, in no mood now to temporize. "Answer me! Where is Procyon?"

* * *

THE SCISSORS HIT the floor. An orchid leaf fell. Brazis himself put a hand to his face and fell into the adjacent chair. The system shielded him, but the tap flash hurt to the roots of his teeth.

"Lord Marak," he said. "I hear you. Enough! I hear!"

"Brazis." Marak was clearly not in a reasoning mood. *"Is there an outbreak of makers in the heavens?"*

"No," Brazis said, too-quick denial of what he could not wholly dismiss as a threat, denial to the wrong party. He amended that. "We don't believe it's actual. It's a fear Earth has."

"Where is Procyon and what has he to do with such things?"

"Lord Marak." Brazis's mind raced. The tap system was adaptive. It tried to cooperate. Even when the system had the spike mechanically damped, its inclination was to respond and attempt to go on working. "The Ila's senior tap is dead, Marak-omi. Be careful. I hear you. Quieter, sir. Quieter. The system is bringing you through quite clearly."

"Where is Procyon?"

Where is Procyon? encompassed a world of trouble. Marak had clearly reached the end of his patience. In answer to that question, he might know down to a quarter block on Blunt *where* Procyon had been, but Procyon was not there, not now. Agents, racing to the area, had failed to locate him. Jewel, stationed with Reaux, reported Reaux's men hadn't snatched him . . . not that Reaux knew about.

"I don't know where he is at this exact moment, lord Marak. I am alarmed by his situation. I do assure you we're trying everything to find him."

A small silence. *"I find no response from him."*

"Nor do we." It was the truth, and it could mean Procyon Stafford was unconscious, or dead. "We're actively searching the system. We know where he was a while ago. He's not there now. How are *you* faring in the meantime, sir? Are you safe? We're extremely concerned about your situation."

"We are not in immediate difficulty, lord Brazis, but the stink of flood is strong on the wind, and the quakes continue, one after the other, bringing down rocks from the cliffs. I am not in great patience as matters stand.

Now I hear trouble in your vicinity and trouble at the Refuge. Is there or is there not an outbreak of makers?"

"Earth fears there is. I entirely doubt it. Complicating our situation, someone has attempted to kill Earth's representative, who was here investigating the matter, but—" Dared he be honest with Marak, who did not forget, or readily forgive? The ground he stood on was less steady than Marak's. "I have a strong suspicion it was another Earthman who did it, a traitor who wants a foothold here, perhaps one of the man's own allies. We have a complex and dangerous situation, and it may involve a ploy to establish someone's power or presence here, endangering the Treaty."

"And Procyon?"

"He was with the Earth representative when the attack happened. We believe he was injured and shaken by explosion. I ask you, lord Marak, be much quieter in the system. Don't wreck us. Let us work. The Ila occupied the system and possibly harmed some of the taps. I don't know Auguste's condition now. You may harm him if you press too hard."

A pause. *"Well enough. But I intend to find this boy myself if you take much longer about it, I warn you, lord Brazis, I am short of time and short of patience. The system is our lifeline, and we are approaching a critical need for it."*

"I well understand that, sir. And I ask you, in all courtesy, report to us what you do find."

Silence, then. Silence so sudden it left a burning sensation in his skull. Brazis rubbed his ears and found his hands were shaking.

He got up from the chair and exited to Dianne's office. She looked up from her desk, clearly unaffected, except by the sight of him. *She* hadn't been within the system, that or Marak's approach had been skilled and surgical, going straight where he wanted it . . . unlike the Ila's blazing entry. Damned right, the Ila's action had been a disruptive attack.

"Sir?" Dianne asked. "Sir, are you all right?"

"I'm not sure," he said. "Fast inventory of the taps. Particularly Drusus and Auguste. Get them to check in." He had a shuddering urge to sit down, but stayed on his feet. Dianne was already talking to the system. It had survived. The government still stood.

"Auguste's lying down on his couch," Dianne murmured. "Drusus has reached his apartment in the last two minutes. Both have severe headache."

"I don't doubt," he said. So had he.

"Are you going to address the Council at all, sir?"

"No. Everything to my proxy. This is far too hot." He had to sit down. His vision kept going in and out. He walked over to an interview chair and dropped into it.

"Shall I get you some ice water, sir? Do you need Dr. James?"

"No. Water." Ice water sounded very good. He wasn't sure, else. The system was under attack, and he had Magdallen, whose credentials he couldn't completely verify—and he had Marak, who right now was in the middle of the wilderness, while the Ila claimed she was on Marak's side. He by no means believed that.

And Luz urgently called Ian in to help her, a 40k trek by truck or beshta.

Help her do what? Silence the Ila, or keep the worldlink to the tap system from collapse?

Worse thought, could Ian possibly be heading into danger, an ambush at home?

He took a chance with his aching head and tapped into security. "Open the system, all relays."

"*All relays, sir, confirm.*"

"You heard me. All relays. Do it but keep the damper in place." If this kept up, if the Ila and Marak grew more insistent in their attempts to get in past mechanisms they likely knew far better than did the technicians managing the net, it could damage the wetware of the critical system, nanisms lodged in vulnerable human skulls—nanoceles that, in his own skull, were already busy repairing the damage, overheating his body, pushing his metabolism at the moment to fever heat.

Which pushed his blood sugar way low. He wanted an orange juice instead of the water, and asked Dianne to get it for him.

She brought him that and a thickly iced danish, taking a subjective eternity to do it. By the time it arrived he was shaking so he could hardly pick up the orange juice.

*   *   *

A GRITTY FLOOR, dim light, towering, dirty facades. Procyon had no idea how he had come to be lying in discarded plastic in system twilight with a hellacious headache, but he was.

Suddenly remembering cleaning robots—stupid robots that couldn't tell him from the trash—he scrambled up.

He got as far as his knees before the pain in his forehead dropped him onto his elbows, momentarily blind. He crawled over against the wall to let his heart settle down and his vision clear. It did, and to his horror he found himself in a service nook facing a cleaner slot, one of those little gates where the service bots went back into the secret places of the station. He'd never paid attention to them. Now he remembered being dragged off inside. If things couldn't fit in the slots, bots took them apart, ripped plastics, shredded metal.

But they weren't supposed to take dead bodies, let alone living people.

Had it happened at all? Or was he hallucinating the whole thing?

He didn't know how he'd gotten here. He felt heat in his face, heat running through all his body.

That wasn't right. Like when he'd taken the Project dose, that was what it felt like, when he'd first acquired the high-tech tap and the visual machines. Beyond the fever, his head hurt, back to front and side to side, a lancing pain that slowly centered on his forehead.

He felt of his forehead, expecting blood. There wasn't. Just a welt. And in a self-preservative moment of clear thinking, he wanted away from that cleaner slot, as far as he could get, in case he passed out again.

He got a knee under him, hands on the wall, and levered his way up to his feet.

There. Nothing broken. Hell of a headache. General sick feeling, from gut to diaphragm.

Then he remembered Gide.

He remembered talking to Luz.

And the Ila.

He immediately tried to make the blood shunt to contact the office. The effort sent pain through the roots of his teeth, total disruption of vision and sense that dropped him where he stood. He tried again, ignoring the pain, and it just wouldn't happen. All he heard was the distant, constant noise of the street.

Then:

"*Procyon.*"

Luz. His heart jolted in panic and he braced himself for the white pain that was the Ila.

But the next sound was a man's voice, a familiar, welcome voice. "*Procyon.*"

"Marak-omi." Relief and terror at once. He was on his rump in an alley in fear for his life and his continuance in the program, and *Marak* had found him again, through Luz—Marak, who had every reason to be upset with his absence in this crazed mess. He staggered to his feet. "I'm very sorry, sir. I've been trying as hard as I can to get back to you." As if he'd just missed a phone call. Fool. And his voice was shaking so he didn't know if Marak could even understand him. "I have a small problem." Twice fool. He'd promised Marak he'd be back before now. Before . . .

He couldn't remember.

"I'm still trying to get home, sir."

"*Are you in safety now?*"

"I think I'm fairly safe now, yes, sir."

"*What is Brazis doing about your situation?*"

"I don't know, sir." He didn't know how much Marak actually knew about Brazis, about the station, or by now, about the craziness that was going on. Marak's question, What is Brazis doing? ricocheted off the completely unrelated fact that flashed into his mind, that some tremendous force had come past him in a doorway, from the outside, from the garden. Not his apartment. The ambassador's.

Security had suffered a massive lapse—if it *was* an accidental lapse. Gide hadn't just blown up. Someone had fired past him. He'd tried to help Gide. And it wasn't his fault.

Very big events were sailing over his head, and one lowly tap, even if he was Marak's, wasn't on that high a priority for survival—not in the scale of governments having an argument. Brazis assuredly wouldn't risk the Project for him.

But Marak, who didn't give a damn about most that existed up here . . . Marak was contacting him, like the Ila, through relays he was sure weren't part of the public system.

"I think I'm in trouble," he confided to Marak, trying not to shiver. "I think I'm in very serious trouble."

"*Explain,*" Marak said, an order from a man for unthinkable ages used to being obeyed; and just as quickly, in the tones of any man having found something lost: "*Hati, I have him. He says he is away from home and in trouble.*"

Hati said something. There was a faint rumble.

"What was that, sir?"

"*Thunder,*" Marak said.

His own pain dimmed. "Have you shelter? Are you in danger?"

"*Dismiss concern for us. Listen. You never should have been involved with this Earth lord. Now the Ila has found a way to reach you, Brazis knows it, others in the heavens may know it, and Ian and Luz certainly know how it was done. This is a dangerous situation.*"

Another rumbling of thunder. He heard beshti call out, that rare and eerie sound, as he sat shivering next to an ominous gateway in an alley nook. His teeth chattered shamefully. But it was a comfort to hear those sounds, to settle his mind down on the world. "I am safe at the moment, omi."

"*Take no chances,*" Marak said. "*Avoid all disputes with the Ila.*"

"Yes, sir," he said. The tap had never hurt, not since his first days on the system, but now it ached from the base of his skull to the roots of his teeth, and his forehead stung as if he'd been burned. The relays out here seemed at the point of overload. So did he. He bowed his head into his arms, intending to follow Marak's advice and not budge or use the tap until he had guidance.

The pain became too much. He lost whatever Marak had said. He lost Marak. He was blind, beset with flashing lights that floated in his vision.

"*Procyon. Answer me. Where are you?*" Marak again.

"Trying to figure that out, sir. A street—near where I live. I have a terrible headache. I'm trying to get home."

"*How far is that?*"

"Not that far." Complications in his situation recurred to him. The lost coat. The dark place. Earther authorities were looking to get their hands on him. "I think it's night." Night was when they took the lights down on the streets, to satisfy the human need for night, for change in the day. White light went down and neon came up, and then a person trying to get home could be a little less conspicuous.

Unless police happened to be watching his apartment. Police had been following him. He thought they had been following him. He had a memory, a quick flash, finding blood on his coat. He'd lost the coat, thrown it away, to avoid detection. What else had he done?

"Procyon, are you safe?"

"I think so, sir. It hurts. I want to let the headache go away. It's hard to think. Give me an hour, sir. About an hour. I'll get on home. I promise you I'll be all right."

AN HOUR ON, the attempt at contact died in a confused flutter of noise and lights, and Marak, sitting cross-legged on the ground, gave Hati a worried look.

"I cannot find him."

"Brazis?"

"I have said all I shall say to Brazis."

Twilight had come down, deep and strange. The contact he attempted kept fading out.

But the storm was coming on. Even near the relay, the signals might grow chancy.

They had not overtaken their fugitives, who had remained elusive and skittish with the weather. Cloud covered most of the sky now, flashing with lightnings, rumbling with thunder. The prospect of the oncoming gust front was what had persuaded them they should drive down the deep-stakes in the last of the light and take what rest they dared. The strange smell on the wind increased with surface air sweeping out of the west, a smell like old weed, wet sand, heated rock. It would be a blow. It would be a very strong blow.

"He is injured, whether by the goings-on with this man from Earth, or by the Ila's recklessness." He was angry at the entire situation. He clenched one hand over the other wrist, arms about his knees, gazing out into the murky distances of the basin below them, the spire-covered descent of sandstone terraces. "I will try again before we move."

The beshti, double-tethered with deep-irons right beside their sleeping mat, grazed on sweetweed that grew in a drift of sandy soil, as content as beshti could be, in this isolate, dangerous place, with the skies muttering warnings and the wind rising.

Their legs ached from their long, generally downward ride, constant jolting against one bracing leg or the other. It should have been a profound relief, too, finally to reach Procyon and prove that he was alive.

"Perhaps we should tell Ian," Hati said. "If not Brazis."

"Neither," he decided. "Neither, until I have some indication where his safety may lie. He claimed he was going home, which by no means sounded safe, if enemies were looking for him. An hour, he said. Now the contact fails. Perhaps the weather. But we have nothing from him. We have nothing from Ian."

"Husband, we have to look to ourselves. Time to go up."

Events pressed hard on them. They had come within hearing of the herd, and lost them. They camped now right at the crest of the rocky slant that was the herd's last and most frustrating escape. Contact with the Refuge had gone. Their terrace was broad and well away from overhangs, which protected them from quake. But that was not saying what layers of soft sediment underlay it, and what the rain might do.

Worse, they were about to lose the tracks, once rain came coursing down the myriad channels that laced across the slopes. They might pick them up after, in wet sand, but that was hoping the rain would stop before the flood overtook them.

"Shut your eyes," Hati said, hugging him in a little shiver of the earth, so slight even the weary, feeding beshti were indifferent to it. "Rest for what time we can, and hope the fog holds off. If we have to climb in a hurry, we climb, and hope the fool beshti out there do the same. The boys will meet us up on the ridge. For now, rest. We have done all we could. We cannot fight the rain. Shut your eyes. Half an hour. Then we climb out of this."

He put his arms around her and they lay down together, he lapping his robes across her, and hers across him.

In the dearth of information from the heavens, who alone had a comprehensive view of the situation, it became the only sane choice: get as much rest as they could before the weather turned, then pack up and climb back to relative safety. They would have to find the boys and walk down off the ridge, at the best speed they could manage, with their two beshti to carry canvas and supplies.

They might see their new sea. They only hoped not to see it yet.

11

THE HALCYON SAID it didn't take credit cards, which was just crazy. Every place in the universe took credit cards. But the Halcyon said it didn't, wouldn't, or maybe the manager just meant this card, which could be risky to raise a louder fuss about, Mignette thought, if her father had finally put a limit, or worse, a trace, on it. So she shut up, near to tears.

She was tired, she'd had a drink, she felt a little sick, and scared, and she and Noble were going to do it together if she could get a room at all, which at this point didn't look as likely as before. Michaelangelo's had turned out to be shut to anybody but current tenants. She was sure her father had done that, likely looking for her and making an untidy amount of noise about it.

That meant all the people that might have been partying late at Michaelangelo's, where they were supposed to meet Tink and Random as a last resort, were all scattered out all up and down Blunt, maybe competing for other rooms, which could mean there weren't that many to be had up and down the street. Someone said all the other places with rooms had raised the single night rate, because of Michaelangelo's shutdown. And they'd only found this one room, here, in a place they ought to be able to afford, a place that wasn't too dirty, and now the stupid asses who ran it decided they didn't want to take her card. She just wanted to scream, and didn't dare. It was only her self-restraint that brought her close to tears. It was pure temper, and the effort not to curse them up one side and down the other.

They had no actual cash, she and Noble. She'd never handled cash in her life, beyond a few chits for street fairs, and here she and Noble were trying to have their romantic night, which was supposed to be so special, and now she was so upset from arguing with a fool with disgusting cologne about a not-very-good room that she felt like throwing up. Now Noble was mad about the room situation—he was scowling and looking off at the bar, with his hands in his pockets. He was about to sulk and get rude to everybody around him, she saw it coming, and he had no sense when he got mad. He scared her.

Desperate, she left Noble and went back to the front desk to try again. "We've just got to have a room," she said, and burst all the way into tears. Tears sometimes worked. They did with her father.

"Well, I could do something for you," the man at the desk said, "if you do something for me."

"What's that?" she asked, and the man got off his stool and moved over to the office door.

"Come in here," he said.

She was stunned. "No!" she said, not half believing she'd just been propositioned by an old man in a cheap sweatshirt. She was outraged. Her face burned.

"Then get out of here," the man said. "Out!"

She was embarrassed to death to be crying in front of this man. "Come on," she said to Noble, and he still stood there like a lump with his hands in his pockets. She grabbed his elbow hard and tried to pull him out onto the street. He stood like a piece of the scenery and resisted going anywhere, being an ass.

"So what are we going to do, walk the streets all night?" he asked her.

She was furious. "I don't know what we're going to do, but I'm not going to sleep with that pig to get us a room!"

Noble took his hands out of his pockets and looked back at the front desk, as if he'd just waked up to the world.

He didn't, however, offer to go back to the desk and beat hell out of the pig.

"So where are we going to go?" he asked her.

"Well, you don't blame me, do you?" Her face had gone embarrassingly red, she knew it had, and people were staring at them, watchers all around the shadowy lobby with its imitation plants and its imitation wood. They'd become the show of the evening. People were sniggering. "They don't take cards, they won't talk, and when my father hears about this, oh, I promise you, that bastard is going to be looking for a ticket to Orb!" She said the last so the bastard would hear, but when she turned around, dragging Noble toward a dramatic exit, she ran straight into a living shadow, one of the Stylists, it had to be, that she had nearly bumped into. One of the beautiful people. Her embarrassment was complete.

"Well," this vision of beauty said.

Male voice. Silken voice. The face was red as blood on the left side, black as space on the right, with tendrils wandering actively between. The eyes glowed with red, inner fire.

And this person, this Stylist, took her hand and held it, a warm, a wonderful touch. "A genuine damsel in distress."

"Just a little trouble," she said shakily, letting go of Noble. She was unwilling to admit to this vision what an embarrassing financial trouble they were in—out of money and out of ideas.

"Do you need a place to stay tonight, lovely?"

"Myself—" She didn't want to admit to this gorgeous creature that she was attached to the sullen, unstylish teenaged lump sulking behind her with his hands in his pockets, but she had come here with Noble and she found herself standing by that fact. Maybe it was a sense of honor, even if it drove this gorgeous being away. Maybe it was fear. Noble was her safety, her barrier against transactions she didn't altogether understand. She said shakily: "*And* him."

"Oh, well. One, two, no difficulty." An ink black, fire-shot hand lifted to brush an airy touch across her cheek. "He can come along, too. But who are you, pretty thing?"

"Mignette." A Stylist thought she was pretty. Her heart raced, fluttered, raced. "I'm Mignette. He's Noble."

"Algol," her vision said, and flourished a gesture toward the outer door.

She walked with him out onto the street. Noble slouched along at their heels.

"An inconvenience, this disturbance up and down the street,"

Algol said, "but not to those of us with forethought and connections. You tried Michaelangelo's."

"It's shut," she protested.

"Oh, not to those of us who live there. You're new to the street, aren't you?"

She had to admit it. "I just arrived. Noble and I—"

"Oh, well, and the police have to show their authority now and again, darling girl. It's this Earth visitor that has them buzzing about. But their orders don't apply upstairs, to private apartments. Dear girl, we who have the keys to the place do as we please. We always have, always will. Such pretty eyes you have."

The contacts were just commercial, off the rack. She didn't feel constrained to blurt that out. She looked really good. She hadn't known how good. Her heart skipped and danced as they walked, together, in beautiful company.

Algol led them not to the front of Michaelangelo's, but around the side of the frontage to the service nook. She was uncertain that was safe, until she saw a delivery door.

He had a key.

"We're supposed to find Random and Tink," Noble objected from the background. She knew it wasn't Random and Tink that concerned him. Clearly Noble didn't at all like the way things were going. He would rather strand them back on the street with no place at all, than take help from a source that cast him in the background. But she didn't pay any attention. They had a personal invitation from a Stylist, and a place to go that had real cachet, and she wanted to go where the beautiful people went. She hadn't deserted Noble. She'd kept faith with him. So he could be mad for an hour. This was important. A prince of the Trend had swooped down for a rescue, because of her. This was a way into a rarefied society.

She stepped through the door that Algol opened for them, and Noble had no real choice but follow.

A LIZARD WATCHED a gnat, bubble-world confrontation above a rotting flower. Reaux, late-night in his office, watched the lizard, distracting himself as best he could from the quandary he had landed in, trying to have caff and a long-delayed sandwich in peace. Jewel was in one outer conference room, silent the last while, fed and supplied with reading material, concealed from any officials who might come and go.

Since Brazis's warning, he no longer dared rely on Dortland— nor dared he rely on Brazis, entirely. He had his own heavily paid plainclothes guard sitting watch on Gide.

Gide's associates on the *Southern Cross* were asking hard questions about the attack, and he had had to admit that there was as yet no word on Jeremy Stafford. So he said—while hoping there wouldn't be.

Dortland's men were watching Stafford's parents. He couldn't pull Dortland's whole force off the search for Stafford without rousing suspicions and getting *that* fact reported to Earth—very directly so, if Dortland was talking to that ship on secret channels. But he had two others of his own bodyguard, men who owed nothing to Dortland, watching down on Grozny, too, with no success yet in finding Stafford. Tracking anyone in the Trend tended to meet with resistance and deliberate misdirection. There were sightings. There had been three. But they didn't pan out.

Find my daughter, he'd asked Dortland personally, hours ago, when he'd gotten him on the phone. *There've been new threats.* Never mind the threats were from his wife. *I want her back. Now.*

Kathy was the best distraction he could offer, and he felt more than guilty doing it—as he felt guilty and frustrated in distrusting Dortland on Brazis's say-so. He felt ashamed of his current situation, and scared, increasingly isolated in the exercise of the power he did have, wondering even what Ernst thought of the orders that had come out of his office.

And increasingly he wondered, now, whether he would find Kathy before something disastrous happened . . . before he got a call from some hospital . . . or before she became a pawn in this covert maneuvering of powers Kathy had no idea of.

To add to his troubles, that phone call from Judy. She threatened to go down to the streets and look for Kathy herself—the very last thing that would help the situation, and she had cried when he told her so. Judy was furious about the police outside the apartment. She was furious that he hadn't dropped everything and come home to be with her at supper. She was doubly furious that he'd had all her calls routed to Ernst. "Not even to you," she'd cried, when he had, in desperation and compassion, talked to her. And at a screaming pitch: "How dare you?"

Well, he dared do it, as other things, because he had no damned choice. What he prayed for was a peaceable end to this situation, one that involved Stafford somehow turning up safely where he belonged, so they didn't have a blowup with Brazis.

And he prayed for a solution that didn't involve Andreas Gide setting up what Gide would try to expand into a shadow government on his station. But in the darkness of the hour, it didn't seem likely that he could prevent Gide trying it, and, despite his speech to Gide, he wasn't utterly confident he could keep power out of Gide's hands.

He wanted his former relationship with Brazis back, uncomplicated by Brazis's confidences. He wanted things the way they had been. Until he had better information, he wasn't sure he could trust anybody in the universe, even Ernst.

He rather thought of sending Dortland to Gide's new office, tied up with a bow, with recommendations of employment, once this was all over and that ship left. But with Dortland wearing his right colors, he'd still have to ask himself constantly which ministers, which councillors were in Gide's pocket—and those pockets, with every annual ship from Earth, could prove very deep indeed.

He could tell Gide privately that Dortland had engineered the attack. That might be interesting.

The lizard snapped his jaws in threat. The anoles never won. The gnats collectively never lost. System in perfect balance, as long as light came into the sphere and the temperature stayed moderate.

So had Concord been in perfect balance, for long, long ages. And did Earth or the Treaty Board itself think it was going to win something new if it came in here disrupting what worked just because some politician on the homeworld had a theory?

He saw the heart of the situation now: distrust had found a way onto his station, distrust of Brazis had moved Earth to send an agent here, Apex had sent an agent for the same reason, and to create their new trustable system—Earth now corrupted his agents, his office, his peaceful situation. No foreign assassins. None from Brazis's office. He was absolutely convinced now that Gide's arrival was a ploy, an elaborate, sacrificial ploy, unknown even to Gide, to land a Treaty Board office on his station and create yet one more power, one they hoped could override him and create trouble for Brazis.

And if Gide hadn't had a clue what they meant to do to him, Dortland being behind the attack made an unwelcome sort of sense. The mobile unit was slagged, to tell them nothing. Gide was only slightly injured. There'd been a launcher in the garden, yes, and yes, there'd been a projectile from outside, but had it killed Gide? No. Could it have killed Gide? Unknown, without examining the machine before the damage its own security systems had done to it. But he doubted it would have. Everything added up to Dortland, who would have killed two of his own men. And that meant Brazis was telling him the truth, that Dortland was working to bring him down.

He didn't want to believe it. He didn't want to deal with it. He'd never wanted to play life-and-death politics. But all sorts of desperate thoughts had nudged their way from the nether side of his brain, where they now established a well-defined architecture and a set of connections.

If Gide had mistakenly died in the attack, Earth would bluster and moan and threaten, and ultimately do nothing about it, since, public face, Earth well knew the hazards of truly ham-handed interference in the Outside, and most specifically at Concord, of all places.

But if someone on the Treaty Board was reckless enough to insinuate an office onto Concord, it was clearly in hopes that their pretense of hysterics and self-protection would dissuade Apex and the *ondat* from objecting too much to a fracture of the very Treaty they allegedly watchdogged.

And if things had shifted this much in the Treaty Board, that body had a great deal to learn about Apex. It was very possible, if Apex decided to counter this move, that Gide would be dead within the year, Dortland with him, accidentally, of course, neatly folding the new office, an unnegotiated folding as it had been an unnegotiated establishment—and he'd have to explain it all to the next Earth ship that called. He could trust Brazis—enough, but not far enough that he was willing to be the first Apex-supported Earth governor in history.

If he let it all play out that way, he could be in for a rough ride. But the alternative was dire. He could well see Earth, under the aegis of what began to look like a newly partisan Treaty Board, begin to play a dangerous third side in *ondat*-human politics, or thinking to do so—possibly getting a presence onto more than one station, creating yet other offices to trouble governors all over Outsider space. If the Treaty Board had gotten actively into politics, no one on Earth stopping them, it meant Earth now didn't trust the governors they themselves had put in office over unwilling populations in the Outside.

Apex had already spoken, via Brazis, a clear warning, hard, clear words.

Worse, they were undoubtedly going to hear from Kekellen once a report about this new office filtered through the translators.

God, maybe *Kekellen* would nix the idea.

Now *there* was a thought.

Apex would object to Gide setting up here—but Earth, who'd take anything Apex objected to as a very good idea, would think very differently if *Kekellen* rose up suddenly and objected. Earth had to count on Kekellen taking ages to understand something had changed. It notoriously took decades to negotiate any change of procedure with the *ondat*, in the delicacies and difficulties of translation, and while Kekellen usually ignored Earth's small shifts in policy—this—

This might prove different, if Kekellen understood that what they did marked a change in Earth's representation out here.

He was incredibly tempted to send his own message to Kekellen, now, before that ship left dock, both to pour oil on those dangerous waters personally and to urge Kekellen to protest before worse happened.

A dangerous, provocative move, to send a message to Kekellen without going through the experts. But his experts were, he had to recall, *licensed* by the Treaty Board.

Oh, that was nice. His translators were about to come under *Gide's* jurisdiction, and operate at his say-so.

Not an acceptable situation.

What he contemplated, however—God, it was dangerous. The *ondat* could take exception, take action, not even limited to Concord . . .

But it might be the most important act of his governorship—to protect Kekellen and the Treaty itself from what looked more and more like his overthrow and the establishment of a new Earth authority out here, at an outpost that meant the difference between peace and war.

What would he say to Kekellen, if he dared? What could he say to Kekellen, without overmuch abstraction, if he could gather the personal courage to risk his comfort, risk his life—risk his station's existence, for that matter? He had a wife and daughter to think of. They had their home, their comforts. He would have the illusion of power lifelong, if he kept his mouth shut and minimized his interference with Mr. Gide, and Brazis, and all the likely agents in a prolonged power game. Or if he strung things along in a series of compromises . . . lose a little, gain a little, playing a tight and narrow game, surrounded by Earth-staffed agencies he could no longer trust . . . he might survive and keep everybody alive, if he used his head. It was a terrible risk, to take direct action. To talk to the *ondat*—

But he had the official translation lexicon, among the books behind his desk. His computer could arrange acceptable syntax, and it routinely did that, when he needed to skim an incoming message. If he just picked the words cautiously and kept to solid concepts . . . not going into the network to tip off the experts as to what he was doing . . .

The rest of the sandwich lay untouched. He stared at the bubble world, chasing thoughts through this and that maze of official protocols, and threat, and weighing not only the possibility of detection after the fact—but before it.

He could do it. He *might* pull it off.

He could at least see if he could compose anything reasonable.

He surfaced his keyboard on the desk and made a cautious initial effort.

Reaux to Kekellen. Gide comes from Earth ship. Someone attacks Gide. Reaux thinks the attack is a trick. Gide wants power on Concord. Reaux asks Gide to leave, but Gide won't go. Gide's office on Concord will be rival Earth office. Concord needs your help to stop Gide.

The computer worked for a second or two with that input and came up with *ondat* script, and a corresponding translation: *Reaux to Kekellen. Gide comes from Earth ship. Attack on Gide unknown origins. Reaux says subterfuge. Reaux says Gide wants govern Concord. Reaux says Gide go. Gide says Gide not go. Gide makes hostile Earth office on Concord. Reaux says Concord wants Kekellen help, wants Kekellen stop Gide.*

A little further editing. Get that word *hostile* out of there.

The computer digested it and spat up something he halfway dared put his name on.

Something that could absolutely ruin him if it got to the wrong hands.

God, could he even trust Ernst?

He ate an antacid. One of the twelve-hour kind. He didn't rate himself reckless or stupid, and on one level, sending this message was beyond stupid, it was criminal. It put him and his family at terrible risk. It put the whole station, the whole situation with the *ondat*, at risk. Their weapons had taken out a planet. A space station, in their territory, was negligible. The end of everything.

But on another—what happened once Gide settled in? Could he even stay in office, once every enemy he had, Lyle Nazrani leading the pack, immediately threw their support to Gide and manufactured charges to bring him down and raise Gide to more and more prominence? He had organized enemies. He could see a challenge not just to him, but to the governorship, leading to the Treaty Board office de facto taking over, with Nazrani and crew power-grabbing all the way.

Which meant Apex would get involved, and then things would get dicey with Kekellen, just the same. With the same result, more slowly, more inexorably, with no way to claim it was a single mistake.

He had this one chance to nip the whole situation in the bud, a short, sharp action that didn't let Gide's organization, like contamination itself, spread through his whole establishment and create more Dortlands.

He had some confidence he *knew* Kekellen's reaction. If he could get the message through, and do it quietly. If it went bad—if it went bad, he could put himself on the line, say it was his mistake. His and only his.

What he sent certainly couldn't go through the compromised phone system, wide open to that ship. They could stop his message cold.

For secure communication resources, he had Dortland. He had Ernst. He had a handful of hired guards who didn't know the systems.

And he had Jewel. He had Jewel Sanduski, and he had Brazis. He *could* get the message out, right under the Earth ship's nose.

"Ernst?" He used the intercom. "Is Mr. Dortland available?"

"He left a written report, sir, and said he'd be back in an hour."

One down. One out of the way.

"Bring his report in. And bring Jewel with you."

"Yes, sir," Ernst said, and broke off to do that.

Less than a minute and Ernst brought Jewel, and simultaneously laid Dortland's report on his desk, for his eyes.

It said: *Your daughter is reported to have changed her appearance radically. The bearer of her card was arrested within the last quarter hour but proved to be a female petty thief, who claims to have picked it up, dropped on the street.*

The antacid wasn't at all sufficient.

In the other matter, we have analyzed the shell fragments. The launcher is a simple tube, locally procured out of Concord Industries. The shell is more exotic, likely out of Orb, where several such attacks have been directed at law enforcement. It was imported. We are checking customs records.

Did he believe that? He believed Dortland already knew damned well where that shell came from.

We have recovered Stafford's coat, the note said further. *It shows residue of blood and explosion. We are checking the origin and integrity of the blood. We have six witnesses who put Stafford on Blunt Street traveling toward Grozny, and have agents in that area, but several locals have manufactured misleading sightings. This is common practice in that district when authorities seem to be tracing an individual. We discount these reports. The sightings we do trust are around 12th and Lebeau.*

We have interviewed Stafford's mother, who claims not to have heard from her son, and his father, who says as far as he knows young Stafford is in the Outsider office complex. We discount his report as ignorance of the situation, but have sent an official inquiry to Brazis. Other relatives claim no knowledge and assume Stafford is at work. The sister alone remains elusive. We have received massive disinformation as to her whereabouts and threats have been issued against our agents.

We have agents on guard in Ambassador Gide's vicinity. He is reported asleep.

Also, one Gifford Ainsford Ames, aged 54, approached the Southern Cross *ramp claiming to have information about irregularities in the arena design selection as motive for the attack on Gide and asking for protection from pursuit, claiming your office has persecuted him. Medical records indicate he has evaded treatment for a mental condition for the last two weeks. Arresting officers have taken him to the hospital, and we have assigned an agent on that case for a concluding report.*

Damn. He knew about Ames. An architect, and a cyclic depressive with a penchant for drink. His arena design hadn't been accepted, and he'd thrown a screaming fit in the offices.

One part of his madly racing brain said damn, he didn't want the word *arena* mentioned in Earth's agents' hearing; and another said fine, so let a lunatic pitch his fit on that topic on Earth's threshold. Nazrani's complaints, recorded with that ship, would lose credibility in consequence.

And Dortland stopped him. Which meant Dortland didn't want that on record, either. So where was truth?

But at a certain remove—he didn't care. He didn't give a damn. He had had all the doubts his mind could hold. He had laid his course.

He looked up at Jewel, feeling himself inexplicably short of breath, about to do something he never could have envisioned doing. At a certain stage of his life he might have considered Judy and Kathy, but they had both distanced themselves from him—deserted him, if he consulted his gut. And fixing this mess was up to him.

To get his necessary moves past Dortland, whose agents could intercept and stifle a message from his communication system, just like that ship, he counted on one conduit, his opposite number in the Outsider government—the very man he should be most nervous about trusting . . . and the one whose physical lines were the most immune to that ship out there, and to Dortland. Everyone considered that Outsider communications flowed almost universally by tap, immune to anything but physical eavesdropping on the sender. But there were internal office nets, well shielded. And a few shielded outside lines, which Outsiders guarded jealously, absolutely licensed to protect themselves and their communications from that ship and from Dortland, by force of arms if need be.

On a station riddled with surveillance, Brazis had the physical lines he needed.

"Ms. Jewel."

"Jewel."

"Of course." Outsider names. No Ms. He copied the computer file, Kekellen's letter, and gave it to her. He wondered where the bugs in his office did reside. But the kind he had to fear now were the kind that could focus their pickup through several walls, the highly professional and elaborate kind that Dortland commanded. "It's important the Chairman understands my official position. Extremely."

"Yes, sir," Jewel said, and took the item into her keeping, in a button-purse she wore at her waist, clearly understanding where that was supposed to go.

"I'm sending Ernst to walk you home. With thanks to Brazis for your help. I hope you'll convey that, personally. Take care."

"Yes, sir." Jewel's eyes flicked left and right, as if a threat might be evident in the walls, resident with the ages-sealed lizards—or she might be aware of electronics he couldn't detect. She might be amped. The ability of some of these couriers was legend. "Thank you, sir. I will thank him for you."

"Good," he said, and relayed the order to Ernst to go with her. Ernst gave him a look—Ernst hadn't gotten such a request since Kathy's last rebellion, in far safer times for the governor to be sitting in his office absolutely undefended.

"Shall I ask Mr. Dortland to send someone to my office for the interim?" Ernst asked.

"No," he said. "I'm sure I'll be fine. That's a firm order, Ernst. Go. Use the lift key. I want you back here as soon as possible."

"Yes, sir."

Dubious, clearly worried, Ernst left with Jewel, who was physically carrying a message for the *ondat*.

He'd done it. And he had to sit and wait, and rethink his course of action, now that it was, positing Ernst's reliability and Brazis's agreement, sliding toward irrevocability.

THE CLIENTELE AT MICHAELANGELO'S was glamorous, even if the place was gray and aged. Glorious creatures enjoyed drinks, and Algol, their rescuer, secured their lodgings, showed them up to a trendy room, then took them back down where the Fashionables gathered, set them at a table and asked them what they would have.

"Blanc," Mignette said, "Couredin." It was what her father always had when he took them out, and she knew it was pricey.

"Beer," Noble said. "A lager."

"Just a lager, modest fellow?" Algol ran a light finger along Noble's stiff shoulder and waved a circular gesture toward the bar. "Couredin for the daring Mignette. A good common lager for this unassuming boy, who makes no greater demands of life."

A ripple of laughter. Several people got up to stand near and stare at them. Mignette stared back at the most extraordinary faces she'd ever seen—green eyes, lavender lips, tattoos that glowed and changed constantly in serpentine patterns. Noble, slouched in his chair, looked miserable.

A hand brushed her shoulders. A white face loomed near. "What are you doing tonight, petite?"

"I'm with Noble," she said. Not Algol. It was scary to be asked by a grown-up stranger. Noble was safe. She'd thought once he was a handsome boy, but Noble lost all his luster among these people, and she saw the sulk that made a hard line of his mouth. She was scared he would blow up at someone and get hurt.

"Well," Algol said, winding down into the next chair. He brushed her cheek, lifted her chin on a finger. "Loyalty. So much loyalty and virtue in such an appealing little package. Let us educate this novice gentleman. Let us provide him critique, and improve him."

"He's all right," she said desperately, but someone else had moved up on Noble, a young man who ran fingers through Noble's hair.

"*This* needs changing."

Another: "The skin needs improvement."

Noble jerked free of the fingers and reached for her hand, pulling at her. "Come on, Mignette. We can find somewhere better than this."

"Oh, I don't think so, little flower." Algol leaned close to her, pinned her other arm to the table. "The streets are very dangerous right now. And there's so little to improve about you, and so much to be done for your friend."

"Mignette," Noble said, sounding desperate.

"I want to leave now," she said, and tried to get up, but Algol was stronger than he looked. He imposed a grip like iron, Noble was pulling her other hand, and they were surrounded by these inhabitants of the place, these glamorous, these suddenly threatening presences.

She fought to get free of Algol's grip. And couldn't. "Noble," she cried, "run!"

Noble tried. They caught him in a net of interlaced arms, harmlessly, laughing at him, and Algol effortlessly held her hand so she couldn't get up to help him. "No, no, no," Algol said, patting her arm above that painful grip. "Little Mignette, stay put. Don't be so silly. You're among kindred souls. Perfectly safe. He had it coming."

A waiter, someone, set the wine and the beer on the table.

She suddenly remembered you should never eat or drink on the street, if you couldn't guarantee the bottle. And the wine and the beer were in glasses, moisture like jewels on the outside of liquid lightest and darkest gold, on a scarred tabletop in a dingy bar, surrounded by beautiful faces.

"Your wine," Algol said, and, releasing her wrist, edged the glass toward her with an elegant fingertip. He smiled engagingly, half red, half black, with patterns twisting across his skin. The eyes flickered from dark to fire. "Dear Mignette. Trust me. It's quite safe."

She conceived a plan to get to the door. She relaxed. She looked in Algol's eyes—one dark, one fire—and let her hand under his go limp. He slid the wine toward her.

She reached out and took the stem in her fingers.

And threw the contents at his eyes, and lunged for her feet.

Noble shoved at the people holding him. She ducked past that struggling knot and grabbed the door latch—latches always had to open from the inside. The law said so.

It was locked.

PLACE TO SIT. Procyon wanted that, just a dark little nook between facades. He found a grimy green molding to sit on, a plastic continuation of a store windowsill around the corner into a false window. His knees were shaky. His forehead hurt. He was fevered. It felt like nanos kicking in, that overheated, overflushed condition, blushing right down to the scratches on his fingers. The blood flaked off. Skin there was pink, scrapes, not scratches, where Gide's nails had raked him.

Flash of Gide, lying there, Gide wanting not to be touched.

Then dark, the bots and the chute. He smelled ammonia, still clinging to him, and a green glow grew in memory. His heart raced, fear flooding his system with chemicals that only made the nano-feeling worse. Maybe the Project nanocele had some hidden tricks. Repair capability outside its ordinary sites. At least that was how he rationalized the sick, fevered feeling in his stomach. He hoped so.

Flashes of that dark kept intruding, trying to surface. He saw a shadow. He didn't know what he'd seen, what had happened to him. He felt rubbery, wet touches on his face, soft and clinging.

His fingers were shaking. He clenched one hand in the other, trying to stop it. He couldn't figure how, step by step, he'd gotten into this mess.

Dark place. And something like shredded cloth. Cloth that moved. He'd seen dim photos of *ondat*. That was what his brain kept insisting. He felt that touch. Smelled ammonia.

He didn't know why the headache became blindingly severe every time he thought of it.

A dark place. A lancing pain.

He sat somewhere else, on the tiles in a service nook, facing one of the service accesses. A cleaner bot darted out, right in his face. He lurched to his feet, back to the wall, avoiding it, and turned and ran.

A shadow blocked his path, an envelopment of cloth, a hard, opposing body and an iron grip on his arm between him and the neon light outside the service nook.

"Procyon!" the man said forcefully—one of the Project agents, he thought, one of Brazis's men, who knew him by name. He struggled, not to get away, only to free his arm, and stared at the black-coated man, who looked to belong in the Trend, but whose grip was damned hard to break.

The man as suddenly let him go, staring at him with green, shocked eyes.

Nothing made sense. But Brazis wouldn't let him go. He began backing away.

"Wait," the man said. "Procyon. Procyon Stafford."

Dark, dark and green light. He didn't trust it. He didn't trust anything now. He took out running down Blunt, hugging the edge of the walk, in the green neon. Normal traffic clogged the street, walkers of every sort. He dodged in and out of the traffic, and took refuge in a dark little bar he recognized from his student days. The Grotto. Low profile. Cheap.

Safe. Safe for the moment. His thinking mind was trying to come back on-line, and he melted back to the wall and into a chair at a vacant table, head bowed, chest heaving while he caught his breath and his balance and tried to get the dark and the touch and the smell out of his head. He didn't look up at anybody, didn't invite being looked at.

He felt as much as saw a shadow come into the place, then, and when he did venture a look up under his hands he saw a shadow that could belong here, just a man in a long dark coat, moving among the Trend fringe and bottom crawlers that frequented the Grotto. Moving with the persistence of a hunter.

It was the man from the nook he'd fled. The man was still tracking him.

Procyon kept his head down, hands shading his eyes, his arms in the pose of a man protecting his drink.

Dark. Pain centered on his forehead.

The man had gone, when he ventured a sidelong glance. He found a breath. A waiter slouched over, wanting an order or else.

He needed his card. He tried to think of something, an order. "Beer," he said, and the waiter went off. But intelligence cut in. Wariness. If he used his card, they could find him.

He didn't wait for the beer. He got up, and tried to walk, and all of a sudden the tap cut in like electric shock through his brain.

"Boy."

Luz. Or the Ila. He gripped the rounded table edge, sank down and discovered the chair, finding difficulty controlling his limbs even to fall into it.

"Boy, listen to me. There's an outlaw tap near you, someone not on the Project system. Shut down! Shut down now!"

He tried to shut down. He tried. He shunted blood away from that the tap toward his fingertips, as hard as he could, and breathed small controlled breaths, feeling the whole world blur as he tried to keep his feet. If the man following him had left, he might have reported to get help. He had to get out of here.

"You." It was the waiter. With the beer. And the waiter backed up. Staring at him.

Flurry of flashes behind his eyes. He recognized pattern in the blinks. He didn't know what it was or what it meant.

He turned full circle. Caught a pale phosphorescent glow in the mirror above the bar, glow on a shadowy figure.

It was him. His forehead glowed with gold light. Looping curls of light, all in a circle on his skin.

Even mirror-reversed, he knew that sign. It was the symbol on *ondat* ships. On doors that should never be opened. On items the *ondat* wanted. Everyone on the station knew it and avoided it.

Ondat property. Don't touch.

The waiter edged farther away from him. Patrons cleared the area, chairs overturning. People yelled.

He was the center of it. He was scared, heart-pounding scared. He tried to organize his pulse in a forbidden, desperate tap to the office, and shooting pain in his ear all but dropped him to the floor. He was in a dark room deserted except for the waiter, and the woman behind the bar.

"Call the cops," the woman said, but he didn't stay for that. He got his feet under him and walked out, back onto the street, keeping to the shadows. Ordinary traffic reassured him. People didn't run.

Until one drunk, coming directly at him, melted aside from his path with a look of horror.

The man in the black coat had tried to grab him and he had run. Maybe that was a mistake. Maybe it had been rescue, back there, and he'd run right where the Project didn't want him—into public, which was the last thing the Project ever wanted its people to do, but other people were looking at him now, people stopping one another and pointing, and getting away.

He couldn't tap in. He needed a public phone. He tried to spot one. Meanwhile he kept walking, trying the tap, desperately.

"This is Procyon," he said to the empty air. His head buzzed, and he thought for a fleeting instant he might have a contact. "I'm on Blunt. I think I'm on Blunt. I need help."

He heard a hum.

He looked down. One of the cleaner-bots raced along near his feet. He shied off from it, staggering, vision full of flashing lights. He hit a window, caught his balance, and ran, knocking into traffic, people crying out in alarm, dodging away from him, one determined to fight, and then dodging back. He ran until his side hurt, and then he walked, weaving as he went, in a street where people stood along the fringes and stared.

Long-dot-dot-dot-long, the signal in his head said: a long-dot-dot-dot-long that sounded like the alarms everybody on the station learned from infancy.

Long-dot-dot-dot-long became a flash, flash, flash of lights in his eyes, then dot-dot, the signal that meant Avoid.

He shied off from the direction he was going, and got the long-dot-dot-dot-long again.

He stopped, stood blind, but thinking maybe Brazis was trying to get through to him that way, audio pared down to its simplest on-off signal. Go, don't go.

He walked, and when he went one way, he heard the run-signal, and when he went another he heard the avoid signal.

"Sir?" he said. "Sir? Anybody? Can you hear me?"

*   *   *

"MARAK!" HATI SAID, and Marak sat still, in the first hard spatters of rain, with beshti moaning and complaining near them, with wind tearing at the tarp that was their shelter. He was cold, but sat bolt upright, after forcing his way through the relays. Makers rushed to his defense, heating his body with fever.

He had confronted the Ila within the system. She had not opposed him.

But something had blocked him. He was angry, and took Hati's warm hand to be sure of Hati's safety while he hurled his indignation at Ian.

"Ian!" he demanded.

And Ian said: *"Luz?"*

"Something is wrong," Luz said. *"Something is very wrong. The Ila says so and I believe her, in this. The boy was absent from the system, and now something else is on the system, something that ought not to be there. There is an outlaw tap. Get off. Get completely out of the system."*

"Marak." That was Auguste, faint and far and wounded. *"Are you all right, omi?"*

"What's happening?" other voices asked, most in the accent of the heavens, echoing into one another.

"Shut down!" Ian said sharply, through the racket. Walls that separated one tap from another were tumbling down. Everything dissolved in a babble of voices, and Marak shut down quickly, seized on both Hati's hands and made sure she was paying full attention to him.

Her braids blew in the gale. Lightning flickered across her face, dark eyes staring into his, deep as the dark, deep as caves into the earth.

"Attack in the heavens," he said to her. "The whole system is threatened."

"Let Procyon go," she urged him fervently, nails biting into his hands, Hati, who had always detested the system. "Damn Brazis and all his watchers. They can go begging a hundred years, and who on earth will miss them? Let us get out of here!"

Spate of rain. Water from the heavens, precursor of an advancing sea. Cold rain, rain like half-melted ice.

The winds of the calamity had reached them. Time was up.

*   *   *

THE WHOLE SYSTEM was under assault. Taps reported in left and right by physical line, taps made ill and disoriented by a strike, this time on every channel. Brazis sat at his desk trying to keep nausea at bay, and Dianne, in no better shape, tried to reach Reaux's office through a physical phone system momentarily jammed by unaccustomed traffic focused on this office.

"I have the governor on, sir. Go ahead."

"Setha? Setha, we've been hit, dammit. Something's hit the whole tap system. Are you doing anything?"

"Antonio? No. Nothing that I know. What's going on?"

"Hell if I know. Luz is claiming there's an outlaw tap. Assure me it's not yours."

"No. No, emphatically not."

"Damned thing's amped to hell and back; it's blown systems, God knows what it's done to flesh and blood."

"I'm not on a secure phone. I'm in my office. I sent Jewel to you with a message."

"The message got here."

"Have you read it?" Reaux asked.

He had the transcript on his desk. Reaux said he wanted it sent to Kekellen, preemptive strike against Gide and party. Scary as it was, it wasn't a bad idea, in Brazis's opinion, but events were moving too fast to give him time to think about it.

"I've got it, I'm considering it. Where's Gide at this moment? Still in hospital?"

"In hospital, sedated and under watch—for his own safety."

"So he's not the one with the illicit tap."

"Couldn't be. Couldn't possibly. You say your system's damaged? Has the problem got onto the public tap? Or only the Project system?"

Good question. He didn't have an answer. "I don't know. It's ongoing. We don't know how or what or even if it's located up here and not down on the planet. We're trying to run down a source."

"My message is extremely urgent."

"I'll think about it." He tried not to get testy about it. Got a breath. "I'll do what I can."

"Listen. Listen. Antonio, I have information on the launcher. The lab *believes it's from Orb. There've been similar attacks against the police there. We're trying to track that down. Unfortunately—you know the problem here."*

The Ila had broken in, warning them of a rogue tap, the system was on the brink of collapse, the head of local security might be a Treaty Board agent firing Orbish shells at a Treaty Board ambassador and now the governor wanted to bring Kekellen into it.

He sipped caff, trying to subdue the nausea, and his hand shook.

"I'll look into that on my end. With all my resources."

"I'll do what I can from this one."

Including keeping Gide quiet, he hoped. Including monitoring moves Dortland might make, if Dortland had any clue they were onto him.

The contact went dead.

The message for Kekellen, Dianne said, had come through Jewel, who was still here, a message hand-carried, not read aloud. Reaux was clearly desperate to send it, equally desperate not to have his fingerprints on it.

It looked like a clean message. More to the point, the message wanted exactly what he wanted, which was Gide out of their systems, and if he kept the physical message as evidence in case of any blowup, it had *Reaux's* fingerprints on it. All Apex could hit him with was being too foolishly accommodating.

But he wasn't, himself, an expert with the *ondat*. The PO had the planet in its charge. Negotiations with Kekellen were much more the domain of the governor's office and his experts.

Experts licensed by the Treaty Board.

He took a strong gulp of caff, summoned up his personal note with Magdallen's tap-code, and tapped in, taking his life in his hands.

"Brazis here. The system is under assault. Can you hear me?"

There was a lot of cross-chatter. Nonsense flashes, like an electrical short somewhere in the system. Foolhardy to be using the system at the moment, but other options were equally scary.

"Your man is walking down Blunt Street," Magdallen said, *"with an* ondat *mark on his forehead."*

"Repeat that."

"It's the ondat *keep-away. It's on his skin, and it glows in any dim light."*
God. "Is it authentic?"

"I have absolutely no idea. It's scared hell out of the street. Nobody's making a move, except staying out of his way and staring, when he goes into shadow, where it glows—you can't see it, else. The boy looks badly shaken up. His movements are erratic. I had my hands on him once. I could grab him again, but I'm not sure you want that to happen in public. The crowd might take its own action. Worse, we don't know where that mark came from."

An *ondat* mark. An *ondat* mark. It could be a human enemy, somebody who wanted the worst kind of trouble.

"Are you hearing me, sir?"

"I hear you," Brazis said. "Keep him in sight. Inform me what he does."

The malfunction on the system created a hell of a headache. He felt a rush of fever near his right ear, which might mean damage to the blood vessels, a chance of stroke. A very great risk of stroke, with spikes and surges running freely through the system.

An *ondat* mark.

And he had that message on his desk.

God, what was Reaux up to? An entity they could only marginally talk to, an entity that could abrogate the Treaty without appeal and reopen the Gene Wars with the whole human species . . .

He should get his own, unlicensed, communications experts in here immediately. He should rely on his committee—

But they weren't administrators, didn't have his clearance, didn't have a clue what had been going on, didn't have a background on the situation, and briefing them adequately was damned near impossible, as fast as events were running. Reaux was much more in the know, at least with the *ondat.*

The mark someone had set on their tap—provocation? Deliberate provocation of a force that could destroy Concord, with all attendant consequences?

The *ondat* were already involved, either challenged by this move or, or, God help them, *already* taking action within the station, on *their* side of the environmental barrier.

He numbed himself to any thoughts of before and after. He

made an executive decision, called up Kekellen's restricted codes with another keypunch, and transmitted Reaux's message over the lines entire, unreviewed by his experts.

Afterward, his hand shook.

He could be right to have trusted Reaux. He could also have just made a mistake that all their experts combined might be unable to get them out of.

12

WIND, WIND THAT HOWLED, tore at the canvas, wind that picked up wet sand and hurled it. Beshti hunkered down, moaning above the gusts. Marak hugged Hati to him, as canvas flattened against his back, poles bowing—it was well lapped under them, and driven down with deep-stakes into the rock, and it held, but his back turned cold, and the insistent headache throbbed with the howl of the gusts.

"Like one of the old storms," Hati shouted against the racket.

"That it is," he said, holding fast to his wife, trusting the beshti, sheltered, like them, behind a sandstone spire, would stay down until the gust-front passed. The wind stank of rot, chilled with antarctic cold—might wear through the canvas, it carried so much sand up from the pans. It rained up, at this edge of the cliffs. Water whipped up from the pans, upward on the gale. Thunder cracked and deafened them and the lightnings were a steady flickering light through the canvas.

It was not a time to try to see, or hear, or do anything but hold fast, breathe only through the weave of the aai'fad, venture no skin exposed, no more than they had to. Fabric would abrade, skin would gall, eyes would be blinded if they faced such a wind.

Like one of the old storms, it was, except this sand blast had an edge of melting sleet, except this presaged a lasting change in the world, no simple march of dunes, but upheaval of the climate itself.

He hugged Hati's face against him, and they breathed in the hollow their shoulders made. His other hand clenched the rope that he had made fast about the spire itself, in the chance the wind should try to sweep them off the ledge, and well he had, he thought. Very well he had.

"*ANTONIO.*"

Brazis reached spasmodically for the desktop control and physically knocked the amp way down on the tap. It was Ian.

"Ian, what in *hell's* going on down there?"

"*An outlaw tap, the Ila confirms it. She denies all responsibility, and says look to those who want war in her name.*"

"What's she talking about?"

"*Movement, apparently. Third Movement, on Concord.*"

At least he was ahead of the game on one thing. "*Third* Movement, is it? I already have a report to that effect on my desk, but I'd profoundly hoped not to hear that word from *you.*"

"*The Ila expresses extreme indignation, insisting she has no relation to these persons, whoever they are.*"

He'd believe *that* when the sun burned blue. "I'm pursuing this illicit tap with all resources. Which are now very scant, Ian. Her blowing through here has put a significant number of taps on the sick list or in hospital. Some may not recover. Her own will not recover. This doesn't fill me with great confidence about her intentions. Be careful." He didn't mention the *ondat.*

"*We'll take precautions.*"

"What about Marak?"

"*Marak is well out of this.*"

"Is he safe?"

"*Safe as a man can be with a sea rushing through the gap. Madder than hell about his tap being taken without his consent. That was not approved, Antonio.*"

"I would have been pushing it, to explain the background of the situation without breaching security. I couldn't gain his consent without explaining more than he wants to know."

"*Maybe you can convince him of that. I marginally suspect he knew the Ila was doing something illicit, and that's why he took this crazy no-*"

tion to ride out and watch the west coast slide into the sea. Maybe he wanted to get out of the Ila's reach, but that's nothing I can prove."

Incredible theory. But one never said incredible, in Refuge history. "Can he have any concept of this Third Movement business?"

"He has his sources. At least for what touches us."

Memnanan. The Ila's longtime head of staff. Those two had passed warnings before. He'd bet on Memnanan having said something, if anyone.

"Are we going to have a feud between them, next?"

"He's not angry at her. But annoyed. That's how I'd describe it. Massively annoyed. When you live this long, Antonio, you have a strangely patient perspective on other immortals' doomed enterprises. There's very little you haven't seen before. If he was in on it, he knew he could only make trouble for Memnanan by spoiling her venture out of hand."

Not angry at her for provoking the governments aloft, yet mad about a personal inconvenience.

Or maybe about what he considered a security lapse and a threat to their safety. He had never thought of Marak as keeping secrets of that nature from his office.

Maybe he was just very good at keeping his secrets.

"A doomed enterprise, in the Ila's case? Do you dismiss it with that?"

"I'm sure the Ila herself thought so from the beginning, but someone at your end decided to act in her name, and it was, yes, a diversion for her. I think so. I still think it's minor and that she didn't instigate it, only took advantage of it to see what would happen. If certain fools wanted to play out their game to your detriment, she certainly wouldn't prevent them doing it."

"I'll accept we're being spied on," he said to Ian, "and I don't know if you know more than you're saying, or if you say what you're saying now with her full knowledge . . . but I have an immediate need for facts up here, Ian. This is all going to hell on us. I do know of one unauthorized tap on station, sent here from Apex, who may be what she's complaining of with this illicit-tap business, but I'm not betting that answers the whole question, not considering what we're dealing with. Has anyone contacted *you* at all, that I don't know about?"

"No."

"Can you make it clear to the Ila in some reasonable way that trouble is proliferating up here, that people have died needlessly, and if she knows anything, or if she's in contact with any illicit tap in our area, she should tell us and give us identities. This Third Movement group has taken her name as their cause, if what you suspect is true, Earth's heard about it, and they're trying to insinuate its own investigation onto the station. They've subverted the governor's security, and the *ondat* may be making some move, and if they haven't yet, they're likely to. Doesn't anything in that set of facts catch her notice? It had damned well better, Ian, or I don't know what comes next up here."

"I'll inform her of all that. And I'm trying to prevent another such outburst on the system. As you point out, Marak is likely going to throw the next hell-fit. He's cold, it's raining, he thought he had the beshti, but they took out to another terrace, just out of his reach, while he was incapacitated with that tap-spike, and his area is becoming more and more hazardous. He's well out of patience."

"I can't help him. He's put himself where we haven't even got good overhead image and we can't get through to him reliably. If we start trying to direct him up that maze and then lose contact, he could be worse off than he is. Best he uses his own instincts."

"He wants the boy back, Antonio. If you could just do that, you could do a great deal toward getting communication calmed down all round."

"I assure you I'm trying to get him back. Ask the Ila, while you're at it. Is there something else she hasn't told us? Has she been passing notes to this illicit tap source, or has she been fighting it? I'd estimate she hasn't been fighting it, if the whole system hasn't blown up. I need to know if that illicit tap is her doing."

"I'll try to get your answer. It all depends on the Ila's goodwill, which may be extremely ruffled at the moment. In any case, I'll be back as soon as I have any information."

"Thanks, Ian."

What else could he say? An honest answer depended on the Ila's personal comfort and how far she thought she could annoy them. It depended on her idea of how much damage she could safely cause them and then back off untouched. He knew of incidents in the past, long before his lifetime, that had wreaked havoc on the powers of Concord, all thanks to her.

And what could they do with her if she'd violated quarantine? Isolate her? She was already isolated. They'd bet everything they held dear that she was isolated.

Now she'd found a way to evolve her tap and God knew what other nanotech into something they hadn't detected until she did it with someone who wasn't even on the planet. His technicians said the thing had hopped frequencies. They'd never seen the like.

And if she was passing notes to conspirators up here—

If there was a cell here, if she'd found her way into the common taps, or if a rogue tap in the Project had helped her—she could have communicated all sorts of technology elsewhere. Her frequency-hopping nanocele, this recent innovation, could be on Orb by now. It could be all the way to Earth.

WOBBLE AND WOBBLE. Procyon knew he didn't hew a straight line down the street. He stopped and rubbed his eyes, trying to drive the lights out of them.

Buzz. Buzz.

And voices. *"Brazisss,"* one said, and he tried to answer it. "Sir?"

"Procyon!" Not from the tap, from behind him. He turned awkwardly, caught his balance, seeing a haze of blue and gold, a presence that reached out and held his arms.

"Brother . . ."

It was Ardath, Ardath, in public, on the street. "I've got troubles," he began to say. "No. Don't be here."

But Ardath had help, one dark, and one gold, who took him each by an arm and told him come along, now, no argument.

Direction, from someone who could see clearly, someone he knew was on his side.

"He's fevered," one said, the darkness. "You can feel the heat in him."

"It's a mod." A female voice, the gold. "No question it's a mod taking hold."

Light flash. The terrible pain in his head made his eyes water as he tried to walk with them. He couldn't coordinate an objection. He just breathed, and walked, and hoped they would get him home.

They went through a doorway, into shadow, a relief, at least for his eyes. He could smell alcohol, old beer, not his sister's ordinary level of establishment. He heard synth-wood chairs moving on a synth-wood floor, voices that echoed around and around. It was Auntie Murphy's, he thought. He knew the older, rougher bars up and down the street. It smelled like Auntie Murphy's.

"Hush," Ardath said, and a chair scraped. "Sit down. Sit down, brother, and catch your breath. Your mods are having a war with this thing. Help them settle. I'll get you something to drink."

He fell into the chair he hoped was under him, finding a welcome table under his elbows. He was so tired. Sickness and fever buzzed in his veins. Mods, they said. And he didn't have mods this fierce. Not what the government had ever given him. Panic beat in his veins, riding his pulse.

Commotion around him diminished. He heard his sister's voice somewhere, giving directions.

A scrape of a chair. "Stupid brother." She was back. She shoved a cold baggette into his hand, and pulled out the straw, bringing it to his lips. "Drink it all down." Her hand was on his back.

He drank it. The stuff didn't taste that bad. Tasted of salt, which he wanted, needed terribly, chased by the complex tang of other minerals.

He grew dizzy. Put his head down on his folded arms. Didn't know how long he sat there, trying to keep down what he'd swallowed.

A little improvement in the nausea. But the flashes in his skull multiplied, blinded him. The buzzing began to make words in his ears, flat-sounding words, like a synthesized voice.

"*Marak,*" it said, or he imagined it said. "*Brazis.*" Over and over again.

Then a different voice: "*No question he's alive, sir. Procyon Stafford is the most notorious face on Grozny right now.*"

"*Procyon! Can you hear? Answer me!*"

Tap. Brazis.

"Yes, sir." He sat up and tried. He tried desperately, and saw and heard nothing but static bursts.

"Procyon," Ardath said, right at his ear, hand on his arm; and he blinked through the illusory lights and saw his sister's face inches from his, the blue and the gold cleared back, now, to show the Arden-mask. "Procyon." Cool, anxious fingers brushed across his forehead. "Who did this?" Anguish. "Who'd have dared do this to you?"

Did he know that answer? Did he know anything, at all? But he remembered what he'd seen in the mirror, that mark, that horrid mark. He'd looked to her for help, and saw by the look on her face he'd brought her more problems than she remotely knew what to do with. Or should deal with. "I fell down. I think I fell down the rabbit hole." Child's story. "But it's not funny, Arden."

"I know." A brush of her cool fingers across his wounded forehead. "I know it's not."

"Somebody shot the ambassador. But I couldn't. I didn't do it. I didn't do it."

"Idiot," she said. "I know that. But they're looking for you all over."

"Down the rabbit hole. Only not full of rabbits. Scary things. Like the old story. Jabberwocky."

"What's this mark?" She touched the wound on his forehead, which felt like a bad burn. "Who's our enemy, Procyon? Who's crazy enough to do this?"

"Bad mods." It was all he could think of, the card that he'd been dealt in a quarrel he didn't understand. And then did. "The Earther. Looking for illicits." A sick feeling, his head aching with pressure and dizziness that seemed to center in that mark. "Found them, found them, haven't I?"

"Algol," Ardath said. "Damn him, *damn* him."

Algol was almost certainly in the middle of it. She was right in that. And if it was bad mods, if his body was trying to organize a defense, he was holding his own. Barely.

"There're slinks out in force," Spider said, a voice from the shadows of the room. "Station security's grabbed a lot of Algol's people. They got Capricorn."

And Arden: "Whoever the slinks haven't got, *we* get. Find Algol wherever he hides."

"No." It was a government quarrel. Not hers. It was an attack on the Project, nothing his sister could deal with. Procyon reached out and took hold of Arden's hand. "No. It's too dangerous."

"That fool's touched my brother," Arden said. "He goes down."

"No. Listen." The stuff that she'd given him was the right thing, to supply the warring nanoceles trying to pull the chemicals they needed out of his bloodstream. Now the threat to his sister roused up his adrenaline, and he began to feel for two breaths as if he could think, as if, doing that, if he could just hold on to his focus, he might be able to function. "No, there's more, Arden. There's a lot more than that. Not street business. Not the Trend. You can't settle Algol. He doesn't care about us."

"Trust me," his sister said, his little sister, his naïve little sister, whose little wars were fought with cold looks and whispers and the turn of a shoulder.

"No, not with this!" He saw her turn away from him, and he seized her arm. "Listen to me. *Listen*, Arden: I work for the government."

She laughed and patted his restraining hand. "Oh, brother, that's old news."

"Listen. There's trouble you don't want to know, I swear to you, you don't want to know. The ambassador's shot, there's something going on with the government taps . . ."

"This ambassador person is alive, in hospital, sleeping off a not very major wound. He's been exposed to Concord now, poor dear, so he has to stay, and he's cursed all the doctors, but he'll have to come around to our view of the universe, won't he, or he'll be very unhappy in his life."

Her information was newer than his, clearly. It made her too confident. "Listen," he pleaded with her. "Someone's shot him. That's the point, Ardath. Someone shot him. This is guns."

"And we know who would bring guns, don't we?"

"Algol's holed up in the Michaelangelo," Isis said, and others had gathered close, listening, a ring of shadows in the dim light of the bar.

"I've got to tell you." He made up his mind to that, because she knew too much, and not enough. "I need to talk to you. You. I need to tell you things."

"*Back*," she said to those hovering about, moving them with a wave of her hand, until there was a clear space, and he had to go through with it. "So say, brother. What? What do I need to know?"

He took a breath, shaky, all over. "It's *not* just Earth. Marak's in a fix out in the desert, the Ila's breaking in on us, and these people, these people who shot the ambassador—we're dealing with the Movement."

Ardath's flickering mask, gold and blue, actually retreated to her hairline and lost itself. "Honest truth?" Childish question.

"Hope to die," he answered, childhood oath, making the old slight move across his heart. "I'm not lying. I'm a Project tap. I've got to get home, Ardath. I've got to call people to take care of this."

"Well, if there's Movement, we know who they are, don't we?"

"Ardath, for God's sake . . ."

"Your government slinks came looking for me, for *me*, brother. They wouldn't say why. They didn't say someone had done *that* to you."

"This." He lifted a hand to the burn on his forehead. Flash of dark. Something moving. He didn't want to see that. "This—no. Not them." She started to turn away from him and he caught her hand, too hard. "Ardath, what I want you to do—what I want you to do is get word to Brazis. Tell Brazis. He'll send someone. He'll take care of Algol."

"And I just drop my brother down another rabbit hole, where maybe he won't come out the same, or come out, ever. No thanks."

"I'm already not the same."

"You listen to *me*, brother. I know where our problems are. I know who'd be crazy enough to have done that to you."

"You don't know! This." He touched the welt on his forehead. "This—I was in a place. I was in a dark place. And it happened there. Ardath, I don't give a damn about Algol. Help me get a message out. Let Brazis handle it."

"No." She wasn't believing him. "Not to take you away where you may not come out. Not to come tramping through the Street, breaking up everything. You'll see, brother. You'll see what we can do about fools."

"Ardath, no."

"Movement? Entirely déclassé."

"No," he said, and got up onto his feet, or tried to. And the buzzes accelerated, like a tap trying to come into focus. Buzz. Buzz. Buzz. *"Brazissss."* Click. Click. *"Kekellen."* Hiss. Crackle.

Brazis.

Kekellen.

A dark gold mask, a purse-mouthed face in the dim light, with the smell of ammonia. Oblong lenses glinted silver, hiding the eyes. Cleaner-bots, all around him, the station's fearsome secret.

And he was aware of something else of a sudden. Of a wild presence . . . a dangerous presence in his head.

Hiss. "*Braziss.*"

"*What is this?*" Angrily. The Ila's voice. "*Who is this?*"

Spike. Procyon felt it coming, convulsed, tangled with the chair and fell back into it, his head near exploding.

"Procyon!" he heard his sister say. "Procyon! Hold on!"

"SIR. SIR!" Ernst broke protocols, broke through the door, pale-faced. "Eberly, at the hospital. The ambassador's having a seizure."

Reaux sat at his desk, stunned.

"They say, sir, they say he could die."

"SIR." Dianne sent Brazis a physical call. "Technical's on."

"Who am I talking to?"

"Hannah Trent," the contact said. Head of Systems. "We've been hacked, sir, major hack. We're on it. We'll get it back. The hack is mutating on us, hopping left and right, not from the uplink. It's coming from somewhere near 10th and Blunt. Shall we send out the emergency vehicles, show of force? We need to find the source."

"Do it," he said.

Their intruder had hit the system.

Stop the Ila from her provocations? Impossible.

Ian take preemptive action against another of their small fraternity? Never yet.

Marak. Never forget Marak, or Hati, or Memnanan—you rule the heavens, they'd say. We rule the earth. Don't read us lessons. *Don't* give us orders. *Don't* bring us your troubles.

Brazis raked his fingers through his hair, wondering if he dared leave the office and go out himself—wondering if he should rely on Magdallen or if he suspected Magdallen of a consummate double cross, maybe even *being* the problem he was hunting.

Magdallen had been ill in the office in the prior incident, as powerfully affected as the rest of them when the Ila came blasting through the system.

Dammit.

"Dianne." He started to ask her questions by tap, as he did a thousand times a day. And stopped himself from what had become a life and death risk. He hurled himself to his feet and went to the door. "Dianne."

Dianne was tight-lipped, alarmed. "Sir?"

"Relay to Langford. Shut the taps down. Shut it all down, common and private. Turn all the relays off. Now, before we have more dead!"

"Contact with the planet, sir—"

"Shut it all down! Now!"

The relays had *never* been shut down from the station, not for two seconds, in all Concord's several existences.

But it would protect the taps they had left.

It meant that Ian and Luz were on their own, except the local planetary net.

If they, in reaction, shut *that* down, then everybody was on his own.

"BROTHER," PROCYON HEARD, felt the table under his face, felt the close physical press around him, a hand holding his against the surface. He tightened his fingers, gripped that hand, got a breath.

"I'm all right." Deeper breath.

"Get those damned things out of here." Ardath's voice. With fear. That wasn't accustomed.

"How?" someone asked.

Procyon lifted head and shoulders, freed his hand and propped himself on his elbows. Ardath was there, with Isis and Spider and a couple of others whose names he didn't know. He wiped his face, hearing a nightmare click-click-click, and looked down, beside the table.

Two bots, two little lumps of metal and plastics, with winking lights, sat right at his feet.

"*Braziss*," whispered the new voice in his head.

"Yeah," he said to it, just him and it, alone, in an inner nightmare. "Yeah, I hear you."

"Procyon?" Ardath leaned into his frame of vision, attracted his attention with a touch on his hand. She was sitting in the chair across the table. "You stay here."

"You're not leaving."

"I'm not waiting for you to die. Or be swept up into some government hospital. I'm not having it."

"You don't remotely know what you're getting into." *Brazisss,* the inner voice said. And: *Marak. Marak.*

"And *you* know?"

And what good was he? What good was he, with whatever had gone wrong with him?

Marak, the inner voice said, but he couldn't reach Marak. He was branded with the *ondat* keepaway. People were scared of the sight of him, that was what good he was.

That was something.

"I think this thing is real," he said to her. "I think this mark is real. There's a war going on. And I'm in the middle of it."

"You stay here. We'll fix Algol, we'll settle with him, and then we'll talk to Brazis, if he wants you back. We'll negotiate."

Brazis wouldn't give a damn for his personal wants.

Marak might. *Marak* would want his own information. Somewhere between Brazis, the Ila, and Marak, there would be hell to pay.

But if the mark was real, if that dark place was real, there was something else. Something with its hand on him. Its voice buzzing in his head.

Something with an interest in him. Keepaway. Keepaway. Set aside. *Claimed.*

Maybe he was still dizzy. Maybe he wasn't thinking clearly. But there *was* something going on in the understructure of the Trend, the shadowy places that fed the Trend with illicits and legitimates alike. The Ila, Gide, Marak, and now him, *him,* become an intruder in his own circles—it was Ardath's whole fragile world about to come under scrutiny because of him. And she *would* be involved. She was in that elite class that rested, like a thin, fragile skin, on the questionable things that, all of a sudden, would be the object of conflict and furor around, of all people who had never intended it, her brother.

But if the Trend could purge itself, if he could keep her and him from being killed, there there was a chance Marak himself, given information, could find him. Could negotiate with the *ondat*, who regarded Marak, Brazis said, as the only honest human, the only one. He had his little robots, his link with that dark place. They blinked and buzzed beside him. They found him, where he went. He had that straight, now.

Where he was, very powerful entities had ears and eyes.

"If you're going, I'm going," he said, trying for steadiness in his voice. "If you're going onto the street, little sister, so am I."

WATERFALLS POURED OFF the heights, and the beshti, on their feet now, in the passing of the gust-front, bawled protests about the weather—justified protests, with the racket of thunder. Marak held on to the tarp from one side, Hati from the other, and they kept the worst of the storm off, warming each other, but the beshti remained on their own, outside, in the lightning-lit downpour. Whether the cliffs above them or under them were stable—that was beyond any precaution they could take, but to stay clear of overhangs.

The momentary confusion in the heavens of Brazis's domain seemed to have settled. That moment when they all, all, from the least to the highest, could hear each other—that was unique in Marak's experience, and not something he wanted to experience again.

But it had passed as quickly as the front itself, leaving the thunder, the storm, and solitude—a sense of quiet for the first time since he was very young indeed.

He hoped the boys up on the ridge had paid attention to the deep-stakes. The gust-front that had run ahead of this storm, particularly up on the exposed ridge, was a test of their skill. There was a knack to tuning the tent to the wind that gave it stability in weather. It had never been this sorely tested. He hoped the boys had learned what he had taught them.

Equally, he worried about his youngest watcher, who he feared was isolated now in a different kind of storm in the heavens, and who had to fend for himself in the mess up there. He had made his opinions known to Brazis. But in this silence even from Ian, now, his watchers had to watch out for each other. He could no longer reciprocate the favor.

He sat snug against his wife and listened to the beshti. Somewhere near them, loose rock gave way and crashed down the slopes.

"I almost had him," he said to Hati, thinking still of Procyon, and that moment that everything had crashed open. "I almost had him. Then it seemed I heard another voice. It made no sense at all. If I tried, I might still reach Ian. That way seems open, still."

"Leave Ian to sort it out," Hati said, hugging his chilled limbs. "Clearly the boy is alive. Folly to move in this downpour. We might at least get some sleep, husband."

Hati was never one to batter herself against the impossible. She snuggled close, and he shifted to increase the warmth.

He heard the other beshti complaining in the distance below their perch, a trick of the wind, an echo, it might be.

"*Marak.*"

Clear and cold. The very man he wanted to hear. "Ian. What happened? What is the sudden racket and silence up there?"

"*We have no idea.*"

"*We have every idea,*" the Ila's voice interposed over Ian's. "*We have a perfectly adequate understanding of what happened up there. The fool director has completely cut us off.*"

"*Ila,*" Luz interjected.

He had been worried because the tap had been silent. Now he had no patience for this bickering. The width of the desert was not enough to insulate him and his wife from the Refuge and its petty politics. "All of you," he said sharply. His arm had gone to sleep under Hati's shoulder, and tingled as she stirred. "Settle your differences. I have no interest in all of this, except the safety of my watchers, two of whom are dangerously affected, if not dead, and one of whom is pursued by Brazis's enemies and now held from talking. Break the system open. Tell Brazis stop this nonsense, use his resources and pull Procyon back to safety. Now."

"That is the very point, Marak-omi," Luz said, *"that the station wants no contact with us at the moment. Brazis apparently detected a Movement cell active on the station. We believe Brazis is the one who shut the link down, for defensive reasons."*

"We are far from certain," Ian said.

"Folly," Hati said disgustedly. She had sat on the periphery of this conversation. But she clearly heard what Ian and Luz said, all on her own. "My husband says it all. We are wet, we are cold, we are at this moment in very ill humor on a cliff that may pitch us down into the basin, and when we get off it, trust my husband will not rest until Brazis accounts for this boy. Ila, we appeal to *you*. Tell us the truth behind all of this."

"About fools who call themselves Movement? Who engage in illicit trade and infiltrate new technology into the system? I know nothing at all substantive."

"We have our deep suspicions," Ian said.

"Enough!" Marak said, beyond angry at this sniping and bickering and insinuation. *"Is* it Brazis who shut us off, or is there some other agency?"

A crack of thunder. A gust of wind carried rain under their shelter, threatening to tear the canvas away from the three irons they had embedded.

"We have not the least idea," the Ila said carelessly. Marak could see the gesture in his imagination, a lift and wave of the fingers, dismissing his strong hint of other interference—or some enemy diverting their attention elsewhere.

"Hati," Luz said, *"Marak-omi, we need you. We need you both. We ask you stay with us."*

Oh, doubtless Luz needed their support in the situation now, Marak thought. Doubtless Luz now repented her bickering with Ian and even more bitterly repented her period of friendship with the Ila. Doubtless Ian and Luz alike dreaded being deserted to the Ila's society without his mediation. Half a year was already wearing on their close, three-sided society . . . without him in the Refuge. They were ready to call him back. And if his and Hati's absence had driven Ian to the far end of the Paradise and actually precipitated this event, he regretted it, but he much doubted that was the case.

Dared he raise the thorny matter of Brazis's personal faults with Ian now? They all had ears to hear. They all would have heard what he had heard in the system, if they had been listening at all. The three of them at the Refuge had all known, if he had not imagined it entirely, that there was something seriously wrong on the system. They had failed to raise the issue or warn him. Subtlety and subterfuge was at work, and he had no desire to fling sand in the soup before he knew what the new alliances were.

"We have no choice but tend to our own affairs, our way," Marak said. "We expect others to do what they can."

With that, he shut the voices down himself, definitively, and possessed a thunderous and rainy silence he had chosen. Let them worry what he knew, and what he might do about it.

He gripped the slit of the tarp against the wind, with his wife warm and close against him, and they looked out on the lightning-lit rain, on rock spires and new streams of water pouring past them—well calculated, where those storm-made streams would run.

The heavens quarreled. At least they knew the relay the boys had set up on the ridge was functioning very well, even in the weather, since the Refuge had come in clear and strong.

This, the thunder and the rain and the constant shivering of the earth, this was reliable and real. The grinding war of shattered sections of the earth were producing something he and Hati had never seen, and despite their danger, even this far away, they shared it. Let the Ila and Ian battle it out with Brazis and the rest. Watchers came and went, sorry as they might be for the loss of three innocents. They could never touch the heavens. They had the earth to watch.

But, then—a small thought slithered back into Marak's mind— if there was in fact someone new in the network, then perhaps something in the long maneuvering in the world above *had* truly changed. Like the cracking of the earth's plates under the hammerfall, like the rupture of the Southern Wall, an event that, over time sufficient to lift mountains, and bring this weather down on them—change could happen up there. They had feared the water rising from below, and instead were half-drowned by water falling down on them from the sky and the cliffs. Surprise could still happen, on the world's scale.

And if something up in the heavens had finally cracked, then they were no longer in an endless loop, one set of known forces against another. If something up there had cracked, then, up there, as below, plates might have begun to shift, bringing chaos and real change in the heavens.

"What are you thinking, husband?" Hati, close against him, could surely feel his heart, and the tension in his arms. It was never a good plan to lie to her.

"A stranger. A stranger seems to have arrived in the heavens. Or something has shifted."

A deep breath. Hati was considering that notion.

"They do not affect us," she said.

"Indeed," he said. "And the uplink is still in our hands."

Brazis might have silenced the downlink, as he could, but not what ascended to the heavens. He knew the Ila's tricks. He knew what she had done to get into Brazis's system: trip switch after switch, locking the relays open, and move like quicksilver, difficult to stop. That was the way.

And use not the ordinary contact codes, but the emergency ones, the ones just very few people alive remembered, the ones intended to allow them to reestablish contact in an inert system if something did go wrong in the heavens.

The master codes. He had never forgotten them, from the earliest days in the Refuge, when the earth and sky were broken. He lived his long life assuming something, at some time in all eternity, would surely go wrong, and he tested his memory of them from time to time.

He did it now. "I think I can get through," he said to Hati.

"Forbear," Hati urged him. "Watchers have died of mistakes. Cannot *we*?"

He sat with his eyes closed, deaf and blind to the storm, quietly testing his limits, probing the relay, running small tests.

The beshti set up a sudden raucous clamor that shattered his effort, a clamor that, under the roar of the rain, found an answer in the dark. Beshti talked to beshti in the storm.

Now—*now*, cold and hungry, soaked and deafened by thunder, their fugitives had become agitated enough to break from the young bull's rule. His own beshta sent out a loud warning into the dark, overruling the young bull's orders to the females.

Hati had not disturbed him with that news. He heard it for himself. He got up, and Hati—after so many years they had no need to discuss the necessities—Hati was right beside him, leaping up into the driving rain, both of them quick to lay hands on the old bull's halter before he ripped the deep-irons right out of the rock, double-tether and all, and ran off to kill the young thief.

"Hyiii-yi-yi!" Hati yelled her own summons out into the dark, and beside them the herd matriarch bawled out her fury at the robbery. The young bull had thought the string were all his females until two arriving senior riders brought in this senior bull and a canny old female that changed the rules on him. There, before the earth ever shook, was the root of their problem. The young bull, opportunist, had done what instinct told him.

So now, fleeing an uncertainty in the weather and the earth, the females who had run off with the young bull had turned, evading calamity they might feel in the earth itself, disaster reeking in that icy wind.

Not at a convenient moment for their return, no. They had rather have found their fugitives by daylight, on easy ground. In the stormy dark, beshti saw ghosts and devils at every turn, and every fleeting notion was an enemy.

The females came, nonetheless.

So the young bull was going to come up that rain-soaked slope. He had no choice.

In the uncertainty of the night, they had left the beshti saddled, the leather under weather cover, and Marak ripped the plastic cover free, losing it to the wind as he tried to gain footing to mount, as shadowy huge figures came bawling and braying up among the shadowy pillars, out of the rain, driving the bull into a circling struggle to get free.

"Let go, woman!" he yelled at his wife, worried for Hati's safety, but there was no chance Hati would let go her hold, though the old bull threw his head up, lifting Hati completely off her feet as Marak grabbed at the rein.

Beshti milled around in the lightning and the rain, squalling and bawling to drown the thunder. One silly cow fouled their tether-line, trying to cross it, tangled and threw Hati half to her knees.

"Unclip!" Marak yelled, half-turning toward Hati as he got a hand on the rain-slick saddle, and Hati risked one free hand, lifted a knife, shining in the lightnings, and began to saw the taut tether-line, no wrestling with the halter clip against the beshta's irate strength.

Marak swung up and landed astride as the bull snapped free with a rolling shake of his long neck.

"Hya!" he yelled, and popped the old bull hard on the rump with his quirt, disabusing him of any thought he was riderless. His vision was all a blur of lightning-lit rain as the old bull spun about, threatened from the dark, with an unexpected problem on his back. He was all puffed up to fight, and had a rider with a loaded quirt and a taut rein complicating his headlong rush for trouble.

The young bull lunged out of the rainy dark toward them, teeth bared.

"Hai!" Marak yelled, pulled his beshta's head aside by main force, jerking himself out of the way, and hit the young bull hard across the face when the youngster tried to sneak a bite.

The young bull, veering off, shouldered them hard in the movement and came in again. Where the cliff edge was, Marak had a guess, but only a guess. Marak laid on a second blow, and a third, the rascal thinking to snake his head under to nip the old bull's throat. The old bull fought to turn under the rein and come full about for a neck-blow that could kill. For a moment it was all a squalling mill of turning bodies and diving heads, and Marak plied the loaded quirt on their young attacker with all the force in his arm, until the young bull finally felt the blows and shied back, flash of the white of one eye in the flickering lightning.

The old bull lunged to give chase. Marak hauled his head around and back, which forced the old bull around and around in a circle. Pops of the quirt stinging his rump kept his rear dodging sideways to escape those blows. This proved too many diversions at once for the old fellow's brain, and he grudgingly resigned the fight, puffing and blowing, on the very edge of the cliff.

There was a great deal of grunting and blowing all around, and complaints out of the dark, complaints from the young bull, complaints from the herd, rumbles of thunder from the rock walls above them. The earth itself jolted, one sharp thump, and the panicky herd milled and squalled in confusion.

Another rider showed in the lightnings. Hati had gotten herself up to the matriarch's saddle, and applied her quirt liberally wherever a beshta showed a disposition to break out of the herd and start a panic or a fight with the matriarch.

They were soaked to the skin. Their tarp with their supplies inside was flat, trampled in the confusion. He had the gun. He had never thought to use it.

But they had the herd back in their control.

13

THE HOSPITAL DIDN'T HAVE a feeling of shattering crisis as Reaux arrived. Two volunteers stood just past the foyer, chatting idly by the lift, then stopped their conversation and stared, openmouthed, recognizing their governor, and security.

Security called a lift car. Reaux rode up to the isolation level, fretting at the ordinary speed, and exited with his minimal escort, the two building security guards Ernst had commandeered for him. No training, no special skills—but no commitment to Dortland, either.

God, what was he into?

The look of crisis manifested the moment he exited onto the Gide's floor and turned the corner toward the isolation units. Hospital security was in plain sight, armed not with guns but with detector wands and hose-down kits. He'd seen the precautions in drill. He'd never seen the reality in his life. He didn't know where the safe limit might be, and pulled up short with his unprotected staff.

"What are we up against?" he asked.

"Governor, sir." The hazmat leader in charge spoke jargon to a collar-com, and a moment later, having heard some sort of answer: "Containment's maintained, sir. It's safe right here."

"Can I see him?"

He didn't particularly want to see Gide, but it was what he'd come to the hospital to do. The first report had said Gide could die.

Reaux was a civilized man—but he had fervently hoped for that event. What he had heard on the way here, however, indicated something far less satisfactory.

He knew the drill with the suit, now. He went into the adjacent room and suited, making the seals tight, checking them twice. When he came out, the men opened the door for him, and he went into the restricted area, leaving his escort in the safe zone.

Faceless, behind another mask, the physician in charge met him as he came through into containment. Waiting for him, clearly.

"Governor."

"Doctor. What's the story here?"

"We've got a problem, but not as life-critical a medical problem as we initially feared. There's a nanism at work, organizing fast. A *sited* nanism, not general."

"Where is it?"

The doctor touched the side of his masked head.

"Are you saying it's a tap, then?" A tap was good news. A tap was a limited involvement, a known mod, with a known progress, a known limit.

"Not commercial. No chance it's commercial. It's a large area of involvement. It's got the ear, the jaw, and the nerves and vessels there, and it's developed faster than anything I've seen."

"Any chance it's contagious? How in hell did he get it?"

"Any breach in the skin. Which he certainly has. Even ingested. It wouldn't matter. The usual administration of the common tap is in a capsule. But we can't readily identify it and we're taking no chances until it's finished doing whatever it's going to do. He, on the other hand, wants out of here immediately. He's furious. And I take it this infection isn't within your knowledge, Governor."

"No," he said, aghast that the doctor had even suggested it, as if his government could have done it.

But Dortland? He could hardly believe it. But he supposed it was possible.

And meanwhile his brain spun its wheels on that word *tap*, getting nowhere he wanted to go. "No, I assure you this is nothing my administration knows about."

"It happened somehow."

"Is he still conscious?"

"Too conscious. Sedation isn't taking. That's one thing that very much worries us. He's got a hellacious headache, understandable with a new mod, and whatever it is, the nanism's sopping up any drug we give him—not uncommon. It's been doing that. But, on the not entirely positive side, his wounds are healing extremely fast. It acts—" A little hesitation. "And this is what makes me nervous—it acts like a general nanism. It acts, in fact, complex."

Complex. *Complex* was not at all a good word. *Complex* put it far beyond the sort of monopurpose illicit the occasional teenaged idiot met and had to have purged out of his system.

If it was a complex nanism, if it was worse than that, sending it to specialists who understood things that didn't have to do with a little body-sculpting . . . that might be a good idea, and, far from offending the doctor, he was sure the doctor would support that move.

Except it bounced Gide, with all the classified things in his head, down to Brazis's territory. All the experts in this sort of thing were Outsiders.

But the facts were, somebody had infected a body too pure to walk Concord streets with a mod he began to fear no hack parlor down on Blunt would dare handle—something that came precapsuled, maybe, that an ordinary hand could handle. Or something injected. Probably not contagious. But it had effects in the bloodstream, by what the doctor said, and that meant it might potentially travel.

"I'll see him," he said.

"Go right ahead," the doctor invited him, more than anxious, he suspected, to get some official order to send Gide anywhere as long as it was out of his containment ward.

Complex, kept echoing in Reaux's brain. Nanocele. The sort of thing only Project labs understood.

Gide had come here to trace smuggling in the PO. Well, he'd found it, hadn't he?

He heard, through the containment suit, Gide shouting at a nurse down the hall. Cursing. He heard some object bang and fall, as if thrown at a wall. A suited nurse exited Gide's sealed door, shaking his head.

He put out a hand to forestall the nurse's resealing that door. Went in.

Gide was sitting up in bed, feet tucked up, hair standing up at angles, hands clenched on the sheets. Whatever had just fallen, a medical bot had nabbed the contaminated article and retreated into the baseboards.

"Mr. Ambassador," Reaux said calmly, "I'm here."

"The hell you say!" Gide tore at his own hair, clamped his hands over his ears, grimacing. "There's something in my head, damn you! There's something in my head!"

"I'm truly afraid there is," Reaux said, with honest compassion. "I wish I could tell you otherwise."

"It buzzes!"

"I'm sorry about that."

"You stand there in that suit, all holy and sanctimonious! This is worse than dead!"

"I wish I could offer you some honest comfort in your situation, Mr. Gide, but the doctors up here are at a loss. I personally recommend you transfer down to Outsider level. Their hospitals have a greater expertise in handling illicits, and the faster they get on it, the better a chance they can do something."

"Damn you! Is that the care I get from my own people? My own doctor doesn't come to tell me this! And now he wants to ship me off to the Outsiders? My God, my God!"

"I sincerely wish I had something better to offer. But I'm sure official Outsider levels didn't do this. There's an outside chance they might even recognize this item and be able to remediate, if you don't delay . . ."

"Considering it was clearly one of their minions that did this, they should know what it is, shouldn't they? Oh, God, the pain!"

"Doctors in this hospital aren't expert at this sort of thing. But by all I understand, by what the doctor believes, the thing is likely a tap, a communication device."

"Communication!"

"Hence the noise I suspect you're complaining of, Mr. Gide, as it infiltrates the ear and the jaw, as a resonance device. It communicates with exterior relays that support whatever system it's tuned to. Whoever did this to you can hear what you say and to some degree hear sounds around you . . . ultimately, can communicate with you, once you habituate to the thing. That's the way they work—which you may know, but I didn't, when I first met Outsider systems."

Gide had a thoroughly distracted look, utter panic, or a spate of activity had just happened in the device.

"It's not lethal," Reaux said further. "Quite the contrary, the doctor says your wounds are healing very quickly, probably through its action."

"It's *complex,* is what you're saying?"

"Yes. That's exactly what the doctor fears. It's one thing for it to draw nutrients from your bloodstream, to build on. They do that. It's quite another to reach out and correct damage elsewhere, in cooperation with the body's own cells."

Gide was stark pale, except a fever-blush around his right ear and along his jaw. His eyes stared, white-edged with fury. "This is sabotage. This is intentional sabotage from the Outsider Authority, and your sole solution is to turn me over to them?"

"On security grounds, I by no means want to send you down there. But you came here to investigate activity that—listen to me, please—activity that the Outsider Chairman absolutely does not support. He's not in sympathy with whoever did this. I believe he would take a hands-off attitude towards information you might contain, under these circumstances. I think you might find him honorable in that regard—potentially an ally in your investigation."

"Ally!"

Reaux kept firm hold of both his nerves and his patience. "A working relationship with the Outsider authority, sir, is an asset—in this place of all places. This is not the introduction to the Chairman you'd have chosen, I'm sure, but, yes, I believe you'd find him a valuable ally."

"Don't lecture me."

"I'm trying to assure you—"

"They're the people who did this!"

"Listen to me, please. What *will* happen once that tap clarifies, is contact with its system, and it doesn't make thorough sense that Chairman Brazis would infect an Earth official with a tap that gives full access to their own highly restricted system. A common tap would be no use to anyone who wanted to eavesdrop. Do you follow my reasoning, sir?" He was far from sure Gide was reasoning with any clarity, at the moment; but he was suddenly reasoning clearly, himself. A moment before, he had held a niggling suspicion of Brazis—but once he followed the logic of the thing, he had far more suspicion of agencies that Brazis might be as interested as Gide in stamping out, agencies they *hadn't* known accessed this kind of technology, agencies that Gide himself had declared existed on Concord. "After all, sir, what did you come here looking for? *Illegal* nanoceles. I think you're right. And I think Brazis will be as upset as we are."

Gide stared at him, disheveled, distraught, but the slack mouth clamped shut. The eyes registered a rational, if agitated, thought process.

"Brazis could do this, I suspect he could, but I assure you he wouldn't," Reaux pursued his logic. "Someone that we know would, we didn't think had the technology, but you did think so, and that's where our mistake was, and where you were right. Unhappily . . . whoever did it is now in touch with you. And will be in touch with you, increasingly so, unless the Outsiders can clean this thing out of your system."

"I can *leave* this forsaken station."

God, didn't he wish. "That might be safest for you, all told, if you can find a place where you know the agencies responsible for this *aren't*. But the hell of it is, you can't necessarily *know* they're not operating wherever you go, and you can't go all the way back to Earth, which would be the only safe place. As soon as this nanism organizes itself, until you assume some sort of control over it, which, again, sir, Brazis's people could teach you, I'd suggest at least confining your more sensitive communications to writing. I'd suggest it, in fact, from now on, and you should insist those who talk to you do the same."

"Damn you!" Gide cried. But it was a less furious protest, more a moan against a very unenviable fate. "Get me released from this place. Never mind hospitals. Just get me released. They're not doing anything helpful."

"You're not likely contagious, that's true. Taps never have been. But there's another reason for keeping you in isolation. Until we know who aimed a missile at you—the station can't know what they'll do next. And if we send you out to a residency, it's very difficult to keep you safe from something worse."

"What could be worse than this?"

"Kidnapping. *Kidnapping,* sir, considering you're from governmental levels. The ones responsible for this attack would ask you a lot of questions, if they got their hands on you, and I don't mean legitimate authorities. No, sir." As Gide moved to protest the idea, Reaux held up a cautioning hand. "No! Panic is not useful here. Look at the positives. You aren't dead. You're not likely to die of this. The tap contact will develop over time. A tap is also two-way. You can use it as well as they can. And if you stay safe, you're a threat to them."

"The hell with that!"

"Hell it may be." Reaux drew a deep breath. This man had threatened him. Now—now, it seemed, it was perfectly possible for him to dictate where this man lived, what he did, with whom he ever had contact. A major threat to his life and livelihood had just become wholly dependent on his decisions. He watched Gide wince and clutch his ears as the fever progressed, and he managed, despite the satisfactions present, a touch of real compassion for the man. "I'm putting you under general security. Another warning. I've reason to suspect my personal head of security is taking orders from your ship, and I wouldn't entirely trust your safety to anyone he picked—if your ship should realize what a security risk it is to them, to have you here alive, and compromised."

"Dortland?" Gide said.

"He is Treaty Board, too, is he?"

"He's not Treaty Board. He's Homeworld Security."

"And you relied on him. So did I. A mistake."

"Dammit." Gide sat with knees tucked up under the sheets, hands clamped over his ears, the picture of a man on the verge of panic.

"Before this thing takes hold, before they can decipher what you say—let me suggest Dortland's probably told your ship everything. And if you are Treaty Board—"

"I am!"

"I doubt under these circumstances you're going to get any official support from your ship in setting up an office here. So I offer you mine. Expert counsel, in how to live with this tap. Medical care, should you need it. Meaningful protection that won't draw any resources from Dortland's office. And, of course, a home here, considering a return to Earth is *not* a possibility for you. If you can get your relatives out here—they'll find a very comfortable life, as comfortable as mine. Your official function on Concord has become beside the point. I've every reason to suspect that Dortland himself engineered the attack on you, if you want the honest truth. The missile was black market, from Orb, and who better to smuggle something so outrageous onto this station? I suspect he did it precisely at the behest of your office—I take it without your knowledge. Your own ship carried the orders *and* maybe the missile itself, all to set you up here and get you past my authority without an argument—I take it by the look on your face that none of this was with your personal knowledge. But I'm increasingly sure he was responsible, and remains responsible, and possibly intended to infiltrate your office when you set it up. But somehow—someone else got to you. One of the police, perhaps. An onscene medic. Someone at the hospital itself. *Someone* who dealt with you, injected you with something that makes you a threat to Dortland, and to that ship, since certainly this kind of technology is very far from anything they'd handle. At this point, your office here is not in question. Your life is. Worse, your sanity. That's a very nasty mod."

Gide, disheveled, distraught, looked up at him—not a weak-minded man, Reaux decided. A tough, dangerous man who'd thought a system governor couldn't stand up to his office, who'd been convinced when he arrived here that the system governor might have been part of the problem.

Wrong, Reaux said to himself, with a coldness of soul that surprised him. Quite, quite wrong. He'd headed into this negotiation with Gide with his hands empty. Now he found they weren't. And Mr. Gide had just learned that fact.

"I do care, Mr. Gide, humanly speaking. And I will help you, personally, with all my resources and good offices. Think about my suggestion you remove to an Outsider facility. It's made with your best interest in mind."

"I expect reports from you."

"I'll be glad to oblige, when I learn anything new. Is there anything you'd like me to relay to your ship?"

"Nothing." Glumly. Dejectedly. "I'll think about this other hospital."

"Rest assured we're taking every precaution for your protection."

Gide said nothing.

Reaux walked out, cleared main quarantine, and stripped the suit. "Get Gide's doctor," he said to his bodyguard when he emerged from the robing room, quite steady and serene. His hair wasn't even ruffled from the hood.

His hands, however, had begun to shake. A thought of Kathy had intruded, the danger she was in, the action that was proceeding on *his* station. Illicits. Rogue nanoceles. Someone who didn't hesitate to attack a high official. Who might not stick at all at fifteen-year-old girls with high-placed parents.

"Governor?" The doctor in charge showed up.

"Dr. Lenn." He read the name, this time, off the uniform tag, and phrased matters as diplomatically as he could. "I agree with you that this poses a serious security problem. I've discussed the matter with Mr. Gide. And I am intending to clear the ambassador to go downstairs, to the PO's own hospital, if I can get them to agree and if I can get him to agree. For security reasons. How much time do you think we have for them to do anything?"

"I have no idea, with a thing like this. Hours, maybe. But I have no objections, medically or otherwise. They're equipped for this. We're not."

"A technical question. *Can* they completely wash this out of him?"

"To our knowledge, not entirely, not a nanocele, if that's what it is. Dr. Kantorin, down there, is an honest man. I'd trust him—professionally speaking, at least. They might be able to limit its effects. There's been some suggestion that's possible."

Trust him, the doctor said. Trust the Outsider government . . . not to take an unethical notion.

"God, what a mess." Even when he looked at his bodyguard, he saw low-level people he'd had to use to avoid the traitor who was supposed to oversee his safety.

The ones he'd stationed outside his house, the ones watching Judy, were Dortland's men.

And did he dare call Dortland on the carpet at this point, tell him outright what he knew and see if Dortland had any bright suggestions at this point what to do? Dortland wasn't a monster. He had an agenda, which right now was going dangerously wrong.

Calling Dortland in might be the best thing to do. It might be the best thing for his own career, before he delivered Gide down to an Outsider hospital, under that ship's witness. He could challenge Dortland face-to-face and see if there were any remaining truths that no one had told him. He didn't think Brazis expected complete collaboration of him. Only a reasonable accommodation, which he might yet achieve, reclaiming certain resources.

He walked. He used his phone, that he hadn't dared use.

"Ernst," he said, and got an answer. "Ernst, call Mr. Dortland, and tell him I want him in my office in ten minutes. Tell him I don't care what I interrupt. This is priority."

MAGDALLEN called—on the phone: that was what they were down to. Brazis grabbed the instrument off his desk and parked on the edge, one foot on the floor. "What news?"

"News, Mr. Chairman? News is your boy is walking down the middle of Blunt at the moment with that *ondat* mark on his forehead, in company with his sister and a collection of the Trend's elite."

Two motions of the heart. Relief and desperation in quick succession. "Good loving God. His sister?"

"Your boy, a fair representation of the practicing Stylists, two little cleaner-bots and one repair bot, all moving right down the center of Blunt. People not involved are not interfering with them. I'll admit I'm not inclined to touch them, either."

̄ The phone was compromised all the way from the governor's office to the ship at dock, but what was happening down on Blunt wasn't exactly secret from the station at large.

Dead middle of the street, and an *ondat* mark on his forehead. If it was gang revenge that had been perpetrated on Procyon

Stafford, it was extravagant and stupid, someone anxious either to turn a young man into a pariah or to provoke absolute catastrophe in politics, not giving a damn if the *ondat* blew up.

But he had this terrible, uneasy feeling, given the intrusion into the taps, and all else that had gone on, that there was some connection between Gide, Reaux's communication with the *ondat*, Dortland's treason, and that keepaway mark, that *claim*, on Marak's junior tap.

"Which way is he going?"

"Straight up to Blunt at 9th, away from Grozny."

"Are you watching him now?"

"From across the street." A picture flashed to his phone, zoomed in on a coatless young man in a black shirt, a young man who didn't seem to feel the ordinary chill of the street. The view zoomed closer, to a shocked, weary face that, yes, Brazis recognized, and a lime green mark that shimmered faintly gold underneath the fringe of disheveled hair as they passed between neon lights.

The zoom backed off again, giving him the entire disturbing picture.

Procyon, no question. With his sister. With a man called Spider. Isis. And three ankle-high bots trundling along beside.

Bots, for God's sake. *Bots.* A malfunction? Three little bots anticipating a cleaning job when this expedition got where it was going?

It wasn't right. It wasn't at all right. Bots didn't just take to the middle of the street.

He tapped keys, coded up his own maintenance manager, typed, *I've got some anomalous bots, around 9th and Blunt. Look into activity. Report triple urgent.*

That query had to go from Outsider maintenance to station maintenance and back. And he still had Magdallen on the phone.

"Suggestions?" he asked.

"I don't have any," Magdallen said. "I'm just tagging along, seeing where they're going. Michaelangelo's, if I can hazard a guess."

His screen flashed up an answer. *No bots within half a block.*

"Shit," he said.

"*Sir?*"

Sweep Procyon up now? It was possible Procyon might even go with Magdallen if accosted, if Magdallen let him talk to his office on the phone.

But that *ondat* mark gave him pause. *He'd* contacted Kekellen. Reaux had asked Kekellen's help, hadn't he? He'd passed the damned message along, without knowing what Reaux had been doing with the *ondat*.

And that mark, shimmering like the highest-priced cosmetics in the intervals of shadow, didn't look cheap or ragged, or bear any of the other hallmarks of illicits that gangs might handle. It didn't look like gang vengeance.

Neither did three bots that didn't show on the maintenance schematics.

"Watch him," he said to Magdallen. "That's all, watch him. Don't stop him."

"*Understood*," Magdallen said.

Brazis stored the image series Magdallen sent, an absentminded press of his thumb. Self-protection. His mind was on another channel, one he'd rather not think of, but there it was: Kekellen. Kekellen.

He came around the side of his desk, sat down in his chair and hand-keyed a fast draft of a message.

Brazis to Kekellen. I see Kekellen mark on man. Yes no? What cause?

He sent it with an entirely uneasy feeling, a second message without consulting his experts.

He drafted a rapid written order to his security department. *Immediately and with all courtesy contact Jeremy Stafford Sr.* Never mind the damn address. Today, they knew it by heart. *Inquire what he knows about his son's current situation and offer him the PO's assistance. Likewise contact the mother, at work or at the residence. Report any findings with all speed.*

That inquiry had a snowflake's chance of turning up anything useful. The parents weren't street people. They wouldn't have a clue what was going on at this moment with their son and their daughter.

He appended another note:

Also check the phone system stat. See whether any call's gone out on Procyon Stafford's card.

The tap system being shut down, Procyon might have gone low-tech. He might have contacted his mother or father with some sort of explanation, might have called one of his friends.

Like hell they were that lucky.

So what now? What in hell did they do?

DORTLAND WAS IN THE OUTER OFFICE, quietly so, with Ernst, when Reaux walked in.

"Inside," Reaux said, not even stopping. He entered his office and held the door for Dortland, who had an apprehensive look.

"Sir."

Reaux let the door shut, sealing them in. "Mr. Dortland, the ambassador has a tap. What do you think of that?"

Honest dismay. He saw that register on Dortland's face. He walked past Dortland to the desk, flung himself down in the chair, leaned back and scowled.

"Where's my daughter, Mr. Dortland? Any ideas?"

"Actually, sir, yes." Dortland drew a deep breath, set his feet. "In a particularly difficult situation, at the moment, in a Freethinker den on Blunt."

Shot for shot. Dortland was trying to unsettle his stomach. And succeeded in making him very, very angry.

"Are you only observing, then, Mr. Dortland? Or do you intend to do something about her situation?"

"Governor, the place is suspect in the attack on Mr. Gide."

"Don't hand me that," Reaux snapped. "I know who attacked Mr. Gide. Is the tap he's got *your* installation, or have enemies gotten to him? The doctors think it's a nanocele."

Dortland's face rarely registered anything. Now it registered worry.

"I think the same," Reaux said, "and I'm not amused, Mr. Dortland. Neither is Mr. Gide. Was it his own agency that planned to strand him here, or was it yours? And why *haven't* you been forward to get my daughter back?"

Dortland didn't say a thing for a moment. He walked over to the life-globe, gave it a cursory look, and looked back. "Your daughter, Governor, has fallen into the company of one Algol, a Freethinker, a grotesque, a perennial problem on the street. It was not a chance meeting. Where she is now—greatly concerns me."

Not a word on the Gide matter. A diversion. A diversion very much on topic.

"And you are doing . . . what, about the situation?"

"I hesitate to say I've been called off the case, sir. I'd like to get back down there."

"And Mr. Gide. The matter of Mr. Gide. An honest answer. Who set him up?"

"I'm not at liberty to say, sir."

"Your own authority, then. You'd answer me, if you could blame some other chain of command than your own."

"Governor—"

"Mr. Dortland, you're not in good favor with me, at the moment, and not with Mr. Gide, either. Did you implant a tap in him?"

"No. No, Governor, I assuredly did not."

"Were you first to the scene?"

"No. The civil police were first, on record. Someone else—"

"Someone else knew you were planning to attack the ambassador and capitalized on the chance, delivering a nanism into an injured man so quickly it anticipated the police. Or perhaps the police themselves were the agency that delivered it."

"It's not at all likely. But that someone got to him in hospital . . . that's possible. I'd look to the very people he's here investigating."

"And *why* did your superiors set him up? To involve the Treaty Board permanently at Concord, to *force* them to establish an office here against their better inclinations?"

One of Dortland's patented blank looks. A shake of his head. "I have absolutely no knowledge of any such thing."

"You only got your orders, did you? Are you that low in the stack?"

"I admit to nothing, sir."

"But you don't deny it," Reaux said with a bitter taste in his mouth. "Did you set up my daughter as a diversion?"

"Your daughter's running off was not an event I planned, I assure you, Governor. I had far rather have come down on these people without a hostage involved."

"This boy she's with. One of them? Or one of yours?"

Dortland shook his head. "A fool. Useless in life. But these people have now contacted *her*, Governor."

"Before or after she ran?"

"That, I don't know. But once she was there, she was not discreet in her identity. She used your card all up and down Blunt. They had no trouble finding her."

His own bright idea, encouraging use of that card. He found himself short of breath, short of accusations. "If you want me to solve this mess with Gide, if you want me to show any forbearance with you, Mr. Dortland, achieve a success on Blunt."

A small, taut silence. "I'd better get back down there."

"Mr. Dortland."

Dortland stopped on his way to the door.

"Awkwardly for us both, at this moment, you can't possibly board that ship to leave this station: being from Earth, it doesn't take on passengers. Gide knows what you are, and he knows what happened, and he will recover. Having a culpable look when one branch of government sandbags a watchdog agency is not, I repeat, *not* a comfortable position to be in."

"No, sir, it can't be."

"I don't want you transferred. I don't know what they'd replace you with. So become faithful to me, Mr. Dortland, and you may find Concord is your one place of safety. Even Mr. Gide may forgive you."

"Brazis's boy is walking down Blunt with an *ondat* keepaway on his forehead and a handful of common service bots following him, and I don't know why." Dortland's face at this precise instant had an uncharacteristic vulnerability. "You should know that. And it's in the vicinity of the place where these people are holding your daughter."

"An *ondat* keepaway." Reaux sat frozen at his desk, remembering his message to that entity.

"An *ondat* keepaway, apparently tattooed onto Procyon Stafford, Marak's tap. The *ondat* venerate Marak above all else, don't they? Looks to me as if they've made a statement about Mr. Gide's actions."

The memory of Gide's face flashed into memory, the pale face, the red flush of fever spreading from the ear to the jaw. He was looking, however, at Dortland, at a traitor only half reclaimed.

"I wouldn't advise you get too close to Mr. Gide, now, sir," Dortland said, "just in case."

He hadn't liked Dortland that much before this. The man's bid to retain power was evocative of a good many reasons not to snuggle close to him. Worse, he'd lay any sum of money on the bet that Dortland's agency had aimed to get inside Gide's, aided and abetted by that ship out there.

"Get my daughter out," he said to Dortland. "Do it. Fast."

"REPLY FROM KEKELLEN," Dianne reported. "On your desk, sir."

Brazis punched the button. It said, with Kekellen's script above and the autotranslation below: *Procyon Kekellen. Kekellen send. Kekellen mark.*"

And: *"Kekellen hear Procyon."*

Gooseflesh crept up Brazis's arms. He reflexively sipped the hot caff he had on his desk.

So the mark was real.

And, Kekellen *hear* Procyon?

Hear wasn't a common verb in *ondat* context, was it? Not one he'd ever run into.

He'd shut the tap system down, and no other taps had gone to hospital since. But he couldn't risk keeping it shut down forever. Hand trembling over the buttons, once and twice hesitating, he called System Control, encoded an order with a furious set of taps, first to warn the techs and then to order them to bring the local system back up. The downlink to the planet only awaited his order.

A graph showed on his screen.

Red to yellow.

Yellow to green. Local was coming on-line.

"Procyon," he said, tapping in quickly, laying himself wide open to whatever was amiss with the tap. "Procyon, do you hear me?"

Flash of light. Pain. The system moderated it, fast.

"What in hell's going on?" he heard from downworld. Never mind his initiating the downlink: the uplink was in Ian's hands, and Ian had come through on it, instantaneously, and loud.

But from the one he was trying to contact, and from the *ondat* themselves, nothing but that flash.

Second sip of caff. He keyed an order, opened the downlink. *"Brazis?"*

"Ian. Sorry about that little glitch. We've been trying to regulate the situation up here. We have a slight emergency. I had the downlink shut down to protect you."

"Incompetence." That was the Ila.

"The *ondat* are involved," he fired back at that ageless presence. "The *ondat* have kidnapped Marak's tap and maybe asked questions of him, for what little he could answer. They may have infiltrated the tap system itself. *They* may be your intruder in the system. So now what can anyone suggest we do?"

There was an unwelcome moment of silence. He so wished that one of the long-lived entities receiving at the moment did have an experience to offer, some ages-old piece of wisdom to moderate the situation.

"Brazis?"

Worse. Marak had just heard them.

"Marak-omi. It is not a good situation. I appeal to you—use restraint. Procyon is physically free. The ondat is talking about hearing Procyon at the moment. Considering everything else that we know about trouble in the system, we cannot afford another spike. What you say or do may reach the ondat, possibly even wound them, to no one's good."

"Through Procyon," the Ila said—who demonstrably knew all about pirating a connection. *"He has become a leak in the system."*

"Isolating Procyon will not solve our problem," Brazis said. "He may not be the only one up here that the *ondat* have laid hands on." Taps were forbidden to discuss station politics or structure with the planet, but the Project Director at his discretion from time to time had to do it, in a limited way, with these few lords of downworld. "The *ondat* have witnessed the intrusion of an uninvited Earth mission in our midst, investigating a possible export of technology that violates the Treaty. *Ondat* have snatched Marak-omi's tap and demonstrated an ability to intrude into our communications system. I strongly suggest—I *strongly* suggest that, whatever our personal innocence in this situation, we have to signal the *ondat* that we are not pursuing whatever actions they took as a severe provocation, or the planet might very soon find an *ondat* authority up here solely in charge. You will not want that."

"Have we provoked this attack?" Trust Marak to ask the head-on question.

There followed another moment of silence in the system.

"We certainly did not transmit technology to the ondat," the Ila said sharply. *"They have breached the Treaty, interfering in our communications."*

Damn her. And he wasn't the first Director to think that. "The Ila knows how painfully slow and erratic our communications have been with the *ondat,*" Brazis said. "And knows how many centuries we have worked to establish certain useful and peaceful boundaries with the *ondat* on this station. I appeal to you for cooperation. If they have intruded into the tap system, this is a new problem."

"And did you not send Marak's watcher to the Earth authority, breaking down certain boundaries?"

Uncomfortable question.

"We did so. It was a serious error."

"Record it," the Ila said, perhaps to an attending au'it. *"We did not precipitate this crisis. The director did. Now do you wish our advice in the matter?"*

No one rebuked the woman, this eternal prisoner of the onworld establishment, this epicenter of all problems that had ever existed.

"Yes," Brazis was constrained to say, keenly aware of Marak's silent presence. "We would be grateful for that, Ila."

"There is an undocumented stranger on your station. He arrived on a ship from Orb. So I hear."

The Ila's lately brain-dead tap could have given more details than that, he was quite sure.

"There is one I know about."

"There is another."

"And where shall we find this person? What is his name, Ila?"

"His name. His name.—Typhon, perhaps."

"Was he in contact with your senior tap, Ila?"

"He might have been. Acquainted with Argent, yes, but not intimately."

Zillha Faron. The Ila's tap. Argent, by chosen name—was brain-dead, resurrection officially failed. Argent was no help to them now—except what items security could turn up in her credit cards and the other detritus of a life cut short. If that contact was in there . . . if there was something in Argent's records that had to do with anyone from Orb . . .

"Thank you," he said, not without feeling.

"Would this Typhon be tapped in now, Ila, hearing us as we speak?" This from Ian. *"Might he be the provocation of the ondat?"*

"By no means," the Ila said airily. *"We have not shared our technology with this person or his followers. We are innocent. What their ambitions thought they might share—that is all their responsibility. The official stranger has provoked the ondat, has he not? Not our doing. Let them fall. Let them all fall. Typhon is a fool. We have no part in his fate."*

Typhon. Brazis's fingers flew on the keyboard.

Typhon. Egyptian name. God of the desert. God of the wasteland. The destroyer of life. The station knew no such legally arrived individual.

"I'll investigate," Brazis said. "Best we break off. We're all exposed, so long as we maintain this link."

A series of flashes and static. Tap-out—from the uplink itself, Brazis suspected. Ian, likely, had shut it down again, while keeping his own on-planet relays up.

He was on his own up here.

"Dianne. Get in here."

As fast as it took to leave a desk and open a door.

"Sir," Dianne said.

"A name. Typhon. T-y-p-h-o-n. From Orb. It may be an alias. It sounds suspiciously like that. Tell the Argent team that's possibly their target. She knew him. Tell enforcement I want an arrest in the next five minutes."

"Yes, sir." As the phone beeped.

Brazis picked it up himself. "Brazis."

"Antonio." Reaux. *"Antonio, the ambassador's been tapped. Infected. They think it's a nanocele."*

Brazis's heart did a skip and a thump. Dianne had vanished back out the door. Jewel was not there. And being an Earther, damn him, Reaux talked with names on a compromised communications system.

"Not our doing. I assure you," Brazis said.

"*I don't think it is. But can one of your hospitals take him? Can they do anything for him?*"

"We're certainly willing to try." That offer was a leap over a chasm of red tape and negotiation. "The faster the better." Damned right he wanted the ambassador in his hands. He wanted to trace the source of that nanocele . . . as if he didn't have a terrible, sinking feeling he knew what it was and from what source it came. He committed an indiscretion himself, aware that ship out there might be listening. He hoped they did hear. "*Ondat. Ondat* may be our source. Handle this with extreme caution."

A little silence on the other end—from the man who'd instigated the message to the *ondat, asking* their intervention. "*Why do you think that?*"

"Because my man is walking Blunt at this moment with an *ondat* sign branded on his forehead."

"*I have the same information. What are you doing about it?*"

"I don't want to answer that on-line."

"*Dortland's headed down there. My daughter is somewhere down on Blunt. He knows where she is.*"

A father's desperation. A hostage. A desperate request that a governor couldn't ethically make.

"I'll bear that in mind." Damn, he thought. Complications.

"*If we get a containment team to bring Gide to your level, where should we take him?*"

"Bring him to Ausford and 22nd." That was dead in front of the Project police station. "We'll take him from there."

"*Done,*" Reaux said. "*I've got to go. I've got to arrange that.*"

"Do it," Brazis agreed, and clicked out.

They were going to have Gide on their hands. Not a willing Mr. Gide, he was well sure.

Meanwhile he tapped in on Magdallen's code, listened for a moment. Didn't hear anything.

"Agent Magdallen."

"*Sir.*" A low voice. "*There's a conference in the middle of the street, our man's group with sixteen others, three more of the Stylists and their particular followings. That's Diamant, Minx, and probably Brulant . . . I'm not sure of him. Diamant and Brulant haven't spoken to*"

Ardath recently. It's a famous feud. It seems to be patched, by what I'm seeing."

Feuds on Grozny were sometimes more smoke screen than fire, masking alliances, confusing external investigation.

"I'll bet it is. What are they doing?"

"Breaking up their meeting, at the moment. I'm sending you the image."

He checked the phone. Saw the conference in question, over against a dark green shop frontage, he assumed on Blunt. If that was Brulant, who had been an informant from time to time, the man had had a few mods.

Procyon was among them, standing beside his sister, looking grim.

"Procyon." He tried to reach the boy. Saw him wince, real-time, shut his eyes and press a hand to his ear. Pain. A still-developing tap.

Did he now instruct Magdallen to grab him? Or did he let the situation run, letting the street do what the street alone had resources to do, finding a way into in places so shadowy and immediately mutable that the police might never penetrate to the core of what was going on.

Dortland's headed down there. Heavy-footed intervention was the last thing they needed in the matter.

"*Sir,*" he thought he heard. He couldn't clearly see Procyon's face to know if he was the one talking. His head was turned. The whole group was hazy-focused in Magdallen's image, with distance and bad lighting.

A burst of static cut him off the tap and made Procyon lift a hand to his ear, as if someone had physically struck him. Ardath turned to her brother, laying a cautioning hand on his arm.

He could shut down the local relays again. But seemingly that didn't stop the rogue.

That meant there was an independent relay station out there. More than one. A thoroughly independent tap system.

If a relay could override his transmission to Procyon, it was either stronger, or nearer. If the *ondat* had reached out into the main station to install relays independent from theirs—

Ondat didn't come onto the human side of Concord, reputedly couldn't do it, for any long periods. They used robots to handle their occasional foraging, lately making rambling, exploratory forays out of their warmer, ammonia-perfumed level. Acquiring orange juice, and chlorine.

Robots could safely do that sort of thing.

Bots. Three of which were in the image Magdallen gave him.

Any one of those . . . especially the repair-bot . . . was conceivably big enough to house the necessary electronics.

Damn. They were looking right *at* their rogue relays.

14

"ARE YOU ALL RIGHT?" Ardath asked Procyon, and: *"Braziss,"* the tap was saying, intermittently, dragging Procyon's attention back and forth between worry for his sister and worry for messages he couldn't get through. They had gathered force. Tap-calls summoned others. Michaelangelo's was across the street, dark and dim, with a police-closing sign on the door—was he surprised, that the place he had shared with Algol was where they were heading, to deal with him? He remembered the inside, the maze of halls, the common room, the back room where the Freethinkers had met, all of it a brown, dingy warren, the only competing color those faded blue plastic chairs. They'd been saviors of the universe. They'd known everything there was to know.

It was shut, police-sealed. But one of Spider's men turned up a key-card, legitimate or otherwise, and no great amazement. Keys came on the market daily, and people had been thrown on the street by that police seal. Michaelangelo's clientele was notoriously low on funds.

"Braziss," the tap said, and Procyon tried to focus where he was. They were going in. Brulant headed across the street to the service nook with six of his people, and as he moved, Isis was talking to her tap, still calling in favors to bring in others off the street. "This is war," Isis was saying. "Be here, do you hear me? Be here, as quick as you can." Diamant, glittering with dust, far from inconspicuous, took her followers across the street, strolling casually

into position at the bolthole entrance, at the adjoining shop frontage.

"There's a rumor out," Isis said in a low voice, at Ardath's side, "that they've snatched kids, upstairs kids, for hostages. Celeste says he's coming in with four of his, fast as he can: he's a block away."

"Good," Ardath said. News flew with the speed of tap-calls from one end of the Trend to the other. Procyon had remembered boltholes even Spider had failed to know: "Carew's, over on White, another at Perle's—" and he was aware, past his headache, that they had gotten people to those, over on other streets: Cepheus, and Lotus, with their people.

But: *"Braziss, Braziss, Braziss,"* the voice in his head kept insisting, and he didn't know what it meant, except the voice thought he was in the wrong place, doing the wrong thing. "I'll go to Brazis," he promised it quietly, and he would, he'd get there, fast as he could; but getting Algol would get what Gide had come for, and bring down what threatened Ardath's safety, she being his sister, and at war with him. Getting Algol would get what disturbed the *ondat,* that no one could reason with. So he resisted the voice, bore down, concentrated, tried to think if he was inside Michaelangelo's, if there was any other possible way out that he hadn't remembered, and couldn't.

"Brulant's there," Spider said, near at hand. Traffic on the street hadn't diminished at all. Bystanders osmosed out of the shops and the side streets, some to see, some to join. It had become a mob around them. Hundreds of them, not coming here for him, Procyon thought: for Ardath, for Ardath, on her say. And he had his own use—to *show* where the trouble in the station was, if Kekellen had failed to find it, to go where the police couldn't. To stand by his sister's side in shadowy places and scare hell out of anyone who threatened her. For his own protection he had a knife out of the bar kitchen. Some of Ardath's allies had more than that. He knew for a fact that Algol did.

Half a minute to draw breath, just enough time for their people to call allies and spread out. "Go," Ardath said, and no more warning than that.

They moved, Spider and his followers a spatter of ink, Isis's in gold and silver, Ardath's young adherents in every shade. Procyon kept by Ardath's side. His three small robot attendants buzzed along, chrome and silver, all in sudden, purposeful motion—where he went, they went; where he went, Kekellen's eyes and ears went.

Michaelangelo's double doors sat catty-angled at the corner of a darkened frontage, and Spider tried the tenant's key, quickly, economically.

Click. Click-click.

It didn't work.

"We have a problem," Spider said on a deep breath, a breath doubled in the gathered crowd. Then someone among the spectators laughed, that most deadly of sounds in the Trend.

Whirr-click. The repair bot, right at Procyon's elbow, hummed. Click-click, went the lock.

"Well," Isis said with a nervous laugh. "So Procyon brought a key."

Spider tripped the latch, softly, then flung the door open on light, on a common room full of laughter and riot—that died as they walked right into Michaelangelo's bar and the bots zipped to one side and the other.

Motion stopped, a tableau of staring faces, not the ordinaries, not the common run of scruffy, self-important Freethinkers. It was a concentrated pack of Algol's allies, fifteen or twenty grotesques and a few sliding down the path to that distinction. Central among them, huddled in chairs, were a couple of juvvies who looked too normal to be sitting where they were.

The girl of the pair sprang up and bolted, throwing over her chair at her tormentors, bolted straight for Ardath and Isis in the doorway. Bright girl. The boy, hesitating, Algol caught, snatched back, a hostage.

"Well," Algol said, passing the boy to his friends, standing there in his red and black glory. There came a distracting thump from back in the farther hall on the left, and again on the right, and then a fight broke out somewhere in the corridors upstairs. "Is this a general break-in? Little dog, bringing his sister to protect him? Your friends back there have run into trouble."

There was shadow enough, and Procyon moved into it. It might not be news, here, that mark of his, but it was there. He saw its immediate effect on the soberer, saner members of Algol's company, who began to look to the edges of the room.

"A cheap tattoo," Algol said. "Is this Brazis's plan, is this little play how he scares fools?"

"Déclassé," Ardath said, stretching out an elegant arm, her fires fading as she walked into bright light, while Isis maintained an arm around the fugitive girl. "Déclassé, Algol. Past and outcast. You're responsible for bringing in the slinks on the street. You're their best friend."

"Silly, *useless* pretty-face! Run away, run, before I change those looks of yours for good and all." Algol's right hand flashed with silver. It was a stinger looped about his ring finger, that weapon of the outlaw fringe, capable of injecting mods or deadly poison. Cries broke out among the intruding audience, a jam-up in the doorway as observers crowded back out the door. Ardath stood her ground, and Spider's hands likewise flashed with metal, two such devices.

But a gray-skinned man walked in from the back halls, a man with burning blue eyes, who wore a soot-gray coat over his shoulders, and unfolded fingers all loaded with stingers.

"Well, well, Typhon," Spider said, who, depend on it, knew the very darkest layers of Concord. *"There's* trouble for us. Back away, back away, all."

"Ardath," Procyon said, "go. Run."

"This boy." Algol flicked his own stinger on, the flash of a green light on its shining top. "Does this foolish boy interest anyone? What is this currency worth?"

"Let him go!" the juvvie girl cried. "Let him go! Please let him go!"

"Friendship. Loyalty. Splendid virtues." Algol reached out toward the hapless boy, who could not budge from the grip of Algol's allies. "Will you come here, little girl? Come and take him—?"

In the same moment Isis's hand lifted from her gold-pleated robes. A weapon hissed.

Algol reacted as if slapped. Looked down at a needle lodged in his black hand, a silver spark in the light. The stinger loosened in that grip, slid. His followers shoved one another to avoid it as it fell. He let go the boy's arm.

"*Kill,*" the *ondat* voice said. That was what it sounded like. Procyon took a solid grip on the knife hilt, prepared to use the only weapon he had as darts hissed, as Typhon made a lightning move at Spider. Stingers spat. Spider jumped back.

A gunshot deafened the air. Typhon spun back and around in a mist of blood and hit the corner wall. Supporters fled for the back hall, trampling one another in their haste. Typhon slid down, and Algol slumped heavily to the floor, the upstairs boy sitting stock-still, frozen, by his side, in a room rapidly vacated, except for Ardath's company, and the dead.

The two cleaner-bots sputtered and hummed into action, rushing about madly, sizzling blood spots into nonexistence. The repair-bot moved to the back of the room, flashing investigatory lights into the dark.

A man in a long black coat, the man from the service nook, walked from the streetside doorway behind Ardath, crossed the floor to nudge Algol with his foot. Algol didn't move. The man kept his right hand in a deep coat side pocket.

The man looked up, then, looked straight at Procyon.

"Procyon Stafford," he said quietly.

"Yes, sir," Procyon said. His head buzzed. "*Braziss,*" the *ondat* voice said, and he believed, this time, that the *ondat* was telling him what he already knew. "Yes, sir. I am."

The man looked around at the rest. "I have names, I have image, and the Chairman's police have the exits blocked. Those of you who don't belong here, show ID as you leave."

Ardath would die first. And being what she was, had no ID.

"Magdallen," Ardath said scornfully, "Magdallen. Are we not surprised?"

"Exquisite, take your people and go. Leave the refuse for the Council police."

The juvvie boy suddenly broke from his frozen stance, leapt from his chair, and fled for the back door, dodging among Algol's fallen followers. He got as far as that doorway, where Brulant, red-gold fires glowing in shadow, stopped him with one outflung hand, a gold metal stinger on the other.

"Procyon." Ardath came to him. Procyon evaded her touch, kissed his fingers and almost touched her face. But he didn't touch her skin with what had touched his lips at all.

"I have an illicit," he said, and drew back the fingers. "And I need some help. I'll go with this gentleman, where I can get it."

"I know a doctor," she said. "I know a good doctor."

"I know others," he said, meaning the hospital inside Project walls. "And I'll be all right, Ardath. This is a friendly intercept. Magdallen, you say. We've met before. If it's a while before I see you again, don't worry."

"He has no right, here!"

"Complications, Ardath. Dangerous complications. Things you don't want to have a thing to do with. I can deal with them, the way you deal with the street. I love you. That's all."

Tears stood in her eyes. He wished he could fix things. He wished he could make everything right for her, and for the parentals. She stood looking up at him, her true face, the Arden face, her blue and gold tendrils faded in the light.

"Sir," he said. "Let me walk my sister out of here."

"Be my guest," Magdallen said. He had a phone in his left hand, so it was a good guess the Project tap wasn't functioning here. Or they were communicating with station police.

He didn't want Ardath deeper involved than she was, not with Earth authorities in the mix. He moved, close by his sister, but not touching, Ardath keeping close the girl who'd run to her for safety, another dubious touch.

Point of good faith, Magdallen kept his focus on the several ex-devotees of Algol who emerged, standing frozen in a clump on the far side of the bar. Brulant moved his group in.

The juvvie boy took his chance and darted to the door, ran to Ardath—not, however, touching her: Procyon interposed his arm to prevent any other contact with his sister, and the boy didn't near touch him, only maneuvered to stay close to her.

The repair bot passed the doors with them. The two cleaner-bots stayed inside, zapping up the blood, clicking in robotic reproach. A small swarm of cleaner-bots arrived and two of *them* joined the repair bot, making up his trio.

Procyon stopped outside with Ardath, in the relative safety of

Blunt Street, in a ring of spectators. A knot of uniformed Earther police waited there, guns in evidence, along with a man in a gray Earther suit.

"Katherine," that man said sternly.

The girl with Ardath ducked to her far side, seeking protection. "I'm not Katherine, and I'm not going with you."

"You have to," the man said. His face could be plastic. It had no expression, not even when Magdallen walked out of Michaelangelo's between them and the police. Magdallen held out an object in his hand, a simple phone.

"You can call the governor. You don't arrest anybody here. This is Council territory."

"Take the boy, I don't care. I'm authorized by this girl's father to take her back."

"And I don't want to go with you!" the girl cried. "I'm with *her*! So is Noble!"

"She's perfectly free to call her father," Ardath said calmly, in a low voice that hushed the crowd. "Let *him* tell her. And we know who that is."

Silence followed. Standstill. The tap buzzed in that silence, a steady, repetitive noise: *"Go Brazisss. Procyon go Brazis."*

"Brazis," Procyon said under his breath, and tried the tap, an effort that dizzied him, as a hand—Magdallen's—slipped inside his elbow. "Sir. Brazis. We need help here."

The man in the suit had one hand inside his pocket. He removed it carefully, and with the same slowness touched a communications unit on his gray collar. "I hear you," the man said to someone, and then, no happier than before, signaled the uniformed police to stand down and put away the guns. To move back. *Outsider* police stayed, still moving about inside, still mopping up.

The girl didn't budge.

"Procyon," his tap said suddenly.

"Sir." His voice shook. It was surreal to speak to Brazis here, in public, with armed confusion around him. He wasn't safe. He might never again be safe. "I've got a passenger. Another tap. I think, sir, I think it's the *ondat*."

While it said, in the same ear, *"Brazis, Braziss. Hello."*

"We thought so," Brazis said. *We thought so. We thought* so, jarred

through him, an of-course acceptance that left him not a known fact in the universe. *Marak,* was what he wanted to ask, the only thing he wanted to know about, for himself. And couldn't. Dared not.

"This is Antonio Brazis." The voice wasn't in his head, it was in the air, thundered like God from speakers all over the area. *"We have visual identification of all persons in the area, with nine active warrants, two of which have already been served by our personnel moving through the vicinity . . ."*

Several individuals in the crowd melted away, fast. Another took out running down the middle of the street.

Then a quieter voice, through the Project tap: *"Report to the office, stat. No delays, no fuss. Just move. Now. No one will stop you."*

"Yes, sir," Procyon said, and turned to the man who had taken his arm. Magdallen, his sister had called him. Slink. High-powered, deadly-armed slink, who'd quietly removed the knife from his hand. "I'm called in. I'm called in, sir." He suspected a slink knew where, and why. Magdallen let go his arm, at least. "Let my sister alone."

"Your sister has no problem with us," Magdallen said quietly, and Procyon turned, threaded his way through a crowd that melted away in front of him, disheveled, coatless—cold, now that the adrenaline had run out.

"Procyon!"

He looked back at Ardath. "Love you. See you." He didn't believe it. He fixed that sight of her in memory, hoping he'd have a memory by tomorrow.

He turned and walked, then, the object of stares and hasty avoidance, and the three bots that dogged his steps zipped and dodged along with him. He couldn't do anything about that. He didn't know what choice he had. Report, not home, but to the office.

The office, he said to himself, and, walking down to the corner of Blunt and Grozny, turned onto Grozny, a very long way from the office, and just kept walking in the right direction.

He heard a hum behind him. An open Council police cab showed up and wanted him to get in.

"Go Braziss," the voice in his head said, and he tapped into the

office. "I've got an escort, sir. Bots. I don't know if I dare take a cab. I don't know what Kekellen will do if I lose them."

"*Can you walk?*"

"I'm doing all right so far, sir," he said, looking down that long, long street, Grozny, that eventually, under various names, led everywhere on the deck. It curved up as it reached a point of indistinction, floor becoming horizon.

It was a long way. But the police made no objection when with a "Sorry," he wandered on. The police just trundled along in his neighborhood, like the three bots, and he kept moving.

SETHA REAUX SAT in his chair looking at the life-globe, watching a lizard catching gnats. Kathy was alive. He didn't know what condition she was in. But Kathy was alive.

"*She doesn't want to come in,*" Dortland had advised him, the dark spot in that most welcome news. "*I tried, sir. I was confronted by an Outsider riot. She's with Procyon Stafford's sister—who does have a clean record. There's another matter——*"

Dortland talked about Freethinkers. About the Movement suspects, both of whom were dead, with bots occupying the place, ripping up evidence, even taking the bodies apart, annihilating traces. Unprecedented. Unsettling to contemplate. He had had a call from Brazis, who had visual surveillance down there, and who proved a far more exact source of information.

Kekellen had answered their request. Hadn't he?

He never wanted to admit to that message he'd sent. Never wanted to, and hoped he never would have to. Whatever those dead bodies contained—Earth authority wouldn't get hold of them, not now.

But Kathy was safe. With Stafford's sister. Safe, with someone who might possibly talk cold sense into her stubborn young head. Kathy had refused to go anywhere with Dortland. Good sense in his daughter.

Dortland was only anxious, he suspected, to be told he was off the hook.

"You did your best," Reaux said. Time to make peace with this man. To warm the atmosphere, at least enough for polite lies to take root and grow. Dortland in his debt might be useful and informative. "She'll call. She'll call when she's ready. Come back to the office. I count it a success."

He hung up. He sat waiting, wondering if he should call Antonio, if he dared call Antonio.

The phone beeped. *"Sir."* It was Ernst. *"The Chairman's courier."*

He jabbed a button. "Send her in."

Ernst let Jewel into the office.

"Are we safe here?" he asked, incongruous question, and she looked about her, seemed to take the local temperature.

"At the moment, sir. Sir, I'm in contact."

"Antonio," Reaux said. "Antonio. What news?"

"Moderately good," Brazis said. *"I can report your daughter is in a safe place. But you've heard that. The young woman is well reputed. A positive influence."*

"Is she safe there, from retaliation?"

"I have a close watch on her vicinity. There may be a few survivors still crawling the corridors, but I think their real desire now is to lie low and wait for a ship bound for Orb or anywhere else in the universe. We're going to watch such ships very closely."

"My full cooperation," Reaux said earnestly. "But my daughter—forgive me: forgive me, sir. Is there any indication—of her health?"

"If there should be anything untoward, she's with someone who can get her expert help. The boy who was with her, likewise. An innocent. Relatively speaking, if stupidity counts."

"Thank God. Thank God for that."

"Algol is dead: he was a known problem. Typhon, likewise dead—an import from Orb, capable of handling exotics, I'm told. Not now. He's done, and every trace of biologicals with him."

"You're sure."

"I hesitate to claim the pieces have all gone into recycling. I think Kekellen's taken them for his own investigations."

"Even the—" He hesitated at the question. "The remains."

"That first. Cleaner-bots have fairly well demolished the place, and police aren't going in there, not yours and not mine."

Bots, for God's sake.

"*Kekellen is involved to the hilt,*" Brazis said through Jewel's lips. "*The fact the local street moved to reject this illicit cell—I think that may have communicated to him. A demonstration of honesty. Kekellen's extremely keen on honesty.*"

It was the theory—that Kekellen had settled on Marak for that reason. "The honest man," Reaux said.

"*Kekellen's seemed to have picked out a* locally *honest man, too—if the notion holds up.*"

Astonishing that he couldn't think of an honest man. Not offhand. He certainly didn't think it was Brazis. Or himself. "Who?"

"*Our young fugitive.*"

"Procyon?" He was a little stunned. In their interview, he could say he'd been impressed, at least, of a certain character.

But he *didn't* like the *ondat's* honest man being an Outsider.

"*He's not the only one.*" Brazis said further. "*If we can count Mr. Gide.*"

"Mr. Gide? Oh, I doubt that."

"*But there is a tap. A nanocele tap. Hospital could tell that in two seconds. The question is, whose. But I think it's much the same as Procyon's situation, however delivered.*"

Reaux's heart sullenly doubled its beats. "But why?"

"*My young gentleman, Mr. Stafford, hasn't gotten to the office yet, and I don't think he'll have any clearer idea than I have. I've been a little careful about contacting him by tap, speaking quite frankly, because we very surely have an intruder in our system, including the one I'm using now.*"

"An—"

"*Listen to me all the way on this one, Setha, and take it for what it is. Cleaner-bots. The bot system comes and goes, does it not? Our friend Kekellen has inserted his own robots through his own system of accesses, bots to mix with ours. Young Mr. Stafford is wearing a mark that we may not be able to purge, and he's attended particularly by a repair bot that won't leave his vicinity. I had the tap system completely shut down for a significant period of time, and we're still getting information on a rogue tap somewhere in the system. I'm convinced he's part of it. And I'm suspecting fairly soon we'll have a second one.*"

"Mr. Gide."

"*He's not savvy of it, not yet. He won't be, for a while. Procyon's fairly expert at handling complex taps, and he's bringing sensible communica-*"

tion through with far less trouble. But that's not the whole point. Kekellen himself seems to be communicating through those two taps—having one internal to himself."

"Good God," Reaux said, appalled. "What do we do, then?"

"Wait and see. That's all I can recommend."

"But Kekellen—"

"He's had abundant reason to complain. We may have settled it. The street may have settled it. And if that fails, Mr. Stafford may be a valuable asset in settling the difficulty. We've never had direct communication with the ondat."

"And Mr. Gide? He's not qualified. He's not prepared for this . . ."

"In a sense it's what eight-year-old kids get done, in our society. Well, excluding the alien intelligence aspect of it. Mr. Gide should find it an interesting experience."

"If you can say so," Reaux said with a shudder. In the life-globe, an anole had climbed the highest branch, lording it over the others. "Intimate contact with Kekellen isn't what I'd call an interesting experience."

"Another tap system. We share one with pop culture. One with the planet. One, it seems, we now share with the ondat, in the head of a Project tap. We're in for a period of adjustment. I think Mr. Gide may be able to communicate a new fact of existence to the authorities that backed this venture."

"If his sanity holds out." He remembered a recent communication. "I've received an official protest over Mr. Gide's transfer to your hospital. Shall I relay your advisement to his ship, about his condition, and its probable source?"

"Oh, by all means. I think it's time to do that."

It was going to be a tense moment, as that ship realized that, with all he knew, Mr. Gide had had a tap implanted, and not by Outsider choice, and not in contact with humans.

But there wasn't a thing a political faction on distant Earth could do about the situation except keep quiet and study the damage a stranded Mr. Gide could do to their political secrets, in close communication with colonials, Outsiders, and *ondat.*

"I'll take care of it," he promised Brazis.

Jewel gave a little nod, indication the interview was over.

"Thank you," Reaux said to her, but he wasn't sure she heard, on her way to the door.

He didn't know what he was going to tell Judy. It wasn't hair color they were talking about, now. It was a daughter down on Blunt—a daughter on Grozny, if they were lucky. A daughter who wasn't going to go back into the best schools.

A daughter who was very soon going to be notorious in her former social circles.

But still his daughter. Kathy. Mignette. He didn't know about Judy, but she was still—after all—his daughter.

RAIN SHEETED, poured down sandy washes, spattered off the rocks, soaked wherever the rain-skins failed to protect—a modern convenience against a modern nuisance, these brown plastic covers, and Marak, disdaining a good many of Ian's conveniences, was glad to have warmth and dryness about them, glad to have the saddles under them kept dry, along with the girths, which took a deal of stress on their slow climb.

They moved, with occasional encouragement from the long quirts. They had moved all through the night, having the young fool ahead of them, driven upward by the wrath of the old bull Marak rode, and the disgruntled females following their laborious path up the cliffs . . . following, because beshti stuck together, give or take riders' intentions, in a vast and otherwise empty land.

And gradually the rock and sand that had appeared only in lightning flashes began to be visible between flashes. It became a sullen sort of morning, gray, wet and noisy with the boom of thunder and the rush of the deluge. Water still poured in diminishing torrents from above, newborn streams rushing down channels in the sandstone toward the pans, which still were dry enough to drink them up. No bright beam of morning sunlight got through the clouds.

But they were alive, and they kept moving to keep warm and to keep safe, climbing up the way they had come down, or finding new ways, where rain had badly channeled the sand slips.

Up by the difficult series of three terraces, while the light grew, with a little rest, then, sheltered from the wind by an outcrop of basalt.

Marak had no watcher at all this morning. Neither did Hati. But they had Ian, who inquired frequently and cautiously after their progress.

"As good as might be," Marak said, informing Ian as little as possible. He was still angry, still asking himself what he would do in response.

Ian would make peace with Luz. Possibly they would become lovers again, possibly not. How both of them would regard the Ila for the next while was a matter of concern, until matters settled out. He was closely evaluating his opinion of Brazis.

"Procyon is safe and asleep," Ian told him finally. *"The ones responsible in the heavens are dead."*

"Is Brazis?" Marak asked harshly. He by no means exonerated Brazis, among others.

"Brazis is still directing matters. He asks me to relay his profound apology, and his gratitude for your patience."

"Patience." He was very long on that virtue, where mountains were concerned. Human beings were another matter. "I will have the boy back, Ian, and I shall have Drusus, and Auguste."

"That seems likely," Ian said, *"but, Marak-omi, the* ondat *seem to have assisted in the fight. And, it seems, they have slipped a maker into Procyon, with which they can contact him—and, through him, you—at will. They have entered the downworld system through this boy. Brazis counsels us all to be watchful, and patient."*

There was no answer to that situation. He was silent for a moment, simply trying to understand what was a very significant move. The *ondat* would touch the world. A change. Another change in the world as it had been.

"This boy is under my husband's protection," Hati said angrily, in his meditative silence.

"And continues to be, Hati-omi. The ondat *have always shown the greatest respect for your husband, above the rest of us. I am somewhat optimistic about this move. The* ondat *protected this boy."*

"It is worth seeing what will happen," Marak said. He was disturbed, but not angry. The blood moved quicker in his veins. He was not accustomed to think beyond the sky. He might have to learn new thoughts, become adept in new horizons. "Where have they gotten this maker, Ian?"

"*A very good question,*" Ian said.

"Indeed," Marak said.

"*I have other news,*" Ian said. "*Your man Fashti broke camp when he heard you were coming up. He is proceeding down the ridge to intercept you.*"

"Meziq?"

"*They are carrying him, as I understand. And the tent, the essential poles, the tack, and considerable supplies. The going is very slow, and they are dragging most of it, but they are making progress.*"

They were going home. And they could ride up the spine to meet the retreat, load up the beshti, and send a party back to collect what they had had to abandon.

"*I can send a plane,*" Ian said, "*to meet you at the edge of the plateau.*"

"You can send your plane to bring Meziq out," Marak said. "If the weather settles. If you wish to take the trouble. If Meziq himself wishes it. He may not. We will tell you which." He broke off the contact, determined to get under way now, the last climb up to the ridge, where the boys and a majority of their equipment would be a welcome sight.

A great deal of help Ian's machines would be, bogged in mud or swept away by torrent in this shift in the weather. But he did not open that argument with Ian, not yet.

Had Luz, meanwhile, apologized for the situation her schism with Ian had created? He heard no hint of that from her.

Had the Ila admitted to her meddling in the heavens? He expected nothing at all from that quarter.

"Procyon will be back," he said to Hati as they started their upward journey. "So will Auguste and Drusus. I shall have that clear with Brazis. For the meanwhile, we have Ian."

Hati cast him a sidelong look in the gloom of morning. A lightning flash showed it clear, and a moment later thunder resounded across the pans.

"I shall have a talk with Luz when we get back," Hati said.

"In moderation, wife."

"Am I ever immoderate?"

A wise husband let that question pass unanswered. And in a moment more, Hati laughed.

The light grew as thunder migrated across the pans. And as they made the last climb to the ridge, a glance down and back showed a strange leaden sheen across the western part of the basin, a sheen that made the air above it thick with fog.

"Water," Marak said. "Cold water."

They had seen their new sea. It was coming, with a rapidity that made them glad they were getting off the ridge soon. If some weakness in the rock began to fountain water through the ridge they stood on, which by then would have become a dam holding the sea from the hollow Needle Gorge, it would be wise to make no long camps on the spine.

"Three days to reach safer ground," he said. "And I think we should go there."

15

Two days answering questions, two days in which Procyon rested in a small hospital room with only the three robots for company; and then the two cleaner-bots strayed out when the meal cart arrived and failed to come back. They had disappeared into the ubiquitous cleaner slots, he hoped. He hoped he wasn't involved in some Project notion of kidnapping the bots and taking them apart to see their circuitry. He still had flashes of dark, the illusion of smelling ammonia. He waked in sweats, with the sensation of a cool, spongy touch on his face.

He sat in front of the small room computer unit and played computer solitaire to keep from going crazy, while the remaining repair bot sat and watched him. He ate, he slept, he answered questions that popped onto the screen, and sometimes he heard one or the other of two competing taps fussing at him, trying to gain his attention. *"Braziss,"* one hissed, sending chills through his spine, and the other: *"How are you doing, Procyon?"* in a warm and maternal voice.

"I don't know when I can see Brazis," he answered the one. "I'm sorry." And to the other voice, clearly a Project tap: "I'm doing all right, ma'am. No problems."

He waited. He answered every detail he could remember, to occasional queries from the motherly voice. He didn't ask about his sister, his family, or the other taps. He didn't want to get any of them into more difficulty than they already had met on his account. Maybe that failure to ask was itself a problem, but if it was, it was his own problem, and he kept up that policy.

He slept again, and the repair bot was gone when he waked up. He worried about it. He never had named it: naming it had seemed to him to be a little crazy. But he had begun to think of it as a presence, and when it left him he felt strangely alone and depressed, at loose ends, even his endless solitaire games incapable of occupying his attention.

"*Procyon*," a voice said. This time it wasn't the woman he was used to. It was another one, younger, harsher. Authority.

"Yes, ma'am. I hear you."

"*The Chairman wants to see you.*"

"Yes, ma'am."

The *Chairman* wanted him. It was a high-level disposition, then, not a quiet disappearance into the hospital and the security system. He experienced a little surge of hope that he hadn't gone invisible, that he might still have some useful function. The wild surmise, which had begun to fade in recent days, that Marak himself might have insisted on his surfacing.

"*Procyon.*" Brazis, this time. Procyon stopped, in the act of dressing.

"Yes, sir. I'm sorry. I'm hurrying."

"*No great hurry. To relieve your anxiety, I'm satisfied with your answers. Everything's fine. Now get in here.*"

"Yes, sir." He had a pair of pants, the ones he'd arrived in, cleaned. The shirt wasn't in great shape, and he didn't have a coat. He put on his shoes. Idiotically, pathetically, he missed the damned robot, which ordinarily would be sitting there blinking at him.

He got up, tried the door, walked out into the corridor and ran into uniformed Project police, to his distress. He said nothing, just went with the two women into the hospital lift system and, through a side hall, over to the restricted lifts, headed for the Project offices.

"HOW'S THE DAUGHTER?" Brazis asked Reaux, through Jewel, who had taken up her post in the governor's suite of offices. "I hear she did phone."

"You know too much," Setha Reaux said to him peevishly, but not with great force, in Brazis's judgment. A small pause. They had been discussing the departure of the *Southern Cross* from dock, an event greatly relieving a number of situations. *"We're meeting at a restaurant. Me, my wife. Kathy.* Mignette, *now. Tonight."*

"I've heard her mentor is counseling her to moderation. To go slowly. Plan carefully. She couldn't be in better hands—where she is."

"Where she is," Reaux echoed him. *"Which is better than where she could be. I know that. We caught another of the group this morning."*

Brazis knew that, but let Reaux tell him, not to expose all his sources, or spoil Reaux's triumph.

"In an apartment on Lebeau. Not a bad neighborhood," Reaux added. *"So I'm told."*

Across Brazis's office, Magdallen sat, source of a great deal of information. Magdallen, with those green eyes and a dark good looks that probably got him more information than the police authority ever could, was still on the job.

"Listen," Brazis said, "the reason for the contact: I'm setting Procyon loose. I *don't* want him bothered."

"I'll make that clear where appropriate," Reaux said. *"Any resolution on the tap—his or Gide's?"*

"Not much activity. It's quieted down. The bots have disappeared, on their own. Gide's become almost cooperative. Have you had any word at all from Kekellen?"

"Not a whisper."

"So," he said. "None here, either. I'll keep you advised. Good luck with the dinner."

"Good luck with your own business," Reaux said, and Brazis tapped out.

"Vanish," he said to Magdallen. "I'll brief you later."

"Yes, sir," Magdallen said, stood up with a fluid motion, and left. It was *sir,* lately. It began to seem that, whatever Magdallen's particular origins, related to the Council at Apex, his reports were going to reflect far better on Concord's business than they had started out to do. The departure of the Earth ship—Mr. Gide irately refusing even to speak to the captain by phone—was a piece of information apt to be cherished there as it was here.

Magdallen left. Procyon Stafford arrived, coatless, a few rips on the shirt, not a physical mark on him but the tattoo, a mark all but invisible in the bright light of the office. Given the rapidity of the healing of other injuries, it seemed likely that that one visible trace was going to remain.

So the doctors said.

"Procyon." Brazis stood up to meet the young man, courtesy to a person to whose resourceful escape they owed, collectively, a very great deal.

"Sir." A reciprocal little bow. "Kekellen's been very anxious I talk to you."

"I know. The doctors have told me." He found the young man's worried intensity disturbing to his own agenda, and he walked over to his orchids, his source of calm and self-direction. It meant he didn't have to look the man in the eye, or lie to him. "It's likely, however, that that ship leaving—"

"It has left, sir?"

A damnable tendency to jump ahead. But the taps were bright. Too bright. Difficult to deal with, to keep under security restrictions.

"The ship is outbound, out of our lives. Mr. Gide remains hospitalized, not adjusting as rapidly as you. But then you've had practice."

"Yes, sir."

"Shall I be honest?" The young man's candor urged him to it. "You're stuck with that tap. There's no way to remove it that wouldn't damage you."

"I rather well suspected so, sir."

"It presents us a problem."

"With Marak, sir."

"Has he contacted you?"

"Is he all right?"

That immediate question, that question that wasn't duty, concern that overrode all questions about his own future. There was a bond between those two. Kindred souls, if one subscribed to such notions. At least a bond that had formed and refused to be broken.

"I've asked Ian to inform him you were too sick to be consulted," Brazis said. "The excuse is wearing thin."

"He's all right?" Right back to the essential question.

"He's all right. So is Hati. They got the beshti back. They've re-joined their party, recovered their gear. They're on their way back to safe ground, out of danger."

A deep, satisfied breath. And no questions about his own future. It was hero worship, maybe. Or something stronger. One could envy the young man that kind of devotion. Or envy Marak, that he'd convinced a young man, who'd never see him face-to-face, that he was worth dying for.

And damn him, the young man had distracted him down his own path.

"Do you hear Kekellen now?"

"Not at the moment. But the bot left this morning."

"You made that connection, did you, that that's your relay?"

"I know there has to be a relay. I don't think Kekellen would pig-gyback on yours."

"Mine. As if I owned them. Don't you feel they're *your* relays, too?"

"I suppose they are, yes, sir."

Brazis gave a humorless laugh, repositioned a bit of fake bark under a green, arching root. "I've damn near drowned these things in the last few days. Time they rested from our crisis."

"Yes, sir." Perplexity. Innocence.

But not naïveté.

"You know you're a security risk," Brazis said. "A tremendous risk to put you back on duty."

"I know that, sir. And I wouldn't risk *him*."

Him. Marak. No question, still no protestation of his own am-bitions.

"Your contact with Marak becomes an interesting question," Brazis said, "since we'll have some notion, via Kekellen's tap, what interests Kekellen, what catches his attention. In a way, it may be a learning experience for both sides. Has he asked any specific ques-tions?"

"He just said your name, sir, as if he had something to ask. Brazis, Brazis, Brazis. But there never was a question."

"Maybe it wasn't a question," Brazis said, realizing that point, himself. "Maybe it was a direction he was giving, for your safety. You're Marak's tap. You were threatened. Kekellen didn't want the program disrupted. Didn't want Marak inconvenienced."

"You think that was it, sir?" Hope, but a great deal of doubt, with it.

Brazis had his own hope. Kekellen was odd, but he had never demonstrated himself aggressive.

"It's a new age in communication, isn't it? If he's talking through that tap, if it *is* Kekellen, one can assume Kekellen has internalized a tap of his own. Does that thought occur to you?"

"I've heard him breathing," Procyon said. "It sounds internal."

As taps from inside did sound . . . internal. Like one's own voice. A man who used the device routinely knew that very well.

"Interesting. But he doesn't get onto our system."

"I haven't caught him trying it, sir. I don't think he does."

"You're the junction point. Gide doesn't own another tap, even the common one. But Kekellen may ask you questions sooner or later. And expect you to relay things to Marak. I wouldn't be surprised."

"I suppose he will, sir."

"Likely that bot will show up when he wants to talk or listen. They get through interfaces in the walls. Places you have to get an architectural diagram to figure out. All sorts of passages that in *our* diagrams don't connect. But repair bots, I suppose, can make little changes we don't know about. Build new routes. Connect others. One wonders what archaeology of the stuff behind the walls could show us, on the former stations."

"I don't know, sir."

The perfect subordinate answer. The opaque answer. But nobody had investigated. The structure of the stations had been on record for ages past. No one ever questioned it not being what was on the charts. Robots did all the internal service work.

"Well, well," Brazis said. "It's all outside your concerns. Except I want a report the minute you find a bot tagging you." It was going to take a little monitor inserted in Procyon's apartment, one that would find intrusions Procyon didn't know about, behind his walls. It was going to be an interesting few decades, his administration.

"Yes, sir," Procyon said.

"Drusus and Auguste have gone back to work. They're still limiting their activities. The doctors don't want them on longer than an hour on, an hour off. We're monitoring via Hati's taps. How do you feel?"

"No effects, sir." A spark of fervent interest. But then a little hesitation. And, worriedly: "I won't contact Marak if I think in any way I'm a conduit for Kekellen."

"I think we can work that out. You'll help us. Marak will. He understands your situation."

"He does, sir?"

"He's not entirely pleased about what happened to you. But he's happier now that you're on your feet. Are you fit to go on duty?"

"I'm fine, sir."

"An hour on, an hour off, until you hear otherwise."

"Yes, sir."

"Dismissed, then. Go to it. It's your shift."

"Thank you, sir." Procyon started to leave. Then stopped. "Where do I go, sir?"

"Home," Brazis said. "Home to your apartment, I suppose. Where your office is."

"I'm known on the street, sir."

"I'd say you are. You'll have to manage that notoriety. I leave that to your ingenuity." A deliberate frown. "And wear a coat in the office."

"Yes, sir." Enthusiasm. Boundless enthusiasm. As if he wasn't a walking communications device for Concord's most dangerous resident. "Thank you, sir. Thank you."

"Out," Brazis said. Gratitude embarrassed him, when simple necessity had dictated the young man's return to work. Keep Marak happy, repair the breach downworld. Keep Kekellen happy—maybe let the old sod ask a few direct questions of Marak, if Marak would deign to answer them.

The one honest man on earth. And Kekellen had found honesty in the heavens, it seemed.

Honesty didn't figure in his own duty. He just did it as he saw it.

* * *

DINNER AT THE *PLANE,* not the place Procyon would have chosen, but Ardath had her standards and her obligations. Procyon wore his best, quiet, against Ardath's blue and gold. The maître d' whisked him to a conspicuous table, saw him seated, and the wine steward was quick to put in an appearance, suggesting his own mid-pricey celebration favorite. Ardath had arranged that, and he didn't fight it. He sat pretending he didn't know the whole room was watching and waiting. He hoped it might be a one-drink wait if he was lucky.

And Ardath swept in early, with Isis and Spider, with little Mignette in close, worshipful attendance. Isis, Spider, and Mignette weren't sharing the table. They had another. But they were always nearby, Ardath's bodyguards, if the need for defense ever presented itself, social or otherwise.

He got up, returned his sister's warm handclasp, sat down again with the whole world watching.

"You're looking good," his sister said. A thousand hopefuls would die for that judgment. He only resisted the temptation to touch the brand he wore forever, in front of all these people.

"You're always good," he shot back, and made her laugh.

They dealt with the wine steward, and with the waiter, and with the owner, who would have fired either the steward or the waiter if they had either one so much as frowned.

It was too much steady smiling. They heaved a simultaneous sigh as they finally found something like a moment of privacy, the two of them alone.

"How *are* you?" Ardath asked him, meaning a world of things, and he gave a little shrug.

"Well, I'm supposed to visit the parentals on the 12th."

"Poor brother!"

"Oh, I'll be completely respectable. Except this." A little shift of the eyes upward. "Except they know, now. The street knows. And they do. It's going to be interesting."

"I can't go." It was an earnest, worried excuse. Halfway an offer to have gone in his place—if she could.

"Sis. You're sweet. But I'll survive. More to the point, I won't scandalize them if I stay in bright light, and I'll play games with the junior cousins. I'll be just cousin Jerry."

"Horrid. You aren't. Everybody knows you're not."

"I am. More than you'd guess. I just live my little life and buy my own groceries. It's my private fantasy."

Ardath set her chin. "The fools on this station can't touch you. *Nobody* dares touch you."

"Security doubts they would, at least." Salads showed up, deftly, quietly. "And you? How are you getting along?"

"Oh, fine," Ardath said. "Really, very."

"That's good."

"Procyon, do you *have* to live at that stodgy nook address?"

"It's comfortable."

"Well, you lend it cachet. No question. They *could* forgo the rent. You should speak to the management."

"I'm kept by the government, but don't spread that around."

A laugh. "I always knew you'd do something sensible."

Kekellen listened from time to time, but said very little. Unlike Marak, Kekellen observed no schedule, interrupting his sleep now and again, but mostly keeping his robots away and his relays quiet while he was working or in public, and he was glad of that.

Drusus was on duty at the moment. They were back in the usual rotation. So he had a private life, such as it could be, with such ties as he had. He actually enjoyed the supper, feeling safe, in a way he hadn't expected. There were two kinds of security, one he'd kept by being nobody and quiet, and what he had now, a notoriety that made people shy of talking to him, let alone bothering him.

That meant he could do what he'd never done, and go where he'd never go, and he didn't have any question he'd stay employed—not these days.

He'd begun to settle in, was what. He'd found a means of living the life he liked.

That wasn't at all bad.

THE AIR HAD a different smell, now, wet sand, wet rock, salt water; and the evenings had gotten much colder.

Change, change, and change in the rules of the world. Marak took a steaming cup of tea, and Hati took one, and they listened to young Farai, who thought he'd seen a fish swimming at the surface of their new sea, and was excited.

Marak himself doubted any fish could survive the plunge the watchers in the heavens described at the gates of the Wall. But who knew? He listened politely, and drank his tea.

The long spine of the Needle Gorge was indeed likely to fail, so Ian said, and soon, taking their relay with it. Well that they were up on solid ground. And they might almost see it from here.

Luz was back with Ian. The Ila had taken to her quarters, with the doors shut. They might stay shut for a while.

Ian's latest rocket was a success. Ian was getting spectacular images from the Wall, which now stood as an island, and they got others, from the edge of the plateau. They sent them to the Refuge, but the Ila refused to come out of her chambers and look.

Ian had tried to entice him to come back, meanwhile, but he was uncertain. Out here, he had no need of Ian's cameras. To see all the history of the waterfall in its glory, it seemed they had a choice, to go back to the Refuge, or at least trek as far as the waystation at Edina, to see Ian's images on a much larger screen.

Meanwhile the shallow rim of their new sea steamed with fog, while the heart of it deepened. The waterfall at the Wall had diminished, the seas equalizing.

As for Farai's precious fish, first would come the chemical adjustment of the water, the algaes, and the weed would take hold, and the one-celled creatures, and the floaters and the burrowers.

Once the food chain established itself, then the fishes might come, long and sinuous, making their living on lesser creatures.

Already the weather reports spoke of torrential rains in the highlands, water which would cut the gorge faster and faster toward the new sea, until it vanished altogether into a chain of islands. When the Needle did merge with the sea, it would sweep down its own different chemistry to a new estuary.

Everything was a chain. And there were thousands of new things to learn.

"I think Farai is imagining this fish," Hati said.

"I all but know he is," Marak said quietly, but he never would deflate the boy's enthusiasm. And, who knew? One might have ridden out the chute.

They were bound for the east, now, at a leisurely pace, while Meziq's leg mended. The watchers in the heavens were back at their posts. The *ondat*, the Ila's great enemies, had established their own tie to the watchers, but Procyon swore it was no great inconvenience to him; and meanwhile the *ondat*, like everyone else in the heavens, simply watched—absorbed, perhaps, in the news of a new sea, new weather, new wonders, in closer relationship with the world than before. There would be no war in the heavens, nor any more troubling by the Earth lord, who had settled into quiet, likewise touched by the *ondat*.

Hati understood the close call they had had. His youngest watcher went on adapting, having the good sense to deal softly with the *ondat*, having all the joy of life in him since his return, describing all the images he saw of the incoming sea.

He could hardly imagine where the boy was at the moment, in a building, in a structure, with this sister of his, at a celebration. Procyon was happy, and new as the morning: that was the bond they had between them. He had sons—he and Hati—sons and grandsons and great-grandsons in great number, besides their descendants; they were all familiar to him.

This one held surprises. Like the desert. Like the sea. This one broke the rules wisely. Like him. Like Hati.

Such a life was a treasure, when it appeared.